10

In common with her heroine, Ann Granger has worked in British embassies in various parts of the world. She met her husband, who was also working for the British Embassy, in Prague and together they received postings to places as far apart as Munich and Lusaka. They are now permanently based in Bicester, near Oxford. Ann is currently working on her eleventh Mitchell and Markby novel and on *Asking for Trouble* the first book in a new series featuring a youthful private investigator, Fran Varady.

A Word After Dying

Ann Granger

HEADLINE

First published in 1996
by HEADLINE BOOK PUBLISHING

First published in paperback in 1997
by HEADLINE BOOK PUBLISHING

10

ISBN 0 7472 5187 8

Typeset by
Letterpart Limited, Reigate, Surrey

Printed and bound in Great Britain by
Clays Ltd, St Ives plc

HEADLINE BOOK PUBLISHING
A division of Hodder Headline PLC
338 Euston Road
London NW1 3BH

I seemed to move among a world of ghosts,
And feel myself the shadow of a dream.

Alfred, Lord Tennyson

From ghoulies and ghosties,
And long-leggety beasties,
And things that go bump in the night,
Good Lord, deliver us.

Traditional Scottish prayer

CHAPTER ONE

There's Gladness in the Remembrance
Memorial to a horse

A SUMMER of drought had baked the ground as hard as concrete. The men's feet in their strong footwear echoed as they tramped across it, as if they were walking across the surface of a drum. Rory Armitage saw how it had cracked open in deep fissures and bare soil showed in patches through a thin, brown, scabby blanket of shrivelled turf.

His lawn at home was in much the same state. No question of watering it. Not that anyone was likely to report you, not in Parsloe St John. But he had a certain standing in their small community and it behove him to set a good example. So he'd let his garden dry and wither. Only the roses had been kept alive by his wife, with an enterprising recycling of washing-up water. Out here, in open pasture, it was much worse. He scraped the edge of his sole along the lip of one crevice and a puff of dust rewarded him.

'Can't get a spade in that!' Ernie Berry announced. He drove the implement down at the earth by his feet, to illustrate the point. It bounced back with a muffled clang. 'It took me and my lad half yesterday to hack out that trial trench of yours with a pickaxe. As for digging a bloody great

1

hole the size you need?' he added, rubbing his brawny arm across his face to erase the pearled sweat. 'Not a chance! You wants a mechanical digger. Me and my lad can't do it.'

The little knot of figures had gathered in the middle of the paddock beneath a venerable chestnut tree. They'd chosen this spot for their discussion because of the shade the leafy branches offered, not because the pit was to be dug here. The root system rendered that impractical. The area designated for the pit was some twenty feet away uphill, marked out with string and pegs. Within it was the trench painstakingly excavated by the Berrys to establish the level of any sub-surface water. The bottom of it was bone dry. They were well above the water-table, thought Rory with relief. That could have thrown a spanner in the works.

However, that was as far as they'd got and that, decided Rory now, was as far as they were going to get without a digger. Berry was right. He eyed the man with a mixture of distaste and wry amusement. There was a distinct resemblance between Ernie and the tree under which they stood. Ernie was squat, powerful, sunburnt and gnarled. He had heavy jowls and not much neck. He wore, as always, work trousers and a grimy singlet stretched over his paunch. Greying hair burst from the singlet and bushed odiferously in his armpits. More hair sprouted along his muscular shoulders and down his bulging arms. Only on his shiny walnut head did hair obstinately refuse to grow at all. A regular fly's skating rink.

Rory suppressed a smile, hardly appropriate in the circumstances, and turned his face into the cooling breeze. They were on the high point of local topography on this hillside, exposed to wind and weather, but offered compensation by way of a truly magnificent view. Rory's gaze absently took in the rolling countryside. He was thinking it was a pity Charles Darwin couldn't have come across Ernie Berry. The great naturalist would've slotted Berry in neatly between ape and man, his 'missing link'.

The vet reminded himself that Berry was a reliable workman. He took good care of Mrs Smeaton's garden and did all the odd jobs about the place competently. Rory knew he was trying hard to suppress his own natural feelings and the knowledge irked. Frankly, he didn't like Ernie because he didn't trust him. The man's shifting gaze, and the way he had of rolling an eye at you sideways when he thought you weren't looking, were warning signs which Rory would have heeded in a horse. Watch out for sly kicks and a sudden vicious snap of teeth, the signs would have cautioned. The meaningless half-grin which always lurked around Ernie's mouth only made it worse.

Beside Ernie stood the lad, a study in contrasts, pale, silent, dull-eyed. He stood waiting to be told what to do next. That was normal. His name was Kevin, but he was always referred to in the village as 'Berry's lad'. As far as anyone could tell, he was a casual offspring of Ernie's loins. He worked for and with Ernie and appeared to have no independent life of his own. Rory looked away from him, and made a determined effort to attend to the far more pressing matter in hand. Village politics, as his wife Gill called them, were best left to villagers.

Rory had lived in the village for twenty years. He held a position of trust and, he had reason to believe, respect. But he knew he was not considered a villager. The true villagers with their intertwined ancestry, had been here since time immemorial. They banded together in a subtle mix of shifting alliances which would have been well suited to mediaeval Italy or long-ago Byzantium, so complex were they and so unfathomable to outsiders.

Demographically, the village was split into four camps, altogether accounting for enough persons young and old to support the school, two or three shops and a pub. Apart from the inner circle of natives already mentioned, there were the inhabitants of the sprawling council estate, a motley crew, some of them kin to villagers and others drawn here for a variety of reasons. The social scale, such as it was, was topped by the knot of professionals, active or retired, such as Rory himself.

Lastly, and quite beyond the pale, were the despised inhabitants of the new houses. Universally scorned, poor souls, not because they were anything but utterly respectable, but because they had no visible reason, by village logic, to be there at all. They didn't work there, but commuted daily in large and noisy cars from and back to their four-bed, double-glazed, double-garaged homes. They didn't have any relatives elsewhere in the community. They certainly weren't what older villagers called gentry. They were thirty-something former yuppies who thought it would be nice to live in the country, safer than the inner city and healthier for the children.

Such pusillanimous reasoning cut no ice with the villagers, although the headmaster of the primary school welcomed the children to keep up his numbers, even though he knew they were only passing through the state system on their way to independent schools elsewhere when older.

But if the natural-born inhabitants of Parsloe St John had anything in common, Rory had long ago found, it was scorn for anyone who tried to change anything. The newcomers were great ones for change. They arrived declaring Parsloe St John 'absolutely perfect' and within six weeks were pestering the council for improved amenities and the serving of a noise abatement notice on old Mr Horrocks's cockerel.

This attitude irritated Rory as much as it did the villagers.

Aloud he said, 'There's not a lot of time. The carcass is deteriorating in the heat.' Sweat trickled across his scalp as he spoke and ran from his thick curly dark hair. He longed to be finished here, get off home and dive under a cool shower.

Berry fingered his jowls and agreed, 'Whiffs a bit, dunnit?'

So did Berry himself by now, what with the heat and all that expanse of hairy skin, and the singlet which looked as if he worked and slept in the same one for weeks at a time. But Berry wasn't referring to the odour of a living body. He was talking of the insidious stench of death.

The urgency of the case inspired Rory with an idea. 'I'll have a word with Max Crombie! He might be able to help us out, seeing it's an emergency.'

Rory left the Berrys beneath the tree and hurried back to his dusty but prized new Range Rover. He glanced towards the house, half hidden behind a fine old red-brick garden wall, its surface dotted with nails which had once supported espalier fruit trees. He hesitated, wondering whether to go in and tell Mrs Smeaton what he intended. But he decided against it. The whole affair had distressed her and, goodness knew, she was pretty shaky these days, even before . . .

See Max first, he thought. Get it sorted out. Max'll help. His daughter's got a pony. He'll be sympathetic. If all else fails, I'll offer to waive the next lot of vet's fees. When it's all done, time enough to tell her. She won't want to be troubled with the unpleasant details.

Max Crombie, a local builder, was a self-made man and proud of it. He lived in considerable style on the other side of the village. But his builder's yard was only a stone's throw from his house. Max liked to keep an eye on things.

He hadn't made his fortune by letting others run rings round him. He knew builder's labourers. Planks of wood, tins of paint, even half a load of bricks at a time would walk out of the place if Max wasn't there breathing down everyone's neck.

'You don't need to be popular, only respected. Golden rule!' said Max to anyone who hadn't already heard him say it a dozen times before, and also to those who had.

But as Rory had guessed he would be, Max was sympathetic to the present situation, even without the offer to overlook the next veterinary bill for his daughter's expensive show pony

'Poor old lady, rotten thing to have happen. Upset our Julie. She cried buckets when we heard about it. It gave her a fright. Now she spends every spare moment combing our paddock for that wretched weed. I'll send a man over with a digger, say in half an hour, all right?'

'As soon as possible, Max,' Rory sighed in relief. 'The carcass is putrefying. The job's got to be finished by this evening if it's to be done at all.'

The digger duly lumbered into the field half an hour later, looking like a perambulating yellow dinosaur with its toothed scoop head bouncing comically at the end of its long jointed neck. Ernie Berry observed its approach mistrustfully. His belief was that machines took away a man's work and were generally to be resisted. Today was an exception, but he didn't want anyone to get the idea that normally, Berry and his lad couldn't manage most any job.

The lad brightened and brief interest at the machine's activities showed on his narrow face as he watched it in his customary silence.

The digger did the trick, gouging out a deep pit between

the marker pegs. When it had been done, Ernie and the lad stepped forward and tidied up the edges, making the whole thing square.

By now the carcass stank, the stuff of horrors, partly eviscerated like a sacred beast of Ancient Egypt being prepared for ritual mummification. It was grotesquely unreal, a nightmare, legs stuck out stiffly like wooden stumps, neck collapsed, the whole surrounded by buzzing flies. Moving it presented considerable difficulty.

'Gawd!' said the digger operator, putting a handkerchief to his green face.

Berry and the lad, of sterner stuff, managed to get ropes round it. They tied them to the rear of the digger and the machine trundled across the pasture, dragging the carcass behind it. Then they untied it, the digger wheeled round, and with the help of its shovel and with Ernie, Rory and the lad all levering like mad with any implement to hand, they pushed the thing into the pit. Luckily, it landed on its side.

Then they all worked like fury filling in the pit. At last, sweating and grimy, they were able to stand back and admire their work. It looked quite neat, a tidy square of raked earth.

'As nice as you could hope for!' said Ernie.

'Job and a half, that!' said the digger operator with feeling. He hadn't enjoyed a minute of it, but Max had promised to 'see him all right' for the unorthodox work. That meant fifty quid in the hand, no questions, nothing for the taxman. And he had a story to tell his mates, too.

'I think,' said Rory with relief, 'we can fetch Mrs Smeaton down to see it now.'

He went to get her himself. He gave her a lift from the house in the Range Rover, even though it wasn't far and it meant bringing her right round the edge of the property by road and depositing her at the paddock fence. But she didn't walk too well these days and crossing the uneven pasture would have been tricky for her.

She was very pleased and thanked them all for their hard work, backing her thanks with beer money for the three labourers.

'Poor old girl,' said the digger operator. 'Nice old lady, too.'

The paddock emptied. The sun went down in a pink fire. The branches of the chestnut tree stretched ever-lengthening shadow arms protectively across the grave. Before they merged completely into dusk, a thrush struck up its twilight song, carolling clear tuneful notes across the deserted scene.

Olivia Smeaton sat at her bedroom window and watched the light fade and evening spread long shadows across the gardens. She sat with her hands folded in her lap and her stick leaning against her chair. Her silvery grey hair stood up in a halo around her head, her pink skull visible and shiny between the roots. Her wrinkled skin was as fine as a baby's and powdered as heavily. Her withered mouth was marked by a shaky line of fuchsia-coloured lipstick and bright blue shadow was smeared above her eyes. She'd been taught to keep up appearances, even when one was alone. A young woman who ran a home-hairdressing business drove over from Long Wickham and saw to her hair.

From here she had a clear view, skimming the weathered walls of the old vegetable garden, in which no one had cultivated anything edible for years, to the paddock. The limit of detail was the chestnut tree, beyond which the gradient dropped away so that the lower reaches of the pasture were hidden. But she could see the square of freshly turned earth because that was higher up, on the house-side of the tree. Beyond all that the distant landscape was a mauve haze of which she could make nothing. The village was down there somewhere, full of people whose lives were a mess of everyday trivia, the non-stop business of living. She was beyond that, almost, had cut herself loose from it years ago and sat here waiting.

Firefly had his grave but she, his owner, would never have one because she had left precise instructions, specifying cremation, for disposal of her own remains. She'd told Behrens, the solicitor, and added that there was to be as little ceremony as possible. She wasn't sure she even wanted a priest, although she was a Christian woman. She was out of tune with the modern church, but she'd remembered the local parish in her will as she felt it her duty to do, the church commissioners having managed to lose so much money and all the rest of it. St John's was promoting its restoration appeal and was a nice old building. It would be a pity to let it fall down.

Mr Behrens, Orthodox in his own religious observances, had been made uncomfortable by the casualness of her proposed farewell to this world. No gathering of friends and relations to sit and sigh, no prayers, no respect for the occasion.

'Really, Mrs Smeaton, are you sure about this? Listen, my dear, I'll find you some nice old-fashioned priest when – not for a long time yet, God willing – the time comes. Someone retired, perhaps? My sister lives on the coast and tells me the place is full of retired clergymen, all faiths.'

'All right, Mr Behrens, if you can find one who's at least seventy and uses the *Book of Common Prayer*. Tell him not to waste time composing an address. There won't be anyone to listen to it if he does. I want no mourners.'

Olivia gave a little chuckle at the memory of Behrens's earnest acquiescence. It died in her throat as her gaze returned to the window and the view of the paddock. It was decent of Armitage to organise the burial party. She'd observed him out there, turning to and lending a hand with the physical work, alongside Berry and his lad. Later there'd been another man, whose name she didn't know, sent by Crombie with a machine to dig out the pit.

Crombie was also a decent sort of man though undeniably a rough diamond. Ernie Berry, too, was a rough—

Here Olivia's mind baulked at the word 'diamond' which suggested something pure and bright. Unable to come up with a satisfactory substitute, she settled for describing Berry as just 'rough'. But a good worker. Yes, that was it. A good worker – under supervision, naturally.

She ought to feel tired. It was late, the day had been long and stressful, she was well advanced in years. But she felt wide awake, sustained by anger.

She was angry because no longer would she see, from this window, Firefly cropping grass in his paddock or dozing beneath the tree, swishing his tail lazily and occasionally shaking his head to dislodge the flies which dared to settle on his long eyelashes. She was angry because Firefly ought not to be dead. She was angry because of the lie, generally believed in the village, that the animal had eaten poisonous weeds. Angry because she knew with absolute certainty that he'd had no need to do such a thing.

That was it, that was the fuel which fed her anger more than any other: the suggestion that Firefly hadn't been adequately cared for. She knew that wasn't true. Some people who were quite ignorant kept horses. It was a sad fact. But she knew about horses. She knew a sturdy pony could live quite well out of doors all year round, provided it was given additional feed in lean months, care was taken over its hoofs, and if the weather turned exceptionally cold, it were provided with a blanket. Firefly hadn't been the first pony she'd kept, though he'd be the last. All his predecessors had thrived as he had during the – Olivia did a quick calculation – during the twelve years she'd owned him.

It was a long time to own an animal and he'd been more than a servant or a pet, he'd been a friend. Every morning before breakfast she'd cross the gardens, enter the walled vegetable plot, cross that to the gate in the wall which led to the paddock. Firefly would have heard her footsteps and the tap of her stick long before she appeared. He'd bustle up to the gate, snickering his welcome, coat steaming gently in the early dew, eyes bright, soft upper lip quivering in anticipation of his treat. Sometimes she took him an apple or a carrot. Generally it was his daily ration of four Smarties. He was partial to the chocolate sweets in their lurid sugar coating, but she was strict with him, because she cared. If Firefly had been lacking feed, she'd have seen it. Armitage would have remarked on it when he called for Firefly's regular check-ups. The farrier who drove out to trim the pony's hoofs would have said . . .

As it was, the pony had been suffering in secret and no one had known until it was too late to do anything about it. She'd miss that early morning routine. Part of her life had been taken away from her. But everything, she knew, was taken away from you sooner or later.

Nevertheless there was a peculiar injustice in Firefly's loss which made it seem more theft than death. Olivia clenched her bony fists and struck them on her knees in impotent rage.

'Such wickedness,' she whispered to the empty room. 'Such wickedness and the world is full of it.' It came in all shapes and sizes, *And I ought to know* . . . she added in her head.

At this, the weariness which wrath had kept at bay swept over her. She pushed herself out of her chair with the help of her stick. She was alone in the house. Janine had left for the day. She was reminded of her housekeeper by the way the loose tip of one slipper sole snagged from time to time as she moved across the floor.

Janine had grumbled about that loose sole until Olivia had been bullied into sending off a coupon cut from a magazine to some company which marketed sheepskin slippers through the mail. The new pair ought to arrive any day.

Janine was a good girl. Well, no, thought Olivia with a cynical little grin, *not* good. Olivia knew a tart when she saw one. But a good worker, like Ernie Berry, only better than Berry because Janine had a kind heart. Olivia played with the words, bouncing them off the sides of her brain like ping-pong balls. Good worker. Good-hearted. The tart with a heart. Wasn't that what they used to say?

She was halfway down the corridor now and deviated from her straight progress to make a semi-circular detour around a worn spot in the carpet runner. It was less prudence than superstitious dread. Two weeks ago, she'd stumbled on that worn patch and fallen forward, landing on hands and knees, her stick skidding away along the floor out of reach.

She'd told no one of the mishap. It had happened after Janine left with no one to see or hear. She'd bruised her knees badly and for a while had remained motionless, in shock, in that undignified position. Then she'd recovered from that shock to get a worse one. She couldn't get up. There she'd been, on all fours, both too weak and too stiff in the joints to remedy the situation. Frightened and perplexed, she'd stared down at the worn Turkey pattern for what seemed an age, seeing its geometric angles and dull reds and blues in an intimacy she'd never done before. What a curious design it was, she'd thought. Whoever thought it up? All those strange shapes.

What she'd needed was a helping hand and there hadn't been one. *God helps those who help themselves!* she'd told herself sternly. She'd crawled to the nearest bedroom door, reached up to grasp the old-fashioned brass knob in both hands and somehow used it to scramble to her feet.

Never said a word to Janine, nor to Tom Burnett when he'd called. Why not? Ashamed, that's why. Embarrassed, you silly old thing, she admonished herself, at being frail and old, as if it were something to be ashamed of.

A pity Janine had left now. A cup of tea would rally her spirits and she'd have to go down and make it herself. Even as she thought this, her ear caught the creak of wood. Perhaps the housekeeper hadn't yet gone home.

'Janine? Is that you?' she called eagerly.

But it was nothing, only the old wood settling at the end of the day. No one there. All alone and, as it was Friday night, Mr Behrens would be settling down for the Sabbath in the midst of his family. But, for Olivia, Friday night meant all alone until Monday morning, because Janine didn't come at weekends.

Olivia set off again, crossing the landing. She looked over the balustrade into the hall below. The chequered floortiles were swept and clean, but dull. No use asking Janine to polish them. Janine would reply that it would be dangerous, when what she meant was she didn't want the extra work. Olivia could remember the days when that highly endangered species, the parlourmaid in black dress and white apron, had been a familiar sight in any house this size. No longer, and she couldn't see Janine agreeing to wear an outfit like that. The very word 'servant' had become taboo. Employer and employee relationship had changed out of all recognition. Janine treated her employer as though Olivia were an elderly, obstinate aunt. Sometimes Olivia didn't mind, mildly amused, and sometimes she did mind, very much.

Either way, she thought, it made no difference. Either way she depended on Janine. Perhaps it was just a more honest age when the Janines knew their worth.

The shifting skeleton of the 250-year-old house groaned again, but Olivia ignored it as she started on her way downstairs.

Rory, looking out of his bedroom window that night as he rubbed salve into his sore palms, thought what a thoroughly unpleasant business the whole episode of the burial had been. Thankfully it was over and done with.

Turning to his wife, he remarked, 'I wish I'd remembered to ask Max whether he'd actually found any dangerous weed in his paddock. We may never get to the bottom of that little mystery.'

Gill mumbled, already half-asleep, as he slid into the sheets beside her. He'd had a busy day of it and went out like a light.

Sprawled at the foot of the staircase of Rookery House, Olivia Smeaton had already been unconscious for some hours and was sliding into eternal sleep.

CHAPTER TWO

When constabulary duty's to be done,
The policeman's lot is not a happy one!
Sir W. S. Gilbert

'I CONFESS it,' said Alan Markby ruefully. 'I am a policeman.'

'There,' said Wynne Carter, 'and they say there's no such
thing as coincidence. Just when I was thinking I ought to
talk to a copper. Just off the record, you understand.'

It was, whichever way you took it, an ominous remark.

Alan cast an apprehensive glance at Meredith Mitchell.
She was on the far side of the room, wedged sideways in the
deep window embrasure with her feet on the sill, and her
knees under her chin. The sill was covered with a blanket,
the usual occupant of which was diligently mousing in
nearby fields. It was early evening. A shaft of russet-tinted
autumn sun reached through the window and brought out
bronze highlights in her mop of dark brown hair. She wore
jeans, a denim shirt and an ethnic-looking embroidered
waistcoat. He thought she looked happy and relaxed, almost
schoolgirlish somehow, as she sipped at Wynne's elderberry
cordial. At the thought she was content, he also felt happy
and relaxed.

15

Although, following Wynne's announcement, not as relaxed as he'd been five minutes ago. It was a hazard known to any professional that people will try to pick your brains for free. They like to do it particularly when you are enjoying yourself and most of all when you are on holiday, as he was now. He turned what he trusted was a stern official gaze on Wynne and said, 'I'm off duty.'

She smiled serenely at him. 'Oh, I quite realise that, Alan! I wouldn't dream of pestering you on holiday!'

Ho, ho, ho! Wouldn't you? he thought. Alarmed, he reflected that 'ho, ho, ho!' was the sort of thing old-time stage policemen said.

'You will have your name and address took!' he added unwarily aloud.

His two companions turned mildly puzzled gazes on him. He had the grace to blush. '*Toytown*, staple diet of my extreme youth. Ernest the Policeman was always threatening to take names and addresses, usually Larry the Lamb's and his friend's, the dachshund's, I forget his name.'

'Dennis,' said Meredith obligingly. 'Dennis the Dachshund.'

'Oh, nothing like that,' said Wynne. 'I don't want you to arrest anyone. It'd be difficult even making inquiries. I know because I've tried and now, you see, the person concerned is dead.'

This was all very tantalising but he refused to be drawn.

Not so Meredith, as he might have expected. 'Who's dead?' she asked promptly. He glared at her.

Their hostess fumbled with a lock of grey hair which had slipped free of her untidy chignon. A forest of pins burst hedgehog-like from the knot of hair, reminding Markby of those defensive circles set up by Cromwellian pikemen. The effectiveness of the pin-formation was undermined by Wynne's habit of rubbing her hand over her head from time to time, presumably to gee up the brain cells within. As fast she returned one errant strand to its place, another fell down. He waited now for this to happen, and it did. He felt an obscure satisfaction.

Alan glanced down at his glass of blackberry wine. Perhaps the satisfied glow was due rather to Wynne's excellent homebrews. The blackberry certainly packed a powerful kick. He was glad he hadn't to drive anywhere tonight, only to stagger as far as the next-door cottage.

Wynne's mind apparently ran on similar lines. 'Let me freshen your glass. Would you like to try the carrot whisky? How about you, Meredith? It's not as though you've got to go far!'

'I'd like to try some wine,' said Meredith, 'this time.' She had made considerable inroads on the cordial. She knew Wynne had heard her question but was choosing her moment to answer it, aggravating though that was to the inquirer.

'Yes, please, wine,' Markby agreed. He wasn't sure about the carrot whisky.

Wynne rattled bottles on her sideboard. 'How about this? Apple. Not a bit like cider, rather more like a German white, or so I like to think. It will make an interesting contrast to the blackberry. Do try.'

There was a break in conversation for trying the wine. But even long-retired members of the fourth estate were not easily deflected. Having plied her quarry with strong liquor to soften up defences, Wynne returned to the attack, albeit in oblique manner.

'Dear Laura told me she had a brother in the police force, a senior copper, in fact.'

'Not very senior!' he objected hastily. 'Only superintendent.'

'That sounds very grand to *me*!' Wynne dealt easily with

the attempt to defuse her interest. She gave him a benign smile to let him know that he, too, dealt with a professional.

Alan felt powerlessness begin to creep over him. (Or too much homemade wine.) A hairpin tinkled to the stone hearth. Wynne stared down at it as if not sure where it had come from.

'I must say you *are* a very legal sort of family, Laura being a solicitor and you a police officer. But then Paul, her husband, is quite different. A cookery writer! His aunt, Florrie Danby, used to talk about it. She was always rather surprised that a boy should have so much interest in cooking. But, as I pointed out to her, look at the number of famous male chefs! I interviewed Philip Harbin once, years ago, when I was a young cub reporter. Do you remember him? He had a beard.'

She sipped her wine. 'He used to go round the country with a little show, cookery demonstrations, in theatres. Before the days of much television but he was an early star of that.'

'Paul's a very good cook,' said Alan generously of his brother-in-law. Or hoped those were the words he spoke. He suspected his speech had become a little slurred. He tried again carefully, 'A – very – good – cook.'

Meredith's eyebrows twitched.

Wynne didn't appear to notice anything amiss. 'Florrie Danby was my neighbour here for years. I miss her terribly.'

There was a moment's pause and an intangible *frisson* of emotion which caused Meredith, ever sensitive to moods, to glance curiously at the other woman. Wynne's gaze had grown faraway and a little sad. Meredith felt a momentary sympathy, resulting in a sense of awkwardness. It was all very well, being a career woman, as Wynne had been and she, Meredith, still was. Life seemed so full, so interesting and rewarding. And then, one day, pouf! It was all over. She gave the glass of wine a hunted look. This stuff was strong. Alan had started to mumble and she was getting maudlin on a couple of sips!

Wynne had rallied her drifting thoughts. 'I was afraid, when she died, the cottage would be sold. It does so matter who lives next door when one is semi-detached and living in such a small community. Florrie had been my neighbour since I moved here, oh, seventeen years ago. So when Paul told me he wanted to keep his aunt's cottage on, and not let it go out of the family, I just jumped for joy!'

'It's an ideal week-end cottage for them,' Markby said. That was better. The words were coming out properly now. With a return of confidence, he grew loquacious. 'With four children, going away is expensive. Coming down here will suit them fine, even though it's not so very far from Bamford. Actually, that's a bonus. No long drive to and fro. You know they mean to let it out for short-term summer lets? In between using it themselves.'

'I know. I don't mind that. It's better than having the place empty. Even if some of the visitors aren't one's cup of tea, it doesn't matter for a couple of weeks. And you and Meredith will be coming now and again. I dare say?' She looked hopeful.

'The fact is' – Markby glanced at Meredith who was holding her apple wine up to the fading light – 'we'd made arrangements earlier in the summer. But work prevented my getting away. No sooner was I free, than Meredith was unexpectedly seconded to Paris for a few weeks – consular department of the Embassy.'

'I couldn't grumble,' Meredith put in. 'It was Paris, after all. Besides, just to get away from that Whitehall desk for a bit! Bliss! Admittedly, it did stir up the longing for a real—' She caught Markby's anguished look. 'Not that I'll get another proper overseas posting now. But it was nice for a few weeks.' She raised her glass again. 'Here's to Toby's broken leg which made it possible.'

'Trust Toby Smythe,' said Markby unkindly, 'to bust a leg and necessitate someone else's holiday plans being abandoned.'

It went against the grain to express any sympathy for someone he couldn't help but see as a younger rival, despite denials from both Smythe and Meredith. Besides, it seemed to Markby that Toby trailed disaster in his wake, rather as a peacock trails his tail feathers. There was that occasion when Toby got himself chucked out of some banana republic and arrived home unexpectedly, which in turn led to Meredith vacating the flat she'd leased from Toby, and moving on to an archaeological site . . .

She was gazing at him reproachfully. 'He didn't want to break it so badly. They had to fly him home. He's still got the steel pins in it. However, he's up and around again and back at work – so here's to his continued recovery!'

They all drank to that.

'Meredith and I at last have two weeks, at the same time, for eating, drinking –' Markby raised his glass in salute '– a little walking. The best of holidays, doing nothing. We could have made the effort to go a little further afield, but the cottage is here and Paul suggested it. We thought, why not? If we went to a hotel, we'd be surrounded by strangers and busy staff. This would be much more peaceful.'

This last sentence wasn't, he hoped, tempting fate. As things turned out, it was.

Wynne was looking reminiscent. 'I miss journalism. I used to think, in my working days, how nice it would be when I retired. I imagined I'd sit here in my cottage, brewing my wine, catching up on my reading, pottering in my garden. Filling up my time nicely. But it's not like that, not really. Not when you've been used to life in a busy newsroom, people rushing about, stories breaking, loads of rumour and gossip and, in those blissful pre-Wapping days, all those boozy lunches!'

'Just as I was thinking not five minutes ago,' Meredith sighed. But Wynne's conversation, always likely to take an unforeseen turn, cut into her words.

'That's why I jumped at the offer to do some work for the morgue.'

This sobered up her visitors who stared in shocked silence.

'The morgue,' she explained, 'is the newspaper's obituary page. The paper keeps the obit notices of the great and the good on file, ready to rush into print should one of 'em turn up his toes. Since I've retired I've written quite a few in readiness – there are always new celebrities coming along. In addition, I've updated several of the existing ones. It's been very interesting and awfully hush-hush. The subject mustn't guess you're doing it.'

'I can understand that,' said Markby. 'Rather a downer to think that some ghoul – sorry, Wynne – some respected scribe is composing your obituary while you're still feeling hale and hearty. Enough to send anyone into a decline.'

'Oh, it's not that!' she assured him. 'They don't *mind*. They're delighted and fascinated. They'd give their eye-teeth to know what you've written, but they mustn't ever see the piece. So it's best they don't know it exists. Once they find out, they'll offer you anything for a glimpse!'

'I can see that it's fun, in a grim sort of way,' Meredith offered from her window.

The thoughtful look returned to Wynne's face. 'Yes, I've

enjoyed it. That is . . .' She fiddled with the cork of the wine bottle. 'Until that business of Olivia Smeaton's horse.'

Meredith set down her glass and swivelled on her windowseat to face the room. Ignoring Alan's frantic signals to disregard this blatant lure, she asked, 'What did it do?'

'Do? Oh—' Wynne smiled vaguely but Markby could have sworn there was a gleam of triumph in her eyes. She'd hooked them and she knew it. 'It didn't do anything, poor beast. That is to say, it died.'

It was make or break time. Now or never. Markby made a last desperate effort to turn the subject away from serious purpose. 'Are you going to tell us you've composed an obituary for a horse, Wynne?'

'No, for poor Olivia who died herself only days later. They buried the pony on the Friday and Olivia was found dead on the following Monday morning. I phoned the paper straight away to let them know. I'd already been asked to revise the obit. On the quiet, in view of her age. But no one expected her to die so suddenly and in the way she did! I'm not telling this very well, am I?' Wynne's apology was spoiled by her smile. 'Shall I start at the beginning?'

'It's getting rather late.' He glanced hastily at his wristwatch.

Meredith slid from her perch and came to sit on the floor by his feet, arms wrapped round her knees. 'Yes, please!' she asked a clearly gratified Wynne. 'Tell us from the beginning, everything!'

Markby stifled a groan and settled back in his chair. It was growing dark outside. Wynne reached for the switch of a table-lamp. It was going to be a long night, full of the telling of tales. The room was filling with ghosts, released from Wynne's memories. And it wasn't even Christmas.

★　★　★

'I had a call from the paper, way back in January,' Wynne began. 'Someone checking the morgue files had discovered an entry on Olivia. Inquiries found she lived here, on the edge of this village at Rookery House. So I was ideally placed to update the obit. The paper knew I'd be discreet. I warned them it wouldn't be easy. Olivia wasn't exactly a recluse, but she lived a secluded life and didn't mix in village society. She was getting on. But then, she never had mixed, not even when she was younger and first came here.'

'When was that?' Markby gave in and asked, reasoning the quicker Wynne got through the story, the sooner they'd escape. He hoped before she got round to why she was telling them all this and what she wanted him to do. Because as sure as God made little apples, this nice old lady wanted him to do something, probably drastic and, who knew, even slightly illegal.

'In 1975. It was the last fact recorded in the original obit. It left a twenty-year gap of nothing since then for me to fill in.'

'Perhaps, after an eventful life, she'd had enough of participating. Just wanted to jog along quietly, doing nothing.'

'No one really wants that,' said Wynne firmly. 'Even if they say so. Old age is bad enough without loneliness. But don't forget, she was only in her early sixties when she first settled here and even then, invitations were politely refused. She never issued any herself. People recall that although she wasn't pally, she was *visible*. She had a pony and trap and drove round in it so she was quite well known by sight. She'd exchange the time of day with folk and occasionally turn up in church. The pony was replaced by another. I think she had three ponies in the end – not all at once, one after the other.

23

'Eventually she gave up driving the trap and the last pony went into early retirement. After that she rarely ventured off her own property. The pony lived in the paddock by the house. Rory Armitage, the vet, used to call and check it over from time to time. In the same way, Doc Burnett used to call and check Olivia. Janine Catto went in every weekday to clean and also did Olivia's shopping. Ernie Berry, our local odd-job man – and he *is* rather odd, poor fellow! – kept the garden straight, nothing fancy, cut lawns, that sort of thing – and repaired anything around the place which came adrift. Max Crombie took care of any major repairs. He's a local builder. He has a daughter, Julie, and for a while the little girl got closer to Olivia than anyone else in recent years, or indeed, that anyone can remember. Julie's pony-mad.'

'Like my niece,' said Markby.

'Just like Emma. Julie wheedled Max into taking her along with him when he was supervising retiling Olivia's roof. She wanted to see the pony closer to hand. She got chatting, in a kid's artless way, with Olivia and the old lady took a fancy to the child. Olivia allowed Julie to ride the pony round the field.

'After that, Julie was down there every spare moment. Olivia didn't appear to mind. I believe she enjoyed teaching the child. I saw them together a few times. Olivia would sit on a chair beneath that old chestnut tree and issue instructions to Julie as she trotted round and round. It always reminded me of a *maître de ballet* and a prize student.' Wynne smiled.

'A pretty pony it was, what they call dapple-grey, just like the one in the nursery rhyme. Julie with her long fair hair and velvet hat, trotting round the paddock, popping over posts laid on the ground was a charming sight! I'd find Max there sometimes, watching, awash with pride. His little girl, apple of his eye, and all the rest of it.

'The child became quite expert and pestered her father to buy a pony for her, of her own. Max offered to buy Olivia's, but Olivia said no, the pony had been retired too long and mightn't be safe in traffic any longer. Besides, it would be better if Julie got a proper show pony, because obviously she was a nice little rider and the show-ring would be the next thing she'd want to try her hand at. So Max – plenty of money there! – went off and bought a beautiful animal, a palomino. Olivia's pony went back to dozing all day in its paddock. Julie eventually scooped the red rosette of her class in every show for miles around. Still going strong, heading for Olympia, I don't doubt, and the Horse of the Year Show some day. Or even the Olympics themselves!'

Wynne paused for breath. 'But actually, I'm getting ahead of myself.'

'What I don't see,' said Markby, 'is what this respectable, quiet-living, horse-loving and evidently kindly old lady could possibly have achieved which would make her passing of interest to the nation. Why an obituary?'

'Ah,' said Wynne. 'She wasn't always quiet-living!'

CHAPTER THREE

The man recovered of the bite,
The dog it was that died.
Oliver Goldsmith

'FOR A start,' Wynne went on, 'in 1937 at the youthful age of twenty-five, Olivia won the Kitwe to Bulawayo rally – ladies' class.'

'Crumbs,' said Meredith, impressed.

'That's not all.' Wynne was well-pleased with the result of her announcement. 'I take it neither of you saw the obituary when it appeared?'

They shook their heads.

'Of course, you were both too busy at the time. Why don't I fetch it? I'll put the coffee on at the same time. Won't be a tick!'

She trotted out to the kitchen and they could hear her clashing utensils. After a moment, the back door screeched on unoiled hinges and screeched again as it was reclosed. Wynne could be heard talking to whoever had entered.

'They're in the sitting room, by the fire. Off you go and say good evening nicely!'

Meredith glanced up with raised eyebrows, but Markby shrugged, having no more idea than she did, who the visitor

27

might be. Whoever it was, with luck Wynne might be deflected from her purpose.

It wasn't to prove so. The sitting-room door creaked and a cat of singular appearance strolled in. If he'd started with nine lives, he must surely be down to his last one. He had one eye and only half of one ear and the result was a piratical appearance. The tip of his tail was also missing. He cast them a look of fierce disdain, defying them to attempt any greeting, and jumped up into the window recess vacated by Meredith, where he began to clean his fur whilst keeping his one eye firmly on the interlopers.

Alan leaned down to whisper in Meredith's ear. 'We should've bolted out the back door when she let that moggie in. Why, oh, why did you have to encourage her?'

'Me? I didn't do anything!' Meredith turned a surprised face to him.

'Not half you didn't! You begged her to tell it all from the beginning – which was what she was leading up to anyway.' Markby slouched back in his chair and stared morosely at the tray of wines. They were all the colours of stained glass. His gaze travelled from deep ruby red, almost purple (damson) and greenish-yellows (gooseberry) to pale amber (apple) and a deep fiery russet. That would be the carrot whisky.

'Oh, rubbish!' The expression in his companion's hazel eyes became aggrieved. '*You* asked questions!' she pointed out, drawing the conclusion, 'So you were interested.'

Cogito, ergo sum, thought Markby.

The cat had paused in his cleaning operations and appeared to be taking a malicious pleasure in the discord between humans

Markby defended himself. 'Only because she was taking so long to get to the point. I was trying to hurry things up a bit so we could nip off home.'

'Alan! Don't be so rude! She gave us a lovely meal – and all that wine.' Meredith's gaze, as was his, was drawn to the glowing array of bottled delights on the tray. 'Actually, I think I've drunk rather too much of the wine. I'm glad she's making coffee. I feel a bit squiffy.'

'Wait until tomorrow!' he prophesied. 'You'll feel worse. Especially after we've sat here half the night listening to the adventures of Penelope Pitstop!'

'Sh! She's coming back!'

Wynne had returned, bustling with a newspaper cutting in her hand. 'Did Nimrod say hullo? No? He's funny with strangers. But when he gets used to you, he'll be very friendly.'

Nimrod sneered from his windowseat and scratched vigorously.

'Here we are. The only photo of her the paper could lay its hands on was years old, unfortunately. Taken during the war.'

'That *is* old . . .' Markby muttered.

Meredith took the clipping. The photograph was clearly a wartime one. It showed a striking woman, wearing her hair in the rolled curl fashion of the day and sporting a uniform cap. She let her gaze drift to the text.

Olivia Smeaton who has died at her home, Rookery House, Parsloe St John, achieved fame, not to say notoriety, in the nineteen-thirties as a rally-driver and society belle. She used to joke of herself, 'They say I'm fast, and I am fast!'

She was born Olivia Adelaide Broughton in 1912, the only child and heiress of the armaments manufacturer, Wilberforce Broughton. She was a debutante and had 'a season' in 1933 during which she was the toast of the London social scene. Though there was much speculation concerning whom she would marry and her name was linked with several eligible young men, it soon became obvious that motoring was her great passion. Her greatest success came in 1937 when she was winner of the Kitwe to Bulawayo rally, despite being charged by an elephant in the African bush, and an attack of fever which, as she explained, played havoc with the map-reading skills of both herself and her co-driver.

The outbreak of hostilities in 1939 gave her opportunity to dedicate her driving skills to the war effort. She became a driver for the War Office and drove many senior officers and sometimes members of the cabinet, often on highly secret journeys. In 1944 she married Colonel Marcus Smeaton. Tragically, he was killed only six months later and his death, so near the final days of the conflict, was always resented by her as an injustice on the part of Fate.

After the war she became involved in charitable work, but in 1958, at the relatively young age of forty-six, she announced she was retiring and going to live in France. She set up house in the South of France in the hills behind Nice, in the small town of Puget-Theniers where she shared her home with a former schoolfriend, Violet Dawson. In 1975, she sold her French home and announced she would be returning, together with Miss Dawson, to live in England. But tragedy struck her life again. On the return journey, their car was involved in an accident in which Violet Dawson died. Mrs Smeaton was badly injured. As soon as she was able to travel, she returned to England and

*settled in the country. She never took the wheel again
but drove about the lanes in a pony and trap. Her final
years were spent in near seclusion. Her end, however,
was to be yet another tragic event. She was discovered
by her housekeeper, on Monday morning, at the foot of
the stairs. An inquest decided she had tripped and
fallen because of a loose slipper-sole and had lain dead
for twenty-four hours before being found. She had no
children and the bulk of her estate goes to charity.*

Meredith passed the clipping to Markby, who read it
through. Wynne watched them both in silence.

Alan put it down. 'Yes, I see what you mean. An interesting, not to say intriguing life.'

'It raises a lot of questions,' Meredith said slowly.

'To which', Wynne returned, 'there are precious few
answers, believe me!'

She gained a militant air. 'That obituary was the most
challenging job of its type I'd ever tackled! There was
clearly so much more to be said. Olivia was actually on my
doorstep, but I couldn't go to her and tell her what I was
about. So I had to try and run into her or call on pretexts and
slip in the odd question. When a person is like Olivia, and
doesn't exactly encourage callers, that's not easy. I had to
take up church work.'

'Wynne!' Meredith teased, 'this is beginning to sound like
the activities of the worst sort of tabloid hack! What did you
do?'

Wynne grinned back at her, unoffended. 'I volunteered
my time to the vicar with regard to his restoration fund. It
gave me a chance to call on Olivia, ostensibly to try and
persuade her to support fêtes and jumble sales and things.
She gave me lots of jumble, clothes, books, vases. She wrote

31

a couple of large cheques. She'd oblige with anything, in fact, except personal gossip! She was too polite to tell me outright, of course, but I could see from looking at her that she thought I was being impertinent with my hints and probing. Believe me, I was cunning enough to make a fox envious!' Wynne added. 'But she was a match for me. There were no flies on Olivia. I miss her.'

Wynne sipped coffee. 'Naturally I tried a second line of inquiry. That's to say I asked Janine Catto. Janine was willing but unable to talk. She told me that "Mrs Smeaton wasn't one for a chat" and so she didn't know anything. She did know that Olivia had spent some time in France but otherwise, Janine was surprised to learn from me that her employer had had such an interesting past. In the end I decided Olivia had learned the hard way that there can be a price to pay for frankness and had built a barrier against intrusions into her private life.'

'I was about to ask,' Meredith said. 'She and Violet were lovers, then? It explains her leaving England as she did. People weren't very tolerant of that kind of arrangement in those days.'

'Olivia never disguised the close nature of their relationship,' Wynne said. 'She wasn't the sort to sneak around in shadows or pretend. You see, I believe they could have remained in London, if they'd been what people then called discreet. But they weren't. Or rather, Olivia wasn't. Violet Dawson might have wished to shelter behind an outward façade of being just good chums. Violet had a rather more modest background than Olivia. She was the daughter of a country vicar and had no money. I understand, before she and Olivia set up house together, Violet had been "companion" to various elderly ladies. Leading that sort of life, she'd learned to be sensitive to other people's opinion, knowing that in the end, it did matter.

'But Olivia had never learned to fear opinion, do you see? And she really couldn't understand why Violet did. Olivia was beautiful, spirited and had her own money. She'd always flouted convention but even in that, there are acceptable ways. I mean, had she and Violet been artistic bohemians, or even believers in radical political and social theories, their behaviour might have been put down to eccentricity. But Olivia was simply a very rich woman who saw no reason why she couldn't do exactly as she pleased. It simply never occurred to her that one day she might take a step too far and someone might be offended enough to do something about it. She didn't imagine there *was* a price to be paid. Much less, that someone else might be called upon to pay it. She simply didn't imagine, in short, that anyone could possibly interfere with the way she wanted to live her life. She was wrong. Someone could and did. She hadn't reckoned with Lawrence Smeaton, her brother-in-law.

'He was furious about her partnership with Violet, seeing it as an insult to the memory of his brother, Marcus. He hounded them. Olivia would have put up a fight, but poor Violet suffered terribly and came near to a nervous breakdown. Olivia was forced to concede there was no choice but to leave the country. I'm sure in my own mind she always intended the exile to be temporary. Not a defeat – something she'd never have admitted – but a strategic withdrawal.'

'It seems pretty vicious of Lawrence,' Meredith mused.

Alan stirred in his chair. 'We don't know, do we, why Lawrence took that view? He may have thought that it reflected on his brother's own sexuality. After all, we don't know what kind of a marriage Marcus and Olivia had.'

'It may have been one of mutual convenience, you mean?'

Wynne nodded. 'Well, we don't know, as you say. Certainly Lawrence showed himself quite ruthless and others followed his lead. Hostesses dropped her name from their lists. There were some quite vile stories going the rounds and nasty jokes. Certain people went out of their way to behave abominably, sniggering in corners, knowing that Olivia or Violet had seen them, that sort of thing.'

Alan suddenly asked, 'Tell us about the horse or pony which died.'

Meredith glanced up at him, and hid a smile.

'The pony? It was poisoned.' On this note, Wynne, showing a fine sense of theatre, got up. 'I have got a picture of the pony, as it happens. I've just remembered.'

'You *are* interested!' Meredith said accusingly, as soon as their hostess was out of the room. 'There are dozens of questions you're dying to ask!'

'I'm human!' he protested. 'Yes, there are a few things which are mildly interesting. But not desperately so!'

'Do you know,' she told him seriously, 'I'd never thought you a hypocrite! Why can't you just own up and admit, you want to know as much as I do!'

'Because I don't! And I'll tell you why!' Alan leaned forward, his hair flopping over his forehead. 'Because Wynne's plotting to involve me in something! She's not telling us all this for no reason at all! She thinks something has gone on which oughtn't. I'm not talking of the past, or not the distant past. I'm talking of the relatively recent. She doesn't have evidence of the sort she can take to the local police – so she wants to set me on to it semi-officially, as it were!'

Meredith frowned. 'I wonder whether old Lawrence is still alive?'

'If he is, he'll be eighty-odd, at least, and we've no reason to suppose his feelings about his former sister-in-law will

34

have changed. He is, however, rather elderly to be poisoning horses! I feel strongly that whatever this is, we shouldn't meddle in it.'

'Max took this . . .' Wynne had returned and held out a snapshot. 'Max Crombie, just last year, before young Julie got her own pony. Here you are. Let's have the gasfire on. It does get a little chilly in the evenings!'

Meredith took the snapshot. It showed a pretty little girl with long fair hair perched aboard a somnolent pony in a paddock. A large tree was in the background. Someone, standing nearby, had allowed his – or her – shadow to get into the picture. It spread across the foreground tantalisingly. She pointed to it as she handed the photo up to Markby behind her.

He took it and nodded. 'Not the photographer,' he said. 'Someone standing to one side. Might be a woman. Seems to be wearing a skirt. Shadows play tricks.'

'That', said Wynne placidly, 'was probably Olivia.'

'I've got a question,' said Meredith, ignoring a painful prod between her shoulderblades. 'About photos. It's about the picture in the obit notice. You said it's the only one and it's a wartime one. But she must have had a passport.'

'She destroyed it – at least, it couldn't be found among her papers. There's no record now of her original passport application.'

'But during all those years in France,' Meredith persisted. 'She must have had that original passport renewed, or a new one issued, probably by the nearest consular authority.'

Wynne shook her head. 'I admit I didn't try that line of research, but she left France in the seventies. There would be nothing kept on record for so long, surely? I mean, any application for renewal of passport?'

Meredith sighed. 'No, probably weeded out years ago.'

'The pony,' said Markby in some exasperation. 'Are we never to get to the story of this wretched animal?'

'It was the hot summer,' Wynne told them. 'No rain for weeks and all the pasture everywhere very poor. I suppose Olivia's pony must have been all right in his paddock in a normal year, but this year wasn't normal. He must have been scraping around looking for anything which looked succulent and edible. Unfortunately he found some ragwort. To be precise, what's called Oxford Ragwort. It's poisonous to grazing animals. Rory Armitage, our vet, was called in as soon as it appeared ill, but apparently the ragwort does its evil business in secret and, by the time symptoms appear, it's generally too late. The pony died. Olivia was distraught. She insisted on the animal being buried in its paddock. That,' Wynne nodded vigorously, 'wasn't easy! The ground was like iron! Ask Rory about it. He was there.'

Markby stretched out his legs and cast Meredith a slightly superior look. 'A very sad affair and I understand Mrs Smeaton was upset. But hardly sinister! The poisoning was accidental.'

Wynne fiddled with a sugar spoon and murmured, 'You ought to talk to Rory.'

'What about this business of the loose slipper sole?' Meredith asked.

Wynne brightened. 'Ah, yes, quite! The slippers were old and one had a loose sole. Janine – the daily housekeeper – had been nagging at Olivia to buy new ones. Janine, a nice girl even if she does dress so oddly and the little boys – No, I won't get off the subject! Janine cut out an advertisement for the sheepskin sort Olivia liked, from a magazine. She took it along to Olivia and told her to fill in the coupon and send it off with a cheque. There was no need to go out shopping, mail order would take care of it. Olivia did that, about three weeks before the fatal fall. That's what's so tragic. The slippers, the new ones, arrived a day or two after her death. The cheque must have been cleared before she died. These mail order firms do often ask customers to allow twenty-one days for delivery, don't they? The solicitor told Janine she might as well have them. With so much of the estate to settle, a pair of slippers was just a minor problem. No one else wanted them and Olivia had left a small bequest, a couple of hundred pounds, to Janine in her will. The solicitor simply suggested she add the slippers to that!'

'Did she remember anyone else in the will?'

'The local church restoration fund.' Wynne grinned again. 'So my efforts paid off there! Two thousand quid. Young Julie Crombie was also left two thousand to help with her equestrian expenses. Apart from that, a smaller bequest to Rory because he'd looked after her animals and to Dr Burnett because he'd been so kind to her, about a thousand each and some little memento or other. Even two hundred pounds each to Ernie Berry and his lad, I believe, although she might just as well have donated Ernie's share to The King's Head direct, because that's where it will end up!'

Wynne shrugged. 'Everything else to be auctioned off for charity. It's been quite a business, sorting it all through. But the house is empty now and up for sale. You'll see it if you turn left out of here and just keep walking uphill. The gardens need laying out again, but it commands a spectacular view. It's a lovely house. I just hope someone will buy it who appreciates it.'

'Wonder what they want for it . . .' Markby's eyes had taken on a faraway look at the mention of the gardens.

'We can go and look at it!' Meredith beamed. 'Tomorrow. Who's got the keys? The solicitor? An estate agent?'

'Both – but they're in town. If you want to view it, Janine

still has a key. She goes in regularly to keep an eye on it. She'll let you borrow it if I go with you and vouch for you!' Wynne smiled happily at them both.

Markby, realising that by his interest in the gardens, he'd displayed an Achilles Heel in his defence, sighed. 'All right, no harm in taking a look. We'll get the key off Janine tomorrow. Now, in the meantime, it's getting late and we must be off! Thank you, Wynne, for a delightful evening!'

CHAPTER FOUR

An enemy hath done this.
Matthew 13:28

'THERE ISN'T any mystery, you know,' he said firmly when they'd reached their own cottage.

'We'll see. No harm in looking over the house, anyway.'

'The house.' Alan sounded thoughtful. 'Didn't Wynne say it had a large garden?'

'Overgrown or more or less. I don't think the handyman, Berry, did very much. Mr Berry the Gardener . . .' Meredith giggled. 'Happy families. You know, Mr Bun the Baker—'

'Good grief, you have had too much to drink!' he told her.

The night breeze caused the trees to rustle. A branch tapped at the tiny dormer window, and Meredith stirred. Alan slumbered, dead to the world. All that wine, she thought still half-asleep. I wasn't the only one.

She opened her eyes, suddenly wide-awake and not sure why. She did feel very slightly queasy. Was it worthwhile getting up to find a digestion tablet?

The window rattled again. Outside came a crack, as of a twig snapping. The breeze tugged insistently at the window catch in a stronger gust. She hoped that didn't mean rain.

Another rattling outside the cottage, as of stones rolling, followed by a scraping.

In the darkness, the window formed a square of grey light. The branch which caused the noise was bowing and swaying against the pane. The scraping came again. It wasn't from the branch – it came from ground level.

An animal, perhaps, foraging around outside? Nimrod slipped out again to renew his patrol, or even a fox? For a few minutes Meredith considered the option of getting out of bed, going to the window to investigate, moving on to the bathroom to find the Rap-eze, finding her way back. All too much like hard work when she was so warm and comfortable here.

'Alan?' she whispered.

No reply. Meredith settled back. Outside came a final flurry of sound, a muted clicking noise. It didn't sound like any animal she could identify. Unless hedgehogs, she thought. They can make funny noises.

She lay awake for some time afterwards, wanting to go back to sleep but unable to, straining her ears though she heard no further unidentified sounds from outside. Fighting wakefulness now became a priority. Alan's continued oblivion made her positively resentful. How could he just slumber on like that?

It sometimes helped one to get back to sleep, if one got up and moved about for a bit, doing something constructive like making a cup of tea. Oddly enough, this was the time of the night when sleep could prove fatal. Between three and four in the morning ran the hour when death gained a natural advantage in its struggle with life. She'd read that somewhere. By four in the morning, the body's temperature has fallen to its lowest point and sleep has temporarily shut down some of its functions. Unaware, the vulnerable drift further and further away, unable to take measures to fight back because they simply don't know . . .

And if that cheery thought didn't get you out of bed and throwing the arms around in a few exercises, nothing would.

Meredith slid cautiously from beneath the duvet and now that it was too late to investigate the noises, peered from the window. It was early dawn, a glimmering light on the horizon and about – she consulted the luminous dial of the alarm clock on the bedside table, Alan's side – just about twenty to five. The danger hour had passed and a new day beckoned.

Meredith padded to the bathroom and found the Rap-eze. That settled the tum. To make tea or not to make tea, that was the question. She went back to the bedroom where Alan was out for the count, just as before. Making tea for one was too much trouble. She slid back into the bed, aware that her feet had become quite chilled. The sudden warmth of the bed-clothes was quite a shock.

And it worked, that getting up and pottering around. Sleep overtook her, quite suddenly. But it was the secondary sleep of early morning when dreams come. Meredith dreamt. A confused adventure, like an old film, had caught her up in its last reel. She was driving very fast in an old-fashioned open-topped tourer car with Alan beside her. Only, when she turned, it wasn't Alan, but someone quite strange, an elderly woman with a pale set face and deepset burning eyes beneath the sort of motoring hat with a veil popular with ladies in the early years of the century. The woman stretched out a claw-like hand and gripped the wheel.

'Let me drive!' she wheedled. The veil fluttered around her face.

But Meredith refused to give up the wheel. It was important not to listen, not to let the veiled woman drive. Because if the passenger took over, Meredith herself would be powerless, chauffeured at even faster rate into the unknown towards some dreadful doom.

'No!' she shouted at the pale face. 'No, you can't!' And she struck out wildly, trying to push the strange passenger away.

'Oy!' said Alan's voice, breaking into the middle of things. 'Wake up!'

It was morning. Sunlight streamed through the tiny window and threw a bright stripe across the bed. Meredith sat up, hair tousled, eyes wild, thoughts scattered. Alan in his dressing-gown stood over her with a mug of tea in his hand. He set it down by her and she rolled over, reaching for it gratefully. 'Thanks.'

'You were dreaming,' he observed. 'Mumbling away. That'll teach you to knock back Wynne's firewater!'

'I feel fine!' she returned defiantly. She sipped the tea. 'I *was* dreaming, something about a car, an old car. I was driving and thought you were beside me, but it wasn't you, it was someone else. It was rather scary.' She sat up straight. 'What are we going to do today?'

The edge of the bed subsided beneath his weight. 'Did you really mean what you said? About going down to see Olivia's house? Getting the key off this Janine person?'

'Did I say that?' Meredith frowned. 'Fair enough, if I said so. We'll have to ask Wynne to introduce us—' Her words were cut short by a sudden commotion from outside the cottage.

'*Ahhhh! Oh, No – ooooh!*'

The scream came from just under the window. A woman's voice, rising in dismay and anger.

Tea splashed as Meredith scrambled out of bed. Alan had already reached the window and had pushed it open. He leaned out, his shoulders filling the gap. Unable to see past him, Meredith hopped about in frustration.

'Wynne?' Alan was calling, 'What's happened?'

'Come down and I'll show you what's happened!' howled Wynne's irate voice from below. 'Vandals! Would you believe it? Here, in Parsloe St John! Just look at what they've done!'

The cottages were a pair, semi-detached. The front doors were on the far left and far right of the block respectively so that the living-room windows of the cottages nestled side by side in the centre. Beneath Wynne's window had been a narrow strip of flower bed, bordered with uneven rocks, and filled with Busy-Lizzies and creeping stonecrop.

No longer. Only a strip of roughly disturbed earth greeted their gaze this morning as, still dressing-gown clad, they gathered with Wynne to inspect the damage. The uprooted plants lay dying in a heap. They hadn't been simply pulled out of the ground, but chopped into pieces so that they couldn't be replanted. The edging rocks, some with bright green stonecrop still clinging, had been dragged out and thrown around the tiny patch of front garden.

'Who would have done it?' Wynne wailed. 'And why didn't I hear anything? I can't imagine when they did it! It was all right when you left last night, wasn't it? And that must have been nearly midnight.'

'I don't think either of us was in a state to notice,' Meredith confessed.

'I shouldn't have thought,' Markby pushed at a clod of earth with his slippered foot, 'that whoever did it, would be bold enough to come up to the cottage while we were all inside, in that room.' He pointed at the window above the vandalised bed. 'Although, it would depend how drunk he

43

was, or they were. It was probably someone reeling home from the pub.'

'The King's Head?' Wynne shook her head. 'No one comes this way home or hardly anyone. Most go the other way, towards the council houses or the new estate – or to the terraced cottages in Stable Row. Besides, it's—'

She broke off and shook her head in disbelief. Nimrod strolled round the corner of the cottage. Seeing freshly turned earth, his one eye brightened and he began to take exploratory sniffs, prodding softer patches with his paw.

'Oh, no, you don't!' threatened his owner. 'I don't need you making things worse!' She clapped her hands.

Nimrod wasn't alarmed by the noise but he got the message and stalked off, his half-tail quivering.

Wynne was already dressed, in baggy slacks and baggier sweater. She and Alan, Meredith was aware as the morning breeze buffeted her bare ankles, were not.

'I'm really sorry, Wynne.' She hugged herself for warmth. 'Oddly enough, I did wake during the night and half-heard a scraping noise. I thought perhaps Nimrod or some other animal. It wasn't really loud enough to make me get out of bed straight away and go to the window. Now I wish I had!'

Wynne heaved her shoulders in a resigned gesture. 'They weren't marvellous flowers. It's just that someone could think it a joke. It's – unpleasant.'

'You haven't quarrelled with anyone recently, have you, Wynne?' Alan asked suddenly.

'Quarrelled? Here in the village, no, no, of course not.'

'Kids did it, then, or someone tiddly.'

'Not at—' Meredith met his eye and something in his expression told her to shut up.

'Some silly kid did it for a bet,' she said.

'I'll bet him!' said Wynne wrathfully.

'We were going to ask you,' Alan turned the conversation. 'If you had a moment today to take us to meet Janine, the key-holder for Olivia's house. We thought we might go and take a look at it.'

Wynne brightened. 'That's no problem. After breakfast?' She glanced at their dressing-gowns. 'Say about ten?' She stooped and picked up some pieces of Busy-Lizzy. 'If I stick these in water, they might root, do you think?'

'I was going to say before you stopped me, quite rightly,' Meredith said. 'Not at a little after four in the morning. Because that's when I heard the noise, the scraping and clicking, which would have been clippers of some sort chopping up the flowers. By twenty to five I was at the window and the culprit had gone. It was just getting light outside and that's far too late for anyone leaving The King's Head or for kids to be out.' She frowned. 'And too early for anyone to be up. Kids wouldn't chop up the plants, only pull them out. Someone thought about that damage. It wasn't spur of the moment. It was planned.'

'I know, but we don't want Wynne thinking about that too much. It was a malicious thing to do. It wasn't too early for someone to be legitimately about. Don't forget this is a rural community. There are plenty of people here who get up with first light. It might have been someone on his way to work. Farm labourer, perhaps? Or even a tramp on his way at daybreak after sleeping overnight in someone's barn or outbuildings? Villages can be clannish places, offence easily given and taken. If it's a tramp, she may have refused a hand-out at the door and thought no more of it. It'd be enough to inspire a spiteful revenge.'

'At least,' Meredith said after a moment, 'we're here, next door, for the rest of the week.'

He was at the window again, staring out at the quiet road. 'Yes, she is a bit out of things here, especially now she's lost her permanent neighbour. I hope Paul manages to arrange a long let for this cottage.'

By ten o'clock the sun was shining and the nasty surprise of early morning had receded into memory. Even Wynne appeared to have come to terms with it.

'It's the end of the summer, after all. I'd have been digging out that bed soon, anyway.' She led them forward. 'Janine Catto lives in Stable Row. She should be there, I don't think she's found another permanent job since Olivia died. There's not much work around here for a young mum. She's been putting in the odd hour or two cleaning for folk, but I'm sure she'd like another job like the one at Rookery House. I was thinking of asking her if she'd do two mornings a week at my place.'

A clip-clop of hoofs sounded and, ahead of them, a girl on a pony appeared around a corner. Horse and rider were beautifully turned out. The pony's coat gleamed like polished brass and its mane and tail were as thick as caramel candy-floss. The girl was about twelve or thirteen, just shedding a young child's podginess for the burgeoning contours of puberty. She made a competent figure in her velvet hat, well secured by a strap under the chin, buttoned green body-warmer and tight-fitting breeches.

'Hullo there, Julie!' Wynne sang out.

The girl raised a hand in salute. 'Good morning, Mrs Carter!'

'Max's girl,' explained Wynne, as the rider moved out of sight. 'A nice child, not yet spoilt by growing up, if you know what I mean.'

'That's the girl to whom Olivia left two thousand

pounds?' Meredith remembered.

'That's the one. Not, mind you, that her dad is short of the readies. There were a few people in the village who muttered "Money goes to money!" when they heard about Olivia's bequest.'

Wynne considered what she'd said. 'It's a funny thing, you know, but money very often does. Now Janine Catto, who's on her own with two growing boys, she could have done with two grand. But Olivia only left her a couple of hundred, though Janine had worked for her for several years, running all kinds of errands which weren't strictly part of her job. But there, it was Olivia's money to do as she liked with.'

They had reached the pub, a low, rambling old building on a corner. Above the entrance a painted sign showed, on one side, the luckless Charles I kneeling before the block. A masked figure stood over him, axe raised in both hands. The reverse showed the executioner brandishing aloft the king's severed head. 'Nice!' said Alan wryly.

Running down the side of the building was Stable Row. Its name suggested that what was now a village pub had once been a grander establishment, housing a livery stables, or even been a changing station for the stage. They turned into the narrow, deserted thoroughfare. Dilapidated terraced cottages lined both sides, but halfway down they drew level with a shop of sorts.

Very much of sorts, noted Meredith. An altogether peculiar place. Curious, she stopped to inspect the dusty window more closely. The shop didn't appear to sell anything which anyone would want, or had ever wanted, to go by the evident age of the brown cardboard packets and film of dirt on the cheap pottery plates. Strings of fly-speckled plastic beads dangled above unattractive ornaments. A black and white cat slumbered undisturbed right in the middle of the display, if such a motley collection of items could be dignified by that description. Perhaps the cat was himself for sale. She wouldn't have been surprised to see a grimy price ticket round his neck. Meredith glanced up. Above the dusty window was a faded legend: YOU-NAME-IT *Prop. S. Warren.*

There was no sign of life behind the window, yet it enticed interest in the way a jumble sale stall does. Realistically, you know everything there is rubbish. But imagination suggests there might, just might, be some unexpected treasure lurking amongst other people's white elephants. Meredith stifled, with regret, an impulse to go inside. Wynne had already moved on and Alan was beckoning. A visit to YOU-NAME-IT would have to be for another day.

Wynne brought the party to a halt before one of the terraced cottages. Before she could ring the bell, however, the door flew open and two small boys shot out as if propelled from a catapult. They were uncannily alike in appearance and dress, their only difference being in size. In their wake came a belligerent roar which filled the quiet lane.

'Bruce! Ricky! You just come back here!'

Bruce and Ricky had skidded to a halt either side of Wynne. They gazed up at her. Both had cropped haircuts, a single earring apiece, washed out black shirts bearing a gruesome image of a razor-toothed robot, jeans and dirty trainer shoes. The expression 'little man' once popular when talking to boys this age, would have applied well to either of the Catto brothers. Neither, except in age, was a child. Their faces were those of wizened adults, knowing, sharp and amoral.

'Morning, boys!' said Wynne with slightly forced cheerfulness.

'Mum!' yelled Bruce, the larger child, 'It's that Mrs

Carter!' The information echoed round the ancient walls of Stable Row.

'You got any sweets?' demanded his younger brother in a voice surprisingly husky for one so young. Meredith judged him about seven and Bruce possibly eight or nine.

'Sorry, not today,' Wynne apologised.

'What, nuffin'?' Disgust entered his face and voice.

'C'mon!' ordered his elder and the pair raced off along Stable Row.

'Can't you just see them?' Wynne asked, *sotto voce*, in a kindly tone. 'In a few years' time? In the juvenile court?'

Reply wasn't called for. The mother of the youthful tearaways had appeared.

When Wynne had first talked of Olivia's housekeeper, the image Meredith had automatically formed had been of someone of middle years, motherly, pinny-clad. Hearing that Janine Catto was a single mother, she'd revised this image to someone younger and more modern. But not, as it turned out, modern enough.

The woman who appeared in the doorway was about twenty-eight. She was clad in black tee-shirt and tight leggings. Black seemed a favoured colour in this household. On her feet Janine wore, incongruously, a pair of expensive red sheepskin slippers. Her hair was cropped short, very like her sons', and streaked purple and dull auburn as if she hadn't been able to make up her mind which bottle of hair colourant to use. From one ear dangled a silver skull. The other ear was festooned round the outer rim with various metal studs. The impression she gave was of pent-up energy, about to erupt with ferocious result.

She was, however, smiling. 'Ullo,' she said. 'You see which way them bleedin' kids went?'

'That-a-way,' the visitors chimed in unison, indicating the flight path of the infant duo.

'That's all right, then,' said their mother. 'They've gone to see Sadie Warren at the shop. They've been off school, sick.'

'Oh? What's been wrong with them?' Wynne asked apprehensively.

'Nothing much,' returned the boys' robust parent. 'Just one of them tummy bugs, that's what Doctor Burnett said. They kept being sick. But they're all right now. They go back to school next week.'

She sounded as if she was looking forward to this. Meredith wondered if Bruce and Ricky's luckless teachers felt the same way.

'You coming in, then?' Janine pointed down her dark narrow hallway in a manner more imperious than inviting. The visitors drew back nervously.

'Actually, Janine, we've come to borrow the key to Rookery House.' Wynne indicated her companions. 'This is Miss Mitchell and—' Wynne hesitated barely perceptibly. 'And Mr Markby. They'd like to view the house.'

'Oh, yeah.' Janine peered at Meredith and Alan. 'You're staying in Mrs Danby's cottage.'

'That's right,' Alan told her, smiling. He was well aware that Wynne had paused to substitute 'Mr' for 'Superintendent'. Knowing he was a policeman probably wouldn't go down well with Janine. She was of that type constantly at war with authority in any form.

'I'll come with you,' Janine said. 'If you'll just hang on a tick. I was going down there myself to check it over. I promised the estate agent I'd keep an eye on things. Hold on.' She vanished indoors.

'You mustn't get the wrong impression of Janine,' said Wynne quickly, as soon as the coast was clear. 'She's a thoroughly decent, hard-working, reliable girl. The children have run rather wild, but that's because poor Janine just hasn't had the time to watch over them. She does her best.'

Janine reappeared. She had changed the slippers for strong lace-up black boots. She pulled the door closed behind her with a slam. 'Right, then, off we go!'

'What about your boys?' asked Meredith. 'Will they – um – want to get back indoors?' She prayed Janine wasn't planning to collect the boys *en route* and bring them along too.

Janine shook her multi-coloured head and the silver skull bounced around in a jolly way. 'Have to wait, then, won't they? They're all right. Sadie will take care of 'em.'

They marched past YOU-NAME-IT in a small band. From inside it now came a muffled childish clamour.

'Tell me,' Meredith asked, unable to resist, 'what exactly does the shop sell, I mean, what's its main line of business?'

Janine rolled a knowing eye at her. 'Anything you want, love.'

'Oh.' There seemed to be no follow-up to that.

But Wynne had one. She moved closer to Meredith and whispered. 'Sadie Warren doesn't so much trade in objects as in the intangible, you see.'

'No, I don't,' said the perplexed Meredith.

'Put it this way,' said Wynne. 'Sadie Warren is a witch.'

CHAPTER FIVE

DON QUIXOTE
Hunted 15½ seasons
24th March 1902 to 11th December 1917
Died 12th December 1917
In his 22nd Year
Sans Peur et Sans Reproche
He never failed me
Memorial to a horse

PARSLOE ST JOHN crept up the hillside in a long finger. Its history could be read in its assorted architectural styles. Entering the village at its lower outskirts was actually to begin at the wrong end, because this was the most modern part. Here mushroomed the council housing and the reviled new executive estate, living uneasily cheek by jowl with each other and a few small manufacturing units.

They belied the ancient origins of the place. Chroniclers wrote of an abbey, a place of contemplation, yet fortified and able to withstand attack in the lawless Dark Ages. It hadn't been able to defend itself against Henry VIII, who had expropriated the abbey and given it together with woodland and farms, to a courtier by the name of Parsloe.

The new owner had razed the abbey except for the church

and the abbot's house. He'd also added his own name to that of the church (St John the Divine) and between the two, created Parsloe St John. He'd been an energetic man with a nose for commerce and the place had thrived under its new materialistic squires. From this prosperous period dated its Tudor centre of low, cramped dwellings and shops huddled around a main street dotted with wider entries to stableyards. These were now given over to car garaging or workshops.

However, the world and the Parsloes moved on and away and so did prosperity. Parsloe St John ticked along nicely, thank you, but it no longer had any expectations.

Wynne and her companions toiled up the steep gradient and backward through the ages. They came first to the church, its massive stones and tiny slit windows recalling its earliest days. A large, newly painted wooden board announced that an appeal was underway for restoration of the tower and roof. A diagram, representing an old-fashioned thermometer, showed the rising level of contributions. Sadly, so far, they hadn't risen even to the halfway mark, but lurked at just under a third in a manner which suggested the generosity of the village had got stuck. Perhaps they hadn't yet painted in Olivia's modest legacy.

The church faced the former abbot's house. That had been taken over and enlarged by the Parsloes as their manor house, so Wynne informed them all. Now it was the home of Dr Burnett, having before that served for a while as the vicarage.

'They bought the vicar a house on the new estate,' said Wynne. 'It seems very odd. He seems to think it practical and reflects the church in the modern world. Not that he ever sees any of those people in his pews of a Sunday! I wouldn't have thought it made good economic sense to buy an expensive new house when the fabric of the church itself is crumbling, but the argument was that a new house wouldn't need expensive repairs, unlike the old vicarage. Tom Burnett got the place for a song.'

Meredith wasn't surprised to hear that, but thought privately that even given that Dr Burnett's house was very old, it was still unnecessarily dilapidated. She was sympathetic, knowing that to do up an old place cost an arm and a leg. Renovating her tiny end-of-terrace cottage in Bamford had taught her that. But no effort at all seemed to have been made to remedy the crying need of The Abbot's House. A modest application of fresh paint would have helped. In addition to which, repointing wouldn't have done any harm.

Wynne led them on until they reached a warm-coloured, kindly proportioned Georgian house, built foursquare to face the road behind a high stone wall defaced by a garish For Sale board. Wrought-iron gates stood ajar, allowing access to a weed-strewn gravel drive.

'Rookery House,' said Wynne.

By common accord they clustered at the gates and peered through, down the neglected drive to what had been Olivia Smeaton's home. It wasn't that large, thought Meredith. Perhaps it had been built for a couple who'd no children. In any case, it hadn't been too large for Olivia. The windows were closed off with what looked from here to be the original internal wooden folding shutters. Rookery House shared one area of need with the church. There was a tarpaulin across an area of the roof and it flapped in the breeze behind an ornamental parapet.

'Bit of water getting in,' said Janine. 'I told the solicitor. He said he couldn't do nuffin'. Mr Crombie, he come down and put that up. Shame to think the old place is being left like it is, just to fall to bits. Old Mrs Smeaton would turn in her grave.'

Markby was already moving forward, his hand out-stretched to push the gate. 'Perhaps we could take a look . . .'

There was a suppressed eagerness in his voice which didn't escape Meredith. She was fairly sure it wasn't Olivia's tragic fate which drew him to the place. So then, what? She felt a twinge of misgiving.

Janine shuffled a bunch of keys and found the right one. The front door opened easily enough in sad reminder of how recently the last owner had quitted the place, and admitted them to a wide hallway.

The shuttered windows meant gloom, but they could see the floor was of chequered marble and a wide staircase ran up to a first floor landing. To the left, a door stood open leading to a drawing room. Janine marched in and in her no-nonsense manner threw open the nearest shutter.

'I do my best to keep the place from getting fusty,' she said truculently. 'Seeing as it's not really my job any more, is it? I don't get paid like a proper caretaker would. I get what Mr Behrens the solicitor calls an honorarium.' Janine looked pleased at mastering this word. 'To compensate me for my trouble.' She spoke the last words in slightly prissy tones which Meredith guessed were meant to mimic Mr Behrens. She suppressed a smile.

Light streamed through, dust particles dancing in the beam, and illuminated the graceful, sensible proportions of the room, the moulded plaster frieze running around the ceiling and the fine classical fireplace. The floorboards appeared to be original, wide, probably oak, and uneven. Meredith tapped her foot on one experimentally.

'Funny to see it like this,' observed Janine. 'All empty. She had a lot of nice things. You see *Pride and Prejudice* on the telly? She had a lot of furniture like that.'

'Pity it's all been sold,' said Meredith. 'Whoever buys the house eventually ought to try and furnish it in keeping with its period.'

'I wasn't too keen on the old stuff myself,' said Janine. 'Too much polishing and regular dust-catchers, all these carved bits.' She ran a finger along the bevelled panels of a folded wooden shutter.

Markby was peering at a wall. 'Well, I'm blowed . . .' he said.

'Oh, it needs a lick of paint,' Janine agreed. 'Gawd knows when it was last done.'

'Last done?' Alan turned to smile at her. 'I'd say it was last painted around the time of the Regency or very little later. Just like you said, Janine, about the time of *Pride and Prejudice*. This shade of pink was usually obtained by using pig's blood.'

'Really?' Wynne moved closer. 'I really hadn't paid much attention.' She surveyed the wall. 'What a dreadful thought!' she said suddenly. 'Not the pig's blood. I mean, the thought that someone might buy this place and paint over the whole lot with modern emulsion!'

'Don't!' Meredith exclaimed.

'Best thing, if you ask me,' said Janine. 'You want to see the rest?'

'They want to see the staircase!' Wynne said loudly and as if in echo to her voice, somewhere in the distance, a door or a loose shutter banged.

Here, then, had Olivia Smeaton died alone. Here she'd lain, possibly unconscious but perhaps conscious for a while but unable to move, possibly for as long as two whole days and nights before being found by Janine on the Monday morning.

'Just there.' Janine pointed. 'That's where I found her.'

They stood in silence, looking down at the patch at the foot of the stairs. Faint chalk marks could be seen on the marble. Meredith shivered.

Alan was looking up the staircase. 'She fell from somewhere up there, you say?'

Janine was clumping up the stairs in her strong boots. 'I'll show you.'

The worn carpeting had been left in place. 'Donkey's years old, the carpet, like everything else,' said Janine. 'She wouldn't ever replace anything. Not that she didn't have the money, but she didn't see no need. Not at her age, that's what she always said.' She stooped and pointed. A wooden balustrade was fractured.

'They reckon she stumbled, grabbed that, it gave way and she went down base over apex.' Janine sat down on the tread. 'And all on account of them slippers. I told her to get new ones and she sent off for them, only too late. But that's how she was. Plenty of money, but mean in little things. Never wanted to buy anything new and, you see, it killed her.' Janine nodded in satisfaction at a point proved.

Alan was examining the broken balustrade and muttered. 'Mmn . . .'

They redescended the stair to the hall. 'Want to see the kitchen?' Janine asked. 'If you're interested in buying, you'll want to see that. It wants all replacing, I can tell you that now.'

Meredith had forgotten they were here in the guise of prospective buyers and hastened to look interested in the kitchen.

It was, as might be expected, enormous. On one side was a huge Victorian range. A more modern gas cooker stood beside it. There was a stone sink the size of a horse trough beneath a window and a door leading out to the gardens.

Janine was looking sentimental. 'I cooked her lunch in here. Not that she ate much. A couple of potatoes and a bit of fish.'

'Did she eat in the dining room?' Meredith asked.

Janine shook her head and the skull earring bounced again. 'No, she'd always come down here. I'd go and call her when it was ready. We had a big table, stood there.'

She pointed and they could all see the four marks on the stone flags where the tablelegs had stood.

'I used to bake once a week, a load of jam tarts and a sponge cake, maybe an apple pie. That would see her through.' She paused. 'I'd been baking that day, the day I gave her the cutting about the slippers. She was sat there . . .' Janine pointed at the empty space where the table had been. 'It was really hot. Sun was blazing down outside and in here, with the oven being on, it was like a sauna. I'd opened the window there and the door, but I was still sweating. I'd just taken the last thing out of the oven, lemon meringue it was. I put it on the table and she came in and said, "I fancy a cup of tea, Janine." I fancied a cold beer myself!' Janine laughed. 'But I made us a cup of tea, we sat there to drink it and I brought out the cutting. "There you are!" I said. "Mail order. You don't have to go out and buy them, the post will bring them to you. You can't go on wearing those old ones," I said. "You'll have an accident." And she did.'

Meredith was sure Janine grieved for her late employer but all the same, she seemed to take a perverse satisfaction in the manner of Olivia's death.

Aloud she said, 'Perhaps Mrs Smeaton didn't mind the heat. She'd been in Africa, hadn't she?'

Janine looked doubtful. 'So they said. But she never talked about it. Never talked about nothing.' Here Janine glanced at Wynne. 'Only right at the end, not long before she had the accident, she said something really weird.'

It wasn't clear whether Janine realised the other three were hanging on her words.

'Yes!' prompted Wynne breathlessly.

'It was when the pony died. She was ever so worried about it. She loved her animals. Animals had true hearts, she said. Not like humans. And she quoted a bit of poetry, lines and lines of it. I only remember one bit.' Janine took a deep breath and declaimed, 'And only Man is Vile!'

'It's a hymn,' said Meredith.

'Thought it a bit strong myself,' said Janine in her normal tones. 'And told her so. Hymn, you say? Not very cheery, is it? Mind you, I've met a few rotten blokes myself.'

'And what did she say?' Alan asked.

'Oh, she said, "People can be so cruel to one another, Janine. I know it. That's why I've turned my back on the lot of them."'

'Whom do you think Olivia meant?' Meredith whispered as they returned to the hall. 'Do you think she meant Lawrence Smeaton?'

'Who knows? Perhaps she meant Marcus Smeaton, her husband! Want to take a look upstairs?'

'Suppose we should.'

Climbing the staircase took them past the broken balustrade again. The others stopped for another look, but Meredith climbed on upwards alone.

There was an open landing, from which it was possible to look down into the hall below, and corridors running to right and left. Meredith paused on the landing and tried to imagine Olivia Smeaton, standing here to keep covert observation of Janine at work.

Not knowing what Olivia had looked like, the only image which came was of Olivia, the uniformed driver to war-time VIPs. It didn't fit the surrounds and she abandoned all attempts to recreate the past.

Instead, Meredith took the left hand corridor. It was ill-lit, long, narrow and had a musty smell. It was lined with a carpet runner of Turkey-pattern, as it had once been called. It appeared every bit as old as the stair-carpet, ruckled in places, and suggesting it had been a bit of luck Olivia hadn't fallen on other occasions before the fatal plunge. Perhaps she had. It might be worth asking Janine that.

But Janine might not know. She hadn't been here all day long and old people, as Meredith knew, tended to conceal information about falls. A fall indicated the person concerned was no longer safe to be allowed to live alone. A fall could mean the nursing home. Olivia would have hated a residential home of any kind, surrounded by strangers, obliged to observe an imposed time-table. But what a size this house was for one old lady. The exterior appearance had been deceptive. It would make an upmarket bed-and-breakfast establishment.

Meredith began to explore the rooms to either side. At the first two attempts, a twist of the huge brass doorknob revealed a medium-sized bedroom. The windows were shuttered but, in the half-light, it was just possible to make out pale rectangular outlines on the walls, marking where wardrobes and chests of drawers had stood. The floors had been covered with linoleum at some point in the past when this had been popular. It had cracked and in some places broken away. That would also have been very dangerous to an unsteady elderly person or indeed anyone. Perhaps there had been a carpet which had been removed for the house clearance sale. It was such a pity all the furniture had been removed. A third door revealed a bathroom. This must once have been a bedroom, because when this house had been built, bathrooms had been unknown. Some late Victorian moderniser had installed this huge cast-iron bath standing regally on lion's paws. There was a wash-basin and a wonderful Victorian lavatory pan, decorated with blue sprigs of forget-me-nots. Half a roll of lavatory paper was clipped into a solid, polished wood and brass holder, itself an antique. The piping for these later hygienic additions ran around the walls, ugly and inconvenient, collecting dust, and held in place by large brackets.

Meredith proceeded on her way to the far end of the corridor. A door faced her, probably leading to a master bedroom, more spacious than the others. She flung it open, eager to see if this were so, and was struck full in the face by such an unexpected blaze of sunlight that she literally staggered back.

For a moment she was blinded. Then her sight cleared and she saw that though this room was as empty as the others, the window shutters had been folded back. The bright light beamed through the window opposite and framed in it, with staring eyes and gawping mouth, was a deathly white human face.

The yell Meredith let out brought the others pounding up to the rescue. They appeared in a confused herd, all asking questions at once.

'Sorry,' Meredith gasped. 'But I saw a face, an ugly face – over there, at the window!'

'We're on the first floor,' Alan pointed out.

'I don't care! I saw a face, I tell you, looking in!'

'Not a reflection?' he asked tactlessly.

'I told you it was ugly! Thanks a bundle! It was very pale, almost white like a clown's, and a bit foolish. Maybe he was as surprised to see me as I was to see him!'

'Sure it was a man?' Alan was walking towards the window as he asked the question.

'Yes – and someone turned back these shutters.' She was growing impatient with all the questions, as if she couldn't be trusted to say what she saw.

'I done that,' said Janine from the rear. 'I come down every so often and air out a bit. I must've forgot to close them all up the last time.'

Alan pushed up the sash with an effort and leaned out. 'You're right! There's a ladder against the wall!' He pulled his head in and turned to face them.

'Of course I'm right,' she said huffily. 'I didn't imagine it!'

'Good heavens, surely no one was trying to break in?' cried Wynne. 'Could it be a tramp?'

'We'll find out . . .'

They surged out again, led by Alan, down the corridor, the staircase, through the hall, out of the front door and round to the side of the building. But when the pack, eager to capture the intruder, reached the spot, they were disappointed. The ladder was there, propped up to the eaves. There was no other sign of life.

'Funny,' said Janine, standing arms akimbo and booted feet planted apart.

But Alan had spotted a movement in the nearby shrubbery. He plunged into it. There was sound of pursuit, followed by a brief scuffle and he emerged, propelling ahead of him a wriggling, protesting youth of about eighteen or nineteen.

'That's the one!' said Meredith immediately.

'I've done nothing!' whined the prisoner.

'Oh,' said Wynne in relief. 'It's only Berry's lad.'

''Ere, Kevin,' demanded Janine, 'What you playing at up that ladder?'

Markby had released his captive on identification. Berry's lad, or Kevin, rubbed his arm, scowled at Markby and looked as if he might take flight again. He moved a little away and treated them to a hunted look. He was scrawny, but muscular, with an unhealthy pallid complexion marred by acne, and ears which stuck out. His teeth seemed too large for his mouth and two of the front ones were chipped. He wore dirty jeans and a tee-shirt. Meredith thought that although her earlier description of 'ugly' was carrying it a bit far, he certainly wasn't very prepossessing, poor kid. The sudden sight of him with the light shining all around him up there, at first-floor level, had been understandably a shock. She wondered about his general intelligence.

'Mr Crombie told me,' said Kevin hoarsely in a defiant way. He flapped his long thin arms either in distress or to indicate the job they were meant to understand he'd been sent to do. 'You go 'n' ask him, Mrs Carter.'

'The leaky roof?' said Janine, putting two and two together.

The youth brightened. 'That's it. Mr Crombie said to go up and check the brickwork round the window there. Damp's got in the mortar.'

They gazed upward, following the line indicated by his pointing fingers. A stepped pattern of dark mortar around some of the bricks betrayed clear evidence of damp.

The youth had gained some confidence and it was making him bolshie. 'How was I to know you were all in there? I was climbing up the old ladder and I'd just got level with the window. I looked in and saw that lady.' He nodded towards Meredith. 'Didn't half give me a fright. Wasn't supposed to be no one in the old house. I nearly fell off me bloody perch.' He was growing steadily more aggrieved.

'Sorry, Kevin,' said Meredith. 'But it gave me a fright, too.'

Kevin ignored her apology and fixed his gaze on Wynne, whom he seemed to regard as the natural authority. 'Mr Crombie told me to check it.'

'Yes, Kevin, so you said.'

'But I haven't checked it,' said Kevin mulishly.

'That's all right, Kevin, go ahead.' Wynne smiled encouragingly at him.

'You oughtn't to go frightening people when they're up ladders,' said Kevin. 'What would Ernie say if I fell off and broke me bloody leg or sumfing?' With a last scowl he shambled off. Meredith wondered whether a fall from the ladder on a previous occasion had resulted in the chipped teeth. She watched as he shinned up the ladder at speed and in a highly professional way, hands gripping the centre of the rungs.

Janine offered, 'If you're interested in buying, you see it's been kept going, by Mr Crombie and me and Ernie Berry.'

They assured her they realised that.

Janine, pursuing the point, went on, 'Mr Crombie, he does all the building work around the village very reasonable as prices go. Ernie does any job you ask him and me, I'd be willing to carry on cleaning.'

'I'll bear it in mind,' said Meredith guiltily. The loss of a permanent inhabitant of Rookery House had adversely affected the economy of the village. Janine out of a job, Ernie and the lad, the gardeners, likewise – and Crombie who had carried out regular maintenance, though unlikely to be sent into bankruptcy by events, had still lost a steady little earner for his building business.

Markby murmured something about the garden and wandered off down a path between shrubs. Meredith hurried after him, before Janine began to discuss terms of employment.

She watched him as he prodded and pulled at bits of vegetation, scraped his foot against the dry soil and, finally, stopped before a lichen-covered statue of a lady in draperies.

'It's been left to fall apart, but it's a wonderful place,' he said wistfully.

Meredith's feeling of misgiving returned, sharper. 'Yes, it is – but a house that size?'

He mumbled and walked on. They came to the erstwhile kitchen garden, sunny and tranquil within its red-brick walls. On the far side was an arched gate. Markby pushed it open and they walked through to find themselves in a paddock.

Hardly a breath of air seemed to move here. The leaves of the fine chestnut tree in the centre hung limply. Alan pointed ahead silently. They walked together over the turf, not yet recovered from the summer drought, to a large square of soil turned not so very long ago, although it had settled and already weeds were beginning to spring up in it. The tiny plants looked to be mostly groundsel and nettles. Though far too big to represent a human resting place, it was obviously a grave.

'I suppose,' said Meredith, pushing back a lock of dark brown hair, 'if she hadn't any human friends, the pony really mattered to her.' She was sweating out here. Her forehead was running with perspiration and her scalp itched.

Alan, his hands in his pockets and his eyes fixed on the square of earth, said, 'It would have been worse if she'd died first. Who would have taken the pony? It might have passed into unsuitable hands. It was probably fairly old and it hadn't worked for years. Been sent off to the knacker's and finished up as petfood, I dare say.'

'Don't!' she protested, scandalised. It seemed blasphemous to say this at the animal's graveside.

He looked up and smiled. 'Think what we could do with this house and the grounds, you and I, Meredith.'

'I knew it!' she exclaimed. 'Well, what would we do? A huge great place, rambling old house with five or six bedrooms and two maids' rooms in the attics, garden, kitchen gardens, this paddock . . .'

'You liked the house,' he said obstinately.

'Yes, I liked it very much. It's the sort of place one dreams of owning – but—!' Her tone gained an obstinacy to match his. 'It can only be a dream! You couldn't get to work from here.'

'I could take early retirement. I've been a copper for years. Too many years.'

'And so what? And what about me? How would I get up to London and back every day? Impossible!'

'You could take early retirement. Before you throw a fit, think about it. Why not? You hate the London desk job. You've only ever liked being out there in foreign climes, doing consular work. And you've said yourself I don't know how many times, you're not going to get another overseas posting. So, pack it in.'

'I went to Paris this summer!' she argued.

'Only because the wretched Smythe broke his leg. It was temporary and a one-off. Unless Smythe is going to oblige by breaking bones at regular intervals.'

'Don't be facetious!' she snapped. 'You've never liked Toby.'

'What's to like? The fellow's a pain.'

There was a silence. The warm air zizzed and a fly had the temerity to settle on Meredith's nose. She brushed it away crossly. 'If I didn't know you better, I'd say you were jealous of poor Toby.'

A growl was the answer. Meredith dropped the vexed subject of Toby Smythe, although, for goodness' sake, she wasn't the one who brought it up. The thought impelled Meredith to riposte with an equally touchy subject.

'You told me that when you were married to Rachel, you had a big old house and it very nearly finished you off.'

'Finished off my marriage, maybe. But that was because I lived in it with Rachel. Here I'd be living in it with you.'

'For goodness' sake, Alan! What should I do all day long if I gave up my job and retired here with you to vegetate?'

'You wouldn't have to vegetate. Parsloe St John could do with a bookshop—'

'A bookshop?'

'Why not?'

'What do I know about running a bookshop?'

'Learn. It can't be that difficult.'

'It would be for me. I know absolutely zilch about it.' Meredith paused as an image flashed into her mind, not of herself surrounded by neat rows of books, but of the dusty frontage of YOU-NAME-IT.

'I don't think,' she said, 'I'd do very well.'

'At least think about it seriously.'

She was going to retort, 'I've thought!' but bit it back. He was standing there, head slightly lowered, hair slipped untidily over his forehead, his expression tense and that look in his eyes which said he'd set his mind on this and wouldn't let it go. It was a look and attitude she'd come to know well. As a policeman it served him well, she reflected. He didn't give up. He wasn't deterred by unco-operative colleagues or wilfully devious witnesses or sheer lack of evidence. If he thought he was on to the right track, he stuck to it, come hell or high water.

But what was such an excellent quality in an investigating officer, could appear as pure awkwardness in private life. She thought ruefully that goodness only knew, she was awkward enough herself on many an occasion. But Alan, unfailingly polite as he was to everyone, even the most abusive interviewee, and diffident though he might sometimes seem in some matters, was as unmovable as a rock when it came to what he believed. And what he chose to believe at this moment, in this peaceful paddock, wafted by a warm autumnal breeze and with an aromatic scent of hay in the air, was that they could live in harmony in Rookery House. The two of them, out here, marooned in Parsloe St John.

'Alan,' she said as reasonably as she could. 'I know what's brought this on. You didn't get a proper holiday this year. You've worked very hard in a new job. You naturally feel a bit fed up with it all and fancy putting your feet up here. But you'd hate it after a fortnight, believe me. So would I. It would finish off our relationship. One of us would murder the other one. It would be a toss-up which of us wielded the breadknife first!'

It must have been subconscious, she afterwards decided. Murder lay on their minds, hidden away, not really mentioned, but there. It was so nice and quiet out here, so peaceful, why should violent crime spring to mind?

There was a long silence. Alan said, in a diffident voice, 'All right, but I think you're being hasty. You haven't thought it through. All I ask is, give it proper consideration.' He began to walk across the turf. 'We ought to be getting back. Wynne will send out a search party.'

Meredith hesitated, looking down at the earth by her feet. 'Are you going to call on the vet? What's his name, Rory something or other. And ask him what killed this pony? How it was poisoned.'

'I might,' he said. 'Tomorrow morning, perhaps. Only to satisfy Wynne, you understand.'

'Absolutely.'

They walked back across the paddock, through the kitchen garden, down the shrub-lined path past the draped lady, and found Janine and Wynne sitting comfortably on a garden seat, gossiping.

'We've seen enough,' said Meredith unwarily.

'Going to buy?' asked Janine.

'Going to investigate?' demanded Wynne.

CHAPTER SIX

'You must not tell us what the soldier, or any other man said, sir,' interposed the judge: 'it's not evidence.'

Charles Dickens

'THERE IS nothing, Wynne,' Alan Markby said patiently (he'd already lost count of how many times), 'nothing at all to investigate.'

'Oh, I don't know,' said Meredith thoughtfully and received a glare which said plainly that he wanted a little support from her in this dispute, not a crossing of the floor to join the other side.

They were sitting by the wide stone hearth in The King's Head, in close proximity to one another around a rather rocky table. It had been getting on for lunchtime by the time they returned from Rookery House and Wynne had suggested they take advantage of the pub's menu.

'Mervyn Pollard is very keen to build up the restaurant side of the business. He hasn't exactly got a restaurant room, you have to eat in the bar, but it's not cramped. His menu is quite ambitious – sometimes,' concluded Wynne enigmatically.

They had repaired to this hostelry, Meredith and Alan

71

certainly expecting a choice of a hearty, rustic list of dishes. They'd been rather perplexed at being offered Indonesian Nasi Goreng, Cod Bordelaise, or, more familiarly, two varieties of ploughman's lunch, cheese or pâté.

'I see what you mean about the menu, Wynne,' Markby said, reading it through. 'Ambitious is the word.'

Some time later, Meredith pushed a lettuce leaf to the side of her plate and contemplated the russet smudge of chutney which was all that remained of her ploughman's lunch. She'd felt unenterprising, selecting this simple dish in preference to the more exotic items, but fried rice in the middle of the day wasn't her personal choice.

The landlord, the celebrated gastronome Mervyn Pollard himself, shambled across and removed the dirty plates from beneath their noses.

'You want the pudding list?' he asked. 'We got a speciality today. We got tirrum-oozoo.'

'What was that, Mervyn?' asked Wynne.

'Tirrum-oozoo, it's Italian, bit like a chocolate trifle.'

They thanked him and declined the tiramisu. Mervyn appeared surprised, and inquired whether they wanted another drink. His manner clearly suggested it would be bad form not to reorder, seeing as they'd turned down the speciality pudding, and they hastened to do so.

'Bring 'em over in a minute,' he promised.

Meredith watched him pick his way across his cluttered taproom. The roof was very low, oak-beamed, and the landlord very tall, a loose-jointed giant. A domestic chore like clearing the table seemed an incongruous task for him; the plates, in his shovel hands, tiny, fragile things. Her gaze rose to a notice pinned up to warn incomers of the hazards of the low ceiling. 'Duck or Grouse' it read wittily. Mervyn, to avoid being brained every other minute, had adopted a curious posture with his head on one side and one shoulder higher than the other, rather like Igor, Frankenstein's servant, in old films. He disappeared through a door into what was, presumably, the kitchen and could be heard exchanging banter with a shrill female.

Mervyn out of the way, Wynne returned to the battle. Her face was flushed, partly with emotion and partly with gin and tonic, and every pin in her topknot was on the point of tumbling on to the table.

'Look here, Alan!' she said vigorously. 'I went out of my way not to spell out what I think. I wanted you to come to the same conclusion by yourself. That's why I just laid the facts before you and let you work it out. I was most careful not to lead the witness, as they say. I thought, surely, as a police officer of great experience, you'd see what I saw, straight off!' A lock of grey hair came adrift and hung down before her nose. She scraped it back crossly.

'But you're not letting me work out my own conclusion,' Markby pointed out. 'You're trying to bully me into accepting yours.'

'I was a journalist for years!' Wynne riposted. 'I have a nose for a story and you, as a copper, should have the same!'

'Ever put a story into print without checking it out thoroughly, Wynne?'

'No, of course not!' She was affronted. The pins quivered and one dislodged itself to a gravity-defying angle. Meredith watched it, fascinated.

'Right, neither do I – I mean, neither do I go haring off without some evidence. And evidence, Wynne, is there none!'

There was that obstinate note in his voice again, thought Meredith. He hadn't really meant it about buying Rookery House, had he? Surely it had only been a fancy of the moment. It was a lovely house, of course. She sighed.

Wynne looked very close to leaping to her feet with frustration but was prevented by the return of Mervyn with a tin tray from which he set the drinks down before them, contriving to present each of them with the wrong order. As he shambled lopsidedly away, they sorted out their drinks, gin for Wynne who'd been given cider, cider for Meredith who'd been given beer, the pint for Markby who'd been given gin and tonic.

Wynne had used the pause to marshal her arguments. 'Now, Alan, you've got to admit that Olivia's behaviour was odd. She was hiding, that's what she was doing here in Parsloe St John.'

'*I vant to be alone . . .*' muttered Markby dramatically.

'You might at least take it seriously! If only out of politeness!'

'Sorry, Wynne.' He was suitably abashed.

Wynne leaned forward and hissed, 'Whatever it was scared her, it found her in the end!'

'Who sez? Oh, sorry again, Wynne. But honestly, you've not a shred of proof for any of this!'

'I do not believe', said Wynne firmly, 'that she accidently fell down those stairs. I know the sole of the slipper was loose, but she'd been walking around on it for ages and we don't know exactly how loose it was. I mean, if someone shoved her down, the first thing the murderer would do, would be loosen the sole a bit more. And the next thing would be to crack that balustrade. She could have fallen any time over the previous week, Alan, and she fell at the weekend when no one would find her before Monday morning. I don't believe it.'

'It's a coincidence, but they happen. She was very old and probably shaky on her pins, even without the worn slipper-sole. The inquest must have gone into all of this. If there'd been serious doubt, it would have been raised then. Presumably it wasn't. As for hiding, I wouldn't put it like that. She was an elderly recluse, certainly. She'd lost her long-time companion and previously to that, her husband. She'd decided to arrange her life without company. She couldn't face another bereavement, perhaps. Is there any suggestion she was unhappy in her last years?'

'Does anyone', Meredith asked mildly, 'want to hear what I think?'

The other two turned to her with some consternation and apologised, both at the same time.

'Didn't mean to leave you out, my dear,' said Wynne, patting her arm.

'Thought you were a bit quiet,' said Alan. 'Come on then, let's hear it.'

'Not if you're going to be flippant! Like Wynne, I consider this a serious subject. We're talking about someone's death here. And of course, her life, too.' Meredith frowned. 'Only we can't inquire into that now. It's too late. Wynne tried when she was updating the obit and got nowhere. But neither of you yet has raised the question of motive. Well, I know Wynne has in a way, someone from her past and so on. But I can't believe someone could still hate a woman in her eighties so much that they'd kill her. Mortal span meant she was nearing the end of her life and *that*', Meredith emphasised, 'is the important bit, or so it seems to me.'

There was a silence. Alan sipped his pint. 'Go on.'

'What do you do at the end of your life? You put your affairs in order and you check your will. She was an awfully rich woman, remember. Someone may have had expectations of her will. But elderly people sometimes change wills on a whim. So someone, needing the money, and believing himself a major beneficiary under her will, may have decided to – make sure she didn't get a chance to change it.'

'But no one did get very much money under her will,' Wynne said thoughtfully. 'Julie Crombie had couple of grand – but Max has plenty of money already.'

'So the supposed beneficiary was mistaken. I still think it's worth checking, if only because of what Janine told us.'

'You mean, when Olivia talked of how badly people treated one another?' Alan was watching her carefully.

'Not that, about how Janine persuaded her to order the slippers and when and where that conversation took place!' Meredith paused for effect. 'In the kitchen on a hot day, when Janine had been baking, and all the doors and windows were open. Anyone, either in the house or outside in the garden, could have overheard it. It might have given someone a very nasty idea.'

Markby put his face in his hands. When he looked up he said, 'You're as bad as Wynne – and I don't apologise! Yes, it's possible. It may have happened. But we have no evidence that it did! We don't know anyone was listening or even around at the time *to* listen!'

'You could talk to Janine again about that,' Meredith pointed out.

'No, not me, I couldn't! This has nothing to do with me!'

'And the other thing you're forgetting', Wynne chimed in, 'is the pony.'

'Oh no, not that wretched horse again!'

'Yes, it is a wretched story. Someone poisoned that animal, Alan. Go and ask Rory Armitage about it! Someone hated Olivia and wished her ill!'

They might have wrangled indefinitely, but Meredith, looking across the table towards the entrance, suddenly asked, 'Who on earth is that?'

The man who'd entered quite filled the low square doorway. He was square himself, of only medium height but with
immensely powerful shoulders and arms displayed to view
by a grimy singlet worn with his corduroy trousers and
strong workboots. The exposed skin of neck and arms was
thick with hair. King Kong in clothes, Meredith thought. His
head, however, was bald, a round, burnished dome, and his
features, tanned to a walnut hue, squashed and dominated by
a friendly grin. On second look, Meredith decided, the grin
wasn't so friendly. It was more a muscular contraction,
something permanent and without particular significance. A
pumpkin head, she thought. If I met him walking around at
Hallowe'en, I'd be terrified!

The newcomer surveyed the bar with his meaningless
smile and greeted everyone with a hoarse, 'Good afternoon!'

A mumble of voices returned the greeting. Hardly anyone
looked up. The newcomer went to the bar where Mervyn,
slowly wiping the top of spilled beer, said, 'Hullo, then,
Ernie. Usual?'

'It's only Ernie Berry,' Wynne said in a low voice. 'Our
odd-job man. He's no beauty but quite a handy person to
have around, a real jack-of-all-trades. Ernie will do anything
for money. No job's too dirty, awkward or unpleasant. They
called him in when it came to burying Olivia's pony. Of
course, he needed help to do that.'

'Kevin's father?' Meredith guessed.

Wynne grimaced. 'One supposes so. Ernie's never married and there have been several women living with him
over the years. He calls them "lady-friends". There hasn't
been anyone there for a while. One of them left a child
behind when she left. If Kevin really is Ernie's boy or
whether his mother brought him with her to Ernie's when he
was only a baby, I couldn't say. He's always lived with Ernie

and works for him. Ernie's quite a good workman. He's not a cowboy, as they call it. He doesn't botch things. But he has his limits. He's best with something manual and without wires. I wouldn't let him near anything involving electricity.'

'Bet he keeps no business books,' said Markby. 'And no, I'm not investigating that either, Wynne! I'm not a taxman. But I've come across a few casual labourers like Mr Berry and they invariably want cash-in-hand.'

'Ernie does,' agreed Wynne. 'But that's partly because he's illiterate. Can't even write his name.'

'So can't give anyone a receipt, you mean.' Markby was unimpressed by the excuse. 'And can swear to having no knowledge of any regulations because he can't read them.'

'He must have to fill in forms occasionally,' Meredith commented. 'How does he manage?'

'Kevin,' said Wynne. 'Kevin went to school in the village and can read and write. Kevin's not very bright but he understands things explained simply. I think Olivia used to help out if either of the Berrys were faced with something they couldn't understand. Read through printed forms for them or any letter they got in a brown business envelope. You see, Ernie wouldn't want any villager knowing his private business, but he didn't count Olivia as a villager who'd gossip. She was a lady and whatever she read, she'd keep it to herself.'

'And she remembered them in her will?' Meredith muttered.

'What's that? Oh yes, a couple of hundred a-piece. Which', added Wynne with asperity, 'was very good for Mervyn's business!'

'She was vulnerable, alone in that great house,' Meredith remarked.

They were alone at last, in the cottage, sitting before the fire that evening with an omelette and a glass of wine each. Alan had cooked the omelettes. Meredith disliked cooking and considered it a jinxed exercise where she was concerned. Anything she put in a frying pan immediately stuck fast to the surface. Alan was no cordon-bleu chef, but having a brother-in-law who was had helped. The omelettes were good. She said so.

Markby received the praise modestly and took up her previous comment. 'Yes, Olivia was vulnerable, as any old person alone is. Your theory about the will might have something in it, but there's no way we could ever prove it now. I've known lots of cases like this. Odd little discrepancies, unsatisfactory explanations, the involvement of unscrupulous people . . . It's not enough.

'Take Berry as a good example. According to Wynne, he's a good worker. He seems to have worked well for Olivia and respected her. Perhaps a bit in awe of her? He took her any official mail to read if Kevin couldn't figure it out. The man's all right in his way. Naturally, I wouldn't trust him. Seen that type before. They have out-of-date tax discs on their vans and keep shotguns without licences and television sets without licences come to that. They're not criminals. They just don't bother with the law. I agree, if I had an elderly relative, I wouldn't like to think she depended on someone like Ernie. But, in this instance, we've no reason at all to believe he cheated Olivia or took advantage of her.'

'But you will go and see Rory Armitage. You said you would.'

He sighed and put down his fork. 'Yes, let it rest, will you? Between you and Wynne I've got a good case for claiming harassment! I'll go and see this vet fellow immediately after breakfast tomorrow, catch him before he sets to work. Coming along?'

Meredith avoided his eye. 'No, you go. Two people turning up uninvited and asking questions might put him off. Man to man stuff, more like it. I – um – I thought I'd go back to Stable Row and that funny little shop.'

'What on earth for?'

She looked a trifle shame-faced. 'If you must know, because Wynne said Sadie Warren, the proprietor, is the local witch. I just want to see her. I've never met a witch.'

'And you won't meet one tomorrow!' he said promptly. 'Only an old dear who believes she's a witch!'

'It's not illegal, I suppose?'

'To claim to be a witch? No, not in itself. Depends what she does. If she just dances round in funny clothes chanting, fair enough. If drugs or sexual abuse of minors are involved, a different matter altogether. She'll probably claim to be a "white witch" and harmless. You'll get a lot of talk of pagan religions and pre-Christian beliefs, green men, the great god Pan, earth mothers, male and female elements of nature, summer and winter solstices and possibly just a dash of the Ancient Egyptian thrown in for good measure. Plenty of people believe that sort of thing.'

'How about selling spells?'

'I wouldn't advise her to do that, or to threaten to put anyone under a curse. That might be deception or extortion and might be a serious offence.' He looked up and grinned. 'You're not going to buy a spell, are you?'

'No,' said Meredith, gathering up the plates. 'I'm going to buy a souvenir of Parsloe St John.'

'Good luck,' he said. 'You won't get anything out of her except the usual ancient religious mumbo-jumbo. You're a stranger. She won't trust you. She might sell you a curious stone or some knick-knack, but she won't make any claims that it can do wonders. They're daffy, these people, but not stupid.'

Meredith, plates in hand, paused by the door. 'Do you think people in Parsloe St John believe in her – as a witch, I mean?'

He nodded comfortably. 'I should imagine quite a few of them do. Never underestimate what goes on in an English village.'

CHAPTER SEVEN

Three young ladies of our Town were on Saturday
last indicted for witchcraft . . .
Witchcraft described and explained, 1709

IT WAS a fine morning with a touch of crispness in the air
which suggested that the extended summer was at its end.
Autumn, with winter at its shoulder, rattled at the door.

Meredith liked this kind of weather. Summer and winter,
each in its own way, inspired a certain idleness or lethargy.
But on days like this the instinct was to get up and go. And
here she was, on the way to Stable Row at just on nine
o'clock, set to catch Sadie in her den before the day got
properly underway.

She'd left Alan back at the cottage, drinking coffee and
reading the paper. But he'd promised to call on the vet,
Armitage, and she was confident that he would. They'd meet
back at the cottage later and compare notes.

In Stable Row, Bruce and Ricky were kicking a football
about, their shouts echoing off the old walls. There was
probably little traffic at any time in this backwater of a
thoroughfare, which made it all the odder that anyone should
choose to open a shop here. Unless, of course, one had good
reason to be discreet.

YOU-NAME-IT was much as before. The window held the same dusty display of unattractive goods and even the cat was still there. In the same position, too, as if he'd never left. Meredith peered at him, wondering whether he was, in fact, alive. She detected a faint rise and fall of his poorly groomed coat. That was a relief. She had hardly time to register this, before she realised that she, in turn, was being scrutinised.

On the other side of the window, beyond the neglected display, stood someone staring out, studying her. Meredith had a fleeting impression of an inquisitive and slightly hostile gaze before a movement indicated the person had moved away from the window. There was no turning back now. With a slight *frisson* of apprehension, Meredith pushed at the shop door.

The room beyond was tiny and made smaller by the shop counter which took up a third of it. Behind the counter, and a large unwieldy Victorian cash register, stood the proprietor.

Sadie Warren was a tall woman, almost as tall as Meredith herself who was five-ten. This surprised Meredith although there was no reason why Mrs Warren shouldn't be tall, short, fat, thin or of any other dimension. But it wasn't just the height, it was the solidity of the woman which impressed Meredith.

Meredith was spare in build. Sadie was narrow-shouldered but bulky of body, her exact outline hidden beneath a pale blue tent sprigged with tiny pink and yellow daisies. An amulet of oriental design hung round her neck. Her face was oval, her nose of the type usually described as Roman and her gaze very sharp, the same gaze Meredith had already encountered through the window glass. Her hair, suspiciously black, was scraped up and secured with two bright pink plastic butterfly clips, one either side of her head.

84

Her lips were smiling at the customer, but her round dark eyes remained unfriendly.

Meredith thought of Ernie Berry. There were too many smiles in this village which didn't reach the eyes. *They share a secret* . . . she thought, and it wasn't a pleasant thought.

'Yes, dear?' said Sadie. Her voice was low, husky with a touch of gravel, suggesting to Meredith a lifetime addiction to gin and tobacco.

'Hullo,' she returned brightly. 'I'm staying in the village for a few days—'

'Yes,' agreed Mrs Warren as if awarding a pass mark for a correct answer.

It stopped Meredith momentarily in her tracks. Sadie clearly knew this already, probably knew a great deal more about Meredith than the other way around, and caution was called for. Did Sadie, for example, know of the visit to Rookery House? Yes, she probably did, because Bruce and Ricky spent some time here and, *ergo*, their mother also. Did she know Alan was a policeman? She might, because the late Florence Danby might have talked about her nephew, his wife and her family. Was there anything connected with Parsloe St John which Sadie didn't know?

'I thought I'd like to take home a little souvenir,' said Meredith. 'Not for me, for my friend's niece.'

'That', said Sadie in the same tone of agreement, 'will be the little girl who likes horses so much.'

'Yes, Emma.' My God, the woman knew everything! It was creepy. Did she have a crystal ball along with all her other witch's paraphernalia? No, reasoned Meredith, Florence Danby had talked in the village. Come to that, Paul, Laura and the children must have visited Parsloe St John enough times and Sadie had seen Emma and the other children. She took a grip on her imagination.

'Emma', she said, truthfully as it happened, 'collects odd bits and pieces of china. If it's got a picture of a horse on it, so much the better. If not, some other animal. Or a figurine of an animal. I saw, through the window, that you seem to have . . .' Her eyes took in the extraordinary assortment of items on the shelf behind Sadie. 'To have pretty well everything,' she finished lamely.

Sadie nodded and turned to the shelf. 'Well, let's see. Nothing with horses at the moment. No, wait a bit.' She rummaged among the stack of dust-laden pottery and knick-knacks. 'How about this?'

She put a plastic packet on the counter. It was labelled *Child's Needlepoint Kit* and contained a square of canvas, stamped with a crude picture of a horse's head, a few small hanks of coloured wool, a bodkin and a folder of paper.

'All the instructions are in there,' Sadie said. 'It teaches them to do something, educational. If she finishes it, her mum can get it framed. Kids ought to be encouraged to achieve something, that's what I believe.'

Meredith didn't argue with that.

Sadie had begun to delve around the shop, producing items from various nooks and crannies. 'Here's a little pottery spaniel, rather sweet – oh, a bit chipped. You won't want that, though you can have it half price if you do. An ashtray with a cat on it? No, you won't want to encourage kids to smoke. They do, quite young, if they can get away with it, like those two.' Sadie nodded at the street outside and, presumably, Bruce and Ricky.

'Where do they get the cigarettes from?' asked Meredith, shocked. The Catto brothers were, after all, very young.

'Pinch 'em, I expect,' said Sadie. 'But not from me. I keep my eyes on them two when they come in here. Now then, animals . . .'

Meredith asked suddenly, 'What's that?' and pointed.

Sadie turned. 'It's a picture,' she said in her literal way.

'But what's it of?'

The painting which had caught Meredith's eye was hanging on the wall to the left of the shelving, between that and a curtain of blue beads which divided the shop area from an inner sanctum. It wasn't clear whether the painting was for sale. There was no price sticker on it. It was, Meredith noticed, quite clean, unlike the rest of the grimy shop contents. She judged it by an amateur hand but competent and from the look of it, painted in the vicinity of Parsloc St John. The subject was an open meadow, surrounded by trees and in the very centre of the pasture, a pair of curious, unidentifiable grey shapes. It was to these that Meredith's question had related.

In some indefinable way, Sadie seemed to close up. The smile had gone, her eyes were blank and she held herself stiffly inside the blue tent. 'That's The Standing Man and his Wife.' Unwillingly she moved towards the painting and pointed at the twin grey shapes. 'It's an ancient listed monument, marked on the Ordnance Survey map. Like Stonehenge, you know, only smaller, just the two stones. The names are very old, too. Always been called that.' She pointed at the nearer stone in the picture. 'That's The Standing Man.' Her hand, small and plump, dropped down by her side. 'And t'other is his wife.'

'That would be a souvenir!' said Meredith.

Sadie shook her head quickly. 'You don't want that, it's got no horses or animals in it.'

'Not for Emma, for me. I'd like it. How much is it?'

'Not for sale!' Sadie hesitated. 'It was a present to me, you see, on my birthday. From an old friend, too. I keep it there because I like it.'

'What a pity. Is it by a local artist?'

Again hesitation. 'Mervyn Pollard at the pub. He paints a bit.'

Meredith was hard put not to show her astonishment, remembering how awkwardly the man had held the plates. That spade of a hand with its thick, clumsy fingers wielding a paintbrush? Apparently so.

'He might have another, then, if I were to ask him, another for sale, I mean?'

'He might.'

Sadie sounded a little annoyed. Meredith wondered, should she return for another visit to YOU-NAME-IT, whether the painting of The Standing Man would still be hanging on the wall where it could catch the eye of curious strangers.

Sadie was waiting.

'I'll take the needlework kit, then.' Meredith indicated it and took out her purse.

'The little girl will like that,' said Sadie as if in some way she was privy to Emma's innermost thoughts which was just the sort of impression Sadie wanted to make, Meredith told herself – and had made successfully for a long time, hence her reputation hereabouts.

'Funny,' said Meredith, picking up the paper bag containing her purchase, 'how little girls go pony-mad. There's Julie Crombie here in the village, I understand.'

'Doing very well round the local shows.' Sadie nodded.

'But learned to ride on Mrs Smeaton's pony, I understand? That was kind of Mrs Smeaton, wasn't it? A pity about that pony. I expect Julie was upset when it died.'

'It was an accident,' said Sadie. 'It ate some sort of weed.' She moved towards the door. 'Both times it was an accident. When the old lady took a tumble down the stairs, as well.' She opened the door and stood waiting.

Meredith took the hint and left.

★ ★ ★

Markby had been told where the vet's house was and set out shortly after Meredith. He knew he was doing so with rather less enthusiasm than she had. The whole thing was embarrassing. How could he just turn up and ask about a dead horse? What possible reason could he give for his interest? Would Armitage take it as criticism of his professional skills?

'Damn . . .' muttered Markby as he strode along, oblivious of the fine crisp weather which Meredith had enjoyed. 'I should never have let myself be talked into this. I need my head examined!'

The vet's house was lower down the hill on the very edge of the older part of the village, just before the beginning of the small, regimented estate of council houses with, beyond them, the bright new bricks of the 'executive development'. The house was of grey stone and stood behind a high wall, but was accessible through a wide gateway giving on to a gravelled forecourt.

As Markby turned in, he heard swearing.

No ordinary, run-of-the-mill swearing, but a rich variety of profanity denoting extreme anger or anguish. He saw that by the side of the house was a lean-to carport and parked under it, a Range Rover. Just in front and to one side of the vehicle stood two figures, a man and a woman. The woman was wringing her hands in a distraught manner and the man was shaking both fists in the air. The front door of the house was open, suggesting they'd just come out. They were, Markby presumed, Armitage and his wife. He opened his mouth to call out, paused and sniffed the air. There was a strong chemical smell which he couldn't, just for the moment, identify.

His footsteps had crunched on the gravel and the woman

heard him. She turned, her rather plain face twisted in dismay.

'Oh,' she said helplessly. 'Oh, are you the police?'

It was, Markby afterwards reflected, rather like the fire engine getting to the fire before it started.

He said, rather awkwardly, 'Yes and no. I am a policeman, but I didn't know you were expecting one. Have you sent for the police?'

The man whirled round, a good-looking, dark-haired fellow about Markby's own age.

'Too bloody true we've sent for the police!' he roared. 'And if you aren't it, what are you doing here?'

'What's the trouble?' Markby moved forward. The chemical smell was stronger.

'Trouble?' yelled Armitage. 'Look for yourself!' He stood aside and allowed the visitor an uninterrupted view of the vehicle.

The Range Rover had been very smart. Its appearance was now utterly ruined. A broad band of blistered, flaking paintwork ran across the roof marking the passage of a mass of bubbling white foam which now trickled ominously down one side. Multi-coloured streaks had broken away and dribbled their own route across the body. The whole reeked powerfully.

'Paint-stripper,' said Markby, identifying it at last.

'Vandalism!' yelled the vet. 'Pure malicious vandalism!'

'Who would do it?' whispered his wife.

'Hooligans! I'll see 'em in gaol! Where are those damn coppers? Hey, listen . . .' Here Armitage seemed to recollect Markby's earlier words. 'If you're a copper, you'll do.'

'Sorry, I won't. Not if you've already phoned the local police. I'm a holidaying copper. I called about quite another matter but, obviously, this isn't the time. I'll come back later.'

'No, wait!' Armitage caught at his sleeve. 'You're the only copper in sight at the moment and I want you here!'

'They're here,' said Mrs Armitage. 'I mean, the others, the real – no, sorry, I'm confused – I mean, the policemen I telephoned.'

Markby saw, with relief, that a police car had drawn up at the gate and two young officers were getting out.

'You're in good hands then . . .' he said, edging away. If these two young eager beavers striding purposefully towards them asked who he was, they might wonder what a stray superintendent was doing here.

'Please wait,' said Mrs Armitage, sealing his fate. 'Rory's in a terrible state and might start yelling at these two policemen and upset them. You can explain.'

It was as well he wasn't asked to explain anything in the end. Armitage explained the situation fairly coherently himself. He'd come out after breakfast, meaning to take the Range Rover down to the garage and fill up – he kept a full tank because he never knew when one of the farms might call him out. Anyhow, out he came and saw the damage. He called out to Gill and she came running out. While they were looking at it, this gentleman here arrived—

At this point in the narrative, a pointing finger drew the attention of all present to Markby, who contrived to look as much like an innocent bystander as he could. The two young police officers gave him a cursory glance and dismissed him. He wasn't a witness except after the deed. He couldn't tell them anything. He sighed with relief.

Rory steamed on. Yes, he usually parked there, under that carport. Yes, he had a garage but his wife kept her car in it. (Don't you, Gill?) It was a smallish garage and the Range Rover would be a tight fit in it. He'd been afraid of

scratching the paintwork so used the carport. Just think of it!
Afraid of a small scratch and now look at it! No, he hadn't
heard a thing. Neither had his wife. (Did you, Gill?) And he
had no idea who could have done it. (Have we, Gill?) No,
they hadn't had any other little incidents of malicious
damage. (Have etc.) And what the ruddy hell were the police
going to do about it? (All right, Gill!)

The officers sensibly let Rory exhaust himself, wrote it all
down, and said they'd be in touch. With this faint succour,
the vet had to be content. He watched the two young men
drive off.

'That's what I pay my taxes for!' he said bitterly.

'You'd better get on to the insurance company,' said his
wife.

'Yes, yes . . .' Armitage scowled, then looked up at
Markby. 'Sorry, who did you say you were? What did you
want? Is it a sick animal?'

'No,' Markby said. 'It's a dead one. Mrs Smeaton's pony.'

'I knew Olivia fairly well,' said Rory. 'As well as any of us
did, I mean. She wasn't the sort of person who liked having
too many people around her.'

They were seated in a comfortable, untidy drawing room,
Rory slumped in an armchair. Gill Armitage had just put
coffee on the low table. She handed a mug to the visitor, one
to her husband, took one herself and sat down.

'I believe', she said, 'that Olivia thought more of that
pony than she did of any human in the world. That's
unhealthy, isn't it?' She glared at Rory who was slurping his
coffee.

'I know what you mean,' Markby told Gill. 'But there are
plenty of people who have no friend but an animal. Of
course it's sad when the situation's caused by loneliness, but

sometimes it's by choice. The person may have lost confidence in people.'

'But Olivia could have had human friends, people who cared for her. She had no reason to be suspicious of any of us. We'd never done her any harm. She didn't want friends. She liked Rory, though,' Gill added as an afterthought. 'She was less keen on me, but that's because I thought she was a cantankerous old biddy, and I dare say she realised that's how I felt.'

'Come on,' protested her husband. 'You were always nice to her.'

'Yes, I was. But she was as sharp as a needle. She knew what I was thinking.'

Markby turned to the vet. 'What caused the pony's death?'

'Grazing ragwort,' said Rory shortly. 'It causes liver damage.'

'No doubt about it?'

'None. I sent the stomach contents for analysis.' Rory leaned forward to set down his mug. 'Look, I'll tell you what happened, even though, to some extent, it's embarrassing for me. Any vet can tell you of an elderly person who's very attached to an old and ailing pet. Olivia's pony was twenty-two years old. She'd owned it for twelve or so of those years. It had been a very hot summer, distressing to man and beast. When Olivia phoned me and told me the animal seemed listless, I wasn't surprised. I'd long had it in my mind that the pony wasn't going to last for ever and when the day came, well, it was going to be a shock for Olivia. I'd even discussed it briefly with Tom Burnett, her doctor.

'Tom agreed. When the pony died or had to be put down, it would be an awful shock. We'd both noticed Olivia had got very frail over the past twelvemonth, even though mentally she was alert. When I saw the pony, it was obvious its condition had deteriorated. I decided the moment I'd dreaded had come. The pony was dying of old age. I had no reason to suspect poisoning. It had lived in that paddock for years without problem and I hadn't had any other cases which might have tipped me off. I told Tom, and while we were discussing how to break it to Olivia, the beast died.'

Rory fidgeted and reddened. 'It was a bit of a shock to me, too, because I hadn't thought it would drop like that. I began to suspect I'd missed something. I got Olivia's permission to open it up. What I found made me suspicious enough to send away the stomach contents. You didn't know Olivia, Markby, but believe me, though physically rocky, mentally she was tough and when she made up her mind, she meant it. When I tentatively suggested it might have eaten something poisonous, she wouldn't have it. She was furious because she felt, quite wrongly, it reflected somehow on her care of the animal. She was as keen as I was on the analysis because she wanted to prove me wrong! She also decided she wanted it buried in its pasture. I tried to talk her out of that. The carcass was deteriorating. I thought it best the knackers came out and took it immediately. But she was adamant and as she was getting increasingly distressed, Tom urged me to go along with the idea and arrange something. So I gave in and called in the Berrys. It was quite a palaver, believe me. I had to establish we were above the water table and wouldn't contaminate any public supply and, even then, we couldn't manage it without borrowing a mechanical digger and a driver from Max Crombie. Ground was like iron after all that hot dry weather. The thin grazing must've led to the pony nibbling the ragwort.' Rory gazed into his mug, frowning.

Gill Armitage opened her mouth, thought twice about what she was going to say, and closed it again.

'So you were satisfied, once you got confirmation of your suspicions?' Markby prompted.

Rory shifted uneasily in his chair. 'Not quite. The thing is, we – Gill and myself – hunted all over that pasture and we couldn't find a single specimen of ragwort growing there. I would have expected to find some more springing up. There wasn't any and no one else found any in their paddocks or fields. We do get the stuff round here but not in abundance. Most people with livestock recognise it and pull it up immediately it appears. Max's kid, Julie, spent hours combing their paddock after Olivia's pony died and didn't find any.' Rory looked up with sudden suspicion. 'Why do you want to know?'

With some diffidence, Markby explained as best he could. 'So you see,' he said, 'it's possible someone deliberately fed the weed to the pony. A kind of vandalism, like pouring paint-stripper over your car.'

'Horrible!' said Gill vehemently. 'A sick mind!'

Her husband looked dubious. 'I've known horses attacked in their fields. It's a curious phenomenon. But generally it's an outward injury that's inflicted – often a sexually significant one. Poison? That's rare. Unless someone trying to be friendly to the pony and ignorant of the danger of ragweed, fed it to the animal?' He shook his head. 'They'd have to have fetched it in specially and fed it to the beast regularly. But if it was malicious, why on earth should anyone hold a grudge against Olivia?'

'I can't help feeling,' Gill said, 'what happened to the pony led to Olivia's death, or at least to the accident. You know she fell down the staircase at Rookery House, Mr Markby? It happened that same weekend, after they'd buried the pony. It must have filled her mind and she just didn't pay attention to the stairs as she should have done.' She paused, looking mildly embarrassed. 'My theory, anyway.'

'Did you go to the inquest on Olivia, by any chance?'

Rory sat upright with a jerk. 'Hey! You're not going to suggest there was anything fishy about that accident, too, are you? The poor old lady tumbled down the stairs, just as Gill was telling you.'

'We both went along to the inquest,' said Gill. 'The police had inquired into it very thoroughly. There was no sign of anyone having broken into the house. It was all locked up when Janine came on the Monday. She had to let herself in with her key. She found Olivia – just lying there. She – Janine – ran across the road and fetched Tom Burnett, our doctor. He lives opposite in the old Abbot's House. Tom reckoned she'd been dead forty-eight hours. She was wearing the same clothes she'd been wearing on Friday and the accident may have happened not long after we'd all left her.'

Rory looked miserable. 'It makes me feel bad. One of us should have called in over the weekend. I should have done it.'

'Don't blame yourself, Rory,' argued his wife. 'Tom Burnett could've gone in. He's her doctor and he lives opposite. You're only the vet and you'd done your bit by the pony. You deserved a rest after all the hard work.'

'I knew she was upset. And you know how Tom's kept busy with a young family. No, I should have called round. It would've been the decent thing and might have saved her life.' Armitage looked obstinate. He'd decided to be at fault and was wallowing in the guilt with a determination with which it was useless to argue.

Markby conceded that he had a point. Knowing how upset Mrs Smeaton had been, someone ought to have called on her over the weekend. But no one had. Had they?

'I understand', he said, 'that she wore slippers with a loose sole, and these were blamed for the accident.'

Gill nodded. 'The sole must have flapped as she walked. She was unsteady on her feet at the best of times, as Rory said. There was a broken balustrade . . .' Gill frowned. 'There were no suspicious circumstances. The coroner said so.'

'I'm not suggesting that there were, you understand,' Markby assured them. 'It's just that, frankly, Wynne Carter has been bothering me. She was upset about Olivia. She'd been calling on her over the previous weeks and had got to know her a little. Nothing can be done about it now, as I keep telling her.'

'Olivia remembered Rory in her will,' Gill remarked. 'She was very kind.'

'Only a grand!' her husband said quickly. He made a gesture of annoyance with his hand. 'Not that it wasn't welcome or that a grand is to be sniffed at! But it isn't a fortune. No one wished Olivia any harm. That's why it seems so – so crazy that anyone would poison the pony!' He shrugged. 'But then, I don't know why we were attacked.'

'Someone pulled up the flowers in Wynne's little front garden and threw the rockery edging around. Not in the same league as pony-poisoning or vandalising your vehicle, but suggesting the perpetrator seeks an easy target. The pony in its quiet field, unseen from the house. Your car in an open-sided carport. Wynne's flowerbed.'

There was a silence.

'I don't like this.' Rory said quietly. 'Someone's got it in for us all, haven't they?'

CHAPTER EIGHT

> It was proved against (her), That she cut off by
> Night the Limbs from dead Bodies that were
> hanged, and was seen to dig Holes in the Ground,
> to mutter some conjuring Words, and bury Pieces
> of Flesh, after the usual Manner of Witches.
>
> *Witchcraft described and explained*

THE INTERIOR of the shop had been claustrophobic and
Meredith was glad to regain the street. Bruce and Ricky had
stopped kicking the football and were consulting together
furtively, planning some mischief, no doubt. If it hadn't been
for the lateness of the hour at which the deed had been done,
she might have suspected them of vandalising Wynne's
flowers.

Her steps had brought her to the corner of Stable Row
alongside The King's Head pub. A side entrance to the rear
courtyard of the pub stood open and through it, providen-
tially, she could see the shambling form of the landlord
himself. He had just come out of the building carrying a
crate of empties which he set down noisily on others already
stacked in the yard.

Meredith put her head through the open gap and called,
'Good morning, Mr Pollard!'

Mervyn stopped work, caught sight of her, and made an effort to straighten up. He still had that lopsided stance, despite no other sign that he suffered from a curvature of the spine. Years of adapting to his low-ceilinged place of work had led to it. He probably lived here too, in the rooms above the bar. A pair of tiny dormer windows were decorously veiled in frilled lace curtains. She wondered if he was married.

He was coming towards her, dusting his broad hands. They were calloused and large-knuckled. It seemed more than ever unbelievable such fingers could wield the delicate hair point of a paintbrush.

'Hullo, there,' he said amiably. 'Taking a look at the village?'

'In a manner of speaking. I was in the pub yesterday at lunchtime.'

'Oh ah, I remember you. With Mrs Carter and the gentleman.'

'That's right.'

'You're staying in Mrs Danby's cottage, as was.'

Trying to gain information from any of the villagers was impossible, thought Meredith in exasperation. They liked to head one off by giving unasked for information about the questioner. It was one way, she suspected, of not answering questions about themselves. This time, however, unlike as in YOU-NAME-IT, she was ready for the ploy and to counter it.

'I've just been along to the shop!' she said brightly. Mervyn twitched a bushy eyebrow but, before he could speak, she went on firmly, 'I was looking for a little souvenir for a child.'

Mervyn looked depressed. 'We're not on the tourist trail here. Other places makes a fortune out of visitors. I've done my best. You'll have noticed that from the menu, the international flavour, up to date stuff.'

'Yes, I – we – noticed the menu was quite wide-ranging.'

'We got historic buildings,' went on the landlord. 'But we're not on the direct route. Main roads take the traffic away from us. Very rare we gets a visitor.' He eyed her as though she were an interesting example of some legendary species.

'Believe me,' she told him, 'you're better off without the traffic and hordes of people. Think how it would spoil the appearance of the place. You'd get fast-food eateries and tea-rooms and probably another pub or two.' Mervyn rolled his eyes at her in alarm. 'I think Parsloe St John has it about right. If people really want to come here, they'll make the effort. It is historic, as you say. Incidentally, while I was in the shop I noticed a very nice painting of some standing stones. I believe it's a local historic site and the painting was by you.'

Mervyn shuffled. 'Ah, I paint a bit when I get the chance.'

'Mrs Warren didn't want to part with that particular painting. I was wondering if you had any others, any local scenes like that one.'

'Only I don't get the chance, much.' Mervyn carried on as if she hadn't interrupted. 'Running a pub is a full-time business. Even when the place is closed, it has to be cleaned up, restocked, a hundred and one jobs. I haven't had time to finish a painting since, oh, early in the year. Come the winter, I may get a chance.'

'You haven't got anything laid by, painted some time ago perhaps?'

'No,' said Mervyn, smiling kindly, 'can't say I have.'

'Oh, what a shame, because I should be prepared, you know, to pay a reasonable price.'

'Oh, I never *sell*!' He gazed at her reproachfully. 'I only ever give them away – to deserving folk, like.'

And that, thought Meredith, is telling *me*!

'Well, if you should ever paint something which would like a good home . . .' she said.

'Oh, ah,' said Mervyn. 'I'll remember.'

He glanced at his wristwatch. 'Coming on ten o'clock. I got to open up the bar. 'Scuse me!'

He moved away but then paused, looking past Meredith. 'What's up, then?' he asked, but not of her.

Meredith turned. Unseen and unheard, a youth had approached and stood a few feet away, watching them.

'Berry's lad,' Mervyn informed her in an aside.

The lad looked much as he'd done before, of unhealthy pallor and lank hair, wary, poised to take flight. He wore a much washed sweater and stood with hunched shoulders and his hands thrust into his pockets, as if he were cold.

When he saw Mervyn look his way, he asked nervously, 'Ernie here?'

'Haven't opened up yet,' the landlord told him. 'He might be along in a minute, I dare say, if he hasn't got a job on.'

Kevin ran the tip of his tongue along his lower lip. 'We have got a job on. For Mr Crombie.'

'Best cut along then, lad,' said Mervyn.

But Kevin remained where he was. 'You seen Ernie at all? I an't seen him.'

The landlord sighed. To Meredith he said, 'The lad's not quite all about, you know. Good boy, though.' Louder he said, 'I told you, I haven't seen him not since chucking-out time last night, right?'

'He never come home,' the youth said.

Mervyn snorted. 'Oh, ah? Got another lady-friend, has he?'

'Just a minute,' said Meredith who'd been listening and watching closely. 'Let's get this straight. Kevin's obviously worried. Are you saying, Kevin, that you've not seen your – not seen Ernie since yesterday evening? That he ought to have turned up because you both have a job of work to do for Mr Crombie this morning?'

Kevin stared at her as he thought through her words. 'S'right.'

In a low but firm voice, Mervyn said to her, 'Best let the Berrys sort out their own problems. That's what we always do.' He walked over to Kevin and patted him clumsily on the shoulder.

'If you've got a job arranged, you go along there and ten to one, you'll find Ernie there waiting for you. He won't like being kept waiting, now, will he?'

Kevin shook his head, running the tip of his tongue over his lips again.

'Off you go, then.'

Kevin hesitated fractionally, then turned and with his hands still thrust into his pockets, strode off at a fast rate, head down.

'And now, miss, if you'll excuse me,' said Mervyn, 'I'll go and open up the bar.'

He made off rapidly and began throwing crates around with great energy. She just wished she could rid herself of that image of Igor, scuttling back from the local cemetery with a sackful of spare parts.

Meredith walked to the corner and looked up and down the street uncertain where to try next. Kevin had disappeared but a clip-clop of hoofs announced a new arrival, Julie Crombie on her pony.

She drew level with Meredith and their eyes met. Meredith tried a smile and Julie returned it shyly.

'Hullo, there!' Meredith called. 'You're Julie, aren't you? I'm staying at the Danbys' cottage. You must know Emma.'

The pony halted, Julie patted its silvery mane and said, 'Yes, I know Emma.'

She was indeed a very pretty teenager. Beneath her hard hat, her flaxen hair hung down in two long braids in a fashion still childish, but there was an awareness about her expression which Meredith hadn't been close enough to observe on the previous occasion. This was a young lady who knew she was pretty. Probably she'd realised, from toddler stage on, that she was attractive and known how to use it. Max would be putty in her hands. In two or three years' time she'd be breaking other impressionable young hearts. Meredith wondered how Max would take to the idea of brash young men paying court to his daughter.

'No school?' Meredith asked.

'My school's got half-term.'

'Oh, where is that?'

'St Faith's Girls' School.' Julie hesitated. 'I'm a boarder.'

No brushing shoulders with the hoi polloi for Max's little girl. Private education, expensive boarding fees, and a social circle well outside this village. That might or might not pay off in the long run.

Meredith patted the pony's neck. 'Mrs Carter tells me you've had a lot of success at local shows.' Julie turned pink with embarrassment and pleasure and wisely didn't attempt a reply. Meredith tried another approach. 'I was told you learned to ride on Mrs Smeaton's old pony.'

She was sorry immediately. Teenage sophistication, so recently acquired, was erased in a second and she was a little girl again. Pain entered her eyes and she looked away quickly, hoping Meredith wouldn't see it. A muffled 'yes' was barely audible.

'I shouldn't have mentioned it.' The contrition in Meredith's voice was real and Julie looked back at her.

'It's all right. It still makes me sad but I've got used to it now.'

'You found none of that weed in your paddock?'

Flaxen braids swung energetically. 'No, we looked everywhere. It was just rotten luck some grew in Firefly's paddock and he ate it.' Julie hesitated. 'I miss Mrs Smeaton. She knew a lot about horses.'

'She knew a lot about motorcars too. She'd been a rally driver in her youth, did you know that?'

But cars were of no interest to Julie. She looked vague. 'She never talked about that. We always talked about horses.'

'I see, well, good luck with the shows and so on.'

'Thanks.' Julie raised a hand in farewell.

Meredith hadn't realised it until Julie rode on, but the din made by Mervyn had stopped. She turned her head. The landlord was standing by the entry to the yard and had obviously been watching her with Julie and probably listening in. Catching her eye now, he turned and went back into the yard.

Meredith walked on, vaguely uneasy. She wasn't sure where to go next, and on the principle that fresh territory might offer something of interest, turned downhill towards Parsloe St John's more modern buildings. She passed by the council housing and in due course came across the executive housing, so new that the developer's board was still in place with pennants flying.

She turned in. It seemed unlikely any units still remained unsold. The houses were quite nice of their type, trying hard to look 'traditional' with their pale yellow building stone. The frontages were open-plan strips and they had little garden land to the rear. All had double garages, however.

Priorities change. The only person about was a man washing his car.

'Good morning!' he hailed her amiably. 'Looking for someone?'

Inspiration led her to pluck a purpose from the air. 'The vicarage. I believe it's around here somewhere.'

He wrung out a sponge, water splattering on to his drive. 'Just round the corner to the left. It's marked up.'

'Thanks. You don't know the vicar's name, I suppose?'

He frowned. 'Can't say I do.' He began to wash the roof of his vehicle with energetic strokes. 'Very pleasant sort of guy, though.'

That one certainly hadn't been encouraged by the presence of the vicarage into taking closer interest in the church. She thanked him again and set off.

Sure enough, on the wall of one of the houses, indistinguishable in other respects from its fellows, was a small notice: *Vicarage of St John the Divine*.

Meredith rang the bell.

The door was opened by a youngish, bearded man in a turtle-neck sweater. 'Hullo there!' he greeted her as if they'd been old friends.

'The vicar of St John's?' It was a little awkward not knowing his name.

He remedied that immediately. 'That's me. Call me Dave.' He beamed at her. 'And come on in.'

He ushered her into a modern sitting room which had little about it to suggest a man of the cloth. It was dominated by a large television set and a guitar was propped against the wall by a chair, suggesting he'd been practising on it before her arrival. There was no bookcase. Perhaps he had a study elsewhere in the house.

'A baptism?' Dave inquired hopefully, hovering.

'Sorry, no. I'm a visitor and I really wanted some information.'

'Ah.' He sat down and put his hands on his knees. 'See what I can do for you, but I'm a relative newcomer myself.'

'So you wouldn't have known Mrs Smeaton who lived at Rookery House?'

'Oh yes, dear old Ollie.' Another beam. 'Did you know her?'

Meredith's heart sank. She suspected this pally attitude would have gone down very badly with someone like Olivia. She denied knowing Mrs Smeaton personally.

Dave broke into voluble speech, confirming Meredith's worst fears. 'One of these grand old ladies, you know. Very old-fashioned and set in her ways, a real relic of the old class-structure. A pity really, because it made her stand-offish and lost her friends.'

Meredith suppressed the wish to point out that there were some friends one might feel happier without. 'I believe she used to attend the church sometimes when she first came to the village.'

Dave nodded wisely. 'Dare say. That would have been in my predecessor's time. He was a nice, doddery old chap, more her style.'

'It's a pity if an older person feels alienated from a church she's attended all her life,' Meredith pointed out, perhaps not altogether politely, but Dave's breeziness was already proving wearing, even after only a few minutes.

Dave, however, was oblivious to criticism.

'I did call on her a few times. Never say die, eh? I don't give up easily. But she was an uphill task, believe me. What she needed was friends. If she'd had friends, she wouldn't have died alone like that, very sad.'

'How so?' asked Meredith, a little more sharply than she'd intended.

Whether it was because he realised that Meredith wasn't altogether in agreement with him, or Dave had been reminded of something else, his chirpiness faltered.

'She'd have had someone calling in on her, see how she was, have a natter and a cup of tea. As it was, she was isolated in that house.' A touch defiantly, he added, 'I tried to get her to come to our club.'

'Club?' Meredith asked weakly.

'Oh yes, we're a thriving community here! Every other Wednesday afternoon we get our old folk into the Parish Centre – have you seen it? Only temporary at the moment, a converted garage back of Stable Row? Still, people are more important than brick walls. We have a really jolly time. Bit of a sing-song around the piano. They love that, the old folk. All the old favourites. W I ladies make us a few cakes and a couple of urns of tea. Sometimes we have a bit of Bingo. They like that. If anyone goes on a holiday, they give us a little talk. Mrs Harris was very good on the Canary Islands and her granddaughter came along to tell us all about Miami. Once a year, we go on a jaunt in a coach. This year we went to Weston-Super-Mare. They like dabbling their old toes in the briny. Tried to get Ollie to come along but she was far too shy. Such a pity.'

'But surely,' cried the exasperated Meredith, 'you could see she wasn't that kind of person?'

'I agree. She was absolutely out of touch in that house. That's another thing, that house. Quite unsuitable. I tried to persuade her to sell up and invest the money in a sheltered flat. She was a very obstinate woman and it was useless talking to her.' He paused. 'She must have appreciated my calling on her, though, because she left the church restoration fund a fair old sum in her will. I had begun to wonder whether she really liked *anyone* calling on her, but it just goes to show. Appearances are deceptive. She always seemed so snooty and really she must have been pleased to have someone taking an interest.'

There seemed no purpose in talking to him any more about Olivia. His smugness sat on him like armour. The sad thing was, he was genuinely a well-meaning man. He had, in his cack-handed way, tried to befriend Olivia, but never paused to ask first what Olivia actually wanted.

As Meredith sat gazing at him, bereft of speech, it seemed to make him nervous.

'That the information you wanted?' he asked. He cast a wistful glance at his guitar.

Perhaps he wanted to get back to playing it or perhaps, thought Meredith with a flash of intuition, the guitar was like a child's favourite toy. It didn't just entertain, it comforted. Somehow, one of her questions had rattled him. He was unhappy. The thing was, which?

'Dave,' she asked gently, because it was important not to frighten him. 'Did you call – or attempt to call – on Mrs Smeaton the weekend of her death?'

He went white. He opened his mouth a few times and just for a moment or two appeared about to burst into tears. She was oddly reminded of Julie Crombie, whose aplomb had been so easily cracked. She'd asked this earnest young man the one question he'd probably been praying no one would ask him and he'd got to answer it truthfully. He couldn't lie. It wasn't in him.

To give him his due, he tackled the unpleasant duty manfully. He sat up straight, put his hands on his knees, turned his eyes resolutely from the guitar, and said, 'It's been on my mind. I'll be honest with you. I've wondered, ever since then, whether I ought to have mentioned it to someone.'

Meredith said simply, 'Tell me.'

Now he really wanted to. The words, pent up for weeks, burst out in the manner of a confession. Suddenly she was the spiritual guide and comforter and he was the troubled penitent.

'Look here, I'm glad you've come. I don't know who you are but I do believe God sent you. No, no, don't say He didn't, because He does work in strange ways. It wouldn't have made any difference, you understand. I went along to the inquest and the medical bloke said she'd probably died on the Friday night or early Saturday morning. I didn't go there till the Saturday afternoon. I don't know why I went exactly. Yes, I remember, I'd gone to the church. I came out and I looked across at Rookery House and thought, I'll see how old Ollie is. I walked up the drive, not a soul about, house all quiet. The shutters were open, though. If it had been all shuttered up, I'd have realised something was wrong. But as it was, the shutters were folded back. They're the old, hinged indoor type, know them? I rang the bell and no one came. I walked round to the back door and knocked, twice at least, no reply. So I thought, either she's taking a nap or she's in the garden. I had a quick look in the garden but she wasn't – wasn't there. So I decided she must be asleep. It was a very warm afternoon and she'd probably dropped off. So I, well, I just left.'

He gazed at her piteously. 'I wasn't to know, was I? A lot of older people take an afternoon nap. She wasn't expecting me to call. For all I knew, she might not have wanted to see me and had just refused to open the door. She was quite capable of that.'

'You weren't to know,' Meredith told him.

He relaxed. 'I'm so glad to hear you say that, because I have been thinking, perhaps I ought to have mentioned it. It would have helped to fix the time of death, wouldn't it? I must say, the medical evidence was on the vague side about that. I thought they could tell these days.'

'Not always. It depends on so many variables. But if the shutters were open, then she'd not closed them the night before and that indicates she didn't go to bed Friday night. The police would've been interested to know that.'

'Oh dear.' He fidgeted. 'I should have thought about that aspect. The fact is, my worry was more that I might have done more – realised she might be ill, even broken into the house.'

Meredith took pity on him. 'That would have been drastic. She might just have been taking a nap, as you thought at the time.'

'Yes.' He perked up then, suddenly cautious, asked, 'May I ask your interest in all this? You aren't a relative, are you?'

'No, more the friend of a friend.' Wynne, after all, counted as much as a friend of Olivia's as anyone else. 'Besides,' Meredith added. 'A friend and I did go and look at Rookcry House with a possible view to buying. But I don't think we shall.'

'Oh, that's a pity. I'm sure you'd like living in Parsloe St John. You're a bit on the young and nimble side for the oldies' club, but we've got a young mums' afternoon on the other Wednesdays, between the old folk's days.'

'I'm not a mum.'

'Everyone's welcome. We do need helpers as well. You look as though you'd be a very good helper.'

'I'm sure the village is very active,' Meredith said firmly. 'Sometimes in unusual ways. I believe you have a resident witch.'

Dave blinked. 'Oh, come on, now! Surely not. In this day and age? Someone's been pulling your leg.'

'I don't think so. I don't mean I believe in witchcraft myself. I was surprised when I was told – about this woman.'

He frowned and scratched at his beard. 'Who is it? Got a name?'

Meredith hesitated. 'Just between us, I was directed to the woman who runs the little shop in Stable Row. I've no proof. Please understand that.'

'I know the shop. Rum sort of female. I might pop in and have a word – don't worry! I won't mention you.' A gleam entered his eye. 'She might come along and give us a talk at one of the clubs.'

'Do you think that would be altogether wise?'

'We mustn't be narrow in our outlook,' he reproved her. He had quite recovered his earlier sang-froid. 'We can all contribute something to the spiritual life of our community. There's much we can learn from other faiths.' A momentary doubt flitted across his bearded countenance, making him again appear younger and more vulnerable. 'Do you think I should have a word with the bishop about it first?'

'I think that would be a very good idea!' Meredith assured him. She gathered herself up for departure. 'Well, thank you so much, er, Dave. You've been very helpful and informative. I believe the church restoration fund is still open? Perhaps you'd allow me—'

'Oh, great. I'll just fetch you a receipt.'

He pattered out of the room with Meredith's tenner in his hand. She thought he must have a study upstairs, but clattering and jangling of cutlery and crockery suggested he'd only gone as far as the kitchen and was rummaging in a drawer there. He returned with the receipt.

'There you go, got to keep the records straight! Now, don't forget, if you want to drop in on a Wednesday afternoon, all are welcome. We do need helpers.'

He stood in his doorway and waved her goodbye.

CHAPTER NINE

But the Parson of our Parish ... will believe
nothing of all this ...
Witchcraft described and explained

WHEN MARKBY got back to the cottage, Meredith was
slumped sideways in an armchair, with her legs over the
supporting arm, a mug of coffee clasped in her fingers.

'I've had a very strange morning,' she said, by way of
greeting. 'I've met a witch, discussed the tourist trade with
the landlord of The King's Head, chatted to Julie Crombie
and a hard-working, dedicated young clergyman, brimming
with bonhomie, who must have sent Olivia screaming up the
wall. How did you get on?'

'I also found rather more than I bargained for,' he told her.
He gave an account of the morning's adventures. 'So, just
possibly, the pony was poisoned. There is certainly someone
out there with a chip on his shoulder, to say the very least.'

'Nasty.' She was looking thoughtful. 'The Reverend Dave
did have something of interest to say.' She repeated the tale
of the vicar's attempted call on Olivia on the Saturday
afternoon. 'It indicates she did die on the Friday night. The
poor chap's been very worried about it.'

Markby gave a hiss of disapproval. 'So he should be! He

115

should have told the police. It was of interest to the coroner.'

'He's more worried that he could have saved her. He didn't exactly say that, but it's what's been on his mind. He's been wondering if she'd just been lying there unconscious and, well, you know.'

'We don't know. It's unlikely. If she fell some, what, eighteen hours before that, no, I doubt she'd still have been alive. I don't say it's impossible but it's unlikely. In any case, there's nothing now to be done about that. It is annoying, though, when people don't come forward with information because they've decided off their own bat, often for some personal reason, that it isn't relevant.'

He had that policeman's martyred air about him, as he reflected on the uncooperative nature of the Public.

'Incidentally,' Meredith said. 'Dave hadn't heard anything about witchcraft being practised in the village.'

'Nobody'd tell him, that's why. He'd be the last to find out.'

'I've told him. I think it gave him a bit of a shock. Still, take his mind off Olivia.' She scrambled from the chair and began rooting around in the bookcase. 'I need a local guide or local map, got one?'

'I can find one. What are you looking for?'

'A prehistoric monument nearby, called The Standing Man and His Wife. Sadie had a scene of it, painted, if you please, by Mervyn Pollard. She wouldn't sell it and he refused to sell me any other painting.'

'Probably just as well!'

'The site can't be far away,' she said. 'I'd like to go and see it.'

'All right.' He hesitated. 'You remember Sir Basil Newton?'

'Certainly, he's the chief constable.'

'He was. He's just retired. They've got a holiday cottage

about ten miles away. When he heard we were coming here for a week, he suggested that if we had time, we give him a ring and go over there for a drink or something. I thought, if you agree, I'd call him.'

Meredith leaned against the table with her arms folded, the look in her hazel eyes serious. 'You now think there's something amiss here, don't you? Just as Wynne does.'

He fidgeted with the edge of the cloth protector on the arm of the chair, straightening it. 'Those are two quite separate statements. I might suspect something's amiss, as you put it. Whether I'm worried about the same thing as Wynne is another matter. I might be looking at something quite different.'

'Wynne's suspicions are all to do with Olivia, how she came here, lived here and died here.'

'There you have it, you see.' Meredith looked puzzled and he hastened to explain. 'Armitage and his wife were both at the inquest on Mrs Smeaton. They're an intelligent, articulate couple with good recall. There was nothing suspicious at all about Olivia's death. It was an accident, sad, but not unforeseen perhaps. Janine had warned her about those slippers.' He relinquished the cloth protector at last. 'As to Olivia's life – yes, one or two points do occur to me. But she's dead. Let the dead lie easy.'

Meredith said suddenly, 'What an odd place this is. Here we are, three people, you, me and Wynne. We all get what might be called bad vibrations from the village but we attribute them to three different sets of circumstance. Wynne puts it all down to Olivia. You put it down to instances of recent vandalism which may be linked.'

'And you?' he prompted when she hesitated.

'I put it down to Sadie Warren not wanting to sell me a picture.'

117

Markby pushed himself up from his chair. 'Well, perhaps it's easier to do something about your misgivings than it is about mine or Wynne's. Hang on, I'll find a map.'

A little later they had located the standing stones on a tattered ordnance survey map. Alan left Meredith studying it, while he went to phone Sir Basil Newton.

Minutes later, he returned. 'He says to come over to dinner tonight, if we're free. I said we were. We are, aren't we?'

'Mmn? Oh, yes, sure.'

'If we set out a little earlier than we need, we'll have time to stop off and visit this prehistoric monument of yours. It's on the way and it will still be light.'

Meredith looked pleased. 'Good!' She glanced up at the calendar pinned to the wall. 'Oh,' she said, 'it's full moon tonight.'

To pass by the historic site meant taking a route along country lanes. Alan, who preferred this to driving on motor-ways, was quite happy. It was a mild and mellow evening and little other traffic was about. They were about halfway to the Newtons' when Meredith, who'd alternately been scrutinising the map and peering out of the window said, 'Around here.'

But Markby had already slowed. 'Water ahead,' he observed.

Running across the road was a shallow moving band of water, emerging from the hedgerows and trickling down the bank on one side and disappearing into a ditch on the other. In a town, it would have indicated a burst watermain. Out here it signified the presence of a nearby spring.

'That's why it's so green around here,' Markby said.

'This countryside looks like Sadie's picture.' Meredith

was studying their surround critically. 'Look, there's a lay-by. We can pull over there.'

Sure enough, a flattened area had been carved out of the hedgerows. Markby parked in it and they got out.

'A district council rubbish basket,' he said, pointing to this article. 'That means people park here regularly. The stones must be just around somewhere. Where are you going?'

His companion was scrambling up the bank with her high-heeled dinner party shoes in her hand.

'Don't forget we've got to turn up looking respectable!' he warned.

'It's all right, there's a stile!' floated back from high on the bank above him.

Markby sighed and scrambled up in her wake. She was already over the stile and walking in stockinged feet across the grass. He strode after her, wondering why he'd bothered to clean his own shoes. One thing for sure, he'd no intention of taking them off and spending the rest of the evening sitting in damp socks!

There they were, the Standing Man and His Wife, sticking up from the rough pasture and reigning over a scene of peaceful isolation.

'In the middle of nowhere!' said Alan.

The only sign that anyone knew the stones were here was a tiny placard poking out of the turf, giving their names and the miserly information 'prehistoric site'. Beneath was added, 'Please do not climb on the stones'.

The man was slightly larger than his wife. 'Mervyn's no good at perspective,' said Meredith critically. 'They look the same size in his painting. How odd to think they've survived all this time and no one has levelled or removed them. No farmer ploughing, for example.'

'Superstition's protected them,' Alan said, examining the sole of his shoe. 'For goodness' sake, look where you put your feet. Sheep have been grazing in this field. Put your shoes on.'

'It's not damp.'

'No, but there might be traces of scrapie or some other animal disease.'

'Don't fuss, Alan.' She was prowling round the stones.

They were of much-weathered limestone, their surface pitted with depressions and uneven with lumps, like a particularly virulent case of acne. The wife was square topped, but the man appeared either to have been damaged at some time, or have been worn down more on one side than the other, so that it appeared somewhat at an angle, one upper shoulder at a slope.

The evening breeze blew across the pasture and brought on it the faint sound of bleating in the distance. The sheep must be nearby. There ought to be a stream crossing the pasture, too, Meredith thought. One fed by the springwater which had crossed the road. But sometimes these ran underground.

'Wonder if there were ever any more of them,' she said. 'A whole circle, perhaps?'

Markby was getting restless. 'Not necessarily. This might be all that's left to mark a burial, a sort of upper tomb. The nearest local library might have some information, or the nearest historical society, if you're really interested. Or even Sir Basil,' he added artfully as a reminder whither they were bound.

'Oh gosh, yes, I was forgetting the Newtons. Mustn't be late.' She set off for the stile. 'Glad we've found the stones. Little mysteries of any kind make me curious, you know.'

'*Don't* I know it!' he muttered with feeling.

CHAPTER TEN

> ... He says, (she) is a Butcher's Daughter, and
> sometimes brings a Quarter of Mutton from the
> Slaughter-house over Night against a Market-day,
> and once buried a Bit of Beef in the Ground, as a
> known Receipt to cure Warts ...
>
> *Witchcraft described and explained*

'IT WAS a lovely joint of lamb,' said Meredith.

Moira Newton looked pleased. 'I'm so glad you and Alan
were able to come over to share it! I said to Basil, just at
breakfast time, that what a shame it was that I'd got such a
nice piece of meat and no one here but us to enjoy it. And
then Alan rang! I hope you didn't mind being asked to come
today.'

They assured her most certainly not. It had been an
excellent dinner. Now they sat in a low-beamed living room
before a wide stone hearth and enjoyed their coffee and a
dusty bottle of port unearthed by their host from his cellar.
Though it wasn't cold a fire had been lit, because Moira
liked the look of it in the evening.

It *was* nice, thought Meredith, in a well-dined and wined
way. Just to sit here in comfort, watching the flames, sipping
the port ... It almost made one long for the quiet life.

She glanced apprehensively at Alan. This was probably how he imagined them at Rookery House. But between evenings like this, stretched long days of what?

As if by some telepathy, Moira Newton said now, 'We bought this cottage, Basil and I, when the children were young, somewhere to go of a weekend. Rather as Laura and Paul will use his aunt's cottage now she's passed on. The children grew up and we didn't need it so much. We let it out a few times. Then Basil pointed out he was nearing retirement and how about retiring here?'

Markby stirred. 'A good idea.'

'I don't know.' Moira pursed her lips. 'We haven't sold the other house yet and I'm not keen to do so.'

'Chance would be a fine thing in today's depressed property market!' growled her husband. 'We're stuck with two dwellings for the foreseeable future! Two lots of council tax, two lots of every damn bill! One of the places has got to go and as we certainly don't need a great big house in town, I'm still for selling that and moving here.'

'We'd be so cut off, Basil, from all our friends!'

'We've all got cars, haven't we?'

'I don't want to drive miles every time I feel like a chat and a cup of coffee!'

'That's how I feel,' said Meredith. 'Alan wants to buy a rambling Georgian manor with huge gardens and a paddock.'

'Ah,' said Sir Basil, rolling an eye at her. 'This wouldn't be Rookery House, Olivia Smeaton's place, would it?'

Markby sat up straight in the corner of the sofa where he had been relaxing, feet stretched to the crackling hearth. 'You know it?'

'I know where it is, seen the place. Never been inside it. Taken your fancy, has it?'

'Taken Alan's,' said Meredith.

'You liked it,' Markby said crossly.

'Yes, I liked it but that doesn't mean I want to buy it!'

'Well, don't fall out over it,' advised Moira. 'It's only a house. Anyhow, you're both years away from retirement! More coffee?'

'Did you know Olivia herself?' Meredith asked. It seemed a safer topic than Olivia's house.

Sir Basil hauled himself out of his chair and lumbered towards the drinks cabinet. 'Can't say I did.' He rattled among the bottles, reminding Meredith of Wynne amongst her homebrews. Perhaps living in the rural seclusion encouraged an interest in strong drink.

'I'm having a drop of scotch,' said Sir Basil. 'Alan? And Meredith, how about you, m'dear?'

'Not a scotch drinker, I'm afraid,' Meredith apologised.

'That's all right, then,' said their genial host. 'Alan can have one, and you can drive home.'

'Basil!' remonstrated his wife.

'I'll drive us home,' said Meredith. 'I don't want any more to drink, anyway, except I will have another cup of coffee, please.'

A few minutes later, when they were settled again, Sir Basil said unexpectedly, 'I saw in the paper Olivia had died. I knew Lawrence, of course.'

He looked mildly startled at the reaction of his guests.

'You knew Lawrence Smeaton!' they cried in unison.

'Good Lord, yes. In my army days, long ago. He was well senior to me, of course. He retired as brigadier. I ran into him later by chance – if I remember right, it was at a racecourse – after I'd quit the military life. He remembered me, asked what I was doing and so on ... He took an interest in my career after that, for a while, anyway.'

'You don't happen to know, I suppose,' Meredith ventured

with bated breath, 'whether he's still alive?'

'Oh lor', doubt it, m'dear. He'd be – oh, I don't know.' Basil paused. 'He'd only be about eighty and these days, that's not the great age it once was. Yes, he's probably still around and active.'

'Honestly, Basil,' said his wife, exasperated, 'I know you never write a Christmas card, but I'd have thought you looked to see who sent them to you!'

''Course I don't,' returned her husband. 'Whatever for? There are always stacks of the things.'

Moira turned to Meredith and Alan. 'The Smeatons, that's Lawrence and his wife, Mireille, live in Cumbria. Mireille is French, actually. Of course, we haven't seen them for thirty years! But every Christmas *I* send them a card and they send us one!' She glared at her husband. 'And every year I open it up and say to you, Basil, that here's a card from Mireille and Lawrence and that they're both still keeping well.'

'Oh, do you?' mumbled Sir Basil into his scotch.

Moira gazed at her guests. 'He never listens to a word I say, at least, not over breakfast! I'm beginning to wonder if he listens any other time! We don't exchange letters, Mireille Smeaton and I, just a note on the yearly card. Although, I might write her a letter. Yes, I think I will.'

Sir Basil said nobly, 'You're quite right, Mo. I should have realised we were still in touch. But you know I leave that sort of thing to you.'

Alan put down his scotch and leaned forward. 'I don't want to talk police business, but while we've been in Parsloe St John, one or two odd things have happened.'

'And one or two happened before we got there!' added Meredith.

'A mystery!' said Moira, delighted and settling back. 'I love a good whodunnit. Basil, put a log on the fire. Alan's going to tell us a nice blood-curdling tale!'

'I sometimes wonder about you!' said Basil to his wife, as he heaved a log into the hearth amid a shower of sparks. He glanced at the sofa. 'Goin' to curdle the blood, Alan?'

'No, not unless you feel strongly about poisoned horses.'

'I see,' said Sir Basil when Markby had reached the end of his story about Olivia's pony, Wynne's flowers and Armitage's Range Rover, with an added account of Janine and the slippers and Wynne's conviction that Olivia's past had in some way caught up with her.

Newton stretched his legs and settled his hands on his generous paunch. 'Right. Well, vandalism is nasty and village feuds can be worse. Put the two together and you've got something really unpleasant, not to say dangerous. Someone might well end up hurt.' He glanced at them. 'Local police should be informed. I mean, of all of it, not just the bit about the paint-stripper on the vet's car, the other instances as well.'

'I'll check on that,' Markby promised.

'About poor Olivia's fall. Of course, I read about the circumstances and it was quite a subject of local gossip hereabouts for a while, wasn't it, Moira? Then people forgot, as they do. Something else happened to take their attention. A case of the usual nine-day wonder. I don't believe any doubts were raised at the inquest. There would be no reason for the police to reopen inquiries and with the shortage of man power, I doubt any suggestion they do so would be well received!'

'I've tried to get this across to Wynne,' Markby said. 'I examined the cracked balustrade myself. It looked a genuine enough piece of accidental damage to me. As to investigating Olivia's past, there's even less reason for that. The only person around who knew her well years ago would be

Lawrence Smeaton, her erstwhile brother-in-law. He disliked her intensely then and probably still does, if he cares about her at all. He didn't, as far as I know, come down from Cumbria for the inquest or the funeral.'

'He didn't,' said Moira firmly. 'Mireille would have rung and let me know if they were going to be in the area, I'm sure of it. But when I write to her, I'll ask her about it, if you like, Alan.'

Sir Basil said delicately, 'Of course, I don't see any objection to your asking around, Alan, off your own bat, as it were. Not official, just with an official nod of approval. I can't give that myself. I'm retired. But I could have a word with my successor and I'm sure there would be no objection. So long as you didn't tread on anyone's corns and I'm sure you wouldn't do that, with your long experience.'

'It's not that I want to get involved,' Markby assured him. 'But Wynne is clearly disappointed in me and by extension, in the reliability of the police force as a whole! I feel I ought to ask a few token questions. Have a word with this Dr Burnett, perhaps, or the builder, Crombie. Apart from that, I don't see there's much else I can do.'

'I don't think Wynne really expects you to do much more than inquire in the village,' Meredith said suddenly. 'You see,' she explained to the Newtons, 'Wynne couldn't do it herself because she lives there and it might be awkward. But Alan and I could.'

Markby hadn't missed the 'and I' and gave her an old-fashioned look.

'A very sad story,' said Moira thoughtfully. 'I shall have to be careful what I write to Mireille. After all these years, though, surely Lawrence still wouldn't be violently angry about something his sister-in-law did so long ago? And especially now she's dead?'

'Sounds as though you're having an interesting holiday break in that village,' Sir Basil chuckled.

'Oh, you haven't heard all of it,' Markby said. 'Meredith reckons she's stumbled on a coven.'

'It's perfectly true,' Moira Newton said, after Meredith had explained her findings, 'that there's a long and quite possibly still active tradition of witchcraft in the Cotswolds. You see traces of it in old place names. There are recorded incidents right up to the relatively recent, say a generation ago. Unexplained events, curious sightings, even the odd murder of someone believed to be a witch. Strange how these things persist.'

Her husband snorted. 'Lot of nonsense as far as I'm concerned! Now, I'm not saying it doesn't still go on – I mean the meeting of like-minded nutters to go through their rituals. I came across instances of it during my time as chief constable and it's amazing how many otherwise intelligent people get involved! Of course, there's often a strong sexual element in all this ritual business.'

He leaned towards Meredith. 'My advice to you, m'dear, is leave well alone. We don't burn or hang witches any longer and they're free to carry on among themselves if they like. Provided, of course, they don't break the law! One has to be sure no under-age youngsters get drawn in, just in case some of what's going on, whilst allowable for consenting adults, would be termed abuse if the very young were taking part. The other thing to watch out for is the use of banned substances. Nothing like an out-of-body experience induced by drugs to convince the user of a parallel world full of strange powers!'

Meredith giggled. 'Neither Sadie nor Mervyn could be described as hippies! Both are middle-aged and, as far as it goes, utterly respectable business people. They show no sign of having been at the magic mushrooms, at least not to me. Mind you, I don't know how Sadie manages to make a living from that shop.'

'She may have other income, say, a pension?' suggested Moira in practical tones. 'A widow's pension, for instance, or something connected with her late husband's employment. Perhaps she had Mr Warren heavily insured, and cleaned up when he passed on?'

'Please!' Markby begged. 'Don't start another hare!'

Sir Basil cleared his throat, recalling their attention to himself. 'As I was saying,' he said severely. 'Without actual proof of criminal activity, it's difficult to justify trying to ban whatever it is they're doing. Some of the adherents, like your Mrs Warren, would claim it was her faith. Paganism is making quite a comeback and, so I'm told, a bid for official recognition. We've no reason at all to believe she's breaking the law. Let's face it, how would we enforce a ban? Witchcraft, if that's what we've got here, was actively and bloodily persecuted for centuries and wasn't wiped out. It's not the only organisation or activity which is secretive about its rituals. Where do you draw the line between what its practitioners would claim was an ancient pagan rite, and what the Tourist Board would describe as an interesting tradition? There's a tendency in out-of-the-way places for such traditions to persist. Pagan festivals remembered by dancing round the maypole, men dressing up in greenery, donning animal heads, all kinds of stuff. Ninety-nine times out of a hundred, those doing it don't really know why. It's just a local custom, something they've always done. People find it rather charming. They send TV crews down to film the merry jinks and run it on the six o'clock news.'

Sir Basil twitched an eyebrow at them. 'You may be right

in your suspicions, Meredith, but I wouldn't quiz anyone further in Parsloe St John about it. I do mean *anyone*. You never know, you see, with these affairs, just who is and who isn't involved. I'm sorry to hear about it, if it's so, but I can't say I'm surprised. Now that you've signalled your interest, you'd be unlikely to get anyone to talk. Let it go.'

They sat for a while, sipping their drinks and staring at the crackling hearth. Then Markby said, 'We stopped off on the way here to look at a prehistoric monument, a couple of stones.'

'The Standing Man and His Wife?' Moira nodded. 'They're probably three thousand years old or more. Isn't it strange how they've lasted so long? It can only be, as Basil says, because locally they're credited with strong magic. There's some buried folk memory of that site being a holy place which mustn't be desecrated or tampered with. Although I believe there was once a third stone. It was moved at some date to the local churchyard, but in the early 1700s, the rector had it removed because it was attracting the wrong kind of attention. It just disappeared after that.'

'What kind of wrong attention?' asked Meredith, intrigued.

Moira looked vague. 'Oh, villagers touching it for luck as they passed by, things like that, I suppose.'

Meredith considered this. 'Hardly enough reason to make the priest want to see the back of it. There must have been something more going on.'

'So, are you going to do as Sir Basil suggested, look into this business unofficially?' Meredith asked as she drove them homeward through the night.

They were taking the same country route back. It was very late, but the moonlight revealed the road ahead as a silver ribbon. The car's headlights seemed almost super-fluous. From time to time, they briefly picked out a rabbit, as it scuttled into the ditch, or caught the reflected gleam of a pair of wild eyes. There was nothing else on the road, no lights of dwellings, leaving them as alone as in a moonscape.

'If I get the go-ahead. At any rate, I'll see Wynne's incident of vandalism is reported and I'll talk to the people who knew Olivia. I don't see I can do much else.' Alan sounded abstracted. His next words showed why. 'They're very cosy there in that cottage, Basil and Moira.'

'Yes, they are. But they do still have a house in town, remember! Moira was right in not wanting to cut herself off from everyone.'

'It's different for her,' he argued. 'She probably has a lot of friends in town. You don't have friends in Bamford, only acquaintances. The same goes for me. Whom do I know well there, except for Laura and her family – and I don't need to be seeing them every five minutes! Besides, they have the cottage now and if we—'

'If we bought Rookery House, we'd see them whenever they came to the cottage? Alan, it's just not on!' Meredith finished for him and heaved a sigh of exasperation. 'I'm not giving up my job, and that's final! You can retire if you want, but you do it on your own. You can go and shut yourself away in Rookery House like old Olivia. You wouldn't last out the month.'

'There's always a surprising amount going on in villages,' he argued. 'People make their own entertainment. You haven't tried to find out.'

'On the contrary, I've had the complete run-down from the Reverend Dave. I've been offered a choice between the young mums and the old folks. It seems I don't need either a baby or a pension book to qualify! Or I could join the tea-making brigade. For that interest which is just a bit different, don't forget Sadie's coven! I don't doubt for a minute people are making their own entertainment in Parsloe St John and how! I just don't see myself joining in any of it.'

He snapped with a vehemence she'd never heard from him before, 'You just don't like to go along with anyone else's ideas, do you? You just like ploughing that lonely furrow! Does it ever occur to you that some people might see you as just awkward? Have you ever thought that just possibly the reason you don't get any more overseas postings is because you are just the teeniest bit difficult to get along with?'

'You have absolutely no right to say that? How would you know? You never had to work with me!'

She could hardly stop the car and tell him to get out, not here in the middle of nowhere late at night, but had they been in a built-up area, she would have done, she was so angry. Instead, she drove on with some disregard for the unlit road until he said, 'Slow down!'

'Ask to see my driving licence, superintendent, why don't you?'

'You're being petty, Meredith. You don't have to drive us into a ditch to prove a point.'

'I'm not trying to prove a point. Why should I? You're the one making all the points – all aimed against me, as it happens.'

'I'm sorry.' She heard him sigh. 'I am, really. I had no right to say what I did. I've never worked with you in an office, as you say. You might be a regular Pollyanna about the place, for all I know.' The car slewed round a corner. 'Look, I love you. I want to live with you in a pleasant house and – and just be normal.'

'I've always thought I was normal, thanks.'

'No one's asking you to spend your days making tea for good causes.'

'As it happens, I have helped James Holland out with his youth club in Bamford.'

'Yes, I know. I apologise, all right?'

The acrimony was cut short in unexpected fashion. Meredith braked sharply and had him grabbing the dashboard. But before he could protest, she asked, 'What's that? That glow on the horizon?'

The red glow hung over the ridge ahead of them. Meredith stopped the car and they both peered through the windscreen.

'A fire?' Alan muttered. 'A hayrick, perhaps? No dwellings up that way, are there? Didn't see any on the way out this evening.'

Meredith pulled into the verge and switched off the engine. 'Come on!'

She already had her hand on the doorhandle as he asked, 'Where?'

'Up there, of course!'

'Hang on!' he protested. 'We can drive on a bit further and take a look from the road.'

She was already out in the road. 'We'll cut across the fields on foot,' she informed him, through the window. 'That fire, I'll bet my boots, is in the vicinity of the stones.'

Markby stumbled after her, up the bank, through a gap in the hedge, and across the field beyond.

It was cold now, and the wind had got up and nipped at their faces and hands. Markby tripped, saved himself and cursed.

'One of us is going to break an ankle,' he advised her. 'We shall probably find a camp of New Age travellers. They have dogs. Thought I ought to warn you!'

But his voice betrayed his own interest. He was as keen as she was to know what was ahead of them.

They were near now. Only a fringe of trees, black giants against the skyline, divided them from the field containing the Standing Man and his Wife. Meredith and Alan negotiated the uneven terrain between projecting roots, becoming snagged on trailing brambles, plunging ankle-deep in soft patches of leafmould, but reaching the further edge of the trees where they both stopped, panting.

Ahead of them the open pasture rose in a gentle swell. Atop of it, they beheld an extraordinary scene.

The prehistoric stones were on the very tip of the rise, illuminated against the skyline by the leaping scarlet and yellow flames of a large bonfire. The wind caught the tongues of fire and sent them leaping unpredictably first one way and then another, so that it seemed that anyone who ventured too near might find himself suddenly licked by the red fingers and scorched. Despite the risk, hand in hand around the ancient monument, moved a circle of dark figures, silhouetted against the sky and the orange glare. Sometimes the circling dancers moved in towards the stones, at other times they eddied back again.

Meredith held her breath, and peered out from behind a narrow tree trunk. 'Don't let them see you!' she whispered.

Beside her, she heard Alan muttering, 'One, two . . .' Then he said, 'I make it twelve dancers. All adult. Can't see whether they're male or female.'

'Alan,' Meredith said in an odd voice. 'There are twelve dancers – and *three* stones.'

CHAPTER ELEVEN

> For my part, I have ever believed, and do now
> know, that there are witches.
>
> *Sir Thomas Browne*

THERE WAS no denying there were three still, silent shapes where there ought only to have been two.

Meredith hissed, 'There's the Standing Man, I recognise the shape, that lopsided way it's worn. And – and there's a *second* Standing Man, just a few feet away.'

'That's his wife,' Alan whispered back, his breath brushing her ear.

'No, *that's* his wife – just over there, the smaller stone.'

They could hear the crackle of the bonfire and smell its smoke. It seemed to Meredith that above the roar of the flames she could hear another sound, a solemn, monotonous chanting as if the wavering line of assembled dancers repeated some mantra, over and over.

A ripple of fear ran over her and she clutched at his arm. 'Alan? Moira said that originally there were three stones and one was taken away—'

He interrupted her. 'It hasn't hopped back under its own steam, if that's what you mean! No, look—'

His hand closed over hers reassuringly. 'It's not a stone,

it's another member of the group, not dancing, just standing there.'

Even as he spoke, one of the two 'stones', as she'd supposed them, moved. Meredith suppressed a squawk of alarm as Alan's hand tightened on hers in warning. The moving shape, while that of a man, still kept that lopsided stance which had made it, in repose, so uncannily like the prehistoric monument. It was as if the Standing Man had taken on human form and, joining the dancers, began to lope awkwardly with them in the ragged circle around the remaining stones.

Without warning, the whole circle stopped. The large, awkward participant left his place and moved towards the larger of the two stones. He stood before it, holding up some long, thin, pointed object. Abruptly he slashed down with it and raised it again, moving it in a complicated pattern before the stone, before retiring. The standing figures swayed and uttered a low moan.

'Thirteen,' murmured Alan in her ear. 'Thirteen revellers or whatever you care to call them. That one, he must be some kind of leader.'

But Meredith's former alarm, rooted in atavistic fears, had subsided with recognition.

'That', she said firmly in her normal voice, 'is Mervyn Pollard.'

Before Alan could answer, there was a fresh movement out there by the bonfire. The circle broke up and the figures clustered together. Two or three then broke away and moved towards the conflagration. The flames bellied out, briefly extinguished and then flared up again, but less forcefully than before.

'They're putting it out,' Alan murmured. 'The ritual's over. Come on, time to go.'

They made their way back through the trees and across the field behind to the car. Both, though neither admitted it aloud, might have wished the night darker. As it was, crossing open ground beneath the bleaching silvery moonlight, they were as obvious as skaters on an icerink.

Scrambling into the car's warm interior, Meredith sighed with relief. Its familiarity and modernity were comforting. Out there had been something ancient, strange, and to them, at least, unfriendly. Back in the car, they were back in today's world, in control again.

In control, too, of her own feelings. 'I'm sorry about the squabble,' she said, adding ruefully, 'I can't help being the only soldier in step!'

He put his arm around her shoulders in comfort and she pressed her face against the rough texture of his jacket. 'I wasn't intending to be as critical as I sounded,' he said, 'I don't want you different. I love you. We'll work something out.' He dropped a kiss on the top of her head.

'Sure.' He was being loyal and she appreciated it. He was also evading the truth which was that he did want her to change her ideas, and she couldn't do it.

Too ruddy honest for my own good! she thought. We mustn't, either of us, ever get into a silly quarrel like that again. The silliest squabbles sometimes did the worst damage. Losing control, the most frightening of all situations, she told herself. Those dancers, were they just celebrating some harmless old ritual? Or did they risk upsetting things, releasing some force which they couldn't return to its prison. Something which might then go rampaging around the countryside causing havoc?

'Whoever they are, they should let well alone,' she said aloud.

★ ★ ★

They drove home past the empty lay-by. Wherever the dancers had parked their cars, they had chosen some secluded spot where no one who chanced to pass by could see them and make a note of numberplates.

They were both relieved to reach the cottage.

Meredith kicked off her ruined shoes and ruefully surveyed holed tights and grimy feet and legs. She sat down on a kitchen chair and watched as Alan filled the kettle.

'The British answer to everything,' she said. 'Even witchcraft. A cup of tea.'

'If it was witchcraft.'

'Oh, come on. It was a coven. I don't know much about it, but an odd number, isn't that supposed to be a good thing? There's something about thirteen, too. Twelve plus one. That's what we saw. Twelve ordinary footsoldiers and one officer-in-charge.'

'Whom you thought was the chap at the pub?'

'Sure of it. What's more, he painted a picture of those stones for Sadie to hang in her shop. He wouldn't sell *me* a painting of them! I'm not one of the initiated. I'll tell you one thing, Alan. Go around this village and find out who else has a painting by Mervyn Pollard, a painting of those stones! Then you'll know who was prancing around out there tonight.'

Alan smiled as he handed her a mug of steaming tea. She took it and clasped it gratefully in hands which were chilled.

'Hardly the sort of evidence a court would accept!' he teased.

'Will you stop going on about evidence?' she asked, exasperated.

'Thank your lucky stars we do have courts which ask for proper evidence, and don't accept oddly shaped moles on your skin, or someone overhearing you talk to your cat!

People were burned or hanged on just such so-called evidence once.'

She sipped the tea. 'All right. So what are we going to do about it? Tell the local police? After all, that's a recognised prehistoric monument. It might get damaged in all the shenanigans out there.'

He shook his head. 'The people out there tonight are the last ones to damage the site. They'll want to preserve it. Nor am I sure about informing the local police.' He caught her eye. 'Look, those are probably local people and, as Basil was saying tonight, you don't know who was among them.' He put down his mug and glanced at the clock on the wall.

'It's late, but I suppose I could call Basil, pass the buck to him. Not that I could say they were doing anything illegal.'

'They must have been on private land, nor can you just go around lighting large fires indiscriminately all over the place. The fire brigades don't like it. Even farmers are no longer allowed to burn off stubble, right? That bonfire could have got out of control. It was pretty breezy out there and the flames were going all over the place. It's still very dry after the long hot summer and just one of those sudden changes in the direction of the wind and whoosh!' Meredith's mug described a wild arc and tea splashed.

'All right. I'll call Basil. But it wouldn't be any use anyone going out there now. It was breaking up when we left and all the dancers will have taken off by now.'

'No names and addresses to be took!' She managed a weak grin.

'What did Basil say?' Meredith asked impatiently a little later.

'Not much.' This aggravating answer was received with a glare. 'What could he say?' Markby protested. 'I had to

139

apologise profusely for disturbing them when they'd just turned in. Then Moira came on the phone wanting to know all about what she's calling our adventure. She says, by the way, that she's sure you're right and thirteen, twelve plus a leader, is the maximum number for a coven and the ideal number. She's got a friend who runs the local historical society and they're going out there tomorrow to take a look. They'll hunt through all the books and try and see if there's any information on record. Basil's phoning his local chaps to send a car out to check on the fire, making sure, as you say, that it's really been properly put out. You, my girl, have started a hare!'

'Me? You were with me. You saw it.'

'Yes, and now I'm going to forget about it. I'm tired and I'm going to bed. Hang a few garlic bulbs around the doors, if you want, and come along.'

Sir Basil was on the phone at nine the following morning. Getting his revenge, thought Markby, for being got out of bed last night.

But Sir Basil had been disturbing others even earlier.

'Called my successor. He's no objection to your asking a few off-the-record questions about Olivia Smeaton. If you turn up anything, naturally, it'll have to be made official. But as you say, the woman's dead and buried and little can be done now. Moira is intending to write to Mireille Smeaton, however, and if you like, we can ask whether Lawrence would be prepared to talk to you. It would mean travelling up to Cumbria. I doubt he'd come down here for that. I actually don't know how active he is nowadays.'

'I might go and see him if all else fails,' Markby agreed, privately thinking, damn!

'The chief constable was quite interested, as it happens,'

Sir Basil was continuing. 'His hobby is motorsports and he knew Olivia's name. He remembered reading the obituary. He hadn't realised she'd been living in the county, or even that she'd still been alive. So when you've finished your inquiries, you might send him a brief report. He'd like to know what, if anything, you turn up.'

So he wasn't the only one, thought Markby ruefully as he replaced the phone, who had started a hare. Whatever he'd accused Meredith of, he'd started one himself, by telling Sir Basil all about Wynne's suspicions. Now he was left holding the baby. He had to investigate, but he hadn't any real reason for doing so – despite an unofficial nod. If he found anything, he'd report it as requested and gracefully retire to let others take it from there. If he didn't, at least he'd be able to reassure Wynne – and the motoring fan they'd apparently now got as chief constable!

'Wish me luck,' he said, as he prepared to set out.

'Where are you going first?'

'Talk to the doctor, if he's free. Go and see that chap Crombie. Meet you at the pub lunchtime?'

'Yes!' she said with what he considered unnecessary enthusiasm.

Only half in jest, he advised, 'Just don't go asking the landlord why he's got bags under his eyes!'

He had, as it turned out, to pay his calls in reverse order. Dr Burnett had already left to attend an early surgery, but would be home in the afternoon.

Markby obtained this information of Mrs Burnett, a thin, nervous woman with lack-lustre hair and washed-out complexion, who clasped an infant to her unmaternally flat bosom. She also gripped a mutinous toddler by the hand, as she addressed him in the doorway of her home.

Markby thought her very young, perhaps no more than twenty-three, and barely coping.

If the exterior of The Abbot's House was dilapidated, a glimpse of the interior suggested that badly needed doing up as well. The hall walls were dingy and marked with the print of small fingers. The carpet was worn to the backing threads. There was a lingering odour of plain food, very plainly cooked, mixed with a steamy miasma of detergent. In the background, a washing machine could be heard rattling at maximum spin speed. This was a large house and he wondered what kind of help, if any, she had. It seemed as if Janine Catto's services might well be needed here.

Markby arranged, somewhat unenthusiastically, to call back in the afternoon.

'What name?' she asked. 'Do wait a bit, Benjy, Mummy's talking to a visitor. Sorry, did you say your name? Is it about a private patient?' A spark of hope gleamed in her eyes.

'Markby,' he said. 'Superintendent Markby. I don't want to consult your husband in his medical capacity.' The gleam in her eyes vanished and depression returned. 'Rather', Markby added, 'in my police one. But please don't be alarmed, my call's entirely unofficial.'

She looked dubious. 'Oh, all right.'

The door was closed in his face a little unceremoniously. Markby stood for a moment on the step, staring at its battered wooden panels. His thoughts were not on Dr and Mrs Burnett, but on something else – nearer to his heart.

He stepped back and scrutinised the frontage. Meredith had remarked what a state it was in and had been right. He wondered how much it would cost Burnett to put the place right, just the essentials. From that, he moved to calculating how much would be needed to renovate and thereafter maintain Rookery House.

A curtain twitched at the side window and he hastened to turn away and set off for the gate. Rookery House, though possibly in better state than The Abbot's House – or at least, no worse – would cost its new owners a packet.

'But it's not as if you're broke,' he muttered to himself. He lived simply. For years now he'd only had himself to look after. At his seniority the pay wasn't bad. 'And it's time I made myself a bit more comfortable!' he mumbled.

Markby's divorce – many years ago now – had been of the clean break variety, largely because at that time, he'd had no money They'd had no children. Rachel, his former wife, had realised there was no point in a protracted wrangling which could only benefit the legal profession. She'd settled for a division of the matrimonial home, an arrangement under which she'd departed with the best of the furniture, most of the wedding presents, and every mechanical device from the television set to the foodmixer. He'd been left with a sofa bed, a camel saddle stool which had been an unwanted wedding gift, the picnic china, three sets of curtains and a set of breakfast bar-stools, for which Rachel had no use. In fairness, most of the wedding gifts had come from her friends and family, and she'd been entitled to them.

Frankly, at the time, he couldn't have bothered less. He'd bought his Victorian villa in Bamford because he'd just been assigned to Bamford station, hung up the curtains, set out the breakfast stools, donated the camel saddle to a jumble sale, and moved in. He'd since acquired a little more furniture, but one pair of the original curtains still hung at the spare bedroom window. He was not, as Rachel had frequently pointed out, very good about the house, a domesticated man. Yet he was a man who enjoyed domestic comforts, when he was offered any. He liked visiting his sister and her family for this reason. He enjoyed the shared time with Meredith. He fantasised about a life together with her, sharing a roof, not just occasionally a bed. It was the improbability of realising his dream which had made him so unforgivably snappish with her on the drive home last night. He was still troubled in his conscience about that. But the dream lived on.

Stepping out the doctor's gates, he found himself staring wistfully at Rookery House, just opposite. He walked over and peered through the gates again, down the weed-strewn drive. The tarpaulin still flapped up on the roof. Crombie hadn't yet fixed whatever was wrong. Crombie. If he couldn't speak to Dr Burnett this morning, he would try and find the builder.

CHAPTER TWELVE

And, certainly, he was a good felawe.
                                        Geoffrey Chaucer

AS HE'D been unable to contact Burnett because the doctor had left for his work, Markby reasoned that it would make sense to try first to contact Crombie at his yard.

He was foiled again. By the time he got there, it was tea-break. He was informed by a labourer eating his way through a doorstep bacon sandwich, that the boss had gone back up to the house for his elevenses.

Markby toiled over to Max's spacious dwelling. A contrast in every way to The Abbot's House, this. A new – not more than fifteen years old, anyway – house, with double-glazing, landscaped garden, double garage, a pair of stone greyhounds flanking the porch and – as he discovered when he rang – musical doorchimes.

Mrs Crombie, plump, cheerful, with a happy-go-lucky air (again a contrast to what he'd found at The Abbot's House!) led him through the house into a sun-warmed loggia where, relaxing on expensive leisure furniture, he found Max himself, feet up on a wicker stool, drinking his coffee and reading the *Daily Express*.

'Take a pew, chief!' offered Max, on learning his visitor's

name and reason for being there.

Markby decided that the epithet wasn't because Max had failed to grasp his visitor's rank, but because Mr Crombie had at one time served in Her Majesty's Navy. He was a sturdy, ruddy-faced man, with sleeked-back hair, who looked as if he enjoyed a drink. Nevertheless, those sharp brown eyes probably missed little and had already subjected Markby to swift appraisement. The superintendent was put in mind of a water-rat sizing up an intruder into its stretch of riverbank. He wondered whether Max was a local man, and asked.

'That's right,' Max agreed. 'Born and bred. Not born in this house, of course. I built this one for me and the wife when we were planning a family. Although our Julie didn't come along for another couple of years, did she, love?'

This last addressed to Mrs Crombie who'd brought Markby's coffee and a plate of biscuits.

'I think I've seen your little girl,' Markby said. 'She was riding a palomino pony.'

Max beamed. 'That cost me a packet and all, didn't it, Sandra?'

Sandra had left them, but could be heard moving about inside the house. Max didn't wait for a response, perhaps not expecting, or caring, whether his question had been heard. He leaned forward and tapped his caller on the knee.

'She's a great little rider, you know. Won prizes, loads of them. Show you, before you go. Got 'em all pinned up on a board in her room. Rows and rows of rosettes – and a couple of cups!'

The cups, Markby thought pedantically, presumably not pinned on a board. 'Olivia Smeaton taught her to ride, I believe?'

'Nice old lady,' said Max. 'Very fond of our Julie. Who wouldn't be?'

'Indeed.' He was learning to cope with Max's rhetorical style. 'I was at Rookery House the other morning. Had a look round it.'

The brown eyes sparked with professional interest. 'Thinking of buying? Needs a bit of doing up. I'm doing a bit of work on it at the moment, as it happens.'

'The roof?' Markby asked. 'I noticed the tarpaulin.'

'Spotted the roof, did you? I can tell you,' Max shook a finger at him portentously. 'I did a load of work on that roof. Then she called a halt, when it still wasn't what I call finished. But old Mrs Smeaton, she was funny in some ways. Old folk are, aren't they? "As long as it will see me out, that's good enough!" she said. So it never got finished off properly, and that bothered me, because I've got a reputation in the trade as reliable. I don't botch jobs. I don't like leaving things half done. But there you are, she was the boss. It wasn't as though she didn't have the money, though, was it?'

Max buried his face in his mug and slurped up the remains of his coffee. He set down the mug. It had a picture of Windsor Castle on it.

'So', he recommenced, 'when the other day, young Janine came to see me and said she'd been in the house, checking round – because she's got the keys, well, you must know that, if you've been in there. Janine is keeping an eye on the place, now it's empty and when she said there was signs of water getting in the brickwork, I was concerned! I went on down there and took a look and sure enough, it was. Made a very nasty stain down one wall and you can't just leave that kind of damage. Gets worse very quickly. I spoke to the lawyer. He wasn't interested. But I still was, my reputation was at stake!'

Max sat back and his wicker chair creaked protestingly as

if it would argue with the last remark.

'No one would blame you,' said Markby. 'Surely?'

'Oh yes, they would!' said Max. 'Suppose now, you bought the place. First thing you'd want to do is fix the roof. You'd look round for a builder. Someone would suggest me. Oh no, you'd say, Crombie fixed the roof last time and look at the water coming in! See?'

'I see—'

Max ploughed on. 'I'd have lost my reputation, you see. You wouldn't want me doing that or any other work, would you?'

'Well, I—'

'So I got a couple of men down there to put up a temporary cover and sent young Kev down to investigate the pointing, where water had seeped down the walls, between the bricks.'

'Kevin, being Berry's lad?' Markby asked.

Max nodded. 'I couldn't spare anyone from the yard to do the job at the moment, but I thought perhaps Ernie and his lad could manage it. Ernie does a proper job of work.' Despite this assertion, Max's cheerful face looked momentarily depressed. 'But it seems to me you can't rely on anyone no more. Take Ernie Berry as a good example. I've given a lot of work to Ernie over the years. He doesn't work for me as employee, you understand. It's more a case of me subcontracting odd jobs to him, when I've not got a man free. He's what you might call an independent. He's never let me down before.'

'And he has now?'

Max nodded gloomily. 'He should've turned up yesterday. I'd told him and the lad to fix that pointing before it started to rain. I told them to come here first and pick up anything necessary to do the work. That way I know what they've

148

used and what it cost. Ernie doesn't bill anything, can't even write, believe it or not. In this day and age, eh? The lad turned up – no Ernie. Nor has he since. I'm a bit surprised, I have to say.'

'What does the lad – I mean, Kevin – say about it?'

'Can't get no sense out of him.' Max snorted. 'He's a few pence short of a pound, you see. He says he hasn't seen Ernie for two days. I reckon, just between you, me and that coffee pot there, old Ernie's got himself another lady-friend. He's always been what you'd call a Don Hoo-arn.'

This seemed such an unlikely thing – given Mr Berry's general appearance – that Markby was moved to murmur that he'd noticed Ernie once, in the pub.

Max, taking the point being obliquely made, chuckled. 'Ah,' he said with a wink. 'You don't know Ernie!'

Which was true. Markby returned to his main purpose. 'You did quite a lot of work for Mrs Smeaton. I understand she was something of a recluse.'

Max thought about this for so long that Markby began to wonder whether the word 'recluse' was in the man's vocabulary. He was about to rephrase the question when Max said, 'I wouldn't call it that myself, no.' He pushed himself up from the wicker chair. 'Care for a lager? I got all kinds in the fridge.'

'Thank you, no – I've arranged to meet a friend at The King's Head at lunchtime. Better not to start drinking now.'

'Then I'll get Sandra to bring another pot of coffee. Oy!' cried Mr Crombie to his spouse. 'Bring us another lot of coffee, love!'

A distant cry apparently agreed to the request. Max returned to his seat, having given himself, as Markby was well aware, time to think about his answer.

'She wasn't very good on her legs, you see,' he said. 'It

wasn't that she didn't want to go out, more that she couldn't walk far. It didn't surprise us to hear she'd taken a tumble down the stairs, did it, love?'

This was directed at Mrs Crombie who'd appeared with a tray of fresh coffee.

'Poor old thing,' said Mrs Crombie comfortably. 'Nasty way to go. But then, it was probably quick. I always think lying for weeks in a hospital bed with tubes and things coming out of you must be worse.'

Markby could have disputed this but merely thanked Mrs Crombie for the fresh coffee.

'P'lice not looking into it, are they, chief?' inquired her husband. His sharp little water-rat's eyes held Markby's gaze unblinkingly. 'There was no mention of any funny business at the inquest.'

'You went along to the inquest, Mr Crombie?'

'I did, as a matter of fact. Went to the funeral, and all. I believe in showing respect. She remembered our Julie in her will, you know. She was a nice old lady. Pity.'

'And a pity she was distressed about the pony, the way it died.'

'Been talking to Armitage, have you?' Max ran a hand over his smooth cap of hair. 'Yes, I agree with you there, that was a funny business.'

'You didn't find any ragwort in your paddock?'

'No – and Julie and Sandra crawled all over it on their hands and knees, looking. Our Julie was really worried. She's devoted to that animal, is Julie.'

'The palomino? She must have been fond of the other pony, too, the one which died.'

'Cried buckets.'

'Mr Crombie,' Markby asked suddenly, 'have you – your home here or your yard – suffered any incidents of vandalism lately? Even something small which you didn't bother to report?'

He knew he'd hit paydirt. There was a silence. Max fidgeted. 'How did you know about that?'

'I didn't – but other local people have suffered malicious attacks and I just wondered.'

The builder ran the tip of his tongue over his upper lip. 'Bloody stupid, really. Someone broke into the yard and the paintstore. Tipped out a load of paint all over the place. Pinched some paint-stripper, too.'

'Paint-stripper!'

'Oh, I heard about the vet's off-roader!' Max nodded. 'But it's not to say it was the stuff pinched from my yard, is it?'

'You didn't report it? To the police?'

Crombie looked mildly uncomfortable. 'It was only a couple of tins. I keep count, you know. You got to keep your eye on things, chase people up. You don't have to be popular,' Max repeated his favourite saying, 'only respected. That's what I say. I didn't make too much of a public song and dance about it, because to be frank, if you do that, it sometimes only gives some joker the idea. Besides . . .'

He shifted uneasily in his chair which creaked again. 'I reckoned I'd try and find out for myself who did it. Seems to me – now, this is strictly private, right! Between us two!—'

Not the coffee pot as well, this time, thought Markby. He nodded.

'Must be someone who works for me, in the yard, got a grudge or something. I got my eye on someone. I bawled him out a while back over something and I reckon he was getting his own back. I tackled him about it and he denied it, of course! But I told him, I got my eye on him and one little thing more, and he gets his cards!'

'And what made you so sure it was someone who works for you?'

'Because the dogs never barked,' said Mr Crombie simply. 'Got a couple of alsatians, guard dogs. They got the run of the yard at night. They wouldn't let no one in there they didn't know.'

Before the visitor left, Max carried out his promise, or threat, and led Markby upstairs to view Julie's trophy board.

'She's certainly done well. A remarkable display,' Markby said. 'You must be very proud of her.' He was being honest. The board was festooned with rosettes, mostly red.

Max picked up a framed photograph. 'There she is, the day she got the pony. Never saw a kid so pleased.'

Nor a father, thought Markby, observing the beaming face above Julie's in the snapshot. He admired the photo and handed it back.

On their way downstairs again, his eye was taken by another picture, not a photograph, but a water-colour. It hung in a corridor running off to the right at the top of the stairs, out of his line of sight on his way up.

'Ah, what's that?' he asked genially and took himself uninvited down the corridor to take a closer look. Max, slightly startled, hurried after him.

'I'm interested in water-colours,' Markby said easily, peering at it. 'Local scene, this, isn't it? I fancy I know where those stones are.'

'Oh, them,' said Max. 'Yes, local site of interest, as they say.'

'You paint it?'

'Blimey, no,' Max sounded shocked. 'Friend of mine, runs the local pub. I did a bit of work for him and he give me that. I was at school with him, as it happens. He was always

152

a bit of an artist, even back then, was Mervyn.'

Mr Crombie slapped his hands together. 'Well, chief, it's been nice talking to you, but duty calls! I got to get back to the yard. Didn't you say you had to meet someone?'

Markby took the hint.

'You might call Nimrod my familiar,' said Wynne indulgently. She bent over her pet and scratched his chin. 'At any rate, I talk to him when we're alone and in his own way, he answers. I'd have been burnt for that, I dare say, once upon a time, just as Alan says.'

Wynne, in her usual baggy slacks teamed today with a startling yellow sweater, straightened up and turned away from the window.

Nimrod, crouched sphinx-like on his window seat, blinked his eyes and looked as if he understood perfectly what was being said, but had no intention of answering anyone on this occasion.

'He sleeps most of the day,' said his mistress. 'After a night on the tiles, or out in the fields in his case. He doesn't like being shut in at night. He yowls.'

Meredith studied Nimrod who was looking particularly disreputable this morning, and might well be rehashing satisfying memories of a misspent night.

'Did you have him as a kitten?' she asked.

'Not exactly, not a little kitten. He was a large kitten when I found him. Not a fully grown cat but halfway between. He was in my garden, injured. I think he must have caught his tail in a some kind of illegal trap. He'd lost half of it and was in an awful state. I rushed him over to Rory Armitage. Getting attention was the first priority, then finding his owner. But I never did find his owner. I put up notices in the village and Rory put the word out but no one ever claimed him. In the meantime, he'd sort of made up his own mind to stay here. He's a Mystery Cat.'

Nimrod rolled over on to his side and stretched out his large flat paws. Wicked claws briefly slid out from furry pads and were immediately withdrawn. The sun moved round to cast a warm beam through the glass over his striped coat.

'I've a cat at home in Bamford, like that,' Meredith said. 'He comes and goes. I don't know where he came from and I don't know where he goes when he disappears. He turns up when he likes, stays for a bit and then pushes off again. I thought he was a stray. Now I'm not sure. I suspect he's got several homes and tours them in turn.'

'Perhaps someone goes on holiday a lot,' Wynne suggested. 'Some owners are surprisingly feckless. They just turn a cat out when they leave the house, even if they're gone weeks, and expect it to be there when they get back, none the worse.'

'Mrs Crouch, my neighbour, is looking out for my cat,' Meredith told her, in case this was a hint.

The two women sat in silence for a moment by Wynne's hearth. 'I can't say I'm really surprised by what you've told me,' Wynne said at last, moving easily to the subject which had occupied them before Nimrod. Meredith had decided to tell Wynne abut the bonfire at the Standing Stones, hoping it might jolt Wynne's memory. But it hadn't.

'Not that I've ever come across evidence of a coven or any rituals taking place around here. But I know that the Cotswolds are full of tales of witchcraft. There are several spots particularly associated with the "old religion". People come from all over the country to plot leylines and so on.' She paused. 'There's Sadie, of course. But I've never really paid much attention to those stories.'

'But the locals believe she's a witch?'

'I'm sure they do. At least, they choose to err on the safe side, and take great care not to offend her! I've always found Sadie pleasant and friendly. She's certainly an intelligent woman. I wouldn't say she was potty. Eccentric, perhaps. But then, where do you draw the line? The world's full of odd religions and societies. There are people who believe the earth is flat; that we've been visited in ancient times by spacemen; that the world is going to end on such-and-such a date; all manner of theories! We tolerate *them*. Whatever Sadie believes in, it's very old. She hasn't invented it. On the other hand, one can't help feeling that it can't be quite right.'

Wynne looked slightly embarrassed. 'You'd think I was a hard-nosed old biddy, wouldn't you? With all my years in journalism. But one does come across odd things from time to time which can't easily be explained.'

'That doesn't mean there is no explanation,' Meredith pointed out. 'So, Wynne, Alan's busy visiting the doctor and the builder. What do you say, you and I visit The Standing Stones?'

Before her eyes, Wynne shed twenty years and became the newspaper reporter she'd never really ceased to be at heart. Her face alight with enthusiasm, she exclaimed, 'What a perfectly splendid idea. And we must go now, or the trail will be quite cold! We shall need a guidebook. Now, let's see, I've got one somewhere.'

'What for?' Meredith asked, bewildered.

'*Raison d'être*, dear. We have to be snooping around for a reason. We're tourists – or you are. I'm just showing you around.'

CHAPTER THIRTEEN

The Anthropophagi, and men whose heads
Do grow beneath their shoulders . . .
                                        Wm Shakespeare

DRIVING OUT to the site on a bright morning was a very different proposition to going there at dusk or by night. They'd taken Wynne's car which, though it was elderly and clanked horribly at every gear change, she manoeuvred in dashing style. Meredith was pleased when they at last drew into the lay-by.

'Here we are!' Wynne scrambled out, clasping the guide-book and Meredith's ordnance survey map as well. Meredith, with some difficulty in keeping pace, followed her up the bank and over the stone wall.

'You're absolutely sure, are you, that you saw no parked cars last night?' Wynne asked as she strode purposefully towards the stones.

'None at all. I know it was dark but Alan and I both looked.'

'But they had cars, must've done. It means,' said Wynne, confidently, 'that they have alternative secure parking arrangements and those aren't so easily come by. We're looking, Meredith, for a local accomplice.'

'There aren't any locals, Wynne.'

'The map, dear, the map!' Wynne spread it out. The wind caught at it, making it crackle and buckle in her hands. Wynne, however, found what she wanted. 'Here we are, Lower Edge Farm. Only a quarter of a mile away. They could easily walk across the fields from there.'

It seemed a long shot, but Meredith didn't want to discourage her. She looked around. Even in the sunshine and with the company of some sheep, it was still a desolate spot. The stones were a disconcerting presence.

'Where was this bonfire?' Wynne asked.

They found the blackened circle of turf. Nothing remained of the fuel used, not a single piece of charred wood. 'Cleaned it up before they left,' said Wynne.

She began to cast about further away and after a while, called to Meredith. 'Here!'

She'd found the location of what would appear to have been an earlier fire. The grass and weeds were growing through the scorched earth, but it was still quite easy to distinguish the area the fire had covered.

'So now we know they come here regularly. We need to go to that farm. The people there would be able to see the glow of the flames, just as you and Alan did. They wouldn't ignore a conflagration up here and if it's been a regular occurrence, they certainly can't have failed to see it! They must have looked into it.'

A sheep wandered up and began tearing noisily at the grass by Meredith. She wondered whether this field actually belonged to Lower Edge Farm. If it did, the farmer would – or should – have been extremely alarmed at anyone lighting a large fire in it. But no one had disturbed the previous night's dancers.

Meredith's ear caught the sound of an approaching car

engine. She raised her head from peering at the scorched turf and looked towards the road. 'Drat!' she said. 'The police.'

The police car was coasting down the lane alongside the field. It stopped. Two uniformed men got out, looked across at the women in the field and engaged in some discussion. One of the men got back in the car and the other clambered up the bank, over the wall, and approached them across the turf. He was very young, ginger-haired, and as he neared they saw he was also nervous.

'Good morning, ladies,' he greeted them.

'Good morning, officer!' Wynne beamed at him.

He didn't seem reassured. 'Might I ask what you're doing out here?' He cleared his throat. 'You're a bit out of the way.'

Wynne brandished her guidebook confidently. 'We're visiting this very interesting historical site. Didn't you know about it, constable? I'm a local resident. I live at Parsloe St John. This lady is a visitor and I brought her out here to see the stones. It's a very important pre-historic monument!'

He took off his cap and studied Meredith. He had the white skin which went with carroty hair, and a tendency to freckles. She gave him a chummy smile. He didn't return it. 'You haven't seen anyone else around, since you've been here?'

'Not a soul,' Meredith told him.

'What's the problem?' Wynne asked.

'We've—' The young man looked back towards the road where his colleague waited comfortably in the car. 'We had a report of some people lighting fires out here. That's a dangerous thing to do.'

'We saw the burnt area,' Wynne told him, pursing her lips disapprovingly. 'We were very surprised, I must say. Such a risk! Just think what would happen to these very old stones if they were caught up in a big fire! They might crack!'

He was backing away. He replaced his cap, tugging it straight. 'Well, right, then. I'll leave you to it.' He hesitated. 'If you should see anyone acting a bit odd – give us a call, eh?'

They promised.

'Poor young man,' said Wynne with a chuckle, as the police car drove off. 'Scared out of his wits he might be tackling a pair of modern-day witches!'

'You handled that very well, Wynne, but perhaps I ought to have told him that I was one of the two people who reported the fire.'

Wynne looked quite shocked. 'Certainly not! You would just have confused him. Besides, I'd told him you were a visitor I was showing around.'

She had a point. It made Meredith reflect that being less than frank with the police always made for problems. The visitor story had been harmless enough, but forced to contradict it, they would have looked fishy.

She walked over to the stones and stood before them, hands thrust into her pockets. There was no denying their fascination. She'd love to know their secrets but those were long lost.

She said suddenly, 'You know, Wynne, I'm not sure I'd agree those people dancing around out here last night were keeping alive some kind of tradition stretching back in unbroken line to pre-history. If there were rituals carried out here in the year dot, no one knows now what they were. Extremely dignified for all we know. It strikes me that last night's worshippers had simply invented a ritual which suited them. The original celebrants, druids or whoever they were, might have been shocked at the modern antics.'

'Last night's revellers would tell you that whatever they

were doing, they'd learned it from others before them,' Wynne pointed out.

'So what? That doesn't mean a thing. When you were a kid, did you ever play Chinese Whispers? You sit in a circle and one person whispers something to the next person who passes it on. The last person to get the message speaks it aloud and it's changed entirely. That's how I feel about Sadie's ideas. There may once have been something to them, but I'm sure a lot's got added on or misinterpreted or just plain changed as centuries went by.'

'One could write an interesting feature on it.' Wynne considered the idea and shook her head. 'Though it's been done before.' She stood beside Meredith and gazed at the Standing Man. 'You know, dotty though it may seem to you, I have to say the stones to have a sort of – aura. Or *I*'ve got a lot of imagination!' She laughed uneasily.

'No, I agree. They do have a kind of power. But I'm not sure anyone ought to try and find out what it is. You and I for example. There's a line to be drawn between investigative journalism and plain meddling. The thing is, I'm not sure those dancers ought to have been meddling, either. It's the feeling that somehow, something might be stirred up which ought to be left sleeping.'

'Absolutely. Only . . .' Wynne fiddled with her hair and a pin fell out. She stooped to retrieve it from the grass. 'I can say this to you, Meredith, because you'll understand. I feel as if it's already been disturbed, the genie let out of the bottle, in Parsloe St John. Olivia's pony, my flowerbed, poor Rory's car . . .' She sighed. 'It was always so peaceful there. Nothing ever happened. Now it's as if some force for mischief is afoot.'

'It's a very modern witch who'd use paint-stripper!'

'Oh, I didn't mean that, I don't believe the vandalism is

down to witchcraft. What I meant – if I'm sure at all what I do mean – is that there's a nastiness in the village which wasn't there before. I don't like it!' Wynne added suddenly in a fierce voice. 'I don't like it at all, I'm afraid of it – something horrid is about to happen. I didn't see that in a crystal ball! I just feel it in my journalist's bones! I've always had a nose for a story, whether it's something which has happened or something just about to happen, about to break, like a storm.'

She was getting agitated and Meredith hastened to reassure her. 'Alan's looking into it, anyway.'

'Yes, I'm so relieved.' Wynne calmed down and smiled. 'Alan inspires such confidence.' She became brisk and businesslike again. 'So, are we going to Lower Edge Farm?'

'We're already here. Why not?' Meredith cast The Standing Man a slightly furtive look as she spoke, in case he – it – mightn't approve. She said, 'Perhaps we shall get a storm, a real one. All this hot weather has to break sooner or later.'

Lower Edge Farm lay at the end of a narrow track. It was a small, untidy place showing little sign of prosperity. The farmhouse was old and had an uncared-for air, the outbuildings ramshackle. The yard itself was dusty and an ancient tractor, so dust-caked it might have travelled through a sandstorm, was parked by a low stone wall on the further side. A man in cloth cap and dungarees was tinkering with its engine but he looked up as Wynne's car bumped across the poles of a cattle grid at the entry and came to meet them.

'Got yourselves lost, then?' he asked. He didn't sound unfriendly, but not particularly welcoming either. Meredith thought him about fifty but he might have been younger. His skin was weathered and lined but such hair as could be seen beneath the cap still dark and curly. He had stooped by the driver's window to ask his question. Wynne let down the glass and gave him her cheerful grin.

'Good morning!' She pushed open the door and he stepped back. Meredith followed her example on her side. As the man watched them emerge, so any latent friendliness evaporated and only suspicion remained.

'Sorry to bother you. We were wondering if the field which holds the pre-historic monument is part of your land?'

The farmer tapped the screwdriver he held against the palm of his other hand, considering first the speaker and then Meredith who was leaning on the roof of the car. 'No, not that bit of land, outside our boundaries.'

'We thought', Meredith said, 'that those might be your sheep. You are the nearest farm on the map.' She raised her hand from below the level of the car roof so that he could see she was holding the ordnance survey map.

At the sight of the map, he blinked. 'Very likely. Doesn't mean it's our land, though, does it?'

'So whose land would it be?' Meredith persisted.

His mouth twisted in dry smile. 'That'd be asking, wouldn't it? Government land, that. That makes it yours and mine, some would say, don't it?'

'But your sheep?'

'What about 'em?' He was growing restless. 'I graze a few sheep on it, keeps the grass down. No one never said I couldn't. Doin' 'em a favour. Got a lot of interest in sheep, have you?'

'No, in the stones.' Wynne took over the conversation. 'Can you tell us anything about them?'

'Not a darn thing. Allus been there. Allus will be there, I reckon. Like I say, it isn't my land and not my affair.' He half-turned away. 'So, sorry I can't help you no more.'

They were being dismissed, but Wynne wasn't so easily dislodged. 'We noticed someone had lit a fire up there very recently.'

He refused to turn back but made for his work at the tractor with an air of obstinacy. He bent over the engine and with his back to them, grunted, 'So coppers said. They was down here earlier on.'

'Do you know who lit it? It was a very dangerous thing to do.'

'Don't know nothing about it. Told the coppers the same.' There was a clang within the workings of the tractor as he dropped his screwdriver. He swore.

'But you saw the fire from here. You must have done, at least a red glow on the horizon?'

Meredith's question, or a combination of their presence and having lost his screwdriver in the tractor's innards, exasperated him. He whirled round, his sunburnt cheeks red with anger.

'Look, ma'am. I don't know what you and your friend want, but I can't help you, right? I may've seen there was a fire up there last night, but 'tisn't the first time and it's not my land, so nothing to do with me!'

'Oh, come on,' Wynne encouraged him. 'Fires spread. So close to your property, you must have been concerned.'

He picked up a greasy rag draped over one huge tyre and came towards them, wiping his hands. 'Now you listen to me, both of you!' He gestured with the rag from one to the other of them. 'If'n it had showed signs of spreading, I'd have got on to the fire brigade. But it didn't. I seen the fires up there before and 'tis gipsies or them hippies. There's only me and my wife here with a fifteen-year-old boy. I'm not going up there and take on half a dozen big fellers and twice that number dogs, when it isn't even my land, right? That's what I told them coppers and that's what I'm telling you. I'm also telling you this here yard *is* my land and I'm a busy man. So you can just take yourselves off and ask your questions someplace else!'

'He knows, all right!' said Wynne as they rattled back down the track. 'He admits there have been fires up there more than once and he must have gone to investigate sooner or later. Either he's scared of them, or they've paid him off, or he's a part of it. If I had to guess, I'd say they paid him something to let them park their cars there, out of sight of the road. It's a nice little earner for him, and just the trick for them. Across his pasture to the stones would be only a shortish walk. Did you notice the tracks?'

'The car tyres? Yes, I did, over by that haybarn. Might have been the police car's.'

Wynne shook her head. 'More than one pattern of tyre. That's the coven's carpark, all right.'

Meredith glanced at her watch. 'So what do we do now? I promised I'd meet Alan at The King's Head for lunch so we'd better get back. Join us, Wynne?'

'No, dear. I've got things to do. But keep me informed of developments, won't you? Tell Alan I know he'll turn up something.'

Alan mightn't appreciate this vote of confidence. 'If there are any,' Meredith stipulated. She hoped Wynne wasn't expecting too much.

'Oh, yes,' Wynne said. 'There will be. I feel it in my bones. Something's going to happen.'

Alan was already in The King's Head, sitting alone in their former place, one hand cradling a pint, his eyes studying the other occupants of the bar with apparent idleness.

Meredith slid into the opposite chair. 'How did you get on?'

'Haven't seen the doctor yet. I had a long talk with Crombie. What are you drinking?'

'Just a sherry, please. I asked Wynne to join us, but she's got things to do at home. She's worried.' Meredith hesitated. 'I've got to admit she worried me. When all's said and done, she is an old hand at sensing a newsworthy story.'

Alan muttered something she couldn't catch and went to the bar to get the sherry. Meredith, alone, looked around the room. She was really looking for Mervyn Pollard, but he wasn't to be seen at the moment. The bar was being tended by a sprightly young woman in a denim shirt and a lot of clanking jewellery. Alan was asking her something in a casual tone. Meredith saw the woman pause, frown as if in thought, then go to the door into the kitchen and put her head through, as if to repeat Markby's query.

A moment later she was back at the bar, shaking her head. Alan thanked her and came back carrying the sherry.

'Thank you. What was all that about? Asking for Mervyn?'

'I've already done that and been told he's gone to see the brewery. I just wondered whether the odd-job man, Berry, had been in this morning. Crombie's been expecting him to turn up at his yard, but he's apparently gone AWOL.'

Meredith felt a stir of unease. 'Kevin was looking for him yesterday.'

'Kevin doesn't know where he is, so says Crombie. Max thinks Ernie's got a ladylove. Don't say it.'

Meredith grinned. 'I suppose he's got a rustic charm. On second thoughts, no, he hasn't. Not more than an old oilcan abandoned in a ditch!'

'Ouch!' Alan grinned. 'Not all are of your opinion. I

rather gather from Max that Ernie's a legend with the ladies.' He looked at her curiously. 'What are you thinking now? You've got a funny look on your face.'

'Thanks, I'm sure! I was thinking that fauns and satyrs and creatures like that which were associated with fertility and general randiness in ancient times were all of them pretty ugly, too.' She sipped her sherry. 'Cheers. What else did Crombie have to say?'

'Not a great deal, when it came down to it. He talked a lot, which isn't the same thing as saying anything. Two things might be of interest and, incidentally, he didn't volunteer either of them! One is that he has had an incident of vandalism at his yard – that was a shot in the dark on my part. He didn't like talking about it. The other is that upstairs, hanging in a rather obscure stretch of corridor, is a painting done by mine host here, of the standing stones.'

'What?' Meredith put down her sherry before she spilled it. One or two heads turned curiously in their direction.

'He didn't seem too keen on my looking at that, either. However, perhaps he merely thought my visit had lasted long enough. He says he was at school with Pollard who was a bit of an artist, even as a boy. I don't think it necessarily proves your theory.'

Markby picked up the menu card wedged in a plastic holder on the table. 'Today's speciality is chicken and mushroom pie with chips or salad. What happened to the exotic cuisine?'

'Mervyn's having a plain food day, thank goodness! With salad, please. Do you believe Pollard is doing business at the brewery?'

'How should I know? That's what the girl said. He may be sleeping off a night of revelry beneath the moon. But he may equally be about his business. We still don't know for sure it was Pollard out there last night.'

'I do,' Meredith said. 'Wynne and I went back there this morning.'

Markby put down the menu with a tsk! of annoyance. 'I wish you'd told me you meant to do that. I'd have asked you not to.'

'What's the harm? The police were out there checking, by the way, but I don't think they'd found anything. But at least Basil's stirred them up. Oh, and Wynne and I found where the dancers had parked their cars. There's a place called Lower Edge Farm, only a quarter of a mile away. The farmer knows more than he's letting on. Surly sort of man.'

'Who wouldn't be?' he retorted. 'With two unknown women arriving out of the blue and pestering him with questions!'

'Solved a problem, though. I was puzzled about the cars. They must have had transport to get out there.'

'Puzzle over the contents of Mervyn's chicken pies for a bit, all right?'

She walked with him, after lunch, from the pub to the gate of The Abbot's House.

'I'll meet you here when you've finished talking to Burnett,' Meredith said. 'I can spend the time over there, in the gardens of Rookery House. That doesn't mean,' she added quickly, 'that I'm changing my mind!' She hadn't missed the brightening of his expression.

'Of course not,' he assured her. 'Go and take another look around. I'll join you later, though it shouldn't take long. I doubt Burnett will have much to say. He's been warned I'm coming and will have worked out just how little information he can get away with!' There was a distinct note of asperity in his voice.

Meredith eyed him. 'You think Crombie will have got in touch with Burnett and relayed the content of your conversation with him?'

'You bet your boots he has!' said Markby gloomily.

Meredith watched him walk up the path to the front door and raise his hand to the bell. She turned and pushed open the unlocked grilled gate to Rookery House and let herself, in her turn, on to someone else's property.

But whose? Wynne had said that everything, apart from the individual small bequests, had been left to charity. Charity, therefore, would be the beneficiary of the sale. But which charity? Had Olivia specified which? Or would that be left to lawyers, deciding between rival good causes? Perhaps it had seemed a good idea to Olivia, but, really, the more specific a will the better, Meredith thought. It could save an awful lot of undignified squabbling.

Someone had been in the house and opened up the upper floor shutters. She supposed it must be Janine, airing the place out. There was no sign that the former housekeeper was still there. Perhaps she meant to return this evening and lock up again. Janine, Max Crombie and the Berrys were all doing their best, but inevitably the building would deteriorate if it weren't sold soon.

She walked slowly around the house between what once had been lawns and flowerbeds. Nearest to the house, the beds had been planted out with annuals. Perhaps Olivia herself had done a little gardening, despite her lameness. Or maybe she had only directed one of the Berrys. There were several things here to remind one of the Berrys. Here was the spot where the lad, Kevin, had rested the ladder against the wall and climbed up, alarming Meredith by appearing at the upper window. She pictured that unfortunate, ill-favoured youth as she'd last seen him, standing at the side entrance to the pub's yard, his hands thrust into his pockets and his body hunched defensively inside his misshapen sweater, as he inquired after Ernie.

Where was Ernie? By all accounts, no one had seen him for two days now. Surely even a passionate interlude couldn't take Ernie out of circulation that long? Not when there was work waiting to be done. Ernie depended on the goodwill of a man like Crombie to keep a steady trickle of jobs coming his way. Not only could the builder withdraw his own patronage, but he could spoil things for Ernie elsewhere. Just a word that Ernie wasn't reliable, that's all it took.

Meredith sat down on a garden seat, once painted bright green, but which had faded and peeled. The sun was warm and the spot sheltered. She closed her eyes and raised her face to the warmth. It was nice here, very nice, but she couldn't live here. There were dreams and there was reality. Alan's dreams and her down-to-earth practicality clashed over this, as had happened before over other things. Had she always been so distressingly sensible?

No, not always, she thought, remembering a time, long ago, when an unwise love affair had almost wrecked her life. Long before Alan came on the scene.

She opened her eyes. A breeze had found its way into this nook and ruffled her hair. She was suddenly disinclined to sit there any longer. She felt an interloper. She had no right. She wasn't a prospective buyer, only a pretender, and was treating the place like a public park. Olivia Smeaton wouldn't approve of that!

Meredith got up and walked back the way she'd come. She looked down the drive, through the gate, and saw that the road beyond was empty. It seemed Alan was still inside The Abbot's House.

Unwilling to return to her lawnside seat, she turned towards the walled kitchen garden. In there it was positively hot, trapped heat bouncing off the old mellow walls, the air stifling. Meredith walked across it, making for the gateway into the paddock beyond, open land and, with luck, a cooling breeze.

But the heat haze hung above the empty paddock, suffocating. The far hedges shimmered and the old chestnut tree out there in the middle cast little shade, the sun was still too high.

And yet, despite that, someone had chosen to sit under it. She couldn't see who it was because he was round the other side, leaning against the trunk. But she could see a leg stuck straight out, and an arm, a bare arm, hanging down immobile, fingers brushing the turf.

She was going to turn away but then something unexpected happened. There was a flap of black wings and a crow soared up from – so it seemed – the lap of the seated man and flew, croaking in alarm, up into the branches above. Almost immediately, another followed it.

Sweat trickled down between Meredith's shoulder blades, together with a prickle of unease. That wasn't right. The crows might have come down, believing the human asleep, but they were prudent birds. They wouldn't – indeed they had no reason – to land on the man's legs.

Unless, of course . . . Carrion-eaters, crows.

No, she told herself. That was ridiculous. But was it? The arm and leg were very still. He might be asleep or perhaps ill. She forced herself to walk forward, nearer to the tree.

The bare arm was covered with dark hair and very brawny. The leg was clad in some kind of workman's corduroy. There was curious buzzing in the air, as if an army of insects swarmed nearby.

That arm and leg, it had to be Ernie Berry. But it ought not to be Ernie, not unless he'd been sitting here for two days. Meredith paused, took a grip on her natural repugnance and increasing fear, and walked around the tree trunk to confront the seated figure.

All at once, a dense black cloud of flies exploded outward from the upper part of Ernie's torso and hung, buzzing angrily in a swarm above his—

'Oh, my dear God . . .' Meredith whispered.

Not above Ernie's head, because Ernie had no head. There were his strong boots, corduroy-clad legs, dirty singlet, dirtier now for the sticky blackened stains which had run down the front of it and dried there. His muscular arms and broad, hairy shoulders . . . and where his head should be, nothing, nothing above what remained of his neck, a tangled, blackened mess of gristle, tubes and flesh on which a few tenacious bluebottles were still crawling while wasps circled and dived above like fighter aircraft, harrying the target below.

Meredith turned aside and threw up violently, chicken pie and salad, on to the turf.

CHAPTER FOURTEEN

*And in the centre of that vale, under a rock, is a
head and the visage of a devil bodily, full horrible
and dreadful to see . . .*

Sir John Maundeville

MRS BURNETT, holding a child's plastic feeding bib,
opened the door. Seeing Markby, she exclaimed in a harassed tone, 'Oh, yes, go on through . . .' and left him to find
his own way.

The place smelled even more strongly of boiled vegeta-
bles, signifying lunch was over. Following the direction of
her pointing finger and his instincts, Markby found himself
entering the drawing room where Dr Burnett strode across
the worn carpet to greet him, holding out a broad palm.

'My wife told me you'd be coming. Sit down, won't you?
What's all this about?'

He was one of those hale, hearty men, who give the
impression of being in the best of health and spirits, even on
occasions when they aren't, and whose age it's difficult to
determine. His boyish, chubby face and good-natured features, together with an engagingly spontaneous manner,
suggested youth. Markby thought the doctor was probably a
little older than first sight suggested, and perhaps as much as

a dozen years older than his wife, say mid-to-late thirties. In Markby's experience, he was the sort of medical man popular with certain old ladies, who saw in him a surrogate son or grandson.

As a police officer, Markby had come across occasions when that fact had proved to have significance. The nice young doctor, solicitor, house agent, financial adviser, next-door neighbour, neighbour's teenage son who had proved, in the end, so unworthy of an elderly person's trust.

He introduced himself and explained the purpose of his visit, as best he could.

'These are not official inquiries as such, you understand. But someone is a little bothered by certain aspects of recent events. As I'm on the spot, I've agreed to look into it. Manpower shortages, you know. I'm supposed to be on holiday!'

Burnett responded to this sympathy-seeking approach as Markby hoped he would. 'Bad luck, old chap. Being a policeman must be like being a doctor. Always happening to me. No sooner do we go on holiday than someone in our hotel suffers a suspected heart-attack or sunstroke or gets a bad dose of Montezuma's Revenge. Before you know it, the manager's knocking on our door and asking, would I mind? Well, of course, I bloody mind. But there you are, it goes with the job.' He chuckled.

In the distance, a child set up a wail. Markby reflected briefly on the difference in appearance between this jolly broth of a boy, and his harassed wife. He reflected too on the shabby room in which they sat. Doctors weren't, as he understood it, badly paid. Certainly Burnett had a young family, but even so, he seemed to be living in what were once called straitened circumstances. Either the Burnetts spent a lot of money elsewhere – the holidays referred to?

Or possibly – an idea which occurred to Markby partly because Burnett seemed older than his wife and partly suggested by his earlier musings on his own situation – possibly, this was not Burnett's first marriage. He might be supporting another set of young children and an ex-wife somewhere.

A man of this type, who needed money, and who had been personal physician to an elderly, wealthy recluse . . . Hmn, thought Markby.

Aloud he said, 'I understand you were Mrs Smeaton's doctor?'

Burnett nodded. 'Yes, she was one of my private patients. I've a couple in the area. She'd lived abroad for years and hadn't got to grips with the National Health. She preferred a private arrangement.'

'That could have proved expensive. Was she a sickly woman?'

'Lord no, fit as a flea – except for being a little dodgy on her pins. As a matter of fact, I suspected we were in for a hip replacement and I was getting around to suggesting it to her. As it happened, well—' He spread out his hands.

'You were called to view the body, the first to see it, I understand.'

'Right. Janine Catto, Olivia's cleaner, found her. She ran over here and got me. But she'd been dead a while. Rigor had set in and already passed off almost completely. We hadn't seen her all weekend, but that wasn't unusual. She rarely left the place.'

'Forgive me for asking, doctor,' Markby said carefully, 'but had you cause to move the body, in order to examine her or check in any way?'

Burnett reddened and bridled like in plump turkey-cock. 'Certainly not. I told you, no doubt she was dead. Naturally

I had to move her arm and turn her head in the course of checking she was dead, but I replaced her arm – and her head – as I'd found her.'

'She was lying on her back or front?'

'Twisted, on her side, one leg forward, the other back. She'd lost a slipper. I saw it lying on the stairs a few treads above us. The stair carpet was rucked up and one of the uprights in the banisters appeared to have cracked. I guessed what might have happened and left everything just as it was. I told Janine to do the same. Evidence, you know, for the inquest.'

'Indeed. Quite right.' Burnett looked mollified but not for long. Markby went on, 'I understand you were in the habit of calling in on Olivia Smeaton, even if she hadn't asked you to do so, just to check how she was.'

'We are supposed to do that, you know, keep a check on elderly patients if we know they're on their own and shaky,' Burnett retorted belligerently. 'Not that it's always possible in a busy, wide-spread practice. There are only so many hours in any day and as you said just now, it's a question of manpower. One can't be everywhere. But as it happened, Olivia was also a neighbour, so it was a simple matter to pop in on my way home or on my way out. My surgery's not here. We're over at the new medical centre in town.'

So much, thought Markby, for having a doctor living in the village. If you needed to consult him, you still had to trek into the nearest town. Such was progress. Aloud he said, 'It must have been reassuring for Mrs Smeaton to have you call on her.'

Burnett nodded and looked pleased. 'I think she appreciated it.'

Too late, he realised he'd left himself open. Markby saw him struggle to bite back the last words, realise he couldn't do it, and decide to face it out. The plump, cherubic countenance grew pink, the round chin tilted, Burnett's gaze met his visitor's determinedly.

'Obviously she was grateful, because she did remember you in her will, I believe.' Markby raised his eyebrows.

'You're bloody well informed!' Burnett snapped. 'Yes, she did! But it wasn't a fortune, you know! She left me a thousand quid and a carriage clock, if you want to know. That little clock, over there!'

He pointed at a carriage clock on a shelf. Markby admired it and said it was a nice thought. Had Olivia known Burnett liked the clock?

'I suppose so, I may have said so,' Burnett retorted truculently. 'One makes conversation – and with old ladies it's not always easy!'

'She never spoke about herself? Her past life? Her exploits as a rally-driver or during the war?'

'Never!' Burnett snapped.

The telephone rang. Mrs Burnett could be heard answering it, against a background of grizzling toddler. Burnett shifted in his chair and looked restless. 'I'm a busy man, you know . . .'

'Yes. I understand. Just a couple more questions, if you don't mind.'

Burnett looked very much as if he did mind. He glowered at his visitor. 'Make 'em brief, then!'

'I'll do my best. I understand that Rory Armitage, the vet, was very concerned about the effect the loss of her pet might have on Mrs Smeaton. I also understand that, before he realised the possibility of poison, he thought the animal was dying of old age. He told me he'd spoken to you about that and you were discussing how best to break the sad news to the old lady, when the pony died.'

'Yes. That's so!' Burnett looked more confident.

'But you didn't,' Markby said gently, 'go across the road and check on Mrs Smeaton during the weekend following the burial of the animal? Surely that was a time to check on her, if any?'

Burnett looked stunned. Then he rallied, his florid features turning dull burgundy in rage. He gripped the arms of his chair and leaned forward pugnaciously. 'She wasn't the only patient on my books, you know! Yes, I could have checked and I would have done so if I'd had time! But, as it happened, it was my duty weekend. I was on call. Two quite separate emergencies came up, one on the Saturday and another on the Sunday. Ours is a rural practice and both these calls were out in the country. You can check that out, if you wish! I put off going to see Olivia until the Monday, by which time she was dead and Janine had found her first. If my wife hadn't been so busy with the kids, she'd have nipped across. But she'd no one to leave the baby with and, frankly, Olivia wasn't the sort of old lady who liked babies!'

As if on cue, Mrs Burnett tapped at the door and showed her harassed face at the crack. 'Sorry to interrupt, Rory Armitage on the phone, Tom. Gill's been taken ill. Can you go over there, right away?'

There was no disguising the way in which Burnett grasped at his wife's words as a drowning man grabs a lifeline. 'Sure, tell him I'm on my way!' He leapt to his feet. 'Well, superintendent, you see how it is! Nice to have met you!' He thrust out his hand again in farewell.

Markby barely had time to shake it before its owner had fairly sprinted out of the room.

As Alan Markby had been ringing the bell of The Abbot's House for the second time that day, Rory Armitage, who'd been up half the night assisting at the birth of twin calves, had settled down for an after-lunch doze in the shabby leather chair which was 'his' and which had survived all attempts by Gill to get rid of it.

He stretched out his long legs, folded his hands on his stomach and reflected that he must be getting old. He was forty-four. There had been a time when being called from his warm bed at three in the morning to spend the rest of the night in a smelly cowshed or stable hadn't bothered him at all. He'd simply come home, showered, eaten a hearty breakfast and faced the next day as fresh as a daisy. That had changed and it wasn't the only thing. He told himself his unwonted feeling of depression was because he was still upset by the attack on his car. Who wouldn't be? And now, on top of everything else, there was this holidaying copper who seemed to hold some sort of troubleshooter's brief to go round asking distinctly disturbing questions.

'It isn't as though,' Rory murmured sleepily to himself, 'there's any reason to suppose he'll find out anything. Wish they could find out who wrecked my car. Don't suppose they'll do that. Dunno what I pay my taxes for.'

Finding, like many another true Briton, an obscure satisfaction in grumbling at this further proof of the waste of his money by the government, he drifted into slumber.

He was awoken by what he afterwards described as 'a God-almighty screech'.

He sat up, gripped the arms of the chair and exclaimed muzzily, 'Whazzat?'

It came again. It was outside in the back garden, and was followed this time by pounding feet coming towards the house. Rory scrambled out of the chair and ran to the French windows which gave a clear view of the rear of the house.

His wife was racing towards him, her face white, her

mouth open, eyes staring. Both arms were raised in the air.

Rory flung open the glass doors and yelled, 'What the dickens is wrong? You look as if you've seen a ghost!'

She stumbled into his arms, clinging to him, sobbing, gasping, unable to draw a proper breath or form words. He hauled her, sagging in his clasp, inside and pushed her back into the vacated chair. She lay there, her eyes rolling and mouth working.

He'd begun to be seriously alarmed. 'Gill? Hang on, love, I'll get a glass of water!'

She let out another shriek and started up, gripping his wrist in fingers like steel clamps. 'No! Don't leave me!'

He prised her fingers loose. 'For God's sake, Gill, what is it?'

She swallowed and attempted to explain, but only managed, 'It's in the—' before hysteria overtook her and she fell to sobbing wildly and rolling about in the chair as if in some sort of fit.

'Gawd!' muttered Rory. 'Look, steady on, darling. I'll phone Tom Burnett and get him over here!'

After all, he himself was only a vet. He'd dealt with a few maddened horses, but maddened women were beyond him.

'It's Gill,' Rory greeted Burnett. 'Sorry to drag you away and all the rest of it, but I've never seen her like it. I can't get any sense out of her.'

'Think nothing of it,' the doctor assured him. 'I'd got some copper in my house, asking a lot of frankly impertinent questions! I was beginning to hope someone would call me out! Has he been to see you? He's been to Max Crombie. Max rang and warned me I might be getting a visit. God knows what's going on in the village of late! Everyone's gone barmy. Oh, sorry, didn't mean – where is Gill?'

Gill Armitage was crouched in the chair. She'd stopped shrieking and was sobbing quietly into a wet handkerchief, swaying from side to side. As Burnett bent over her, she gave a squeak and cowered away from him.

'OK, Gill, it's only me,' he said in a tone of professional reassurance. 'Let's have a look at you. What's all this, eh?'

She peered up at him, recognition dawning through panic, fingers clenched on the sodden rag. 'Oh, Tom . . . where's Rory?'

'Here, love,' said her husband.

Her mouth worked soundlessly for a moment, then she whispered, 'Have you found it?'

Burnett glanced sideways at the vet. 'Know what she means?'

'Haven't a clue. She came in from the garden, screeching blue murder and went beserk.'

'Mmn, well, she's clearly had a bad fright.' Burnett stooped over his patient again. 'It's all right now, Gill. We'll take care of it, whatever it is. Look, I'm going to give you something to make you sleep for a bit . . .'

Her hand shot out and grabbed the startled doctor by the lapel of his tweed jacket. 'No! You've got to call the police!'

'Oh lor',' muttered Armitage. 'Not again.'

'Police?' Burnett raised his eyebrows. 'Just left one of the blighters back at my place, Gill.'

'Well, go and get him!' she yelled in his face with such force that he reeled back.

'Here,' said Rory, 'let me talk to her.' He shouldered the doctor aside. 'Gill, is it more vandalism? Is it in the garden—?'

She let out a piercing scream and he clapped his hands to his ears.

'I think,' said Dr Burnett, 'we may assume it's in the garden.'

There was a crunch of wheels on gravel outside. Rory glanced at the window. 'Here's Polly,' he said. 'Polly Desmond, my assistant. That's a bit of luck.' He went to the door and could be heard calling. When he came back, he was accompanied by a brisk young woman with long fair hair braided into a single plait.

At the sight of her, Gill Armitage wailed, 'Oh, Polly, I've had such a dreadful experience – I've seen an – an awful sight!'

'What was it?' Polly sat down beside Gill and took her hand, but Mrs Armitage, at the renewed memory, had fallen back, shaking her head wordlessly.

'She should be all right here with Polly for a few minutes,' Burnett whispered. 'What say, you and I go and take a look? That may solve the mystery.'

'The roses . . .' Gill Armitage croaked, her grip on Polly's hand tightening.

'Come on,' said Rory. 'This way.'

He led the doctor through the French windows and down the lawn. 'Garden really suffered this year,' he observed. 'But Gill kept the rosebed going. She's a keen gardener, you know, and her roses have always been her pride and joy. She's got a little rose garden over there . . .' He pointed towards a large, circular bed of rose bushes.

They approached it with care. 'She came running out here, by the looks of it . . .' Burnett pointed at the broken sprays and scattered orange petals of a Christingle rose. An abandoned trowel and secateurs lay on a patch of scuffed earth.

'Mind the thorns,' Armitage warned, negotiating his way between the bushes, and scrutinising the ground for the source of his wife's distress.

He stopped suddenly, causing Burnett to cannon into him. 'Strewth . . .' he whispered.

'What is it?' Burnett tried to see past him, failed and manoeuvred his way around a flourishing Peace. They were in the very centre of the bed, which was marked by a standard rose, a crimson-flowered Alex, and at the foot of it, lay the thing, the reason for Gill Armitage's hysteria.

Armitage hadn't answered, and only pointed at the object with a shaking hand.

Burnett gulped. 'Hell's bells . . . I haven't seen anything like that since I was in anatomy class . . .'

Rory said in a small, quiet voice, 'It's Ernie Berry, isn't it?'

Beside him, his fellow medical man, showing admirable clinical sang-froid in the circumstances, replied, 'Yes, but only his head.'

Bewildered, and looking wildly around the garden, Rory demanded, 'Then where the deuce is the rest of him?'

At that very moment, Meredith, stumbling out of the gate of Rookery House into Markby's arms stammered out the answer to his question.

CHAPTER FIFTEEN

I have often thought upon death, and I find it the
least of evils.

Francis Bacon

'HOW IS she?' Wynne asked.

She hovered anxiously on the threshold, clad as she'd
been earlier in the day, in baggy trousers and baggier
hand-knitted canary yellow sweater to which she clasped a
bottle of elderberry cordial.

He stood back to allow her into the cottage. 'At the
moment being very British and buttoned-up. Coping mag-
nificently. The burst of panic when she found – it – has
subsided. Now she's detached. The shock will surface later.
She's in the sitting room, go on through.'

'My dear!' Wynne exclaimed, bustling in and taking the
seat beside Meredith on the sofa. 'How are you? You look
pale. What a truly terrible experience!' She thrust forward
the bottle of elderberry. 'A little restorative!'

Meredith took the offering with thanks. 'It was nasty but
Alan's plied me with enough brandy to cope. Anyway, I
understand I'm not alone in getting a shock. The – the rest of
Ernie has turned up elsewhere.'

She was disinclined to say the word 'head'. It conjured up

the gruesome image of the decapitated figure beneath the tree, with the buzzing insects attacking the congealed stump of the neck. She put the bottle of cordial on a nearby occasional table and repeated, 'This is very good of you, Wynne.'

'In Rory's garden, can you imagine?' Wynne clucked in decent dismay but a gleam in her eye betrayed the habit of a lifetime, which saw a wonderful headline in all this. Wynne, to give her credit, struggled with this instinct and managed, almost, to suppress it.

'Poor Gill found it in her rosebed and had hysterics, so I heard! You do seem to be taking it very well.' She nodded approvingly.

'As it happens, I've seen dead bodies before.' Meredith gave a wry grimace. 'That is, other than laid out neatly in a bed. Road accident victims and rather nastily mutilated. I just didn't expect to see something like that sitting under a tree in Olivia's paddock!'

She attempted a dispassionate view. 'I don't know how long he'd been there. But then, I suppose whoever left him there wouldn't have expected him found soon. Who had cause to go into an empty paddock? Whereas the – the *head*,' Meredith named the missing piece of Ernie's anatomy firmly, 'the head turned up, as you say, in Mrs Armitage's rosebed where the person who put it there might reasonably expect it to be found sooner rather than later.'

'Oh dear,' said Wynne, absently picking pieces of fluffed wool from the front of the canary yellow sweater. 'One does wonder what's going to happen next!' She looked up as Markby held out a glass. 'Oh, thank you, Alan. I must say, I feel I could do with a dram.'

She promptly knocked back the contents with a practised

flick of the wrist and held out the empty glass. Markby obligingly refilled it.

Meredith let her gaze rest on the glowing bars of the electric fire which had been brought in to heat the room. Despite their orange rays, she shivered and rubbed her folded arms. She wasn't nearly so recovered from her experience as she'd assured Alan and now Wynne. But the fact of the matter was she'd had to pull herself together quickly. Alan had called the local police who'd arrived and taken a brief, preliminary statement. The scene had been one of utter confusion, made worse by the fact that the police had received two separate calls, virtually at the same time, one reporting the discovery of Ernie's body and the other that of the unfortunate man's head.

They were now awaiting the arrival of an inspector from the area serious crimes squad. It was half past six. The sun was beginning to go down, but work was only beginning.

'An Inspector Crane,' she said. 'We're waiting for him. He's coming here.'

'Someone you know, Alan?' Wynne asked.

'Afraid not. I'm regional squad, you see. We don't normally deal with local murders unless we're asked – or unless it ties in with something we're working on.'

Wynne was looking disconsolate. 'So there's no chance you'll be put in charge of this?'

'None whatsoever, I shouldn't think, Wynne.' The telephone rang outside in the hall. 'Excuse me . . .' he murmured.

'Now, dear,' said Wynne briskly when he'd left the room. 'In the course of your consular work you had to deal with such things as people injured in road accidents, as you said. Just as I did, in my journalist days. You'll know as well as I do that one must try and keep routine going. Important to eat, for example, even if you don't feel like it. Just a bowl of soup or some Marmite sandwiches, anything. Have you had something?'

'I don't need *food* yet, Wynne, honestly. My stomach hasn't settled down and, if I tried to eat anything, I'd throw up again. Though I should eat, I know, because I've been sitting here drinking! I will have some soup when this Inspector Crane has been. I just hope I'm not tiddly by the time he gets here. All I can tell him is that I went to the paddock by chance and found Ernie. I saw nothing else.' Meredith's voice faltered. She paused, screwed up her forehead and went on. 'I'm sure I saw nothing else. No sign of how long he'd been there but I don't think two days.' She drew a deep breath. 'Foxes and rats would have found him. There were crows, but they'd only just – I'm sure . . .'

'Let the police worry about it, dear.' Wynne patted her hand.

'I'm worrying about it. I've been racking my brains. Wynne, you know more about the village than we do. Crombie told Alan that Ernie might be missing because he'd got a new ladylove. Lord knows, it seems incredible to me, but I suppose it's possible. Have you heard any gossip? Ernie's name linked with anyone's?'

Wynne's topknot quivered as the numerous pins began to work their inevitable way loose. 'I wouldn't know a *name*. I hear a certain amount of gossip. I know Ernie looked unattractive but he did have a name as a philanderer. But if Ernie had been boasting about a conquest, he wouldn't do it where women were listening. It would be more in the nature of men's talk.'

'But if men were listening, then it might get to the ears of a jealous husband?' Meredith persisted. 'He could go looking for revenge!'

Wynne pushed up her canary yellow sleeves in thought.

'He might go round and beat Ernie up. That would be the village style,' she adjudged. 'I don't think he'd go and cut his h— Oh, sorry, dear—'

Meredith had twitched violently.

'I mean,' Wynne went on a little hesitantly, 'that would be a bizarre revenge. If such a murderer, motivated by sexual jealousy, wanted to mutilate his victim he'd aim for, um, quite another area, don't you think? I do remember a case long ago when I was working on the . . . but we won't go into that now! Besides, we don't know that Ernie did have a new girlfriend. That was just an idea that seemed to get about. If I've learnt anything, it's that one must always check one's facts.'

'But it was two people's idea, and they put it around quite separately. Mervyn Pollard mentioned it to me, and Max Crombie to Alan. Why should they both say it?'

'Because of Ernie's reputation, which I can assure you was a sort of running joke in the village!' was Wynne's response. 'Look at all those women who've lived, on and off, at his cottage and – oh my goodness!' She suddenly looked horrified. 'Kevin! Will anyone have told that poor lad?'

'I should think the police have found him and told him,' Meredith muttered. 'He's Ernie's next of kin, after all. He is, isn't he?'

'There's no one else, at any rate.' Wynne began to look agitated. 'They won't ask that poor boy to identify the remains, will they? I don't know that he could handle that.'

'I've no idea. Perhaps Dr Burnett could do it. He was there when the—' *Say it!* Meredith ordered herself. 'The head turned up in the rosebed. In any case, I'm sure they'll make the – the whole thing look tidy, if you know what I mean, before anyone else sees it. Cover most of it with a sheet.'

'I suppose you're right, but perhaps I ought to have a word with this Crane fellow? You know, explain to him that Kevin isn't used to any responsibility. Someone is going to have to keep an eye on him until he's had a chance to get used to being alone. He's never had to manage without Ernie. Although it's true that Ernie—'

Wynne fell silent and fiddled absently with the topknot, pushing back pins at random until they stuck out like the long needles from a geisha's wig.

'What about him?' Meredith looked up curiously.

'Oh, well, nothing really. I was just thinking that you might say Ernie didn't look after Kevin very well, at least, not when he was a child. He was always grubby and badly dressed. There was just no one to care, really, his own mother having left them and all the other women being temporary. The Berry cottage isn't a salubrious place and I'm not surprised none of them stayed very long. There's always one family in any village which seems more dysfunctional than most. The Berrys were it in Parsloe St John.'

'Sounds like a case for the social services to me. Didn't anyone ever take an interest in the child?'

'Oh no.' Wynne looked a little embarrassed. 'In villages, you see, they like to take care of their own. A family may be feckless, but it still survives somehow. The point I'm making now is, however ramshackle a home Ernie gave Kevin, it was a home – and now Kevin is there alone. He isn't a *competent* sort of youngster. Ernie always told him what to do. He's never had to make any decision.'

As they'd talked, Alan's voice, murmuring on the telephone, had sounded in the background. Now they heard the click of the receiver returned to its rest and Markby came back into the room. He looked part relieved, part embarrassed.

'That's it, then. I'm off the job. My inquiries in Parsloe St John are to cease forthwith in case I get under the feet of the murder inquiry team – or confuse any witnesses. Sorry, Wynne.' He smiled at her.

'That's all right, Alan. Thank you anyway. You had made a start and if you'd been able to carry on, I'm sure you would have turned up something.' Wynne looked wistful. 'You didn't, I suppose, turn up any leads?'

He shook his head. 'Sorry, can't say I did.'

'Oh, well, can't be helped.' Wynne got up and tugged the sweater straight. 'I'd better go home before your Inspector Crane arrives. Don't forget I'm just next door, so if you need anything . . .'

They thanked her and she went out, still looking disconsolate.

'Poor Wynne,' said Meredith. 'You really didn't, did you? Turn up any leads, I mean?'

'What? No, unless there's a connection with her will, as you suggested. She was wealthy and had no family. Someone may have thought . . . On the other hand, because she remembered those who'd befriended her isn't a reason to suspect foul play. She was returning the favour to Armitage, Burnett, and to Crombie, through his daughter. Crombie's fairly well off, as it is. Armitage likewise, I'd guess. Burnett's house gives the impression of an owner strapped for cash, but that may be an entirely false impression. If you're chatting to Wynne, you might slip in a question as to whether Burnett's marriage is his first.'

There was sound of a car drawing up and sharp knock at the door.

'And that,' said Alan, preparing to answer it, 'will be Inspector Crane. Get ready.'

He went out and Meredith prepared herself mentally to repeat the story of her macabre discovery. Footsteps sounded in the hall, Alan's voice, an answering murmur in treble tones – not Wynne, surely? She'd left.

The door opened. 'Meredith,' Alan cleared his throat. 'This is Inspector Crane who is in charge of inquiries.'

A tall, smartly dressed redhead in a dark business suit, severe white blouse and high-heeled shoes marched into the room and set down a document case. 'Miss Mitchell? I'm Amanda Crane. How do you do?' She thrust out her hand.

After the slightest pause, Meredith shook it.

Inspector Crane opened her document case, took out a small sheaf of papers clipped together, snapped the case shut, crossed her legs, smiled, and said, 'Now, Miss Mitchell!' in an encouraging voice.

Markby, sitting discreetly at the back of the room, slid down in his armchair and leaned back his head, out of the ring of light from the standard lamp nearby. The subdued glow flattered Crane's copper hair which had been cut by an expert hand. She no doubt represented the shape of things to come, but he wondered whether the police force would manage to retain such a dynamic young woman for long. It was all very well offering the graduate intake – he guessed she was one of them – fast-track promotion. But much policework, by its very nature, was painfully slow, repetitive, frustrating, time-wasting and dull. Over the years, the force had sadly tended to retain some officers who displayed similar qualities. Not all, thank God. But all the more reason why it badly needed to keep Crane and her kind.

Leaving aside her intellectual abilities, she wasn't a pretty young woman in the usual sense, but she was very attractive.

The glowing copper wings of hair skimmed her prominent cheekbones as she looked up and down from her notes. Despite vigorous efforts over recent years to combat the canteen culture of the average police station, old habits persisted. Since they represented human nature at its most basic, they probably always would to some degree. He didn't dare imagine what kind of remarks, heavy with innuendo, were made behind Inspector Crane's back. She didn't look the type to tolerate them being made to her face. He suspected she'd made few friends in the force, which was all the more a pity.

It wasn't yet dark outside, but inside the cottage the remaining daylight had become suffused with a pall of grey. For the sake of Inspector Crane's eyesight, the standard lamp and another smaller table lamp had been switched on.

'How are you feeling now, after the nasty shock?'

The nannyish tone was the wrong approach, thought Markby. It would work with a lot of witnesses, but not with Meredith. He could see her bridling, metaphorically rolling up her sleeves for battle.

'I'm feeling better than I did. The first shock is fading.'

Let it go at that, Markby silently begged Crane. But his prayer went unanswered.

'I can arrange for some counselling, if you'd like that.'

'No, I wouldn't!' snapped Meredith. 'Thanks all the same.'

'Well, think it over and if you change your mind, let me know. I've got your statement here,' Crane went on, 'which you made to one of the officers at the scene of the crime.'

'I can't add much to it,' Meredith told her.

'Well, we'll just go through it, shall we? Do you feel up to that?' Amanda asked her kindly.

Markby, in his shadowy corner, imagined – or hoped he

only imagined – Meredith growl. He was beginning to feel apprehensive. The love of his life was sitting bolt upright on her sofa, arms folded. At least, he reasoned, taking a positive view of the situation, it's perked her up. Perhaps Crane's approach wasn't so disastrous after all, though more by good luck than good management.

'What took you into the field?' The inspector looked bright and interested.

'Paddock,' said Meredith sourly. 'There's a pony buried in it. I went to look at the grave. I find it rather touching.'

Inspector Crane met the surliness of the interviewee with a professional smile. 'That was your purpose in going on to the premises of Rookery House?'

A neat way, thought Markby, of asking Meredith why she was trespassing. Maybe Inspector Crane just liked to live dangerously.

With snapping hazel eyes, Meredith was replying, 'We had already visited the house with a view to possible purchase. We were told it's for sale and you probably saw the estate agent's notice on the wall. The local key-holder showed us round. Alan was calling on someone else this afternoon and I decided to go and have another look at the grounds while I waited for him.'

Inspector Crane turned her long, pale intelligent face towards him. Her looks were of the kind sometimes unkindly classified as horsy. A very English look, as any gallery collection of Old Master portraits would demonstrate.

'Would that be in connection with the inquiries I believe you've been making, sir?'

'That's right,' said Markby. He was well aware that the inspector was in a delicate situation here and appreciated that she was walking a tightrope. She was in charge of the conversation, but he was the senior in rank. She had to phrase her questions carefully. He was interested to hear how she'd do it. 'I was having a word with Dr Burnett – until he was called away.'

'That was when he was called to Mr Armitage's house?'

'Yes. I understood at the time that Mrs Armitage had been taken ill. I didn't know she'd found – some of the remains.'

'I understand, sir, you've been looking into the circumstances of the recent death of the elderly lady who owned Rookery House.'

Markby made a deprecating sound and waved a hand. 'No reason to suppose it anything but an accident. However, there were some curious points – more concerned with the old lady's life than her death, you might say.'

'And you'll be continuing, will you, sir? With these inquiries?'

'No, inspector, I shall not. Not now you're here.'

Crane looked at him doubtfully, then turned her attention back to Meredith. 'It says here, Miss Mitchell . . .' She consulted the sheaf of notes. 'You told the constable you recognised the deceased as Ernie Berry, a local casual worker. Yet I understand this is your first visit to Parsloe St John and the deceased was without—' Even competent, poised Inspector Crane hesitated.

'Without his head,' supplied Meredith bluntly.

'Quite. The body was headless. How could you be so sure it was Berry?'

'I couldn't have sworn to it, I suppose, but I was sure enough in my mind.' Meredith reflected. 'I had seen him in the local pub. He was of distinctive build. He – his body – wore the same clothes as when I saw him. Besides, I knew he was missing.'

Finely arched eyebrows were raised. 'Indeed? How was that?'

Meredith repeated her conversation with Mervyn Pollard and Kevin. 'Kevin said he hadn't been home all night.'

'And Pollard suggested Berry might be with a woman friend?'

'Yes, he did. He was the local Romeo, believe it or not.'

'Hmn.' Crane looked as if she didn't believe it.

For which, thought Markby, she couldn't be blamed. But he said, 'I was also told Berry was missing, by a local builder named Crombie.'

'May I ask on what occasion that would be, superintendent?'

More polite, that, than a blunt 'when?' Markby supplied the answer graciously. 'This morning. I understand Crombie had expected Berry yesterday to come and do some work for him. Only Kevin Berry turned up. Same thing happened today.'

'Did he seem surprised? Was Berry normally reliable?'

'Apparently. Crombie also suggested a woman friend might be detaining the man.'

'Crombie . . .' murmured the inspector and wrote it down. Meredith met Alan's eye across the room.

She asked a question. 'Has anyone found Kevin Berry and told him his father is dead?'

'Yes,' said Inspector Crane briefly. There was a silence. A little unwillingly, she added, 'He doesn't appear to be very bright. As I understand it, there is no other family. He's of age, nineteen. I could pass it over to social services, even so. However, they're busy and it might be better if someone in the village, someone he knows and respects, could keep an eye on him for a few days.'

'You could ask Mrs Carter,' Meredith suggested. 'She lives next door.' She pointed in the direction of the adjoining cottage.

'Mrs Carter,' murmured Inspector Crane and wrote that down.

'Have you found a weapon?' Markby asked from his corner.

The inspector looked startled then slightly defiant. 'No, sir. Not yet. We began a search of the field – paddock—' She cast a furtive glance at Meredith. 'But when light began to fade, we stopped. We'll begin again tomorrow, first thing. If we don't find it there, we'll spread out and search the rest of the grounds, but they are extensive and largely overgrown.'

'Any idea what you're looking for?'

'The doctor thinks some heavy, large blade. It was more a hacking job than a cutting or sawing job. We'll have to await the post-mortem report.' She turned away, cutting short the topic, folded the sheaf of papers and returned them to her document case.

Without looking at Markby, she said, 'I understand, sir, there have been some instances of vandalism in the village?'

'To my knowledge, three,' he said. 'Unless, of course, you include the poisoning of the pony. But that might be unconnected.'

'The pony buried in that field – paddock – sir?'

'Yes,' said Meredith. 'And then, there's the witches' coven.'

A pause. Crane turned a suspicious face to her. '*A coven* . . .' she repeated, rather as Lady Bracknell might have said, '*A handbag?*'

'I rather wish,' Markby murmured, when Inspector Crane had taken herself and her document case, off, 'that you hadn't mentioned the coven, not just yet. We don't know that's got anything to do with it.'

'She ought to know. She's the sort who wants to know

everything. She can write it down.'

'I suppose,' Markby said resignedly, 'I ought to be glad you didn't just tell her to take a running jump.'

'Well, she niggled me.' But Meredith had the grace to look slightly abashed. 'I wasn't aware I'd let it show.'

'You were fine. It's just that I know you rather better than she does! I thought she handled the interview well. Difficult for her, having me sitting here.'

I thought she handled you rather well, thought Meredith, but didn't say so.

CHAPTER SIXTEEN

What surer Signs of Poverty,
Than many Lice and little Bread?
Verses addressed to
Lewis le Grand, 1709

ERNIE BERRY sat under his tree. In some mysterious way
he'd got his head back again. He'd fetched it from Gill
Armitage's rose garden, or someone had fetched it out here
to him, and he stuck it back. Not very well, because
Meredith could clearly see the join, running all round his
neck in a black ring. But well enough, because he was
grinning at her in his meaningless way.

It was very hot in the paddock. Meredith, standing before
him, said, 'You oughtn't to be here, Ernie. This is Mrs
Smeaton's garden.'

But Ernie just grinned, mocking her. Then he raised one
brawny arm, pointed to his head – at which point it fell off
and rolled, still smiling up at her, across the turf.

At this point, blessedly, she woke up.

Going to bed at all that night had required some courage.
She had been afraid the memory of the day's events
wouldn't let her sleep and equally afraid that despite them,
she would sleep – and dream. And of course, as she'd feared,

that was just what she'd done.

Meredith blinked up into the darkness, grateful to be out of the nightmare but still physically with one foot in it, heart fluttering, limbs and forehead running with perspiration. She thought, *I've got to get the better of this, right away. I can't let Ernie haunt me.*

Inevitably he would for some time yet. But she could, with effort, keep him in his place. Her skull throbbed as she frowned in the darkness, trying to remember what had happened after she found the body. She must have turned and run like the wind across the paddock. No, she'd been sick first – though she had only the haziest memory of it. After that she'd run and of this flight she had no memory at all. All she recalled was finding Alan outside the main gates and of being more pleased to see him than she'd been to see anyone, anywhere, in her life before.

Of actually crossing the paddock, nothing. Of the walled garden and the other gardens around the house, nothing. Yet there was something to be seen or experienced, if only she could conjure it to view. Meredith screwed up her eyes and tried to visualise Rookery House. Irritatingly, it appeared in a haze, just a general shape. The drive and the wrought-iron gates were equally vague. The road itself outside, the church and The Abbot's House beyond were all swathed in a sort of fog.

Inspector Crane had annoyed her not just by her bright manner and trim form, but because she expected her to chatter away about finding Ernie and recall every detail. Contrary to received popular belief, every detail wasn't printed on Meredith's memory, as she'd discovered. All she could see was Ernie and he, wretched man, kept putting his head back on. So much for accurate recall! She was being unfair to Crane who had been sympathetic and offered, of all things, counselling.

'I don't want counselling, I want to remember whatever it is I've forgotten!' Meredith muttered to the darkness.

Alan stirred. 'Meredith, all right?'

'Fine, thanks. Just mumbling.'

'Dreaming?' He propped himself up on an elbow. 'I'll fetch an aspirin.'

'Just a bit. Nothing to worry about. I don't need the aspirin. Ernie got his head back – in my dream.'

'Ernie's gone and you can forget him. You've given your story to Crane. Let the whole thing go now. You don't have to worry about it any more.'

I do, she thought, I do. But she didn't tell him so.

Wynne was back again in the morning, appearing at the front door just after breakfast time. 'How is she today?' she asked kindly. With a touch more tension, she added, 'Have they found any clues yet?'

She wore the same baggy slacks as the day before, but the canary yellow sweater had been replaced by one of oatmeal-hue in complicated stitch and festooned with multi-coloured wool rosettes.

The comfortable image didn't deceive Markby.

'Wynne, with all your contacts in the newspaper world, would I tell you? *If* I knew, which by the way, I don't! Early days yet, anyway. As for Meredith, she had a restless night, but she's better this morning. Come in and see for yourself.'

Wynne stepped past him into the hall. Nimrod, who had been lurking at her heels on the doorstep, saw a decision to enter had been made and darted past his mistress, up the stairs. Wynne apologised for his behaviour, which she put down to cats being curious by nature. Markby led her to the kitchen, where Meredith dawdled over a last cup of coffee.

'Don't worry about the cat. I'm not so bad. I've had coffee and cornflakes so I don't think I've gone into a decline.' Meredith essayed a wan smile.

Wynne took a seat at the table and leaned across it, as if about to impart a confidence. 'You're a very brave person. That smart young woman came to see me yesterday, after she'd left you.'

'Oh, Inspector Crane!' murmured Meredith.

'Very competent.' There was a silence during which unspoken comment hung in the air and it was clear their minds ran along similar lines.

Wynne ventured to give the thoughts spoken form. 'They look sort of different nowadays, don't they, policewomen? As I remember them, they were, um, rather well-built and not, well, not at all fashionable.'

'It's like policemen,' said Meredith. 'They get younger and younger. Isn't that what they say?'

'Very true, dear. Inspector Crane did strike me as a very high-powered young woman. I don't know what the village will make of her.'

Markby cleared his throat and inquired a little plaintively if all this meant he was a harmless old codger, well past his sell-by date, and due to be put out to grass?

They hurriedly assured him this certainly wasn't so.

'Thank God for that,' he said. 'I was getting worried.'

Nimrod reappeared, having presumably checked out the house. He strolled over and sat down by his owner's feet. Meredith made encouraging overtures to him. He flattened his whole ear, which gave him the appearance of a scowl, and ignored her.

'Now seriously,' said Wynne. 'What I came to tell you was – once I'd made sure you were quite all right – the inspector asked me about Berry's lad and whether I'd keep an eye on him. I promised her I'd go along to their cottage this morning and see how he was fixed. I hope he's managing.'

'I suggested you, Wynne, hope you don't mind,' Meredith told her apologetically.

''Course I don't mind! But I am just wondering whether I can deal with it all that well. The fact is, and I feel awful asking this after all you've been through, but is there any chance you'd come too?' Wynne cast a nervous glance at Alan. 'I dare say you don't want to and for all I know, you've got other plans or just want to be left in peace. But you've got experience in dealing with distraught persons. I have too, but in a different way. In my day, I was always badgering the poor souls for their stories.'

Nimrod was beginning to look restless.

In fact, Meredith thought, being left here with nothing to occupy her mind was perhaps more to be feared than almost anything else. On the other hand, Kevin, with his associations with Ernie, was the last person Meredith wanted to see. But there, she'd suggested Wynne's name to Crane and thereby landed Kevin on Wynne's plate, as it were. It hadn't been fair, not without asking permission first. She owed Mrs Carter at least support on her mission. And seeing Kevin might, with luck, lay Ernie's ghost.

Meredith glanced at Markby. 'Have we got any plans?'

'Not this morning. I think we shall have to hang around the village in case we're required to add to our statements. But going as far as the Berrys' cottage still counts as being in the village. It's up to you, if you feel you can. But, if you don't mind, I'll stay here. I thought I'd give Basil a call, put him in the picture. See you back here, later.'

'Better idea, I'll buy you both lunch at The King's Head!' Wynne insisted. 'Yes, yes, don't argue! The very least I can do!'

She placed her hands on the table top to push herself up. Nimrod marched to the front door with his stumpy tail upright, and stood there expectantly.

'He's beginning to accept you,' said his owner, though it was difficult to see on what this optimistic judgement was based. 'When you're ready, Meredith, just knock on my door.'

When I'm ready, thought Meredith glumly, *ha!*

'If you don't really feel like it, you should have said you didn't want to go.' Alan's eyes were searching her face anxiously. 'Want me to nip round and tell Wynne you've changed your mind?'

She straightened up in her chair. 'No, I said I'd go and I will. I'll be all right. In a way, I feel I owe it to Kevin to pay my condolences and see if he's OK. What are you going to tell Basil?'

Alan grimaced and tilted back his chair, stretching his arms above his head. The chair tilted forward again with a thud, and he leaned his elbows on the table. 'I shall play it by ear. I was thinking of asking him to set up a meeting for me with Lawrence Smeaton. I know I'm no longer at liberty to ask questions in Parsloe St John. But I could drive up to Cumbria. You could come along. We can stay overnight somewhere.'

'When?' she asked.

'That would depend on Basil and on Lawrence, if he were willing to see me at all. That, in turn depends on how he feels about Olivia, even after all this time. Also, he mightn't be in good health and not want a stranger pestering him about the past.' He looked a little shame-faced. 'I'm not saying I agree with Wynne. But I don't like leaving a job half done. I started inquiries here and they didn't turn up anything. All the same, I'd like to finish them so I can sign off. Wynne would appreciate it. I told Crane I wouldn't trespass on her patch and I won't. This is a personal search conducted for curiosity's sake. Like Nimrod, I want to see what's behind every door. A bad habit, but ingrained in me, I fear.'

'Talking of Wynne,' Meredith pushed back her own chair. 'If I've got to go and pay a good Samaritan visit on Berry's lad, I'd better get it over with. See you at twelve in the pub.'

The Berrys' cottage was outside the village, situated at the end of a long, narrow, rutted track. There was no other dwelling in the area, only fields. The cottage, when they came to it, didn't so much seem built there, as to grow there. Its old walls were earth-coloured, its thatched roof nibbled by rodents and dark brown with age. Patches of moss grew along its lower edge.

The Berrys hadn't a garden in any recognisable sense. They had a fairly large piece of ground which, where it wasn't overgrown with every imaginable grass and weed, was littered with derelict vehicles. There was an old ambulance without wheels, resting on brick blocks. Two old cars rusted away nearby and a yellow painted pony-trap thrust its shafts skyward.

'I think Ernie ran a bit of a scrap business, on the side,' said Wynne.

'That trap,' said Meredith, pointing at the uptilted shafts, 'looks in better condition than the other things.'

They approached it, taking care where they put their feet. Nevertheless they were taken unawares as, with a flurry of feathers and a burst of cackling, a hen flew up from inside it. It dropped to the ground and strutted away, uttering low protesting clucks, to join others which Meredith now saw beneath the trees, pecking and scratching at the soil. She looked into the trap and exclaimed, 'Phew!'

'Found any eggs?' asked Wynne with a snort of laughter.

'No, just a load of chickenshit, actually. What a disgusting mess. Ernie was an old horror.'

She examined it further with caution. The trap, though dirty and smelling strongly of manure, was probably still serviceable despite the fact that the hens had taken it over. A tarpaulin had been thrown over the rear part of it. Its large wheels, half-buried in dark green weeds with yellow flowers, appeared in good condition.

'I think,' Wynne said quietly, 'that was Olivia's. Ernie must have bought it off her when she gave up driving. Whatever did he want it for? If he was thinking of selling it on, he ought to have got it under proper cover. The upholstery is cracking up and the chickens have ruined it. What a shame. It's leather.'

They turned aside and made for the front door. As they reached it, Meredith's eye caught a movement behind the dirty glass pane of a nearby window.

Wynne knocked but there was no reply.

'He's in there,' Meredith murmured.

Wynne knocked again, more loudly, and called, 'Kevin? It's Mrs Carter. Open the door, please!'

Her firm tone must have had some effect on Kevin, who was used to following orders. There was a rattle, as of a bolt drawn, and the door opened.

Kevin stood before them. He appeared to have neither washed himself nor changed his clothes since Meredith had last seen him in the yard of The King's Head. He stared at them both, wild-eyed, and then fixed a terrified gaze on Wynne. Putting both hands behind him, he declared, 'I never done it!'

'Of course not, Kevin,' said Wynne. 'We've come to see how you are. Can we come in?'

Kevin backed away from them and with a strong feeling of repugnance, Meredith followed Wynne into the cottage.

Originally there must have been a tiny hall with a stair leading upwards. Someone, presumably Ernie, had knocked out the wall between hall and sitting room, so that they stood in an open-plan living area, with a staircase rising in the far corner to the upper floor. There was a wide stone hearth containing an old-fashioned iron range. The range had been lit and emitted a thin ribbon of strong-smelling woodsmoke which was trapped in the room and mingled with the other odours, sweat, dust, burnt fat, beer dregs. Meredith suppressed an urge to gag.

The top of the range was covered in blackened cooking pots. Grimy rags were draped along a rail fixed to the hearth above it, together with a pair of socks.

There was a lot of furniture, far more than necessary. Some of it, for all it was undusted and grease-spotted, was of good quality and quite old. Meredith wondered whether Ernie had frequented local salerooms. The TV set held pride of place, as in many homes. Its screen flickered with sound turned down.

Kevin stood before them, his hands still behind his back, and his feet slightly apart, in a grotesque version of the stance called by the military 'at ease'. The youth was clearly anything but at ease. He kept his eyes fixed on Wynne with the same expression of panic in them.

'We're very sorry about Ernie,' Wynne told him. 'How are you managing, Kevin?'

He ran his tongue over his upper lip which, Meredith noticed, was split. The injury was half-healed and scabbed. She caught a glimpse of his broken front teeth as he answered.

'That p'licewoman's been here, asking me questions.'

'Inspector Crane. It's her job, Kevin.'

'I told her, Ernie never come home. Two nights he never come. Mr Crombie, he was cross about it. I told him too. I don't know where Ernie went. He never told me.'

'There were other times he – Ernie – hadn't come home?' Meredith asked.

Kevin dragged his gaze from Wynne and stared at her. 'He never said and I never asked.'

And he also impressed on you that you shouldn't tell, Meredith thought.

Wynne had moved over to the range and was surveying the assorted pots and pans. 'Have you had any breakfast, Kevin?'

'I had a tin of beans,' Kevin mumbled. 'I had a tin of beans last night.'

'Yes, but this morning? Oh dear . . .' Wynne gazed in despair at the cooking arrangements. 'Have you got a – larder or a fridge?'

Kevin crossed to a door in the corner and opened it, standing silently by it and waiting for them to inspect whatever lay beyond.

Unhappily, his visitors went to take a look. It was walk-in store room and larder, stone-floored and dank. There were several crates of bottles on the ground. On the shelves were various dishes and bowls, one containing dripping, some bread in a plastic bag and a bowl of unwashed eggs.

There was also a musty, acrid smell which Meredith suspected meant mice. She picked up a small tin plate and put it over the dripping bowl as a lid. Better late than never.

Wynne took possession of the eggs. 'I'll make you an omelette, Kevin, all right?'

She went back, bearing the eggs and bread, and busied herself, searching through the pans for one which was usable.

Meredith asked in a low voice, 'Have you got any money, Kevin, to buy food?'

Kevin's gaze slid to a brown-glazed jug standing on the crowded surface of an Edwardian chiffonier. 'Ernie kept the house-keeping in that.'

Meredith inspected the jug. It contained three pound coins and a twenty-pence piece.

She hunted in her bag and produced a ten-pound note. 'This is to buy some food, Kevin. Or would you rather I bought the food and brought it out here to you?'

Kevin took a hand from behind his back and twitched the note adroitly from Meredith's grasp. 'I can go to the shop.' He stuffed the note into the pocket of his dirty jeans.

'What about the future? You'll need a job, to earn some money.'

'Mr Crombie says he'll give me a job.'

Glancing over her shoulder from the range, Wynne observed, 'I expect Max will see to it. But I'll check with him.'

'Perhaps one of us better ring social services,' Meredith muttered.

'No, it will be all right!' Wynne said firmly. 'The village will take care of it somehow.' She lifted the frying pan from the range and ordered, 'Bring a plate, Kevin!'

'Ernie and I, we usually eat it out of the pan,' said Kevin.

'Then it's time you started eating off plates!' snapped Wynne.

Kevin went to a nearby dresser and returned with a rather fine willow pattern plate of considerable antiquity.

They stood over him while he ate the omelette and three slices of bread.

'I'll come back again tomorrow, Kevin,' Wynne promised.

Kevin looked up from his plate. 'You don't need.'

'All the same, I'll come.'

'Kevin,' Meredith said gently. 'Have you burned your fingers?'

Kevin snatched his hands away from the table top and hid them in his lap. 'I done it on the old range over there, when I was trying to clean it out t'other day.'

'The whole place needs cleaning,' Wynne declared. 'I'll organise something later on. Perhaps if I paid Janine enough, she'd come over and straighten it up.'

'We don't want no one here,' Kevin said. 'Ernie and I, we don't want no one here.'

'But Ernie's dead now, Kevin,' Wynne said gently.

Kevin hunched his thin shoulders. 'He never come home, he never come home two nights. I don't know where he went. He never said and I never asked.'

His gaze slid furtively towards Wynne. 'I never did it!' he said.

'I can't say I'm sorry to get out of there. What a dreadful place.' The words burst from Wynne's lips as if under some impetus of their own. She shook her head immediately after she'd spoken and strode on, eyes fixed resolutely ahead.

They were walking away from the cottage, along the track. Meredith remarked, 'I thought he was in shock, which is understandable. But he doesn't strike me as backward exactly.'

Wynne glanced at her. 'He knows his way around in a general sense. As long as most of his old routine can be preserved, he should be all right. By old routine, I mean, as long as he stays on in his home and works for Max or does odd jobs for other people. Just as he did before with Ernie. I agree, he isn't retarded. He's simple in the old-fashioned sense. Virtually no education, no experience of the outside world, but fine in his own limited world.'

These words, spoken with comfortable assurance, contrasted with those she'd cried out wildly as she'd left the cottage. The last words, Meredith thought, sprang from the head: the previous ones from the heart. The feeling of unease which she had felt in the cottage increased. Not for the first time since arriving in Parsloe St John, she felt she was being presented with a hidden agenda. Even Wynne, utterly reliable, kind and experienced, seemed to be hiding something. She was afraid or unwilling to speak her real mind, deliberately creating some scenario which was more acceptable, less worrying. There was obstinacy in her insistence that Kevin was all right, would come to no harm, needed no outside interference in his affairs.

'I dare say you're right,' she said, not because she believed it, but because she sensed this was what Wynne wanted to hear.

Alan Markby had made his way to Rookery House, shown his identification to the officer at the gates, crossed the gardens and arrived at the garden gate into the paddock.

They were still searching it for the weapon. He watched the line of men and women, moving forward slowly, picking over the ground. They had almost reached the far side. When they'd finished there, they'd start elsewhere, probably here in the old kitchen garden and after that, if nothing were turned up, in the rest of the gardens. It would be a long job and he sympathised with the inevitable frustration this would cause.

Crane was standing some little distance away, near the chestnut tree, talking to someone he thought probably the sergeant in charge of the search. She turned aside, looked across the paddock and saw Markby at the gate. She began to walk his way.

He opened the gate and went to meet her. 'Good morning.'

'Good morning, sir.' She looked wary. She wore flat shoes this morning, suitable for the terrain, a tartan kilt and a quilted body-warmer sprigged with tiny flowers, over a bottle-green sweater. Her red hair had been severely brushed back from her face and secured by an Alice band.

'How are you getting on?' he asked cheerfully.

A tense smile touched her mouth and disappeared. 'No luck, yet. We'll start on that kitchen garden this afternoon.'

'I haven't come to get in your way,' he reassured her. 'I just wondered if there's been any word on a post mortem yet.'

'It was carried out yesterday evening, sir. There's no sign of any struggle before – before he died. The body contained a large amount of alcohol, some of it produced naturally. The pathologist thinks he may have been drinking heavily during the twelve hours before death. He might – it's only a theory of course – have been sleeping it off under that tree. It's a nice quiet spot. Someone came up and took one good swipe at his throat, shearing through the windpipe and jugular vein, inflicting fatal injury, without his even realising what was happening. Then the killer finished the job, hacking through the rest of the neck and spinal column possibly after a short delay. He may have intended to cut up the body in order to remove it bit by bit, and then abandoned the idea. We don't know why he took the head away. It couldn't be to delay identification, because he left the head where it was almost bound to be found.'

She spoke briskly. She wasn't, Markby thought, insensitive, but she had good control of her nerves. She was a senior police officer.

'What made you choose the police?' he asked suddenly.

She hesitated. 'What I usually say, when I'm asked that, is that I wanted to do a worthwhile job.'

'As far as I'm concerned, that's good enough reason.' Markby nodded at the distant chestnut tree and, by implication, the ghost of Ernie Berry. 'How long had he been dead?' he asked.

She relaxed, relieved, he was sure, to be spared further personal questioning. 'Doctor estimates no longer than five or six hours.'

'He'd been missing longer than that. He hadn't been home for two nights. He has to have been somewhere during all that time. Possibly not in this village, or someone would have spotted him.'

His remarks were casually meant. He hadn't intended to sound as if he was doing her job for her, but she froze.

'Yes, sir, we're still looking for a woman friend. But that might be a red herring.' Her gaze took in the paddock and the square shape of the grave. 'He helped dig out that grave for the animal. Then he came back here and died. It's almost as if he came back here *to* die. Funny place to choose to sit down and take a nap, beside a buried horse.'

'He knew he wouldn't be disturbed?' Markby suggested. 'He did know this place very well, having worked for Mrs Smeaton on and off for a number of years.'

'I suppose so.' She pushed her hands into the pockets of the body-warmer. The searchers had reached the limit of the paddock and were returning.

Markby nodded in their direction. 'I'll let you get on with it.'

213

Unexpectedly she said, 'I hope Miss Mitchell's feeling better today.'

'She's fine,' said Markby robustly. 'She's gone with Wynne Carter to see Berry's lad.'

Crane pulled a face. 'It's a real dump of a place, that cottage. If she hasn't been there before, she'll get another shock.'

'I shall hear all about it at lunchtime. We're having a bite at the pub, The King's Head. Join us?'

She hesitated. 'If I'm free. You know how it is. Thanks, anyway.'

'Not at all. Good luck. Hope you turn up the murder weapon soon.' He left her to her work.

Amanda Crane watched him walk away and turned back to survey the team searching the paddock. The superintendent seemed a nice man but it was a real nuisance having him here. He didn't mean to interfere. He was on holiday and this wasn't, in any case, an inquiry overseen by him. But she realised he couldn't help it. He was professionally intrigued and she had been over-sensitive in taking everything he said as a criticism. She'd allowed herself to be flummoxed by having him stand there at her elbow. The knowledge annoyed her further.

She'd only half answered his question as to why she'd chosen the police as a career. People always asked and she'd got used to that. She rarely told them all of it, because it was difficult to tell and sounded too personal, almost petty – except that there was nothing petty about a death.

It had been her brother's death, victim of a hit-and-run driver, many years before. He'd been ten at the time and she had been eight. Stevie had gone out on a simple errand and failed to return. Searching for him, they'd found his body, high up on a grassy bank, where it had been thrown by the impact.

The driver had turned himself in, coming to his local station with his solicitor to protect his rights. He said Stevie ran out in front of the car. He'd driven on because he was in shock. Nothing like it had happened to him before, said his solicitor, insisting his client was deeply shaken by the incident and wanted to express his sorrow to the family. It had been a shrewd move, turning himself in once he'd had time to get hold of a lawyer and get the story right. It made a good impression on the court which believed him. There'd been no witnesses. He'd acted contrition well.

He'd been pointed out to her by her aunt, as they sat in the family car outside the court, waiting for the re-emergence of her parents. 'That's him!' Auntie Jenny said. She'd seen a big, confident young man with incipient podginess about the jaw and waistline. His shifting blue gaze had briefly touched the car and its occupants and she, with a child's unerring instinct for when an adult is pretending, knew he was a liar. She also knew it because Stevie had been so careful about crossing roads, always telling her to use the pedestrian crossing, press the button, wait for the green man. If there wasn't a crossing, look right, look left, look right again. Even now, after so many years, she could hear his childish voice, echoing in her ear as he delivered her the lecture, holding her tightly by her hand.

A week after the inquest, a friend's mother had taken Amanda and her own daughter shopping. As they pushed the trolley of groceries across the car park, Amanda saw him. They were walking straight towards him. The friend's mother didn't recognise him and he didn't recognise Amanda. She was just another kid. He was talking to a couple of his mates, standing by his car. A car with a brand-new headlight and a dent still in the wing. The car which killed Stevie. They were laughing and joking. They hadn't even taken away his licence. Not that she knew much about licences at the time, but she realised it now.

The pain of it remained. Even now, thinking of it made her wince. He hadn't a care in the world. He'd got away with it. He jumped in the car, roared out of the car park, a real jack-the-lad. She wasn't very old but old enough to think, *if I'd been in charge, if I'd been the policeman who'd come to visit our house to tell us what had happened, if I'd been sitting on the magistrates' bench that day, I'd have found out the truth!*

She didn't tell people this because it sounded as if, in her choice of career, she'd had a personal axe to grind. It suggested the sort of police officer who had a closed mind, fixing on one suspect and setting out to nail him, no matter what. She didn't do that. She knew mistakes were made that way.

She couldn't afford mistakes. Too many people were waiting for her to trip up. Not Sergeant Morris though, who was walking towards her. Morris had been suspicious of her at first, but had come around. They'd worked together several times and a mutual respect had emerged. Sometimes, to her secret amusement, Morris treated her rather as he might a favourite niece. He showed signs of being proud and protective, sometimes worrying, and always expecting her to do well.

That didn't mean he always expected her to get everything right first time. Quite the reverse. He had a habit of giving a diffident cough behind his fist and murmuring, 'Excuse me, ma'am . . .' when he thought she was haring off on the wrong tack. But, like a precocious child, she was aware that at the end of the day, she was expected to practise until perfect and then pass all exams with flying colours. She wasn't afraid of slipping up in front of Morris – she'd proved herself to him now – but she was worried about Markby.

Unwarily, she said aloud, 'We've got to find that murder weapon soon!'

'We'll find it, ma'am,' Morris told her reassuringly. 'It's only a village, not that many places it can be. I'll tell you something about country folk, too. They don't throw anything away. Real old hoarders, they are. If it's a good knife, it'll be kept. Hidden, maybe, but kept.'

Amanda Crane hoped he was right.

'We got that Italian thing today,' said Mervyn Pollard. 'All in one dish. Lasagne, they calls it.'

'We'll wait till Mr Markby joins us,' said Wynne.

'Or we got the usual ploughman's,' Mervyn went on, ignoring the interruption. 'Still got a couple of the chicken pies and we got a pudding list. We got apricot crumble, icecream and a brand new speciality.'

'What's that?' asked Meredith, giving way in face of the ruthless roll-call of delicacies.

'It's what they call a Mississippi Mud Pie,' said Mervyn. 'Funny old name, ain't it? Chocolate, mostly.'

'Do you make all these things here, on the premises?' Meredith asked, entranced.

'No, gets it all in bulk from the freezer centre. I'll come back in a minute to take your orders, when your friend gets here.'

'Whatever happened to home-cooked meals?' asked Wynne, as the landlord shambled away.

'I'd rather not think about home-cooking at the moment,' Meredith replied, remembering the Berrys' kitchen. 'I gather

Mervyn is hoping to attract the passing international tourist trade.'

'You still think it was Mervyn you saw – out there?' Wynne asked tentatively.

'I'm sure: Alan isn't.'

Markby had arrived as they spoke and was taking his seat. 'What isn't Alan? If you mean, do I still doubt that you-know-who was the person we saw you-know-where, then all I can keep repeating is that I don't identify anyone by a silhouette against the night sky, a hundred yards away.'

A very old man nearby, hunched over his pint, observed loudly. 'Never did this fancy food in pubs in my young days.'

'I expect they did pasties or sausage rolls,' Wynne said, diverted from the mystery of Mervyn's nocturnal pursuits.

'No, never did nothing like that. Used to have big jar of pickles up there on the counter. Nothing else, 'cept pickled eggs, they sometimes had them.'

'You've got to admit, the freezer centre has its advantages!' whispered Meredith.

'Then they took to selling crisps.' The ancient's memory had moved on. 'Not the fancy crisps what they've got now. Plain 'uns, with the salt in a little bit of blue paper.'

'That's right,' said Wynne bravely. 'I remember those.'

'They got fancy crisps now,' persisted their informant. 'They got cheese 'uns and chicken 'uns. They got some taste of hedgehogs.'

'Are you sure about this?' asked Meredith, worried.

'You ask Mervyn there. They got crisps what taste of hedgehogs.'

'Don't,' begged Wynne. 'Don't ask.'

'So how did you get on?' Markby asked, determinedly ignoring the Oldest Inhabitant. 'The kid all right?'

'Middling well,' Wynne answered him. 'He's all right, for the time being anyway. We'll get something sorted out.'

It was clear from her tone she didn't want to discuss Kevin, at least not in here where they might be overheard. Mervyn was coming back.

'You decided what you want, then?'

They settled for two lasagne and one cheese ploughman's. 'I'm sorry,' said Meredith. 'I can't seem to face anything cooked just at the moment.'

The room was filling up fast and it was clear what the topic of conversation was. Wynne was right, thought Meredith, not to mention Kevin Berry. Many of the people here had clearly come expressly to find out if there was any news.

Mervyn was shambling in their direction carrying the ploughman's lunch in one hand, and a basket of bread rolls in the other.

'You'll have lost a good customer, Mervyn,' said the old man unexpectedly, as the landlord set down the rolls and plate of cheese and pickle, decorated with half a tomato and one lettuce leaf.

'I have that,' Mervyn agreed.

'He liked a pint or three, Ernie!' the old man chuckled.

'He did,' said Mervyn, pulling a wry face at the others.

'You'll very likely go broke now, Mervyn!' The old man seemed in imminent danger of choking on his laughter. 'You'll very likely have to put up shop, now Ernie Berry's not spending all his money in here!'

'Still got you, spending your pension,' retaliated Mervyn.

'Government don't give me the sort of money Ernie spent in here,' said the aged one. 'And beer being the price it is.'

'For goodness' sake,' said Markby, 'give him another pint, my shout.'

219

There was nothing wrong with the old man's hearing. 'Thank you very much, sir! You're a gentleman, you are.' He pushed his empty glass towards Pollard. 'Here you are, Mervyn, you fill it up like the gentleman said.'

Mervyn scooped up the glass in his giant paw and made his ungainly way to the bar.

As he reached it, a hush fell on the bar-room. Heads were turned towards the door. Looking across, Meredith saw that Amanda Crane had entered and was walking towards the bar.

A low whisper ran around the room. They all knew who she was.

'She's a trim one,' said the old man appreciatively.

Crane turned from the bar, and came towards their table, carrying a glass. Eyes followed her and heads put together in her wake as whispering was renewed.

'Coming to join us, inspector?' Markby asked, getting to his feet.

'Thanks, no, I don't want to take the time. I've asked the landlord to cut me some sandwiches to take away.' She raised her tomato juice. 'Cheers. How did you get on at the cottage, Mrs Carter?'

'Don't you worry about it,' said Wynne. 'All in hand, as you might say.'

'Good. How are you feeling today, Miss Mitchell?'

'Fine, thanks. Please call me Meredith.'

''Ere!' called the old man. 'You found out who done in old Ernie yet?'

You could have heard a pin drop in the bar-room.

'Not yet. We're working on it,' Crane told him crisply.

'He'd have approved of you,' said the old man. 'Ernie would've approved of you. He liked a fine-looking woman!'

A ribald chuckle ran around the room. Crane flushed.

Fortunately, the barmaid in the denim shirt and jangling jewellery appeared, striding across the room, bearing the hot lasagne dishes, clasped in oven-mitted hands.

'Mind!' she ordered, setting them down with a crash. 'They're hot! Just come out of the microwave! Got your sandwiches, miss! Up at the bar!'

'Leave you to it!' said Crane with a dry glance at the room. '*Bon appétit*!'

Another ripple of rustic mirth followed her exit.

This was Friday lunchtime, and afterwards remembered as the lull before the storm.

It began innocuously enough, early Friday afternoon, shortly before Mervyn shut up his bar for his mid-afternoon break. A strange car appeared in the village containing two sharp-faced young men. It was closely followed by another driven by a girl in a red jumpsuit, accompanied by a stubble-chinned individual with an expression of acute boredom and carrying expensive camera equipment. Before long, cars with London registrations littered the High Street. The press had arrived.

It was against such invasions from outsiders that, long ago, the abbey and its church had been fortified. Parsloe St John of modern times was unprepared. Like a Dark Ages horde bent on pillage, the journalists roamed the village, hunting singly and in packs. They brandished notebooks and tape-recorders. They gabbled into mobile phones. They hailed one another with the breezy informality of old acquaintances, followed by cautious fencing intended to discover whether a rival rag had got in ahead of them. 'Try the pub!' they cried, and descended on the oasis of The King's Head like a band of legionnaires lost for days in the desert and seeking both liquid sustenance and intelligence.

Mervyn Pollard, bemused, abandoned his afternoon rest period and told the girl she could forget hers. They were staying open.

'Well,' said Meredith, kneeling in the window embrasure of their cottage to watch a brace of eager newshounds trot past looking for someone to interview. 'Mervyn did want to be on the tourist trail.'

'Not, I fancy, like this!' mumbled Alan. 'And come away from there before someone sees you and comes haring up the path to bash the door down. The first question they'll be asking must be, "Who found the body?" '

This was soon proved prophetic. A hammering at the door was followed by a face at the window, grimacing and holding up a tape-recorder. Shortly thereafter a voice cried wistfully through the letterbox, 'Miss Mitchell, could we have a word?'

Meredith and Alan took the phone off the hook and retired upstairs. When the coast was observed to be clear, they slipped out into the street. At the pub, Mervyn had had enough. With arms aching from pulling pints and throat hoarse from parrying questions, he had locked his door. A sign hanging on it announced the pub wouldn't be open again that day, though Bush Telegraph, it turned out, was alerting the regulars that this didn't apply to them. They could gain admittance that evening by tapping at the back door and having identity verified by Mervyn, peering through a chained gap.

Most of the inhabitants had already followed Mervyn's example and barricaded themselves indoors. If trapped outside, they feigned ignorance, simplicity or deafness. A few enterprising younger ones demanded unrealistic sums for headline-making details. But these deals soon fell through when it was established by the hard-nosed hacks that the purveyors of these tantalising gems had more imagination than genuine information. If Parsloe villagers really knew anything, they were keeping it to themselves.

Meredith and Alan beat off several approaches and attempted to take refuge next door with Wynne. Mrs Carter was located by a furious rattle of typewriter keys and discovered hunched over an elderly portable, shedding hairpins in all directions.

'I can't stop, my dears! Those others will pinch my copy from under my nose! It's my village and my story!'

'Not any more!' said Alan, as he and Meredith made their way discreetly across the fields on a long and, with luck, lonely walk.

CHAPTER SEVENTEEN

Whereat with blade, with bloody, blameful blade . . .
Wm Shakespeare: A Midsummer Night's Dream

ALAN RETURNED from the tiny post office cum news-agent's shop on Saturday morning with an armful of papers.

'You ought to see the scrum in there!' he panted. 'Nearly every copy is sold out!'

They spread the sheets of newsprint out on the floor.

'Oh dear,' said Meredith. 'I don't think Parsloe St John will like any of this.'

'GRUESOME MURDER SHATTERS IDYLLIC VILLAGE CALM,' Alan read aloud. 'Do you think that means idyllic village or idyllic calm?'

'This is worse,' Meredith told him. 'RITUAL SLAUGHTER AMID COUNTRY PEACE.' She put down the sheet to ask seriously, 'Alan, do you really think it's a case of ritual killing?'

'How should I know? It makes a good headline, whether it is or isn't. Oh, here's Wynne's piece. MURDER VILLAGE: AN INSIDER SPEAKS. Hmn, well, nothing she's written is going to rescue property values!'

'Alan!' she insisted. 'This could be very bad news for

Sadie and the others. Once a story like this is printed, everyone believes it.'

'Crane's problem, not mine,' he returned heartlessly.

They weren't to be let off so lightly. In mid-morning, Markby's sister, Laura, rang, ostensibly as part-owner of the cottage and kin to the present tenants. Closer attention was soon promised.

'I thought we'd drive over and lunch with you tomorrow, Sunday, if that's OK with you. Say if you've got other plans.'

'Come by all means,' said Markby into the phone, attempting at the same time to signal the intelligence to Meredith. 'It's your cottage. I don't know about lunch here. We can all go to the pub. I think Pollard is open for business again. He took fright at some of the Press questions and shut up shop.'

'Oh, you don't have to worry about that! We'll bring it all with us. Paul will put up a picnic basket. A friend will look after Emily. The two older ones have gone back to school. We shall have to bring Vicky.'

'I'll put away everything breakable,' he promised.

'She's much better than she was, Alan. I think going to nursery school has helped. We won't stay late. But really, hearing about all the things going on, we felt we ought to come.'

He put down the receiver and turned. 'It was only to be expected, I suppose. You will have gathered from that we're about to receive a visitation. Paul, Laura and one daughter, tomorrow. Paul's bringing the food.'

From the sofa, where she reclined with her feet up, Meredith murmured, 'Good . . .'

'Good, they're coming, or good, they're bringing the food?'

'Both. I don't think Paul would appreciate Mervyn's offerings from the freezer centre and I think I've had enough of pub food for a while.'

Markby's brother-in-law, a dedicated cook who had trained at a hotel school and worked for a while in some famous restaurant kitchens, had achieved moderate fame ever since he'd had a series on regional television. His recipe books were beginning to sell well, on the back of the TV series, though they languished in the shade of greater culinary luminaries. On the whole, though, Paul was a happy man, who spent his days pottering around his own kitchen, emerging to preside over demonstrations to women's groups, when not planning the next book or series on the box.

His wife Laura, Markby's sister, was a partner in a busy firm of solicitors in Bamford. Representing the law, as they did, in different aspects, Laura and Alan wrangled occasionally, but generally got on well. Meredith and Laura had hit it off from the start. If Markby felt slightly apprehensive at the prospect of his family drawing up at their gate, it was on account of his niece.

He was fond of all Laura's kids and that included young Vicky. The trouble was that Vicky, aged four and of angelic appearance, had what is popularly called 'a touch like a weight-lifter'. Things came apart in her small hands. Quite robust things which ought to have been child-proof. Her older brother and sister had quickly learned to hide their belongings from her if they wanted to keep them intact. Baby Emily was just beginning to realise that not even her soft toys were safe and set up a wail as soon as she saw sister Vicky seize one.

Before going to bed that night, they put all small objects out of reach.

★ ★ ★

This time, when Meredith awoke in the early hours, her senses were immediately on alert. She sat up. Not this time those confusing little sounds from outside the cottage. This time, she was sure of it, the sound had come from inside, downstairs.

'Alan?' She shook his shoulder. 'Alan, there's an intruder.'

'Are you sure?' asked a voice muffled by the duvet and expressing deep reluctance to be hauled from sleep.

'Of course I am! You're a policeman. At least show a bit of interest!'

Beside her, the duvet heaved and a dimly outlined form said crossly, 'I can't hear anything.'

'I did.' Meredith thought about it. 'I must have done. I woke up.'

'Dreaming again.'

She was about to deny this when, from below in the area of the kitchen came a clang.

Meredith was going to ask, 'What about that? I didn't dream that!' but she had no chance.

Alan was out of bed and heading for the door. She scrambled out and after him.

'Stay there, Meredith!'

'Not likely!'

'Then keep quiet, for Pete's sake!'

This rankled. He was hijacking her intruder. First he showed no interest, then he wanted to be in charge. There was something very male about all this.

Alan had pushed open the bedroom door. The cottage seemed to be holding its breath, although, Meredith realised, she was the one doing that.

From below came another rattle, as if someone had knocked tins together.

'Torch?' Alan's voice breathed in her ear.

Meredith retreated to the room, hunted in her bag thrown on a chair, and returned with a pocket torch she kept in it.

They crept downstairs, Indian file but with less than a woodsman's skill. The old wooden treads creaked noisily. It didn't seem, however, that the intruder in the kitchen had heard. He was still rattling around in the cupboards, or that's what it sounded like. There was a sudden, extra loud crash.

Alan leapt for the kitchen door, threw it open and switched on the light.

The back door swung open, letting in a cool draught of night air. The kitchen presented a scene of devastation. The cupboards had been opened and every tin or jar tipped out, either on the floor, or over the furniture and work-surfaces. The fridge likewise swung open, buzzing madly in a hopeless attempt to regenerate escaping chill air, and emptied. Spilled cornflakes crunched beneath their feet. Flour rose in white clouds. Milk dripped from the draining board. In the middle of it all, sat Nimrod, doing his level best to open a packet of sausages. He looked up crossly from his task, annoyed at being disturbed.

Alan swore vigorously and ran to the open back door. He was back in an instant.

'Long gone, I reckon. He, whoever our visitor was, did this about half an hour to an hour ago and we didn't hear a thing! Look at that tin of syrup there, lying on its side. It's had time to drain out completely. Then Nimrod strolled in through the open door and started investigating. He made the noises we heard. He must think it's ruddy Christmas! Look at him!'

'Who did it?' asked Meredith, bewildered. 'And why?' A thought struck her. 'Alan what about Wynne?'

'Phone her – no, wait, hang on, I'll go round there!'

He ran back upstairs and returned within minutes in trousers and pullover. He went outside and could be seen investigating the garden. The thin inadequate beam of the torch flickered over bushes and tree trunks. He went round the side of the house.

Nimrod, who all this time had been concentrating on his packet of sausages, had succeeded in chewing it open and was dragging the contents across the floor in a long, pink string. It looked uncommonly like intestines.

'Shoo!' Meredith clapped her hands at him. 'Take the wretched things and scat, cat!'

Nimrod bounded away into the dark of the garden, sausage links bouncing along the ground behind him.

Meredith turned round, thinking to herself that all the trouble they'd taken to secure doors in here ahead of Vicky's visit, had certainly been wasted. They hadn't checked the sitting room. She left the kitchen and went in there.

She switched on the light. 'Merry hell!' she muttered. He'd been in here too. He'd tossed soft cushions from the chairs and sofa to the ground and slashed them open with a knife. Feather fillings had burst out and covered the floor as if someone had slaughtered a chicken in there. The image of slaughter was intensified by the letters 'DETH' printed in wonky scarlet capitals across the wall.

She supposed he'd meant to write 'DEATH,' but in his hurry, or because of the darkness, had missed a letter. The medium used looked so like blood that, for a moment, Meredith feared she was going to do something she'd only ever done once before in her life – faint. She didn't. She forced herself to approach the gory message and peer closely at it. Tentatively she touched the bar of the H. Raspberry jam. She was so relieved that, despite the grim circumstances, she laughed aloud.

She could hear Alan's voice, outside. calling up to Wynne's bedroom window. After a while, a crunch of footsteps on gravel heralded his return, Wynne puffing along behind him wrapped in an exotic royal blue garment heavy with oriental embroidery.

'Meredith? Oh, my dear, what a mess! We checked my place and no one's been in there. Whoever is doing these awful things?'

Meredith pointed at the wall and the jam. 'Recognise the handwriting, Wynne?'

'Not from that! What is it? Not—?'

'No, it's jam.'

'Oh, thank God.'

They spent the next two hours clearing up. There was nothing which could be done about the cushions, except to gather up as many feathers as possible, stuff them back, and put towels over the slits. The back door had been jemmied open.

'Not difficult,' said Markby. 'Simple lock and not very well fitted. Get it fixed first thing. Max Crombie must be able to send someone down.'

It was just on six and the sun was well and truly risen.

'Fortunately the tea's in bags,' Meredith said. 'I'll make a cup.'

'You'd better have breakfast with me,' Wynne decided. 'It's nearly time, anyway.'

The Danbys burst into the cottage in noisy confusion, Paul bearing the picnic hamper. It was half past eleven.

'Hullo there, are you all right? This'll buck you up. I've got roast chicken with apricot stuffing, home-made Grosvenor Pie, mushrooms in sherry and cream sauce wrapped in puff pastry – they're frozen and will need popping in a very hot oven – salads, strawberry shortcake gâteau and cheese straws . . .' He was heading for the kitchen as he spoke.

'We've been living on Alan's omelettes and Mervyn Pollard's pies and lasagne,' Meredith told him.

'Alan's omelettes are all right,' said Paul generously, adding, 'as for Mervyn's grub, it doesn't matter what it is, it all tastes the same. Close your eyes when you're eating and you wouldn't know whether it was meat pie, chicken stew or one of those things he optimistically calls puddings!'

He began to unpack his own basket of delicacies. 'I've told Pollard I don't know how many times, I could draw up for him a simple menu of dishes which could be prepared entirely on the premises. Any half-ways competent local woman could manage it. No charge. I'd consider it an act of public service.

'He told me—' Paul paused, a foil-wrapped brick which was probably the Grosvenor Pie, in hand. 'He said, if you please, that his customers "like the specialities"! "What sort of specialities?" I asked him. "How do you choose them?" Do you know what he does? He goes over to that freezer centre and he picks them out by the picture on the box. He hasn't got a clue what they are. The man's a culinary philistine. I doubt he eats anything other than sausage and mash himself. Hullo!' Paul had spotted the swinging back door. 'What happened to that?'

'We had an intruder last night,' Alan told him. 'Don't panic. We didn't confront him. Wish we had. Crombie came down this morning to see if the lock could be fixed and advised a new door. I know builders like to do that sort of thing, but in this case, I think he's right. The old one had warped and made it easier to jemmy the lock. I'll pay.'

'Of course you won't. Good grief . . .' Paul examined the

damaged lock. 'Did he pinch anything?'

'No, tipped out the contents of the cupboard and fridge and did a bit of damage in the living room. You'll see.'

Laura, who had been in the living room, had already seen. 'What on earth happened to the cushions? And has someone been scrubbing something off the wall?'

There were more explanations.

'Never mind,' said Laura. 'It was a very old suite. We would have replaced it anyway. So long as you're all right. But I must say, it's scary.'

'If Crombie was here, the whole village will know by now,' Paul put in.

Vicky, during this time, had wandered into the back garden where, as her father fell silent, she could be heard addressing someone in a stern voice.

'Let me take you indoors,' she was saying in clear child's tones, 'let me take you inside – no, you've got to come here and let me pick you up. Stay still, cat! I want to pick you up!'

'Oh no, Nimrod!' exclaimed Meredith. 'I really think she oughtn't – he's not the sort of cat—'

Vicky could be heard approaching the back door, huffing and puffing as if in a struggle. She appeared.

Nimrod, it seemed, had met his match. Perhaps having eaten a pound of sausages during the night had made him less fleet of paw. Vicky had grasped him firmly around his body beneath his front legs, and held him aloft, his back pressed against her chest. Nimrod dangled in undignified fashion, his front legs pushed upwards, framing his squashed and furious face. The rest of him hung down in an elongated stretch of striped fur, his back paws attached limply to the far end. His stomach, in the middle, bulged with sausage-meat. Unable to lash for want of length, his stumpy tail waggled angrily back and forth. He looked, Meredith thought, rather like one of those foxfur fashion accessories so popular with Edwardian ladies, complete with head and baleful glass eyes. Vicky was staggering along – he was a heavy cat even without extra food in him – and had succeeded in her purpose of hauling her trophy indoors for display.

'I've found this cat,' she panted. 'We can take him home.'

'Don't think so, sweetie,' said her father. 'I think he lives next door. Better put him down.'

Vicky's face was red with her efforts and now set as mutinously as her captive's. 'I found him. He was in our garden. We can keep him.'

'Put him down, love,' said Paul, returning to the unpacking of his picnic basket. He took out the roast chicken and set it on a plate.

Nimrod, from the headlock in which Vicky held him, opened his eyes in so far as he was able, and his whiskers quivered. The scent of the chicken had reached him and even in his present predicament and notwithstanding his full stomach, he was interested.

'He's a nice cat!' shouted Vicky, aligning herself with the minority interest group which constituted Nimrod's admirers.

The argument had detracted her from her grip which had slackened. Nimrod effectively dislocated his entire skeleton, sliding down between her arms to land with a thump on the floor. He picked himself up, reassembled himself in a trice, and fled.

'Come back, cat!' yelled Vicky.

'Let him go,' said her father peaceably. 'And wash your hands, there's a good girl.'

'Is that Wynne's cat?' asked Laura, returning from another

visit to the damage in the sitting room. 'We'll have a cup of coffee or something and then I'll nip round and ask her if she wants to join us for lunch.'

'The coffee was one of the things tipped out. But I think,' Markby said, 'I'd rather settle for a glass of wine, in any case.'

'Brought that too!' Paul produced a couple of interesting bottles.

They retired to the sitting room and opened the wine. Vicky, supplied with a carton of orange juice, had wandered outside again.

'So.' Paul raised his glass. 'Here's to crime! What have you two stirred up down here? When my Auntie Florrie lived in this cottage, the village was as dead as a doornail. By which I mean, nothing ever happened. No gruesome corpses littering the place. No house-breaking maniacs. What foul spirit have you roused from slumber?'

'Things were happening,' said Meredith, 'but your aunt didn't know about them, or she decided not to tell you.'

Paul sipped his wine. 'I remember old Ernie Berry. Odd-looking bloke. He could fix most anything, though, so he was a handy chap to have around. I think he mended auntie's guttering.'

'I remember him very well. Quite hideous and never seemed to wear a shirt,' said Laura. 'Not even in winter. He used to have a weedy youth always in tow, fetching and carrying for him as a sort of plumber's mate.'

'Kevin,' said Meredith. 'We think he's Ernie's son.'

'Very likely,' mumbled Paul. 'One of 'em, anyway.'

'One of them?' This aspect of things hadn't occurred to either Meredith or Alan.

'Sure. The village is full of Ernie's bastards. That much I do know. As far as I've ever been able to make out, it doesn't worry anyone. They were all rather proud of Ernie's prowess.'

'How well', asked his brother-in-law, 'do you know other people in the village, say the vet, or the doctor, or that builder fellow, Crombie?'

Paul thought that over before hunching his shoulders. 'I really only know the people auntie dealt with. The doctor, Burnett, you mean? Yes, I've met him. He hasn't been in the village all that long.'

'He's got a young family,' Markby said.

'That's right. But he's also got a daughter about thirteen or so, at boarding school. Previous marriage.'

Markby murmured. 'Shelling out school fees, is he? That could explain it.'

'Crombie's a rough diamond, but a good sort. Emma gets on well with his girl, Julie. Pony mafia. Armitage and his wife we've met, haven't we, Laura? Nice couple.'

'How about Olivia Smeaton?' Meredith asked.

'Old Olivia? Florrie used to talk about her.' It was Laura who spoke. 'I think Florrie tried to be friendly when Olivia first came to live here, but didn't get very far. She used to say that Olivia had built a ring of defences round herself, wouldn't let anyone through. Florrie thought perhaps Olivia had had a string of bad experiences and was frightened of being hurt again.'

'She took a fancy to Julie Crombie, I believe,' Alan said.

'Makes sense,' Laura nodded. 'Elderly lady, end of her life. Bright, pretty little girl, life before her. A sort of passing the baton, as in a relay. Olivia was about to drop out, Julie just starting the race. Didn't she leave Julie some money?'

'Two thousand,' Alan said. 'But less than that to her housekeeper, a single mum who needed the cash more.'

'Ah,' said Paul wisely. 'Don't forget that Olivia was a

grande dame of an older generation. Janine Catto, for all the combat boots and independent style, was a servant. Sorry, but there it is. Janine wouldn't see herself like that, but Olivia did.' He got up to refill everyone's glass. 'Janine cleaned for Auntie Florrie, too. She wasn't above a bit of gossip. Apparently Olivia hardly ever got any post, except official post, but once she got a letter from some relative or other of her late husband.'

'Lawrence Smeaton?' Alan looked up in surprise.

'Janine didn't know exactly who it was, but it was the same surname, Smeaton. Olivia was very upset. Wandered round the house all day, muttering "how dare he?" Wouldn't eat any lunch. Apparently, she refused to answer it. Janine heard her on the phone to her solicitor, instructing him to answer it on her behalf, saying she wished nothing to do with whoever it was, and not to contact her again.'

Markby held his wine up to the light, admiring the ruby glow. 'Now that is very interesting. Old Lawrence trying to make amends, eh? Offering the olive branch, excuse the pun, but being given the cold shoulder. Any idea when this happened, Paul?'

'Quite a while ago. Couple of years, at least. Long before she died, anyway.'

'But he didn't come down to the inquest or the funeral,' Meredith remarked.

'Would you?' Alan asked her. 'After being given the legal brush-off?'

There was a crash from the kitchen, followed by Vicky's voice, upraised and scolding.

'Naughty cat! Bad, bad cat!'

The others abandoned their wine and conversation, to hurry to the scene of the commotion.

Nimrod was nowhere to be seen. Vicky was standing by

the table, holding the chicken, or rather, holding the bulk of it clasped by her left hand to her summer dress, leaving plentiful grease marks, and brandishing a drumstick, torn from the carcass, in her right hand.

'Oh, Vick,' exclaimed her harassed papa. 'What have you done now?'

'It wasn't me!' she denied indignantly. 'It was that cat. He was on the table. He pulled off its leg.' She waved the drumstick at them.

Nimrod, to his joy, had discovered that this kitchen offered unexpected opportunities for raids.

'He can't possibly be able to eat another mouthful now,' Meredith protested in wonder. 'Perhaps he was going to hide it for later.'

They examined the bird. The drumstick and part of the thigh on one side showed teeth marks and there was a score, as of a claw mark, along the breast on the same side.

'That side'll have to go,' growled Paul. 'Damn moggy. It doesn't look as if he's touched the other side, confound his greedy guts!'

'We'll have to put it all out, Paul,' argued his wife. 'I'll give it to Wynne and the cat can have it for his dinner – last for days. We've got plenty without it.'

'Wanted you to try the apricot stuffing,' moaned the cook.

They all tried to console him, but he was not to be comforted.

'If I see that ruddy animal again today,' he promised, 'I'll brain the brute! Teach him to keep his thieving claws to himself!'

Constable Darren Wilkes had joined the police with high hopes, and encouraged by his Uncle Stan.

Uncle Stan had been a serving police officer for thirty

years and retired with the rank of station sergeant. He approved of his nephew's career decision, even though the police force wasn't what it used to be.

'All these whizz kids,' said Uncle Stan disapprovingly. 'All these university graduates, fast-track promotions and what-have-you. They may have degrees, I grant you, they're bright enough. What they haven't got, Darren, is experience. You don't learn experience in schools. You learn it out there on the beat!'

Uncle Stan usually accompanied the last words by pointing out of the window into the far distance, rather like the tale-spinning mariner signalling *westward ho*! In the painting, *The Boyhood of Raleigh*.

'Experience, Darren, that's what tells in the end!' Uncle Stan would conclude his homily.

Whilst not venturing to contradict Uncle Stan – with whom, in the main, he agreed – Darren had begun to wonder if, for his own part, he hadn't been a little over-optimistic when imagining himself rising to the dizzy heights in the police force. He knew himself to be keen and willing to learn. But whenever he looked at Inspector Crane (and let's face it, she was a stunner), doubt began to grow in his breast, as in the heart of the Victorian clergyman reading *The Origin of Species*.

Progress in his career would mean competing against the university intake, with their degrees, grasp of English grammar, sleek grooming, guaranteed promotion and names like Amanda, Sebastian or James (never Jim). A handful of GSCEs and a name like Darren didn't provide the same basis for confidence – certainly not the kind of social confidence – which allowed the Amandas, Sebastians and others to look a chief constable in the eye, and converse with him politely, with just enough deference, but at perfect ease.

There were some of his colleagues who, in the canteen, made unkind jokes at Inspector Crane's expense. Half the time, so Darren decided, because they fancied her something rotten. The other half of the time, because they saw her as a threat, resented her intelligence and dimly realised she represented The Future.

Darren did respect her sharp brain and the skill with which she dealt with the sniggers and the winks. He was desperate to impress her – not in the man/woman stakes – but as a police officer. He wanted to show her he wasn't just another youthful plod. In his favourite fantasy, he played Watson to her Sherlock Holmes. Well, a bit brighter than old Watson, in fact. Darren hadn't read the stories, but he'd seen the old black and white films on telly, with Basil Rathbone and Nigel Bruce.

But now on a Monday morning, very early, with dew still dampening the ground Darren knew he had a lot to prove to Inspector Crane before he could assume such a role. The search team had reassembled, coughing, snatching a quick drag on a cigarette behind a bush, exchanging gossip, lamenting no one had won the lottery, the usual Monday morning, in fact. Out here in the open or indoors in the station, the conversation was always much the same.

'All right, get to it!' ordered Sergeant Morris, breaking up the small groups. 'We'll tackle that walled garden first and move on to the main gardens. Any questions?'

No one had any questions. A voice was heard to mumble, 'What's to ask? We're looking for a bloody knife in a sodding jungle.'

'It may well have blood on it, Henderson!' observed the sergeant caustically. 'I take it that's what you meant?'

'Yes, sarge. On our way, sarge.'

'Inspector Crane's car just drawn up by the house, sarge.'

'That'll give us something else to look at . . .' muttered Henderson, but took better care this time that the sergeant didn't hear him.

Darren Wilkes set off for the walled garden with the rest and was assigned what looked like the dankest area of it. Uncle Stan, who was a gardener, would've liked to have a go at this lot, knock it into shape. Must've been great in the old days living in a big house and having a load of people running around the place doing all the work. If he ever won the lottery . . .

Frankly, if ever he'd won a fortune, Darren wouldn't have had a clue what to do with it, other than buy a fast car and go on an expensive holiday. Winning the lottery wasn't one of his daydreams. It couldn't hold a candle to his favourite, involving triumphs of detection at the side of Amanda Crane. He picked over a pile of moss-covered plantpots in a corner, dislodging a variety of creepy-crawlies, and indulged himself in his dream scenario.

'Wilkes!'

Yes, that was her voice. He allowed himself a smile and moved on to a broken vegetable frame.

'*Wilkes!*'

'Oh, blimey!' Darren jumped. 'Yes, ma'am. Sorry, didn't see you there.'

'We're going to have to finish in this area this morning and move on. It's taking far too long. I don't mean skimp the search, but try and speed things up a bit, can you? You looked as though you were drifting off there, smirking to yourself.'

'Sorry, ma'am,' repeated the hapless Darren, scarlet-faced.

She moved away. He hoped no one had overheard her criticism. She was right, no time for daydreaming! Uncle Stan wouldn't approve. Frowning in concentration, he hunched on his heels over the frame.

What had enabled a proud Victorian gardener to raise prize cucumbers and marrows had been reduced to a sorry state, wood split, panes broken or missing, caked with grime. Taking care to avoid the jagged edges of glass and expecting the whole structure to disintegrate, Darren raised the lid and peered into the frame's dank interior. It smelled of decay. He muttered 'Pfah!' and wrinkled his nose in distaste.

Ancient, rotten straw lay at the bottom, a factory farm for slugs and snails, beneath more plantpots. It didn't invite further investigation and he was about to replace the lid when it struck him that, unlike the plantpots he'd just been moving, these were muddy but free of moss or green slime. Perhaps because they'd been sheltered by what remained of the frame. He picked one up. There was moss on it, but on the underside.

A prickle ran up his spine. Someone had disturbed these old pots recently, picking them up and replacing them, but omitting to put moss-side upwards. He began to pick them all out, very carefully, one at a time. When they were all standing on the path at his feet, he gently moved aside the rotten straw.

'Inspector Crane, ma'am!'

His voice, in his excitement, broke awkwardly. But he was beyond noticing it. He raised an arm. 'Over here, ma'am. I think I've found something.'

She was hurrying towards him, as was Sergeant Morris, suspicion writ large on his dour countenance.

'What's all this, Wilkes?' growled the sergeant.

But Darren, true to the storyline of his daydreams, ignored him to address himself to the inspector.

'Pushed down under the straw, ma'am.'

They put their heads together, Amanda's against his, with Sergeant Morris attempting a frustrated look-in. Metal gleamed in the straw bed.

'Knife of some sort, ma'am!' exclaimed Morris. He elbowed the mortified Darren aside. 'Mind out the way, Wilkes!'

It was lifted out with care. A big thing, more like a machete than a knife. The solid blade, honed to a razor-edged sharpness, was fixed into a haft bound round with string to make a secure grip.

'Homemade, I reckon,' said the sergeant. 'Seen this kind of thing lying around after gang-fights. Vicious damage it does, chop an ear off, easy.'

The implication of his words wasn't lost on any of them. Morris's voice shook slightly. 'Could be the weapon, ma'am. Hidden away like I said it'd be.' He peered at it and grunted. 'Be a job to get any prints off the string-covered handle. But it's got some stains on the blade here, might well be blood.'

'Right.' She sounded relieved. She'd been more worried than she'd been prepared to admit even to herself that they mightn't find a weapon. 'Get it bagged up.' She turned to Darren, fidgeting in the background.

'Well done, Wilkes.'

'Thank you, ma'am.'

Just wait till you hear about this, Uncle Stan!

CHAPTER EIGHTEEN

. . . a notorious Piece of Sorcery, long practised by
Hags . . . which had a sympathetick Power . . .
Witchcraft described and explained

MEREDITH PAUSED before YOU-NAME-IT's chaotic window display. The cat still slumbered there, but today had chosen a far corner for his snooze. A painted paper fan was flattened beneath him. The impression he gave was still that he needed lifting out and dusting down, to be returned with his price ticket replaced around his neck. But at least he had demonstrated he was capable of movement.

Meredith glanced at the door of the little shop. A notice hung lopsidedly against the glass, announcing it was closed. There was no other sign of life behind the glass. The cat had the place to himself.

She walked on down Stable Row. The Danbys had packed up and returned to Bamford the previous evening, still expressing concern for the welfare of Alan and Meredith in the cottage. Before leaving, Paul had insisted on nailing a board across the interior of the kitchen door, securing it to the frame and rendering it unusable until replaced.

'That'll keep anyone out!' he'd announced, hammer in hand.

'What if there's a fire?' inquired his brother-in-law.

'You can hop out of a window, can't you? You can't just leave that door open all night long with a nutter running round the place. You're going to report the break-in to the local cops, aren't you? It was definitely malicious. He didn't take anything. We checked.'

Markby was doing that, even now, this Monday morning. Meredith was carrying out her own investigations. Whatever was going on here, she'd had enough of it. Especially since it had now turned its attention most definitely to them.

Stable Row lay empty in the early morning sunshine. No Bruce and Ricky today. Presumably they were back at school making their teachers' lives a misery again. Meredith hoped, as she knocked at Janine's door, that this was the case and she wouldn't find the Catto brothers at home. She wanted to talk to their mother and doing so with Bruce and Ricky nearby, listening, their sharp little old men's faces alight with malign intelligence, wasn't something she fancied.

She could hear a distant cacophony which sounded like a television set, going full blast. But no one came to the door and it was possible Janine had gone out and left the set on. Just as the silent TV set had been flashing up a colourful jumble of pictures, all ignored, in the Berrys' cottage, so Janine too probably switched her set on first thing in the morning. It then ran all day, flickering energetically in the corner, until bedtime. Sometimes no one in the household, in all that time, would have actually sat before it and watched a programme right through. People all over the country treated a television like a household pet. It lived with them. It had a right to express its normal nature. Meredith could never understand this attitude, but was resigned to it.

As if to confound her thoughts, the sound stopped, apparently in mid car-chase. Shuffling footsteps approached and a voice called belligerently through the panels. 'Who is it?'

Meredith shouted her name and a reminder that she had called previously with Mrs Carter.

The door was dragged open and Janine appeared, in dressing gown and the sheepskin slippers, sporting a magnificent black eye.

Confused and appalled, Meredith gasped out an apology at having disturbed her.

''S'all right,' Janine told her. 'I thought you might be one of them newspaper scribblers come back again. That's why I was a bit slow opening the door. Comin' in?'

The interior of the little house showed that particular kind of modern poverty which Meredith always found both depressing and frustrating. Few and cheap essentials contrasted with costly luxuries which earlier generations, similarly strapped for cash, would have done without. Priorities had changed. Janine's furniture appeared to have been picked up at second-hand dealers. There was no central heating system, only a coal fire in the hearth. It was lit despite the mild weather, because it provided heat for general use. Before it an old-fashioned wooden clothes horse was draped with washed-out boy's denims, steaming gently. This basic lifestyle was undermined by the presence of an enormous television set. An expensive video-recorder lay on the threadbare carpet beneath it. The general impression was untidy, though very clean.

Janine had been propped on squashed but regal plum-coloured velvet cushions, piled haphazardly on the worn brown moquette of a sagging sofa. She was strategically placed before the fire and her telly. She'd been reading a magazine devoted to the world of pop music and culture – and eating cheese-and-onion-flavoured crisps.

It was impossible to ignore the black eye and yet politeness seemed to forbid any questions. Janine solved the problem.

'See you looking at my shiner, here . . .' She raised a hand and touched the area around her eye gingerly.

'It's certainly a bad one,' Meredith agreed.

'Coming out,' said Janine. She moved to a mirror placed, in defiance of safety, above the open hearth, and peered into it. The clothes horse rocked, threatening to tip its load into the fire. Meredith reached out and grabbed it.

'Yeah, turning yellow,' went on Janine. She dusted off crisp crumbs and sat down amid her imperial cushions. 'I was in a fight. My last boyfriend but one turned up out of the blue. I told him to f—' Janine cleared her throat and out of delicacy for her visitor, amended her words to '– told him to clear off. He only come to borrow some money anyway, or see if there was anything he could pinch to sell.'

The video-recorder, perhaps. Janine had defended her property vigorously and successfully but not without suffering physical hurt.

'Were you harmed in any other way, Janine?' Meredith asked in some concern.

'No, like I said, we had a bit of a scrap but I threw him out. He won't come back again for a while.' She sounded confident.

Meredith's gaze fell on the denims. At the same time, Paul's words echoed in her head, and his claim that Ernie's progeny were to be found all over the village. An alarming thought struck her. Surely not Bruce and Ricky, too?

'This, um, former boyfriend, would he be your children's father?'

Janine nodded. 'But he don't come to see them. Don't pay no maintenance, nothing.'

'He's not a local man, then, from Parsloe St John?'

'Not him,' said Janine, adding, 'Nor am I local, really, come to that. I come from Long Wickham – 'bout ten miles away.'

Around here, ten miles was enough to make you cease to be a local. 'You prefer Parsloe St John?'

'Not really. Much the same, nothing going on. Here we got a couple of shops and the school. Over Long Wickham they haven't even got a shop much less a school, so I'm better off here, with the kids and everything. You want a cup of tea?'

She was already on her way out to the kitchen where she could be heard filling the kettle. She came back and leaned against the doorjamb. 'Won't be a sec. Just waiting for it to boil. What was it you wanted?'

What she really wanted was to talk about Olivia, testing Paul's claim that Janine gossiped, but the subject had to be approached obliquely.

'My friend and I will be vacating the cottage at the end of this week, Sunday afternoon. Mrs Carter has a key and I wondered if you'd have time to go in sometime on Monday next after and give it a good clean round, so that it's really fresh for the owners. I'll leave it tidy and it shouldn't be too much work. I'll pay you now.'

'Sure,' said Janine, screwing up her face as she calculated. 'Won't take me more than a couple of hours, tops, and that's with the windows. Say a tenner?'

'I'll give you fifteen.' Meredith said, opening her purse. 'Just in case it takes you longer for some reason.'

And because ten pounds was little enough to her, but for Janine, to be earned by two hours' hard grind, polishing and window-washing. Meredith, no fan of housework, appreciated what was involved.

It was doubtful that Olivia had. Rookery House with its large, high-ceilinged rooms and wealth of carved wooden balustrades and moulding had been kept immaculate by Janine, single-handed. It had been labour beyond duty. Yet old-fashioned snobbishness had led Olivia, otherwise a kindly woman by all accounts, to leave her housekeeper a derisory amount and to give £2,000 to a spoiled little girl, the only child of a wealthy man. Somehow or other, whenever she thought of that, Meredith's feelings towards the dead woman hardened.

She looked at the video-recorder again and wondered whether Janine had other income, less advertised than her cleaning skills. If she did, it wasn't surprising; with two youngsters to support and no money from their father, she needed every penny she could lay her hands on.

And supposing . . . whispered a little voice in Meredith's brain. *Just supposing, Janine needed money very badly and thought that Olivia had left her rather more than a measly couple of hundred?*

Janine twitched the ten-pound note and five-pound note out of Meredith's hand and tucked them in her dressing-gown pocket. 'Don't worry about it. I'll see to it. But you're not going yet, you got the rest of this week. I'm not that booked up, you know.'

'You know how it is,' said Meredith obscurely.

Janine disappeared into the kitchen and returned with two mugs of tea. She handed one to her visitor.

'Gonna buy the old house?'

'The old? Oh. Rookery House.' Meredith hoped she didn't sound guilty. 'I doubt it. Lovely place but too big – and all that garden.'

Janine sat down on her sofa again and tapped the plum-coloured cushions. 'These come from Rookery House, when all the stuff got cleared out and sold. Everything was numbered and valued, but before the bloke came, I brought these home because who was going to buy a couple of cushions?'

Defensively, she added, 'I asked the solicitor. It was when I asked what I should do with these slippers.' Janine stuck out a foot. 'Mr Behrens, that's the solicitor, he said I might as well keep them and he didn't see why I shouldn't take a couple of old cushions if I could use them. Made a difference to my old sofa here.'

And what else? wondered Meredith. With or without the knowledge and blessing of Mr Behrens? Did it matter? It was all to be sold. Perhaps Janine had felt entitled, having looked after these things for years. Olivia had no relatives. But she'd received a letter. It all led nicely into Meredith's real reason for her visit.

'A great pity when someone dies like that and a whole house has to be stripped and disposed of. I'm surprised she had no one at all.'

'Her husband, he died in the war.'

'Oh, she told you that?'

Janine reflected. 'Not until I'd worked there for a long time. She wasn't one to talk about herself. It was when a letter came from someone called Smeaton who must have been one of her husband's family. She told me then, he'd died in the war and she'd had nothing to do with his family since.'

'She quarrelled with his family? Or just drifted apart?' asked the devious Meredith. 'That can happen when there are no children.'

'Didn't say, but I reckon they'd had a bust-up, because

she was really upset. The letter upset her, I mean. Her face went dead white except for two little red spots up here . . .' Janine touched her cheekbones. 'I'd never seen her like that. She was all of a shake. I thought she might have some sort of turn and fetched her a glass of water. She got on the phone to Mr Behrens and told him to answer the letter for her. She didn't want to see whoever it was. So he, whoever wrote the letter, must have wanted to come and visit her. I don't think he ever wrote again.'

'There was no other . . . she didn't do anything else, after she'd had the letter?'

Janine's eyes glinted with sudden intelligence and she gave Meredith a sharp look. She's on to me! thought Meredith ruefully. She's guessed I came here to talk about Olivia.'

'You got an interest?' Janine asked coolly.

'In a way.' It was best to be frank.

'Something wrong?' Janine's whole manner had become wary.

'I don't know of anything wrong,' said Meredith truthfully.

Janine drained her mug, looking thoughtful. Almost unwillingly, she said, 'She did do one odd thing, after she had that letter. She went right through the house, all the drawers, cupboards, everything. She burnt a lot of old papers and things. Having a clear-out, she said. Not that I'd have thought there was much to clear out. She'd told me she'd done that all her life, cleared everything out from time to time. She said that she did it so that when she went – she meant, when she died – everything would be in order.'

In order all right! Not a clue left!

'And after she received Smeaton's letter, she had another of these clear-outs?'

'That's what it looked like. Burnt some old letters and a photo.'

Meredith fought back her excitement. 'Photo?'

'Not of a person,' Janine said quickly. 'Of an old house. A bit like Rookery House, it was. I came into the room while she was kneeling in front of the fire, tearing up the old letters and pushing them into the flames. I told her to take care. I picked up this old photo. She'd put it on one side, as if she meant to burn that too but had left it till last, perhaps to take one more look at it, you know? I handed it to her, just being helpful. She said, a bit snappy, "I can manage, thank you, Janine!" and snatched it away. Into the flames it went. A shame, I thought, because it was a really old picture. It looked like it was somewhere in the country, a bit like around here, lots of trees, a church tower sticking up behind them, like the church over the road from Rookery House. Very like it, in fact. I would have asked her if she'd been less tetchy. No point in inviting someone to bite your head off, is there?'

'No people in the photo?'

'Only a kid,' said Janine. 'A little girl, old-fashioned dressed with a hat and everything.' Her gaze met Meredith's steadily. 'I can't tell you no more, sorry. She was a funny old girl. I got on with her all right. But you couldn't be friendly with her, know what I mean?'

Only too well, thought Meredith. Paul was quite right. Olivia was of the old school and Janine was a servant. One didn't gossip with servants.

'More's the pity . . .' said Meredith unwarily, aloud. Janine gave her a suspicious look.

Back at the cottage, Meredith and Alan lunched off the remains of the food brought the previous day by Paul and Laura.

'You did pretty well,' Alan said generously if indistinctly. He was chewing a cheese straw. 'The photo is an entirely new element. It must have meant a lot to the old lady, because it seems to have been the only one to survive, until then at least, the obsessional clearances she went in for!'

'Yet she was frightened enough by Lawrence's letter to burn it.'

'You think she was frightened by his letter? Not just angry?'

Meredith shook her head. 'She was scared. It's a guess, of course. But I'd say, that old photo was probably of her childhood home and Olivia was the little girl in old-fashioned dress, as Janine described it. That's why Olivia later bought Rookery House.'

'How so, Holmes?'

'It was similar in appearance and situation to her old home. Janine had time to notice that before Olivia snatched the picture out of her hand. Sentimental reasons cut across common sense. People keep articles which are just junk, broken, useless, totally without any monetary value – why? Because of *sentimental* value. Olivia kept that picture because it was the last link with her childhood, but Lawrence's letter had her throwing it into the fire. She was frightened, all right.'

Meredith neatly removed the last of the cheese straws before he could get to it. 'Even after so many years, old Lawrence remained a threat. You're going to have to talk to him, Alan.'

He sighed acquiescence. 'I thought I'd drive over and have a word with Basil this afternoon, see if he can fix it up over the phone while I'm there. Coming?'

She shook her head. 'I thought I might ask Wynne if she's

paying another call on Kevin Berry. I'll go along with her, if so.'

'She won't be going this afternoon. I saw her drive off in her car, just before you got back from Stable Row.'

Meredith thought about it. 'I'll go anyway. He seemed utterly bereft the last time we went. I don't know what Amanda Crane is doing about it, if anything, but Kevin needs someone looking out for his interests. He could just stay in that tumbledown cottage and starve.'

The Berry cottage looked no better this afternoon. The weed-infested yard was as it had been before. The chickens pecked and scratched around the part-wrecked vehicles which lay about like the aftermath of a battle. Meredith paused by Olivia's old pony-trap and tried to imagine it as it had been when in use. The grey pony between the yellow shafts, rattling merrily along the road, Olivia sitting up there, holding the reins. Probably happy, thought Meredith. She would have been as happy as she'd ever been in her latter years when driving the pony around and still notionally part of the community. The very last years of her life, isolated in her self-imposed house arrest, must have been sad and lonely.

To turn to the purely practical, the trap was probably worth a bit, even in this state. Kevin clearly needed money. She would suggest to him that he advertise it – or get Wynne to advertise it for him. Meredith stooped and pulled aside some of the tall dark green weeds with the yellow flowers, rather unattractive she thought them, and peered at the wheels they hid. The wheels were sound enough. Definitely she'd suggest Kevin sell the trap with Wynne's help.

The door of the cottage was ajar. From behind it came

faint sounds of movement and a tinny clatter as if someone had dropped a saucepan.

Meredith pushed at the door and peered in. The open plan interior, created by Ernie in a burst of home-improvement which had fizzled out afterwards, was as cluttered and grimy as before. Kevin, she was a little surprised to see, was on the far side of the room, back turned to her, at the range, cooking. He wouldn't, at least, starve, as she'd feared.

Perhaps he'd always done the cooking? He might, for all she knew, be a reasonably competent cook, when not in shock. She opened her mouth to call out his name.

At that moment, Kevin turned from the range, holding a hot baking tray with the aid of two cloths. He carried it towards the table with care and was about to set it down when, alerted perhaps by a draught, he looked up and saw Meredith, watching from the door.

The result was unexpected. Kevin let out a yell and dropped his baking tray with a clang on to the table. He backed away, clasping his oven cloths to his thin chest, and stared wildly at her.

'It's all right,' she said quickly, stepping into the room. 'I'm sorry I scared you, Kevin.' A thought struck her, something which might explain his nervousness. 'Were the newspaper people here? Did they bother you?'

Her assurances didn't help and her steady gaze led him to drop his own eyes. Head down, he muttered, 'I kept out of their way. I went over the fields.'

'Good idea. My friend and I did the same. I only came today to see how you were getting on. Obviously you're doing fine.'

Kevin shook his head and husked. 'I don't want nothing.'

Meredith felt a twinge of embarrassment. She was an intruder. Not even an old acquaintance like Wynne, but a do-gooder, come prepared to patronise him. Instead, she'd found him properly busy in his admittedly sordid home. Since he didn't mind the gunge, who was she to criticise it? He was managing perfectly well.

She couldn't just turn and walk off. She had to go through with her lady bountiful visit. Like the squire's lady of old, she had to conduct a formal, uncomfortable and one-sided conversation, before putting down her charitable contribution and fleeing to healthier surrounds. Get it over with.

Meredith walked in briskly. 'Can't stay long, Kevin. I promised Inspector Crane I'd look in on you.'

She was compounding her errors. To mention the police in any way was a mistake. Kevin licked his lips, the broken teeth coming disconcertingly into view. 'Why? What does she want?'

'Nothing—' Meredith ordered herself not to make it any worse and desperately seeking another subject of conversation, turned her attention to the baking tray. 'What are you making? Oh, biscuits – gingerbread men, aren't they?'

Kevin let out a high-pitched yell, dropped the oven cloths and leaped towards her. She thought, for a moment, he meant to attack her and threw up her hands. But his mind was only fixed on escape and she was an obstacle in his path. Pushing her aside, he bolted past and out of the open front door.

Alone in the room, Meredith pulled her startled wits together. 'What on earth?' she muttered. 'What did I say to make him do that?' As an afterthought, she added, 'Perhaps he is barmy.'

She looked down at the tray. To find Kevin cooking was perhaps just understandable. To find Kevin engaged on such dainties as fancy biscuits, astounding. Meredith peered down at the gingerbread people.

Not gingerbread, just baked dough. Inedible in appearance, greyish, roughly moulded rather than stamped out . . .

Meredith caught her breath.

Not biscuits at all – nor anything intended for eating. Quite another purpose, if she guessed right. Each figure was different to its neighbour and the females distinguished from the males by the addition of round dough breasts. Not just any dough figures, but specific people. They were too hot to touch. Meredith bent cautiously over them as she tried to identify each one.

Starting at the left of the line and judging by the small knob of dough atop the bigger knob which formed the head, the figure represented Wynne with her bun of hair. Two larger male figures. Armitage? Crombie? A female one in a skirt with long thin legs and a rough pattern of strands imprinted around the head and some box-like object attached to the end of its arm was Amanda Crane with her document case. Another female figure, as tall as the male figures. Meredith picked it up with care, juggling it in her palm to avoid being burnt. She gazed ruefully at its grinning dough face.

'You,' she said to it, 'are meant to be me, aren't you?'

CHAPTER NINETEEN

I asked them privately what those things betokened.
Sir John Maundeville

SHE WASN'T, Meredith told herself, superstitious. But standing here alone, in this isolated cottage, with a trayful of grotesque little dough figures as her only company, would be guaranteed to send a shiver down the most resolute spine.

After this initial reaction, cold reason took over. She went to the door, but Kevin had disappeared. It was possible he hadn't gone far, but was hiding out there among the abandoned vehicles and tangled vegetation, waiting for her to leave.

She returned to the table. Leave she had to, but not without these little charmers. Meredith picked up one of the cloths dropped by Kevin in his flight. She spread it on the table and began to transfer the dough figures from the tray to the cloth. They were still hot to the touch. What had Kevin planned to do with them? And what had given him the grotesque idea in the first place?

'He's heard,' muttered Meredith reassuringly to herself, 'of others doing something like this.' But she knew he could be more involved. There was one person who could tell her.

She supposed what she was proposing to do was technically theft. But if she left the figures here, Kevin, on his return, would surely destroy the evidence of his amateur witchcraft. Meredith rolled up the cloth with care and carried her booty to the door.

'Kevin!'

Her voice echoed around the desolate patch of ground and was trapped in the surrounding trees. An ungainly black shape, perched insecurely high in the swaying branches of one of them, cawed a hoarse response.

'If you're Kevin's familiar,' Meredith said to it with jocular bravado, 'tell him I've got his horrid little toys here.' She lifted the bundled cloth.

The crow spread great jet wings and flapped away, uttering his discordant cries. The superstitious prickle of unease returned. She had given the creature a message and it had duly taken off to deliver it to someone, somewhere.

'Rubbish!' said Meredith aloud as firmly as she could. She raised her voice again. 'Kevin, if you can hear me, I've got your biscuits here with me. I'm taking them away.'

If Kevin were out there, she was fairly sure this would make him surface. But there was no response, not even a tell-tale rattle among the rusting metal hulks or a shiver of leaves in the bushes.

If nothing else, her conscience was appeased. She had told Kevin she was taking away his baking efforts and it wasn't her fault if he'd run off out of earshot.

The closed notice was still in the door of YOU-NAME-IT. Undeterred, Meredith rapped loudly. The hanging notice shivered at the violence. She waited a little, then rapped again.

After a moment or two, she was rewarded with signs of

movement within. Meredith pressed her nose against the dusty glass. At the back of the shop, the bead curtain had parted and a bulky form was coming towards the door.

Sadie appeared on the other side of the glass, dressed in another tent-like gown. She mouthed inquiry as to the reason for the disturbance.

Meredith lifted the cloth-wrapped package and pointed at it.

Sadie couldn't know what it contained, but curiosity, Meredith was sure, would make her open the door, and it did.

'What is it?' Sadie asked disagreeably. She might have meant either the package, or Meredith's errand. 'I'm taking a day off. I've got a headache.'

You'll have a worse one, chum, when I've finished . . . thought Meredith unkindly. Aloud, she said, 'I think you ought to take a look at this. I'm sorry to disturb you,' she added for formula's sake.

Token observance of courtesy didn't mollify Sadie who stared at the bundle resentfully. 'Can't you come back tomorrow?'

Meredith remained where she was. 'We should talk now.'

'All right.' Sadie stepped back and allowed Meredith into the tiny shop. She closed the door immediately behind them and bolted it. Meredith reflected that she was shut in here now with someone who was quite possibly the local lunatic, and no one knew of it. She hoped she hadn't been rash.

Sadie had turned and was plodding ahead of her towards the bead curtain. They passed through it, down a narrow corridor and arrived in a comfortable sitting room.

Comfortable, that was, in furnishings. In decoration, it was highly disconcerting. Sadie appeared to be a collector of what might be called either folk art, or ethnic curiosities.

261

Carved wooden masks hung on the walls at irregular intervals. A wooden dresser was laden with crude pottery bowls, some tri-legged, jugs and primitive figurines, the latter mostly all-too-female, wide of hip, enormous of stomach and breast, but in some cases with incomplete arms or legs. Amongst them lurked other sinister and unattractive items of bric-à-brac of obscure but possibly occult significance. A picture on the wall, a garishly hand-tinted print, showed women in seventeenth-century dress dancing. The dance appeared similar to a Scottish reel or a square dance. The dancers gestured with arms and clasped hands as they exchanged places.

Meredith was about to comment on it when Sadie said loudly and in an accusing voice, 'I don't know what you want, but I've had my fill of upsetting visits lately! It's left me quite ill and I can do without being badgered any more by people too ignorant to know any better!'

'I haven't come to badger you,' Meredith told her, perhaps not quite truthfully. 'I've come to ask your advice, if you'd like to put it that way. I think you can explain something for me.'

Fury glowed in Sadie's dark eyes. 'Advice, is it? You mean information. Well, there's none I can give you or anyone else about anything, all right? People seem to think I can explain every wretched thing which has happened here. Seems to me that someone other than me has been pretty free with information of a sort! Telling tales, lies, about me, to the police! Not only the police, either. The papers, too. You've seen what they've written? It's slander, that's what it is and I ought to sue whoever's responsible!' She fixed a meaningful look on Meredith.

Meredith hoped she didn't look guilty but supposed she did. Sometimes it was as well to brazen things out. 'I was told you were recognised locally as a witch and that it was no secret. You didn't try to hide it. It surprised me and I didn't altogether believe it. But I did mention it to Inspector Crane. It came up in conversation.' (Sadie sniffed.) 'It's all I told her because it's all I know,' Meredith finished.

(Well, not quite, she thought. But it's all I'm going to admit to.)

Sadie was looking partly appeased but still suspicious. 'I didn't say it was you,' she said grudgingly. 'But someone's been telling evil stories. Ritual murders, indeed! Lot of spiteful nonsense put about by those who don't know the difference between the old religion and satanism!' A sort of satisfied smile played across her mouth. 'But we've had to put up with slurs and slanderous attacks of that nature for centuries, so it's not surprising if I'm suffering what others have suffered before me.'

'Who are these others?' Meredith asked her.

Sadie reached out a pudgy hand and silently indicated she should sit down and took a seat herself. Between them was a low table on which stood the remains of a snack meal. Pot Noodles and a mug with a sodden tea-bag in it, modern debris which looked incongruous among the other artefacts. Possibly Sadie was genuinely feeling under-the-weather following a harrowing interrogation by the police, and it was unkind to bother her. Meredith crushed these sentiments.

'Yes, I am a witch,' Sadie said calmly. 'I've never denied it. It's entirely my own affair. I am not a satanist, and that's as much as I'm prepared to tell you about it.'

She didn't add 'so there!' but her manner did.

Meredith reflected that she'd been in some odd situations but this had to be one of the oddest. Here she sat in this really very ordinary back sitting room, leaving aside the unusual nature of the ornaments, with a self-confessed witch, engaging in a surreal conversation. It didn't matter that she, Meredith, didn't believe for a moment that Sadie had any special powers. As for the 'old religion', something to do with Nature, no doubt – Sadie herself clearly believed in it with such an intensity that one couldn't simply smile and dismiss her obsession. It ruled her life and directed her decisions. That meant that if one dealt with Sadie, one dealt, willy-nilly, with her beliefs, however eccentric.

Sadie had dispensed with the pink butterfly hairclips today and her black hair was secured rather more smartly with a green velvet Alice band. She had folded her hands in her lap and Meredith noticed that her fingernails were very well kept. She clearly meant it when she said she had no intention of expanding on her statement.

'I haven't come to accuse you of anything, Mrs Warren,' Meredith assured her, 'certainly nothing in connection with the murder of Ernie Berry.'

'Obliged, I'm sure!' Sadie's mouth opened to release the words and shut like a trap after them. Getting any information from her was going to be very much a matter of breaking down a defence. Not only was the woman uncooperative, but she was set on actually thwarting any inquiry out of sheer perversity, if nothing else. Supposing, that was to say, there was no other reason . . .

If Meredith wanted information, she was going to have to surprise it out of her.

Meredith placed the bundle on the table. Sadie's eyes moved their pebble-hard gaze from Meredith's face to the cloth shape.

'Why have you brought that to me?'

There was a faint lilt to her voice, perhaps Celtic in origin. Meredith hadn't thought to ask whether Sadie was a true local.

'You don't know what it is,' she retorted. This was Sadie playing tricks again. The impression she gave by the question was that she did know. But it was going to take more than that to unsettle Meredith this time.

'It's something which worries you.' There was a malicious glint in the dark eyes.

'I think it ought to worry both of us.' Meredith scored with that reply. Sadie blinked. The pudgy fingers twitched and tightened their clasp.

'I have no reason to be uneasy in my mind.' Sadie was fighting back and gave her visitor a look of scorn. 'I told you I am a follower of the old religion. If that disturbs you, it's not my fault, nor, in modern parlance, my problem. Perhaps it is a problem for you and others like you, who don't understand and can't be bothered to inquire. You prefer popular myths and the imagination of pulp fiction writers. Wallow in your ignorance. It's nothing to me.'

'I would like you, if you'd be so kind . . .' Meredith ignored the put-down and stretched out a hand to the cloth. She was amused to see that Sadie's superior attitude wasn't proof against a quiver of anticipation. The woman tilted her body forward. Her voluminous dress, a brownish-colour with a geometric pattern on it, similar to African prints Meredith had seen, rustled. She smelled of violet cachous. '. . . to take a look at these. You might be able to explain them to me. It shouldn't take up much of your time.'

She unwrapped the cloth.

Sadie drew in her breath sharply. The anger returned to flood her eyes and fixed Meredith in a way which uncomfortably brought to mind the old saying 'if looks could kill'. 'Who did this?'

'I'd rather not say,' Meredith declined, shaking her head.

'You've seen similar things before? I was hoping you had and could tell me about them.'

'Were you indeed?' Sadie sat back, suddenly relaxed. She'd been furious for a moment, but had got it under control. Meredith had the obscure feeling that somehow she'd lost the initiative.

'And supposing that I know anything – or have seen such things before as you believe – why should I tell you?'

'Because these were made by someone who is both very unhappy and vulnerable. Someone who needs help.'

'That's obvious.' Sadie's lips curved upward in what ought to have been a smile, but wasn't. 'This person, whoever he or she may be—'

Sadie paused fractionally, but Meredith wasn't giving away the sex of the offender – and offender Sadie clearly saw the maker of the dough figures to be.

'This meddler,' Sadie's voice hardened, 'should leave well alone.'

'What would be the purpose of such things?' Meredith asked bluntly.

'That would depend on who made them.' Sadie moved and the geometric print rustled again. 'But I can see that whoever made those is so ignorant that in fact they could serve no purpose.'

'But where would the maker get the idea from?'

This time Sadie laughed aloud, a curiously light sound. 'Where? Television? Films? The sensational literature I mentioned before? Gossip? Malicious slanders? I suppose whoever it was had some idea of sticking pins in the figures. I can tell you now, it would have been a waste of time. This is a child's game.'

'I see.' Meredith wasn't sure quite what she'd expected Sadie to tell her, but she'd learnt one thing. Kevin wasn't part of Sadie's circle. He'd heard of it and he'd thought he'd have a go.

'Well, thank you, Mrs Warren. I won't bother you any longer.' Meredith reached out to remove the cloth and the figures from the table, but Sadie had got there first, her pudgy fingers closing, Meredith was alarmed to see, on the dough figure which she'd taken to be Meredith's own representation.

'They must be destroyed!'

'Sorry, no,' said Meredith. 'I have to return them. All of them, that one as well, please.'

'They are an insult!' Sadie's voice shook and her calm had suddenly deserted her. 'Someone is playing a foolish game, meddling! Someone who has no right!'

'I'll pass the message on.' Meredith twitched the dough figure from Sadie's grasp. Its head fell off.

There was a silence. Sadie gave an odd little snort, either of derision or glee, it was hard to tell which.

Meredith collected up the broken dough doll and rolled it, together with its fellows, in the cloth. 'Just as well you say they have no power!' she said with forced cheerfulness.

'*They* don't.'

The implication was clear but Meredith wasn't to be rattled. There had been a moment there when she'd been alarmed by Sadie but now she was satisfied she dealt with eccentricity.

'I'll have a word with the person concerned. I don't think it's a healthy activity myself – if not for the same reasons as you may have. Don't worry, they'll be destroyed.'

She got up and made her way to the door.

Moving with a speed and agility her bulk wouldn't have indicated, Sadie got there first, barring the way. 'You must tell me who made them!'

Meredith shook her head. 'I'm not going to. I know I've bothered you with this and you probably feel entitled to be told, but just believe me, it won't happen again.'

Sadie said quietly, 'You shouldn't promise what you can't be sure to deliver.' She indicated the bundle. 'Tell whoever it is, it must stop. It is, in any case, quite useless unless one understands . . . Tell this person that what he, or she, is doing is offensive.'

She stood aside, allowing Meredith to pass. Much, it had to be said, to Meredith's relief.

The relief was short-lived. As she stepped down into the street, and Sadie prepared to close the door behind her, the woman said, 'It makes no difference whether you tell me or not. I shall find out, in any case.'

The door slammed, glass shivering and the little closed notice danced on its string.

It was quite possible that she would, thought Meredith uneasily. If Sadie thought about it, knew, for example, that Meredith and Wynne had visited Kevin, she might work it out for herself.

Just to complete Meredith's concern, a large black crow, which had been perched on the roof of YOU-NAME-IT, launched itself from its roost and swept across the narrow lane so close to Meredith, that she felt a caress of disturbed air from its passing wings.

There was no sign of Alan's car at the cottage and she supposed he hadn't yet returned from the Newtons. Meredith hesitated with the bundle of dolls in her hands. She had promised Sadie, foolishly as Sadie had pointed out, that she'd ensure these were destroyed and no others would be made. The destruction would be easy enough: she had only to drop it to the ground and they'd shatter.

It would also be high-handed. Kevin had modelled them. Kevin should be persuaded to destroy them and a promise extracted from him, at the same time, not to carry out another such experiment.

It meant returning to the cottage. She was disinclined to do so alone. Meredith went to Wynne's door and knocked. There was no answer and when she looked around the side of the cottage, Wynne's car hadn't returned. Only Nimrod sat on the windowsill, waiting for the window to be opened so that he could resume his favourite seat within. He miaowed crossly at her.

'Sorry,' said Meredith to him. 'I can't oblige. What's more, I certainly owe you no favours!'

Nimrod gave her a look which said he'd expected nothing more. She wasn't a useful human being.

There was nothing for it but to set off alone. Well, she'd faced up to Sadie in her den. Kevin shouldn't be a problem.

He wasn't a problem because he wasn't there. The cottage door was firmly shut and no one answered her repeated hammering on its thick oak planks. It brought forth only that peculiar empty echo which comes from a deserted dwelling. Meredith walked around it and peered through grimy windows. He might be hiding upstairs but she felt sure he'd left again. Again was the operative word here. He'd been back. The door, left open, was now closed and she didn't think it was the wind. Upstairs, a casement window, which she was sure had stood ajar at her first visit, was also shut.

That left her with the bundle of biscuits in her hands and no notion what to do with it. She could just leave it, put it on the windowsill. Meredith put it there and then picked it up again. The hens might fly up here and discover it and eat the lot before Kevin returned. She'd take it back, wait for Alan to return and show it to him, then come back, with Alan for company, to the cottage.

She walked quickly back along the dirt track which gave access to the Berrys' home. The banks on either side were high and thick with grasses, brambles, wild plants of all kinds. There was even a small patch of wheat ears, spilled over from nearby fields or grown from seed dropped by birds. Amongst it grew another of those rather plain dark green weeds with the small yellow flowerheads. Meredith, struck by an idea, stopped and tugged at it. It was well-rooted but snapped off in her hand. Glancing over her shoulder, because in all this she'd had the odd feeling she was being observed, she put it with the bundle of pastry dolls, and carried it home with her.

Home, the cottage, was still empty. No Alan's car. No Wynne's car. Meredith entered via the front door and carried her trophies through to the kitchen, where the barred damaged backdoor was a bleak reminder of the unwanted visitor. She switched on the electric kettle and, while it hissed companionably, went into the living room to search among the books in the solid Edwardian bookcase. There had been a number on the natural world, fauna and flora. She found the picture dictionary of wild plants and took it back to the kitchen.

The kettle had clicked itself off. Meredith made a pot of tea and settled down to turn the pages of the book. She had set out the weed alongside it and cross-checked from time to time. About three-quarters of the way through the volume, she was rewarded.

'There it is,' she murmured.

Tap-tap-tap.

Meredith started. Someone had rapped at the front door. She hadn't heard Wynne's car return and Alan had a key.

She got up, went quietly to the sitting-room window and peered out. It might be a journalist returned. Or, in this village, it might be anything.

Get a hold of yourself! Meredith admonished herself. It won't be the intruder. He works by night. Nonetheless, she opened the door with caution. It was Inspector Crane.

'I'm sorry he's not back yet. He's gone to see Sir Basil.'

Meredith had brewed up afresh and poured out a cup for her visitor who sat across the kitchen table from her.

She saw, as Alan had done, that since her first visit in city garb, Crane had adapted to country circumstances. At the moment she wore an Aran-knit pullover over her tartan skirt. Her hair today, as Sadie's earlier, was kept tidy by an Alice band. The comparison caused Meredith momentary amusement. Even in her distress at being questioned by the police, Sadie had taken note of the more upmarket hair-ornament and adjusted her own style accordingly.

'Thank you.' Crane took the cup of tea offered and fiddled with it. 'I dropped in to tell him – to tell you both – we've found the murder weapon. Or that's one reason I'm here.'

Meredith detected a note of triumph in her voice. She expressed her congratulations.

'I thought you'd like to know. It was hidden in the kitchen garden alongside the paddock. The lab's run tests on bloodstains and they match up to the deceased's. Someone had made an attempt to wipe the blade but it's not so easy to clean up something as people sometimes imagine!' Crane allowed herself a brief smile.

'Fingerprints?' Meredith asked hopefully.

Tenseness returned accompanied by a shake of the head. With manifest reluctance, Amanda Crane said, 'No luck there. The whole thing was a homemade effort and the

271

handle had been bound around with string. We weren't able to get a print off that. But it's a positive step forward. It's a distinctive object and someone may be able to identify it.'

'That's very likely.' Perhaps it was, but if someone did, there was no assuming that person would give the police the information.

Crane gave Meredith a slightly awkward look. 'I meant to ask after you, also. I mean, how you're feeling. You did, after all, find the deceased.'

'Most of him.' She hadn't forgotten it. Gallows humour helped.

'Quite. You were obviously very shocked when we first met.'

'I don't want the counselling, thanks.'

Crane flushed. 'No, I realise you've probably been used to dispensing help rather than being on the receiving end. But it doesn't mean – that is, we all need help from time to time. But I won't mention it again. If you change your mind, Superintendent Markby would be able to advise you.'

'Look,' Meredith said bluntly. 'I didn't mean to be rude to you. I was upset when you came here last time. It's not an excuse.'

'It seems a pretty good excuse to me!' Amanda Crane relaxed and smiled. 'And believe me, you weren't rude. I get all kinds of reception from witnesses and people I call on generally. You were coping remarkably well, I thought.'

Meredith accepted that in the spirit it was meant, though one couldn't help thinking, ungratefully, what else she'd been supposed to do. Sit on the floor and howl?

'I've read the press reports, of course,' she said.

'Who hasn't?' said Amanda Crane gloomily.

'Is it just tabloid hysteria, or are you taking the ritual idea seriously?'

The inspector sipped her tea and set it down again. 'We're obliged to consider the possibility of a ritual murder, given the sequence of events. You and the superintendent witnessed some kind of celebration at the Standing Stones, and Berry was found next day, mutilated. But nothing has suggested Berry had any direct dealings with the supposed coven. The man was illiterate, a drinker and womaniser. No sensitive society would place its secrets in his hands! Nothing places him at the site of the Standing Stones. There are no traces of blood out there.'

Meredith hesitated. 'There's a farm, Lower Edge Farm. They must know something. Wynne and I called there but the farmer was unfriendly and definitely nervous.'

'I've been there. It's the nearest habitation and whatever went on regularly at the Stones, I agree the people at the farm must have at least have known of it, even if they didn't participate. The farmer, his name is Cleggs, eventually admitted he let "visitors who come late at night", that's his description of them, park in his yard for security. He has, he says, nothing to do with the goings-on. He charged them a fiver each per stay. That was around sixty quid for an evening and not bad, tax free. He knows none of their names and took no record of any licence plates.'

'I – that is, Mrs Carter and I, thought that might be where they parked.'

'We took a good look around the farm,' Crane went on, 'and found nothing to suggest Berry had been there, or that anything untoward had taken place there. If we could trace Berry's woman friend, that would settle it, of course, and we could forget the witchcraft angle altogether! In the meantime, I've checked out the shop in the village here. I went to see that woman, Warren. Now that was a reception and a half!'

Crane grimaced. 'She tried the lot. Rampant indignation, the steely-eyed brush-off, mysterious hints at things better left unasked and unanswered! This is strictly off the record, I shouldn't be telling you,' Amanda added hastily, 'but in the end, she didn't deny that she was a witch – or claims to be a witch. I suppose, if you say you are one, you are.' She smiled drily. 'I got a long spiel about old religions. She does deny, most emphatically, that she practises anything illegal and says it's no part of her beliefs to go in for ritual killings of any creature. She wouldn't admit to knowing of any other followers or co-practitioners, whatever you care to call them, in the neighbourhood. So far, I can't tie her in to this, and I should tell you that frankly, I'm doubtful that Berry's killing is in any way connected to the whole jiggery-pokery. If the man was a philanderer, however unlikely it might appear to you and me, then my money's on a jealous husband.'

'I went to see Mrs Warren this afternoon,' Meredith admitted.

The inspector sat up straight, cup clattering in its saucer. 'I hope you didn't do anything to complicate my inquiry! This is a police matter and a very serious one. It concerns murder. I really must ask you to stay away from someone who might have valuable information.'

'I wasn't asking her about Ernie Berry,' Meredith told her. 'I had something I wanted to show her – you'd better see them too.'

'Well,' said Amanda Crane a little later after she'd examined the collection of dough people. 'It looks as if I ought to put social services on to Kevin Berry, after all. This suggests to me he's gone mildly off his rocker. Shock at his father's gruesome death? Panic at finding himself alone in the world? People do strange things after a traumatic bereavement – but this must be among the weirdest I've come across.' She touched the broken doll with the tip of a manicured fingernail. 'Sorry yours lost its head – if it is yours, as you say.'

'It's mine – and I can make a guess at some of the rest. The question in my mind is why? What's he got against us all?'

Amanda Crane smoothed a hand over her already immaculate hair. 'More precisely, have you any idea what he or anyone else might have against you specifically? You and the superintendent appear to have upset someone in the village. I'm supposing, as a working theory, that the person who broke in here on Saturday night and wrecked the kitchen, wrote on the wall in the other room and did other damage, is the same person who vandalised, for example, the vet's car. Armitage and the other people are residents. You and the superintendent are visitors. So, why you? Have you had time to make an enemy?'

'I think,' Meredith said slowly, 'we've been condemned by association. It's not what we've done. It's that we've consorted with those the vandal hates. It makes us one of them. He hates them and we like them. So he hates us. Those who are not for him are against him. It's a common enough attitude for an angry and confused mind to take.'

There was a silence. 'You sound,' Crane said, 'as if you think you know who the vandal was.'

'I think you know, too. Or, at least, you're as much in a position to guess as I am. We've been talking about him.'

Crane said nothing and Meredith went on, 'The various acts of vandalism and these dolls are linked. When I saw Kevin in the yard of The King's Head, the first time he reported Ernie missing, the kid kept his hands firmly in his pockets. Later, when Wynne and I called at the cottage, he kept his hands behind him for as long as he could. When he finally had to use them to eat, I noticed his fingertips were blistered, as if burnt. He said he'd done it on the old-fashioned range. It might have been caused by unwise handling of some caustic substance, say paint-stripper?'

'The vet's car?'

'Right. It was damaged by paint-stripper almost certainly stolen from Crombie's builder's yard. Crombie's guard dogs didn't bark at the intruder. Max realised that meant the animals knew him and he jumped to the conclusion the culprit was a man he'd had trouble with earlier. But the Berrys had done work for Crombie on and off. The dogs would have known Kevin.'

'It's possible.' There was, in Inspector Crane's eyes something of the pebble-hardness Meredith had seen in Sadie Warren's.

'Another thing,' Meredith said. 'When Kevin saw Wynne walk up to his door, the day she and I made our mercy call, he was terrified. Yet he knows Wynne well, and previously, when we found him in the gardens of Rookery House, he addressed nearly everything he said to Wynne. He wasn't scared of her. He saw her as some kind of authority. At the cottage, not only was he scared, but he yelped out "I didn't do it!" I thought at the time, because the police had been asking him about Ernie, he was frightened of being accused of his father's death. I think now, he meant he hadn't uprooted her plants and destroyed the bed. He thought she'd found out and was coming to tax him with it.'

Crane tapped her fingertips on the table. 'Perhaps. But if he thought he'd been rumbled, why did he come here and wreck this place, after that?'

'Because Wynne didn't accuse him and he realised she

hadn't guessed. To Kevin, that just meant he had got away with it. Really, I should have guessed as soon as I saw the word "death" spelled d-e-t-h on the sitting-room wall. It wasn't because he was working at speed or in the dark. It was simply because he can't spell. Ernie was illiterate. Kevin's able to read and write but only just.'

Crane said slowly, 'I agree. It all holds together well. But it's not proof. I need proof. The dolls aren't enough. I need proof of involvement in vandalism.'

Meredith prepared her *coup de grâce*. 'Well, how about this?' She swivelled the open plant book to face her visitor, picked up the green weed and placed it on the relevant page. 'Oxford Ragwort, the plant which was used to poison Olivia Smeaton's pony. It's not common hereabouts, which was what puzzled Rory Armitage. But the Berrys' front yard and the lane leading to their cottage are both full of it.'

CHAPTER TWENTY

For things passed out of long time from a man's
mind or from his sight turn soon into forgetting . . .
Sir John Maundeville

'AND SO,' Markby said, 'Sir Basil and I will drive up to
Keswick tomorrow to meet Lawrence Smeaton. Sorry to
exclude you from the visit, but it's Basil's show. It'll be a
long round trip and I don't know how much time we'll
spend with the Smeatons. If it gets late, we'll find a B and B
along the route, drive back early the following day.'

It was a little after six o'clock that evening. Amanda
Crane had left before Markby's return, taking the dough
figures with her. Meredith glanced at the window. Clouds
had begun to scud across the early evening sky which
suggested rain in the offing. She expressed her doubts about
the weather.

'All fixed up, can't change arrangements now. Incidentally, Moira's asked you over there to lunch. We thought, as
you and I have only one car between us here and you won't
want to be marooned in this village until I get back, you can
drive me over to Basil's tomorrow morning. Basil and I will
go on in his car and you can come back later in the day here
under your own steam.'

'Fair enough. It's kind of Moira.'

Alan had opened the ransacked fridge and was peering inside without much optimism. 'Are we going up to The King's Head to eat tonight?'

Meredith hesitated. 'I ought to go back to the Berrys' cottage first, just to see if Kevin's come home and to tell him I gave his pastry efforts to Amanda.'

'If you're right about Kevin being the one who broke in here, then I'd like to talk to him as much as you do—'

'You oughtn't to scare him, Alan! He's already very frightened.'

'Hold on, let me finish. The thing is, it would be better to leave it to Crane. And if you're worried about scaring him, then the knowledge that Crane has his pastry dolls will panic him completely and mess up any interview Crane may wish to have with him. Crane's having the dolls is her ace in the sleeve. All in all, it might be as well to leave the wretched lad in ignorance for the time being.'

'You make me feel very guilty,' she muttered in dissatisfaction.

'At what?' He picked up a piece of cheese in cellophane and studied it, assessing its potential as main ingredient of a meal. 'Giving the dough dolls to Crane? Telling her about the ragwort? You couldn't have done otherwise. If you had, you'd have been withholding information. If you hadn't told her, I should.'

'Then I wish you had! I shouldn't feel so bad about it.' Meredith added, 'Amanda's very pleased to have found the murder weapon. She glowed when she told me about it. She wanted to tell you. Pity you weren't here.'

'You told me.'

'I mean, she wanted to tell *you* in person. She wanted to bask in your approval.'

He put the cheese back in the fridge. 'She doesn't need my appro. If she needs anyone's, it's that of whoever runs her division.'

Meredith thought he was beginning to sound tetchy and dropped the subject. 'I should still go back to the Berrys' place. Kevin went running off quite crazily and he is in a very strange state of mind.'

'That would seem to be permanent,' Markby muttered.

She told him that was an unkind comment and as Wynne had returned home, she'd ask Wynne to walk over to the Berry cottage with her.

Markby pushed the fridge door shut and straightened up with a sigh. 'We haven't got any food, not to speak of, unless you want beans for your supper. We'll stop off and check on Kevin Berry, if that's what you want. But don't mention Crane, all right? Then it's heigh-ho, to The King's Head we go. Pollard ought to be making a mint. He's got a monopoly of dining establishments in this village.'

Receiving no reply, he turned round. She was propped in the doorway, arms folded, jeans-clad legs crossed at the ankle, sleeves of her sweater pushed up to her elbows and a combative look in her hazel eyes. He knew that look well.

'Is it possible,' she asked, 'that you are just slightly out of sorts?'

'No!' he denied indignantly.

'I'm not going anywhere to eat with you if you're going to sit there like a bear with a sore head. Is it the prospect of driving up to Cumbria with Basil? Or seeing old Lawrence? I'd be dying to see the old chap, if I were in your shoes.'

'Well, you're not in my shoes,' he told her. 'I'm sorry if I sound short-tempered. I didn't mean to take it out on you. Look, Meredith, you know the expression, let sleeping dogs lie? I've a strong suspicion that's what Wynne should have done when she started out on updating that obit. All she had to do was tack a short paragraph on the end of the existing piece the paper had on file. A sentence would have been enough. Something like, "Olivia Smeaton spent the last years of her life in seclusion." Who, after all these years, cares? Who asked Wynne to stir things up? Start turning over stones and dislodging all the happy little beasties living there? Involve me, involve Sir Basil . . . And for what? To find we've dislodged a very large beastie, that's what! And its name is Lawrence Smeaton. I am not looking forward to meeting Lawrence. I have the strongest possible misgivings.' A touch wistfully, he added, 'And I'm on holiday.'

Her mop of dark brown hair quivered with transmitted emotion. 'Don't you want to know how she died?'

'I know how Olivia Smeaton died.'

'You're going along with the findings of the inquest, then? Even after all the other things which have happened in this village?'

Markby walked over to her and put his hands on her shoulders. 'I said, I know how Olivia Smeaton died. I believe these are circumstances in which both the dead and the living should be left in peace. Asking questions and resurrecting old memories, perhaps things which ought to have been left forgotten, it can only harm those still alive and do nothing for those who aren't. Forgetting isn't something we do just because we grow old. We do it to protect ourselves. Ask any doctor. Ask anyone who's had to deal with post-trauma. After tomorrow, it's not going to be possible for anyone to rest as easy again. Let's leave it there, all right?' He kissed her lightly on the mouth. 'Where did you get that weird sweater?'

She unfolded her arms and surveyed the sweater. It was dark blue and had a knitted motif of three pigs.

'In a sale.'

'Ever wonder why no one else had bought it?'

'I'm most definitely not going out to eat with you!'

'Yes, you are. We'll go now. Come on – and we'll stop by the Berrys' place. We'll spend a whole evening during which we won't talk about the Berrys or the Smeatons or anything remotely murderous.'

'Not even my maligned sweater?'

'You,' he said gallantly, 'would look wonderful in a potato sack.'

She pulled a face and adopted a stage cockney accent. 'Lawks, sir, how you do go on . . .'

The Berrys' cottage was as she'd last seen it, doors and windows tightly shut and not a sign of life. They walked round it, Markby muttering at the general state of the yard and making uncomplimentary remarks both about the late Ernest Berry and Kevin.

'Look at this junk. Not just old cars, but old mangles, old farm machinery, two old-fashioned baby prams – which, incidentally, I've been informed by my sister are now highly desirable – a supermarket trolley and this—'

He dived into long grass and emerged holding a ship's wheel. 'When did Ernie ever go to sea? I suppose someone might want this.' He was examining it. 'A regular scrap yard, but Ernie seems to have hoarded it rather than dealt in it.'

'I was going to suggest Kevin sell some of it.'

He grunted. 'You're right to think along those lines. Kevin should get a reputable dealer in, if only to clean the place up! But I imagine it's worth a few quid. I'll have a word with Wynne. Belay there, me hearties!' He tossed the wheel back into its grassy bed.

'You should see inside the house,' she told him. 'It's chock full to the ceilings, all in a muddle. Ernie must have dragged stuff home like a demented magpie. It seems more like an animal den than a human home, although it could be made very comfortable. I'd guess Ernie made a botched attempt at doing it up at some time, knocking out internal walls. He's got some old but good furniture in there but it's all filthy. I'm not surprised he couldn't get any of the lady friends to stay long. Someone could make something of this whole place, though.'

'If that same person was prepared to spend a small fortune.'

When they'd completed their circuit of the cottage Markby frowned and looked up at the sky across which dark silhouettes of clouds were skimming in a race to bring in the rain. 'Kevin'll come back at nightfall.'

'Suppose he doesn't? He was very scared. We ought to tell Amanda Crane.'

'What's she going to do about it at this time of night? You or Wynne can check again tomorrow. If there's still no sign of him, I agree you should tell Crane. But it's too early to go jumping to conclusions. The weather's breaking up and that, if nothing else, will make him seek shelter. He's probably waiting until it's dark and no one likely to come calling on him, as you did!'

Dissatisfied, she tapped her foot on the ground. 'I feel responsible.' She sighed and pushed back a hank of brown hair. 'I meddled, didn't I? I should've done as you said – let sleeping dogs lie.'

'Come on.' He slipped his arm through hers comfortingly. 'You were trying to help the kid. He knows his way around here and the whereabouts of half a dozen places to lie up if he's caught away from home in bad weather. He's a countryman. He'll be all right.'

They walked away, en route passing the pony-trap. Suddenly Meredith's memory sparked. 'Wynne recognised that as Olivia's. I find the sight of it in this state very sad. Old Ernie was a horror, all right.'

'Is this where you got the weed?' He tugged at a spray. 'Yep, that's the villain, all right. But why on earth did the wretched youth do it? *If* he did do it – and all the other things he probably did.'

'I picked my specimen of weed out there in the lane. But there's more than enough of it.' She paused. 'It was a vicious thing to do,' she said emphatically. 'Kevin's ill, Alan. He has to be. We should try to find him.'

'Ill? Possibly, but not necessarily. I'd say a damaged personality, disposed to acts of spite and thoroughly unpleasant.' Markby, gazing at the ragwort in his hand, didn't add that experience told him Kevin was a ticking timebomb who'd progressed from petty vandalism to a serious act such as the pony's death. In time there'd be other acts of criminal damage such as arson and, sooner or later, worse. All who had to deal with young offenders knew the pattern well. He tossed the plant into the gloom. 'Let's go and eat.'

But on arrival at The King's Head, they encountered a hitch in their plans. By now the pub was busy with its evening trade. A buzz of voices could be heard from the bar, even before they pushed open the door. The moment Meredith and Alan stepped inside, however, complete silence fell.

Faces were turned towards them and then quickly away. No one spoke. The atmosphere of hostility was palpable.

'Oh-oh . . .' murmured Meredith with sinking heart.

Mervyn Pollard came out from behind the bar and loped

towards them. The landlord looked both shame-faced and determined.

'Evening, sir.' He ducked his head at Meredith. 'Evening, ma'am. I wonder, sir, if I could have a word with you and your lady outside, maybe, private like.'

They found themselves outside again in the High Street, aware that as soon as the door swung closed behind the three of them, conversation broke out within, twice as lively as before.

'Right, Pollard, what's going on?' Markby asked crisply.

Mervyn shuffled about and ignoring Meredith, addressed his questioner. 'Well, sir, I know now that you're a policeman – quite a top-notch one as I hear. So I'm hoping that you'll understand and not take it amiss. It's the honest truth that it goes against my nature to ask anyone to find somewhere else to do their eating and drinking. I'm a hospitable chap and it makes me feel bad. Besides, business isn't so good that I should turn good custom away. You've been good customers while you've been here, which I appreciate. But after all, The King's Head probably isn't what you'd be used to. Like as not you'd be happier in a fancier place than mine, anyway.' Mervyn, sweating profusely, paused for breath and to observe their reactions.

'We're banned?' Meredith exclaimed.

Mervyn rolled his eyes at her but continued to address himself to Markby. 'I'm in a difficult situation here, sir, and I hope you'll help me out. The thing is, feelings are running high in the village. I don't say old Ernie was the most popular bloke around, but he was a true villager, and everyone knew him. He'd done work for most folk at some time. So they take it personal, almost like he was family. Fact is, as I recall, he was by way of being a second cousin of my old mother's. We all of us have a few relations we're not proud of, don't we? But they're family all the same when something goes wrong.'

'We were in your pub the other day,' Markby remarked, 'when Inspector Crane came in at lunchtime. There was no open animosity then. Rather a jolly atmosphere, if anything. I realise the journalists who were here gave you a rough time, but they've cleared out now.'

'And gone off and printed up a lot of nasty stories,' said Mervyn. There was a silence. They looked steadily at him and he grew more agitated. 'You read 'em. We all did. The whole country did. Them journalists didn't make it all up out of their heads. Someone musta told them old Ernie was done in as a result of some ritual. No one here believes that and we don't like it being put in black and white for the whole world to read, like it was proved! People have been questioned by the police. That might not seem like much to you, but to people here, it's shaming and we all want it stopped. You'll oblige me, sir, if you'd tell all your police friends so. I dare say it makes a good old yarn for the newspapers, but we got to live with it. I'm sorry, you being a copper and all. It puts me in a funny old spot. But I wouldn't want to see you or your lady insulted under my roof. Some of those folk are a mite outspoken. They don't know no better.'

Nervously he added, 'I hope no one is going to object to the renewal of my licence on account of this. But I got a right to say who comes in my pub and, well, you're a temporary visitor, be going home soon. Those others in there are my regulars. They're my living. I don't want to see them all trailing over to Long Wickham to do their drinking. Not but what The Wheatsheaf over there don't sell as decent a pint as I do, but Parsloe villagers has got their principles.'

'Say no more, Pollard,' Markby told him. 'We'll take our custom elsewhere. Although I should make it clear that neither Miss Mitchell nor I spoke to any member of the Press, right?'

'Ah,' said Mervyn, visibly relieved. Almost immediately, he became apprehensive again. 'I'm making no accusations, but it's them, in there. I hope you won't bear a grudge now. I need my licence.'

'Blacklisted by the village pub!' exclaimed Markby, when the landlord had gone. 'I hope this never gets back to regional HQ. I'll never hear the last of it!'

'My fault, I suppose,' said Meredith ruefully. 'Telling Crane about Sadie and going to see the woman myself. But it's unfair to be blamed for the Press reports.'

'Crane had to know. Anyway, I've had about enough of village company and Pollard's menu. There are dozens of nice little places within a ten-mile radius. Let's go back and get the car.'

They found a small, comfortable roadside restaurant some five miles out of the village. It was on the way, so a signpost told them, to Long Wickham.

'I'm almost inclined to go there to The Wheatsheaf, just to spite Pollard,' Markby grinned. 'But I think we'll do better here.'

'Janine Catto comes from Long Wickham,' said Meredith.

'Then we'd probably get the boot there, too. What made her move to Parsloe St John?'

'It's got better amenities.'

Markby grimaced.

'It's true.' Meredith suddenly became Parsloe St John's defender. 'It's got a school for Bruce and Ricky. You know, there was an awful moment when I thought they might be Ernie's kids, in view of what Paul said. But their father seems to have been one of several casual menfriends in

Janine's life. One of them had been to the house and tried to take the video-recorder. She fought him off.'

'A tough one, Janine,' said Markby. 'A matriarch.'

'He'd given her a black eye.'

'Did anyone see *him*? He probably had a few bruises, too.'

'It's not funny, Alan,' she said crossly. But she wasn't of a mind to argue. The interior of the restaurant was cramped but cosy. The tables were prettily laid with crisp white table-linen and the old stone walls blessedly free of touristy gimmicks. No ancient kitchen implements or supposed memorabilia of a lost rural way of life.

The food was good, too. 'Mervyn did us a favour!' said Alan.

They relaxed after the meal with their coffee and smiled at one another across the table in the way of people who are at peace.

The promised rain arrived overnight and by breakfast-time had set into a steady patter of drops against the window-panes. As they drove away from the cottage, they passed Wynne's home and saw that Nimrod sat in the window, a prisoner of the storm. His normal rakish air gained more than a touch of superiority when he saw them out there in the wet while he was inside in the dry. Wynne appeared behind him and waved a farewell.

Sir Basil was waiting for them, togged up ready to face whatever the weather might throw at them. He wore a tweed suit of ancient cut and carried an even more ancient raincoat and a trilby hat. Moira was packing boxes of sandwiches and thermos flasks into a picnic hamper.

'There's nowhere on the motorway but those fast food places. Basil hates them. The seats are always too close to the tables and he can't sit comfortably and, anyway, he doesn't like the food. Hamburgers and things, not his style, and far too many people sitting around him while he's eating.'

'Families with kids, chucking spaghetti around,' said her husband with some emotion. 'Gloomy-looking business blokes working up an ulcer.' He paused and brought out the worst offence, 'Low-alcohol lager . . .'

He and Markby drove off in a cloud of spray.

'It couldn't be a worse day, could it?' said Moira. 'And the weather's been so nice, too. Come and have some coffee and tell me how your investigations into the world of witches are going.'

Some time later, after they'd had coffee and Meredith had brought Moira up to date, they sat before the open fire in silence. The long-case clock in the corner ticked gently, the only sound other than the continual rattle of the rain which continued to trickle down the windows.

Meredith felt obliged to utter a token sympathetic comment with regard to the travellers.

Moira, her mind on other things, murmured, 'Oh, I dare say they'll drive out of it.' She leaned forward, took a piece of wood from the wicker basket in the hearth and added it to the fire. It blazed up, crackling.

'I suppose,' she said, as she straightened up and sat back, 'that the woman Warren does no harm.'

'That depends,' Meredith pointed out, 'on whether you consider the influence she's had on Kevin harmful or not.'

'But she didn't set out to influence him directly, did she? Or not as far as we know. He may not have got the idea of making the dolls from her. Was there a television set in that cottage?'

'The Berrys' place? Yes, there was – is.'

'There you are then. He could have watched some film on

that which showed someone sticking pins in a doll. They show some very odd films late at night.'

'I don't even know,' Meredith confessed, 'that Sadie does that sort of thing. It's all very serious with her. I think she considered the doll aspect frivolous and insulting. Offensive, was the word she used to me.'

'I did ask my friend who has the interest in local history,' Moira went on. 'She lent me this.' She leaned across to the bookcase against the nearby wall and produced a battered volume. 'It's one of these county guides which Victorians liked to produce. I always feel they had a mania for information. It tells you the population of every hamlet, the height of every church steeple and the inscription on every tombstone of note. But they were very good on local history. Unfortunately, I couldn't find out what happened ultimately to the third standing stone – the one which was removed from the fields to a churchyard and then taken away again.'

Moira was leafing through the book. 'But there's a reference to it and even a drawing of it – ah, here it is. Sketched by some other indefatigable visitor in 1721, shortly before it was banished by the parson as unsuitable.'

She handed over the open tome. Beneath the heading, 'Ancient carved stone formerly in the churchyard of St Nicholas-Below-Wold.' The stone, to go by the sketch, had been much like the other two, the Man and His Wife, except that it appeared to have been roughly engraved with a partial set of features, eyes and a mouth. The writer of the book thought it might have been a fertility goddess and the devotion shown to it by parishioners during its time in the churchyard had been in this connection. As the writer primly put it, ' "Countrywomen were wont to touch the stone and place flowers before it, believing in their simplicity, that their childless state might be remedied." '

'One can't be surprised the parson threw it out,' said Moira.

' "The present whereabouts of this ancient stone are unknown," ' read Meredith aloud. ' "But it is believed by some to have been broken up on the orders of the then incumbent, the Reverend J. S. Murgatroyd, but in secret, lest the villagers object." '

She put down the book and smiled. 'He took their local goddess away. I should imagine he was unpopular after that.'

'I think he showed considerable courage,' Moira said. 'He risked being reviled by every childless woman in the village thereafter! In fact, any bad luck striking the community would have been blamed on him. But as a Christian priest, I suppose he felt he had to do something.'

Meredith leaned back on the cushions of her comfortable armchair and watched the pattern of rivulets down the window glass. 'When the weather's like this,' she said, 'it's somehow easier to understand how the old beliefs survived. Before modern roads, this part of the world must have been cut off, especially in the winter, a landscape of secret little valleys and tucked away hamlets, sealed in by snow or mud. They sat indoors on days like this, huddled round the fire, and told the old tales, frightening each other witless with yarns about ghosts and curses and goodness knows what else!'

A gust of wind rattled the windowpane. 'Would you like to stay here tonight?' Moira asked. 'I don't like to think of you on your own in that cottage over at Parsloe – not with all the unpleasant things which have been going on, and that dreadful youth on the loose.'

Kevin was still on Meredith's conscience. She had mishandled the whole thing, ought not to have taken away the dough figures. It could only have served to panic the boy even more. She wondered where he was and hoped against hope that Alan had been right, and bad weather would have sent Kevin scurrying homeward at nightfall.

'I'll be all right. Anyway, if I don't go back, Wynne will be on her own. As long as I'm next door, we can lend one another support in an emergency.'

'Think about it over lunch.' Moira got up. 'I popped a casserole in the oven and I expect it's about ready.'

CHAPTER TWENTY-ONE

Those obstinate questionings . . .
William Wordsworth

WHILE MEREDITH and Moira Newton were lunching off the casserole in comfort, Alan Markby and Sir Basil were sitting cramped and very uncomfortable in a lay-by, munching sandwiches and watching the rain wash over the car windows.

'Not chosen the best day for it,' observed Sir Basil gloomily. He opened up his sandwich and peered into it. 'She forgot the mustard. I can't abide ham without mustard.'

'Mine's got mustard in it,' said Markby unwarily.

He received a suspicious look. 'Then she made up two kinds, with and without. You've got mine.'

Markby apologised, although he wasn't sure for what. It seemed expected of him.

His companion accepted the apology graciously and began to unscrew a vacuum flask. 'This is coffee. Have you got tea?'

Markby checked the other flask, found it held tea, and quickly handed it over before he was accused of unlawfully making free with that as well as with the ham-and-mustard sandwiches.

'I haven't seen old Lawrence for years.' Sir Basil, now that he'd got the tea flask, was able to turn his mind to the object of their journey. 'And it occurs to me that if he ever knew anything, he will have forgotten it by now.'

'He can certainly tell us whether he was ever successful in getting in touch with his sister-in-law after the failed attempt we know about. Did he write again? Perhaps to Behrens, the solicitor? Why did he want to meet Olivia after all those years and such a bitter quarrel?'

'As to the last,' said Sir Basil, 'he might not want to tell us. I can't help feeling we're pushing our noses into his business. Frankly, I'm rather embarrassed about this whole trip.'

Markby grimaced. 'I'm sorry – I didn't realise my enquiries would lead us so far afield.'

'Oh, I'm not grumbling at you, my dear chap. More than willing to set it up for you and help out and I'm rather looking forward to seeing both the Smeatons again. But what happens if he tells us something which upsets the applecart, eh? Do we really want that?'

'We might not want it,' Markby said as rain beat afresh on the car roof. 'But we shan't be able to prevent it.'

They sat sipping tea and coffee respectively in silence for a few minutes.

'Then what shall we do?' asked Sir Basil.

They reached their destination in the early evening. The rain had stopped but dense cloud had descended over the fells, shrouding the high ridges and spectacular scenery and sealing in the travellers at ground level. Huddled long-tailed, black-faced sheep emerged like dirty ghosts from the mist and disappeared again with disconcerting suddenness. Derwentwater lay grey and grumbling in the surrounding leaden gloom, its further shores invisible. It was as if the place rebuffed the intruders, defending its inhabitants against those who would question and pry. Everything added to the unease Markby had felt from the outset. To know Sir Basil shared his misgivings did little to console him.

It wasn't easy in the circumstances to locate the Smeatons who lived outside the town. But at last they found the long, single-storey, stone cottage, pressed against the steep fell behind it, the low-lying mist curling around the ridge-tiles of its slate roof. They tramped up the narrow path and rapped chilled fingers on the door.

A beam of yellow electric light enveloped them, warmth flooded out and a man's voice exclaimed, 'Good Lord, we thought you would have given up! Come in, come in!'

Markby had visualised Lawrence Smeaton as a large, overbearing, blustering figure. In fact Smeaton was a small man, once stocky in build but now showing the frailty of old age. He had kept the military man's bearing and neatness. His tweed jacket, though every bit as old as the one worn by Sir Basil, looked as if it had just come from the dry-cleaner's, as perhaps it had. His trousers had a knife-edge crease to them and his shoes were polished up to a mirror-shine. His wife was a tiny bird of a woman, with expressive features and large dark eyes, peering up at them from beneath a heavy fringe of iron-grey hair.

They both bustled around the new arrivals, ushering them into a cosy sitting room and seating them directly before a roaring fire.

'Very good to see you again, Basil,' said Lawrence, when satisfied his guests were comfortable. 'And to meet you, Markby. I just hope I can be of some help.'

Mrs Smeaton had betaken herself to the kitchen, murmuring about the dinner. From that direction came a beguiling scent of garlic, herbs, shallots, good coffee and wine vinegar . . . the aroma of a French kitchen. Markby, on whose stomach the ham sandwiches lay heavily, wished he hadn't bothered with them, given the prospect of a delicious meal later.

He murmured his gratitude at being allowed to trouble the Smeatons. But it was clear that visitors here were few, and whatever their errand, they were welcome for the novelty's sake. He looked around the room. The furniture was old but comfortable. There were some nice pictures on the walls, local scenes, probably by a local artist. Perhaps Smeaton himself painted? Books were packed along built-in shelving. The firelight gleamed on a profusion of polished brass knick-knacks. On show was the accumulated garnering of a lifetime. Olivia had cleared everything out, keeping nothing. Lawrence and his wife had kept the lot.

'We should have got together before now,' Sir Basil was saying. 'You must come down and stay with us, you and Mireille.'

Lawrence Smeaton moved his hands restlessly. Thickly corded veins ran in ridges beneath the parchment-like skin. He wore a heavy signet ring which had become loose on his finger. Perhaps seeking to control his hands, he placed them together and rubbed them as if to warm them. The friction of dry skin made a soft shu-shurring sound.

'I had planned a trip to your part of the world a few years back. It was when I was attempting to get in touch with Olivia again. I believe you know something about that.' He raised his eyebrows and stopped, Markby was pleased to see and hear, the distracting rubbing of his palms together.

'I understand you wrote to her, brigadier,' he said. 'But that she refused, forgive me if this is personal, refused to see you.'

'I don't mind talking about it!' Lawrence added wryly. 'You seem already well acquainted with most of it!' He gave Markby a very direct look. 'Nothing fishy about her death was there?'

'Not as far as I know,' Markby said truthfully.

'Good. I don't mind telling you that's a relief. I would have come down for the funeral but my wife wasn't well at that time. I felt badly about missing it. I'm old-fashioned enough to believe one ought to show respect towards death. She – Olivia – didn't want to see me when she was alive, of course! But I think she'd have appreciated my turning up at her funeral. I sent a wreath.'

'Do you have any idea why she didn't want to see you?' Sir Basil asked bluntly.

'Still hated my guts, I suppose.' Lawrence was engagingly frank. He got to his feet and proceeded, with obvious approval on Sir Basil's part, towards the whisky decanter on the sideboard. 'Normally,' Smeaton went on, unstopping the decanter, 'one would hesitate to rake up old gossip, disputes, misunderstandings . . . A painful business. But in fact, your visit has come as something of an opportunity to me. You'll take a dram, both of you?'

They would, indeed.

When they were all supplied with a glass, Lawrence resumed his seat. 'The opportunity, if you like, to say some of the things to you which I wanted to say to Olivia, and which I wasn't able to say.' He sipped his whisky. 'I'll have to go back to the beginning.'

Markby settled down. The wind rattled at the panes and the fire spat. An additional presence seemed to have joined them in the room. It, too, was listening with interest. Perhaps Lawrence was to get his opportunity to speak to Olivia, after all.

'She was an extraordinarily beautiful woman.' Lawrence glanced at the door a little guiltily, lest his wife hear him express such unqualified admiration for another. 'But dashed wilful. My brother, Marcus, fell for her like a ton of bricks. He was a fine man.' Lawrence paused, his eyes seeing far away, into the past. 'The marriage was heading for total and utter disaster. Had he not been killed in the war, as he was, they'd have ended in the divorce court, no doubt about it.'

'Clash of personalities?' ventured Markby, as Smeaton had fallen into reverie again.

The brigadier gave a start. 'What? Oh, yes, call it that if you like. There was more to it, of course. I'm not a trick-cyclist.'

'Quite,' said Markby, suppressing a smile.

'Shrinks, good fellows no doubt, seem to explain everything by saying someone's had an unhappy childhood. Olivia didn't. Her parents had adored her and she'd been thoroughly spoilt. As a result, she thought everyone else ought to admire her, too. Most people did. Those who didn't were – run down, squashed flat like a poor hedgehog in the path of a juggernaut! She absolutely dominated everyone around her. Look at that poor little mouse, Violet Dawson. Wouldn't say boo to a goose, carried being self-effacing to an extreme. Not that Dawson wasn't a pretty girl, might even have given Olivia a run for her money in that way. I met her first at their wedding where she acted as bridesmaid. She had dark hair, like Olivia, but was slighter in build. In fact, I thought she was equally attractive, but lacked the personality to go with it. In strength of character she was no match for Olivia. At first I couldn't understand why Olivia wanted to tow the wretched Dawson around in her wake, like a trophy. Unless it was that she wanted a foil for her own brilliance.'

He gave a little snort. 'There used to be a comic song with the refrain, "And her mother came, too", or something like that. Well, when Olivia married Marcus, the Dawson came too. They set up a blessed *ménage à trois*. I thought it rum at the time. But on the other hand, I imagined it was a short-term thing. It was wartime and a lot of people were living in temporary accommodation, bombed out and so on. Friends and family took people in. Olivia had taken in Violet Dawson, fair enough. Besides, single women didn't live alone in those days. It was thought a bit fast. So for Olivia to have given her old schoolchum a home wasn't perhaps as unusual as it would seem nowadays. I soon rumbled that it wasn't quite as simple as that.'

Lawrence shifted in his chair. 'Marcus hadn't twigged what it was all about. I was pretty sure of that. After all, he'd just married her himself and so he didn't think she – well, she might prefer *la* Dawson to him, to put it bluntly. But he did feel the friendship was a bit intense. On the other hand, he supposed that perhaps women did have friendships like that, for all he knew. That's what he said to me. Didn't know much about women, Marcus. Naïve sort of chap in the worldly sense. Brilliant intellect. All set for a fine academic career at the outbreak of war. It was shelved for the duration, as so many people's careers were. But he'd have taken it up again. He had a university post waiting for him. The waste of all that – war is a bloody business but it's the waste that's so particularly criminal.' Lawrence shook his head. 'I'm not just talking of bright fellows like my brother. The loss of any life is a pitiful waste of what might have been. The French writer, Saint-Exupéry, he understood that, if you've ever read him, you'll know that. If you haven't, give it a go.'

Markby ventured to interrupt. 'Why do you think she

married your brother, if you're so certain her heart wasn't in it?'

'Women did get married then,' said Lawrence simply. 'It was the accepted thing. Someone like Olivia, good-looking, educated, plenty of money, known about the social scene, had been presented at court, name linked with several decent chaps before the war – people were beginning to wonder why she'd never made it to the altar.

'Then the war came and people rushed to get married. It was a case of *carpe diem*. You don't hang about if you think you're about to be blown to kingdom come. Young couples dashed to the register office when the chap had a week's leave and made hay while the sun was shining! Girls in Olivia's circle were getting married at the drop of a hat and often to fellows they scarcely knew. Someone like Olivia, who was a driver to the top brass, was surrounded by healthy young chaps living each day as if it were their last, as sometimes it was. She had ample opportunity to get down to Caxton Hall with one of 'em and make it legal. Lots of fellows took a shine to Olivia. She'd encourage them up to a point and then freeze them out when they got too keen.

'In the circumstances, it was seen as playing ducks and drakes with the emotions of young men who were laying their lives on the line for their country – and her reputation suffered. I know it for a fact that a couple of dowagers saw it as their duty to take the girl aside and read her the riot act. In essence, what they told her was, pick one of them, turn up on the day with a corsage pinned to your frock and wearing a hat with a veil – and let other admirers know you were thereafter out of bounds.'

Lawrence gestured widely with one hand. 'Marcus must have appeared like an answer to a prayer. I really believe – and God forgive me if I'm wrong about this! – but I believe she thought Marcus was a good-natured, trusting sort of chap who'd allow her to move Violet into the matrimonial home and never suspect a thing. I don't say she wasn't fond of Marcus. People were . . .'

Again Lawrence fell silent and gazed into the fire. 'Damn fine man,' he muttered. 'Deserved better.' He made a visible effort to pull himself together. 'He never knew. At least, I don't think he guessed and I don't believe anyone told him. I thank God for that, at least.'

Lawrence drew a deep breath. 'But after the war, and his death, Olivia just cast convention to the four winds! For her to set up house with a chum would have been perfectly in order. There were a lot of women left alone in the wake of the war and quite a few of them tackled both the loneliness and the post-war economic austerity by sharing a home and expenses. But Olivia seemed set on going out of her way to let it be known that her relationship with Miss Dawson was far closer than that. People simply didn't wish to know about that, and she insisted that they did. It was unforgivable, not least because poor little Violet Dawson suffered so horribly from the gossip and being cut dead by society hostesses. There was always a strongly selfish side to Olivia or rather, an obliviousness to anyone else's feelings. However, it was up to her what she did with her life. I wouldn't have interfered but for the memory of Marcus.'

Smeaton turned faded but fierce eyes on them. His voice cracking, he said, 'It made my brother appear to have been a damn fool! That made it my business. I couldn't allow people to whisper that poor old Marcus must have been blind not to see what was going on under his nose and all the rest of it! There were even some—' Smeaton faltered, pulled himself together with a visible effort and continued, 'Some who began to suggest that the marriage had been one of pure outward convenience which would allow both parties to pursue their sexual preferences without scandal!'

Markby, who'd suggested something very like that to Wynne and Meredith, had the grace to look mildly embarrassed. Smeaton was fortunately beyond noticing.

'If I could do one thing for my poor brother, it was make his wife behave with respect for his memory in his own country amongst his friends! Protect his reputation from her antics. She might have been expected to have given a thought to protecting it herself! But not Olivia, oh no! I made it clear to her that if she wanted to live in *that* way with *la* Dawson, she wasn't going to do it in England!'

He relaxed and settled back in his chair. 'They went to France. You know what happened. They stayed there for some time and for reasons I don't know, decided to come back. If I had to guess I'd say that Olivia found life in a French village very boring. She was used to London. There would be few opportunities for her to show off, as she so liked to do!' Smeaton snorted.

Then he grew sober. 'There was a fatal accident on the way home, in France. Violet Dawson was killed. Olivia came back alone, set up home in Parsloe St John on her own and just disappeared from all human contact as far as I knew. Years went by. I began to think – one does, as one gets older – that I'd been harsh. Grief for Marcus had made me unjust. After all, she'd suffered a double bereavement, first Marcus, then Violet. I began to think how lonely she must be. I thought I'd try and make it up, put things right. I wrote to her suggesting a meeting. She wouldn't see me. She got her solicitor to write to me making it clear any communication from me would be unwelcome. That was that. One makes mistakes. All of us make mistakes. I made one. Tried to put it right. Wasn't allowed to.'

The three of them sat unspeaking for some time.

Markby asked, 'Did the terms of her will surprise you?'

Lawrence looked up, surprised. 'No – I knew nothing about her will. She and Marcus made wartime wills, as people did, leaving everything to the survivor. I witnessed both those wills, as it happened, so I knew about them. Violet was the other witness, needless to say. Later on, she must have made another. She was a wealthy woman in her own right. Left it to charity, didn't she?'

'Most of it, except a few small bequests, to people who'd worked for her and a couple of others who'd shown her kindness.'

'Glad someone showed her kindness,' Lawrence said. 'I didn't.'

The dinner was all it promised to be. Aromatic celery soup, pepper steaks with *sauce béarnaise*, a delicious apricot tart. It wasn't until after dinner, as they relaxed around the fire with a liqueur, and Mrs Smeaton had joined them, that talk turned again to Olivia.

'I met her two or three times,' Mireille Smeaton said. 'She was a very –' She waggled her fingers. '– A very spiky person. You couldn't discuss things with her. She would say, she would do this, or that – and her mind was made up. I was sorry for her then because she was very unhappy. Something had gone wrong for her. I tried to talk to her, be friends, she didn't want that. I don't like to think of her, all those years alone in that great house in Parsloe St John. It was so strange, I've often wondered why she didn't drive the car any more.'

'Oh, my word, yes,' her husband said. 'Demon driver. Violet's death must have shaken her confidence.'

'That isn't what I meant by strange,' said Mireille.

Markby's spine tingled. There was a draught blowing at the back of his neck. Maybe a draught, maybe imagination, the knowledge that Mireille was about to tell them something which perhaps, it might be better they didn't know.

'I read the obituary,' Mireille said. 'I cut it out of the newspaper and kept it. It said she used to drive about the country in a pony and trap.'

'That's right,' said Markby. 'The last pony was retired and kept as a pet. When it — it died, she had it buried in its paddock.'

Mireille was shaking her head. 'But she told me once — I am sure of it, I remember it quite distinctly — she told me she was allergic to horses.'

'What?' That was from Sir Basil. He's been dozing off by the fire and now jerked awake. 'What was that, Mireille, are you sure?'

'Yes, I'm sure! One day, some friends wanted to make up a party to go to some event with horses there, some show-jumping and dressage . . . not the races. I forget quite what now. Anyhow, I thought, maybe Olivia would come. She said no, no, it was impossible. Just to be around horses, to be near them, she came out in a terrible rash.' Mireille rubbed her arm in demonstration. 'An allergy. And it wasn't just an excuse not to go out with us. Her allergy was how she began her interest in motorcars. Horses, they brought her out in big lumps, her eyes itched and watered, everything. Really unpleasant. I simply can't imagine her driving a pony and trap.'

CHAPTER TWENTY-TWO

Light thickens . . .
Wm Shakespeare

THE WEATHER had cleared in the afternoon and allowed Meredith and Moira Newton to go for a walk. It hadn't been a particularly pleasant outing, wet underfoot and dank. They came back and sat before the fire to toast crumpets and drink tea.

A phone call around six informed them (a) that Sir Basil was wedged inconveniently in a wayside public phone booth; (b) that the aforesaid booth was in the neighbourhood of Keswick; (c) it was almost impossible to see a hand in front of your face out there; and (d) after visiting the Smeatons, the travellers' intention was to find a small hotel and return the following day.

'All's going well,' said Moira, returning to the fireside. 'We can forget about them and make ourselves snug.'

The result of all this was that Meredith left the Newtons' home rather later than she'd intended. The original invitation to lunch had somehow spread itself to reach eight-thirty on a dull night. As she prepared to leave, Moira had again urged her to stay over.

Barely a mile into the drive homewards and Meredith was

reflecting that she might have done better to have accepted the offer. Though she'd enjoyed more than enough generous hospitality from Moira that day and, in any case, should Alan phone the cottage that night, she would like to be there to answer. There was also Wynne to consider. Wynne was all alone in the pair of cottages and was probably keeping an anxious eye on her window for the return of Meredith's car.

There was no other traffic on the narrow country road. Everyone was sensibly indoors. Cloud cover had brought evening gloom forward, something for which she ought to have allowed and hadn't. Meredith reflected that the nights were drawing in and the Indian summer they'd been enjoying was an illusion. They were on the threshold of a brief autumn. The leaves, just beginning to turn colour, had been brought down during the day in quite some quantity by the rain, and a good stormwind would shake out many more.

The high camber of this winding country backroad had caused rainwater to drain down to either side where it lay up in wide puddles. It forced her to drive on the dry central strip, watching out for traffic approaching in the opposite direction. She met none and began to wonder if the road ahead was passable. It ran past the Standing Stones and in that area, as she recalled, there was a permanent water splash across the road. The addition of the rainfall might have turned it into a regular flood and she could find herself obliged to turn back.

The failing light played tricks in this deserted countryside. Wayside trees seemed taller, denser, their outstretched arms hovering over her car as she passed beneath. The fields were hazy with a gathering mist. Time seemed strangely out of sync so that she had to keep looking at the dashboard clock. The wildlife had vanished. She felt herself eerily alone and was unduly relieved when she saw, walking along the middle of the road ahead of her, a solitary pedestrian.

He was a countryman by his clothing, sturdily indifferent to poor weather conditions. He wore some kind of waterproof jacket, far too large, and clutched it around him as if he sheltered something beneath it. A woollen hat was pulled down over his ears. She didn't know where he might have come from, out here, far from habitation. Perhaps from a farm. She tapped the horn by way of warning.

He had already heard the car's approach behind him, and begun to move over. At the toot, he scrambled up the bank. There was something furtive about him, his movements less those of a man avoiding traffic than of a man avoiding observation. It occurred to her he might be a poacher.

Curious, as she passed by the spot, she looked in the mirror to catch a reflected front view of the figure high on the bank. At the same time, he raised his head and looked after the car.

It was Kevin Berry.

He had recognised her. As Meredith slewed to a halt, he leapt up over a low stone wall into the field beyond and disappeared. She didn't hesitate, but threw open the car door and jumped out – straight into an expanse of wayside puddle.

Cursing beneath her breath, Meredith extricated herself and scrambled inelegantly up the bank after him. The long wet grass wrapped itself disagreeably around her legs. She reached the top and found her way barred by the ancient dry-stone wall. Less athletic than Kevin, she sought for a toe-hold and managed to hoist herself over it. She could see Kevin well ahead of her by now, in the middle of the field, running awkwardly across the rough turf, one arm swinging free and the other pressed against his chest, clasping fast the unseen object beneath his jacket.

She put her hands to her mouth and yelled, 'Kevin!' But the wind snatched her words away. She set off in pursuit, probably a fruitless endeavour, but if she could only get a little closer, she might be able to make him hear. She felt a personal responsibility for his plight and, if nothing else, could at least offer him a lift home in her car to spare him a long, wet walk.

The terrain wasn't designed for sprinting. The pair of them struggled along unable to make any kind of rapid progress. Feet sank into ruts and twisted or even broken ankles were threatened. Unable to gain any real purchase, each spring forward was stillborn. Running strides became a series of abbreviated lolloping gambols like those of new lambs trying out their wobbly legs. The muscular effort needed to stay in this comic cuts race was unbelievable.

Once or twice Kevin looked back, his whole attitude one of panic. When he did, she shouted his name and beckoned to him. He only plunged on. She couldn't abandon him in his terror. She had to explain to him that he could trust her, that they all wanted to help him.

They had crossed most of the open field and were nearing a patch of trees. Meredith realised this was where Kevin was headed. He was, in the hunting phrase, going to earth. If he did, she wouldn't find him again easily. She redoubled her efforts, but an agonising stitch began to announce its presence in her side, her lungs ached, her heart threatened to burst out of her chest and her legs were weakening.

The terrain was taking its toll of Kevin, also. Without warning he stumbled and almost fell. He stopped, gathering breath.

'Kevin, wait! It's all right, there's nothing to be afraid of!'

But he set off again, making his way doggedly towards those trees. There was something familiar about them.

Suddenly, she realised where she was. The Standing Stones were in the field just beyond the line of trees. Further along, at the far end of the copse, was the spot where she and Alan had hidden to watch the dancers around the bonfire.

She had managed somehow to close the gap on Kevin, but too late. He disappeared into the copse and was lost.

Meredith panted to a halt, doubled over drenched in sweat, hands on knees, struggling to control her breath. She might as well turn back. On the other hand, he was in there, somewhere, and now she knew more or less where they were, she was disinclined to give up the chase. She made her way, at a more sedate pace, to the trees and paused there by the first creeper-swathed trunks.

'Kevin, can you hear me?'

It was very dark among the trees and she didn't fancy going in after him. She strained her ears. There was a sharp crack, as of a snapped twig.

'Kevin? There's nothing to be afraid of. You can come out. I'll take you home in my car.' Silence. 'I'm sorry if I gave you a fright at the cottage. I didn't mean to. Kevin?'

She moved forward uncertainly, into the first line of trees. Gloom enfolded her, as suddenly as if someone had switched off the dim light outside. There was a path, wending a narrow way between undergrowth and lined with briars and nettles. Her foot kicked against a fallen branch. She pulled it aside and tore off a piece to use as a guide. Holding it ahead of her to locate bramble sprays across her route or any other obstacle, she made her way on, pausing at intervals to listen.

'Kevin, if you can hear me, please come out. I can take you home. It may rain again. Did you go home last night? You can't stay out here, living rough.'

A rustle away to her left. Perhaps Kevin, perhaps water falling from the overhead branches, perhaps an animal.

Damn kid. Let him stay there. There was light of a sort ahead. She'd made her way through the band of trees and was about to come out into the field on the other side. She stepped out thankfully, glad to be free of the claustrophobic tree presence.

And there, would you believe it? There was Kevin, walking nonchalantly across the field ahead of her. He had assumed she wouldn't follow him into the trees and that she'd turned back. Considering himself free of pursuit, he wasn't even hurrying.

He was making a fool of her. Meredith set off after him grimly, her footsteps silent on the wet turf.

Kevin had no idea she was behind him until he had almost reached the two stones. Then, either sixth sense or a faint squelch of sodden earth alerted him. He whirled round. His mouth fell open. His face, in the half-light seemed to have an eerie white sheen on it. He fumbled beneath his coat and brought out the object he'd carried so carefully shielded.

Poacher she'd thought Kevin to be when she'd spotted him walking ahead of her along the road, and she should have realised that poachers had guns.

Meredith had frozen in the position she held at the appearance of the sleek metal barrel. They were about ten feet apart and she could see that the gun was an expensive rifle of what appeared, to her untutored eye, to be an up-to-date model. She supposed it must have belonged to Ernie, the type of man – as Alan had rightly guessed – who kept unlicensed televisions and guns and untaxed rattletrap vehicles. To turn to poaching would be natural for such a man. For Ernie and the lad it had probably been a profitable sideline, to judge by such a modern weapon, lightweight and accurate.

Kevin was holding it in both hands. The muzzle, she was relieved to see, pointed downward. He spoke, in a high-pitched, terrified voice, 'Don't you come no nearer!'

'Look, Kevin,' Meredith said as reasonably as she could in the circumstances. 'You know who I am and that I'm harmless. I'm sorry I frightened you at your cottage, but you can come home now. I know what you did in our kitchen and at Mrs Carter's and Armitage's. Inspector Crane knows, too. But we understand. We know that whatever reason you had, it made you see us as enemies. But we aren't your enemies. No one means you any harm, Kevin. We all want to help you. It's getting late, and dark and it's very cold now and will rain again before dawn. My car is just down the road back there—' Unwisely she lifted her hand to point back the way they'd come.

The barrel of the gun jerked upward. 'Don't you come near me. I'll shoot!' She could see his ugly broken teeth as he spoke. The coat he wore was much too big, its volume indicating it was lined with poacher's pockets.

'All I want to do is help you!' Meredith repeated more urgently.

Kevin's face twisted into a sneer. 'No one ever helped me!'

'We all realise you're upset about your father's—'

'He wasn't my father!' The words were shouted out with unexpected violence. The gun barrel jerked again, veered back and forth and then, thank goodness, drooped earthward. She realised he'd momentarily forgotten he held the weapon.

But the words had intrigued her. 'Not your father? I'm sorry, I was told Ernie was – was your dad.'

'I never had no dad. Don't know who he is. My ma, she was in the club with me already when she moved in with Ernie. He told me so, Ernie did. Over and bloody over, right from when I was little till the end, before he died. "You're a bastard and no one knows whose", that's what he used to say. I was what she brought with her – and left behind when she left!'

There was such a heartfelt anguish in his voice as he shouted out the final words, an abandoned child's years of agony and despair finding expression, that Meredith automatically moved forward, her hands held out to console.

Kevin immediately took a step back and warned, 'Stay there!'

'I'm staying here, Kevin. Put the gun down.'

He gave a cunning, wild grin. 'No – I'm in charge now, ain't I? I give the orders and you do like I say. I was never in charge before. I was just Berry's lad. He treated me like dirt, did Ernie. Knocked me all over the house just for the hell of it, when I was just a nipper – no reason for it. Because he didn't like me – and he did like knocking me around. She never stopped him, while she was there – and then she went.' Kevin frowned. 'Some people, they leaves behind old clothes and things they don't want no more. She left me. She was a real bitch. But they were all the same. All of 'em has always treated me like I was a piece of rubbish.'

'I'm sorry . . .' It sounded weak but what could she say?

'Ernie carried on kicking me around right to the end.' Kevin had a grievance and finding his voice, meant her to know all of it. 'I allus had the bruises – but no one done nothing. No one took me away from him.'

The broken teeth, broken no doubt by a blow from Ernie's fist at some time past, flicked into view as Kevin's mouth twisted in that sneer again. 'There were plenty as knew and did nothing. People as could have helped me, but they didn't want to know. She could've helped, old Ma Carter. Likes doing good works, don't she? Goes round collecting for the church? Never did nothing about me. Or him, the vet. Sitting there in his big house, with his big car . . . He knew. Never did nothing. That bugger, Crombie – worst of the lot. He saw Ernie hit me over at his yard once, and he laughed, Crombie did. He laughed.'

Meredith thought, *this is awful* . . . as it was. A catalogue of lifelong abuse. Kevin was about nineteen, she supposed. Nineteen years of beatings and curses and taunts about his origins. Long enough indeed for people to have noticed. But no one had wanted to become involved. They assumed the boy was Ernie's son because his mother had been living at the cottage when he was born. Besides, Ernie, in his way, was a useful person about the place, the man you could get to fix anything. A tough character, too, not easily tackled.

'You wanted revenge,' Meredith said quietly. 'That's why you pulled up Wynne's plants and ruined Armitage's Range Rover. You even poisoned that pony. That was wrong, Kevin. That was harming another living creature which hadn't possibly harmed you. It was only a poor beast in a field.'

'It was hers,' said Kevin sullenly. 'The old lady's. She was no better than the others. She could've helped. Ernie was afraid of her. She was a toff, spoke posh. She could've told him to let me alone and he'd have listened. She never did anything.'

'Kevin . . .' A night breeze had sprung up and ruffled Meredith's hair. It was twilight now, and Kevin's features indistinct. The words stuck in her throat but had to be spoken, even though she dreaded the answer. 'Kevin, did you push Mrs Smeaton down that staircase?'

'What?' He sounded puzzled, then burst out angrily. 'Of course I never did!'

'Thank God,' Meredith said. 'Because she did try and help you, Kevin. She left you money in her will.'

'Two hundred quid,' Kevin's voice came bitterly across the intervening space, issuing from his silhouette etched against the deepening purple of the sky. 'Two hundred sodding quid. I never got it. Ernie had it. Took it off me. He'd got a new fancy woman over Long Wickham way and he spent it all on her. I could have left him with that money, gone off somewhere on my own. But he took it off me. I swore I'd get even with him for that.'

'And you did, you killed him.' Meredith drew a deep breath. 'You did, didn't you, Kevin? But any court would take a lenient view. You were horribly provoked.'

'You're potty, you are!' Kevin shrieked, his anger turning against her. 'Why do you keep on about me killing people? I never killed no one. I never killed Ernie. I was too bloody scared of him. He was already dead when I found him, by that tree. Someone had been there before me and cut his throat. Seems like someone else wanted to get even with him! Had done, too. But I thought, I won't be cheated out of my revenge. I went and got a big knife we used for pruning back bushes in the gardens round Rookery House. We kept it in a shed there. I hacked off his head.'

Kevin chuckled, a mirthless, vindictive sound which made Meredith's blood run cold. 'I cut it off and I put it in the vet's garden, in them rose bushes. The vet's old woman, she's always swanking about them roses. Bet it give her a fright.'

It was a mind, as Markby had said, completely twisted out of true, warped beyond repair. But it needn't have been. Not if just one person had reported the abuse the child was suffering at Ernie's hands in that lonely cottage – and made sure that social services, or the police or the NSPCC or anyone had followed up the complaint, taken the child into care.

But people had turned their eyes aside. Incomers like Wynne and Rory had considered it a matter for the true villagers to sort out among themselves, knowing how resentfully outside criticism was received. The natives, for their part, considered that family matters belonged in the family and 'the social' had no business to interfere.

There was something more important to get straight now. If Kevin was speaking the truth – and she was sure he was – then he had found Ernie dead, murdered by someone else. Who?

It was then she remembered something she'd quite forgotten. Finding Ernie as she had, running to tell Alan, to fetch the police, making statements, the horror of it had completely erased all memory other than that of the mutilated corpse. Shock had slammed shut a window in her mind which now re-opened, allowing her to see the whole scene clearly.

She saw herself, walking up the drive of Rookery House that dreadful afternoon. The building lay ahead of her, graceful in its Georgian proportions. All along the upper-floor windows and shutters stood open, just as she'd seen them then. She recalled thinking to herself that someone had been there to air the place out. All this she'd forgotten. Now she remembered not only this, but what it signified.

From the upper floor, the opener of the windows would have been able to see right across the garden wall into the paddock. Could easily have distinguished the unique figure of Ernie, making his way towards the chestnut tree and settling down for his nap.

Only one person in the village held the keys to Rookery House and visited it regularly as caretaker. One person by her own admission was in the habit of opening up the upper windows now and again, to air the place out. Janine Catto.

Janine Catto of the mysterious black eye. A black eye supposedly given to her by an ex-boyfriend. Alan had asked, when Meredith told him the story, whether anyone had seen the boyfriend in question. Well, had anyone? Or had he come and gone, elusive as a will-o'-the-wisp, seen only by Janine? Unlike Ernie, always about the village and notoriously free with his fists . . .

'Kevin,' Meredith said huskily. 'We must go back to Parsloe St John. It's very important. We've got to phone Inspector Crane and tell her how you found Ernie.'

'And tell her I done him in, as well, I suppose?' Kevin shouted. He was moving, lifting the gun.

'No – I know you didn't—'

'You said just now I did. You said I killed Ernie and the old lady. According to you, I bloody well killed everyone!'

'Yes, but I was wrong and now I know who did kill Ernie.'

'You're not going nowhere.' Kevin's voice was hoarse and ugly. 'You're not going to tell people lies about me! You keep reckoning I killed them people. Perhaps I oughta kill someone? Perhaps I oughta kill you!'

In the distant sky above Parsloe St John, there was a sudden flash and a rumble. In the brief moment of light, Meredith saw Kevin clearly. He was just in front and a little to one side of the Standing Man. He was holding the rifle to aim point-blank at her. His face was white, eyes staring – but not at her. At something behind her which had been revealed to him in the crackle of the lightning.

'Don't be silly, Kevin,' said a familiar, lilting female voice.

Meredith, skin a-tingle with the electricity in the air and with a sense of something she didn't understand, managed to turn her head. A second flash of light across the sky revealed Sadie Warren, standing a few feet away, prosaically clad in a yellow plastic mackintosh and sou'wester, with brim turned up above the forehead, and down around the nape of the neck.

'Don't you go coming anywhere near me!' Kevin called out shrilly.

'Put the gun down on the ground, Kevin.' Sadie's voice, though even and not raised, carried a ring of authority. 'It's no use to you now. No use at all against *me*.'

'I never done nothing to you!' Kevin whimpered.

'But you have, Kevin. You've been very naughty. Playing with dough and making those dolls, meddling in things you don't understand. Coming here with a gun, threatening violence. Here, in this sacred place! That's more than foolish, Kevin, it's wrong! You're desecrating this ancient place of worship and I can't allow it.'

Kevin mumbled something to the effect he hadn't meant to come here, but Meredith has chased him all over the sodding field. He finished by retaliating, 'How did you get here, anyway?'

'I came here, Kevin, because I was drawn here.' Sadie's plump form floated nearer, emerging like a yellow plastic balloon from the gloom at Meredith's elbow. 'Drawn here because the sacred stones are in danger. Now I am here, and you must do as I say. Put down the gun.'

Kevin uttered a stifled sob. In a final blaze of lightning across the sky, they saw him turn to run. But instead of fleeing, he let out a great shriek of terror, leapt into the air as if he'd received an electric shock, twisted and fell. There was a deafening roar as the gun went off.

CHAPTER TWENTY-THREE

Let's choose executors and talk of wills.
Wm Shakespeare

'I CAN'T say what happened,' Meredith said. 'I can only describe what I saw and explain what I think happened.'

'Fair enough,' said Rory Armitage.

They were crowded into Wynne's sitting room. The impetus for the gathering had come from Markby.

'We've leaving on Sunday,' he'd explained to Meredith. 'And I don't want to leave a lot of rumour and misunderstanding behind. There's been altogether too much of that already in this village. I want to clear the air, once and for all, and set the record straight. We'll need Wynne's help. I want everyone there and I fancy that by now they are all suspicious of me. Burnett certainly wouldn't accept any invitation from me directly. But he was Olivia's doctor and a beneficiary under her will and he was with Rory when Ernie's head was discovered. I want him to hear it, too. So the invitation will have to come from Wynne, if she wouldn't mind.'

'I'm sure she won't,' said Meredith. 'She's itching to hear all the details.'

So here they were, Rory and his wife, Meredith, Alan,

Wynne herself and Tom Burnett. Mrs Burnett had been invited but had declined, giving a teething infant as her reason. Max Crombie who'd also been asked was the other absentee. 'Got a job on!' he'd said.

Two days of rain had cleared the skies and the sun had returned, a little more watery and faint, but still pleasant enough to give a pale glow through the window. Basking in it sprawled Nimrod, his front paws tucked tidily under his chest and his back legs spread out sideways. With his one whole ear cocked for any interesting sound in the room, his eyes watched the world go by outside. From time to time his half-tail beat on his blanket as a dog or bird or – anathema – another cat crossed his vision.

Wynne's wine had been brought out, tasted more than once, and declared more than satisfactory, also more than once. Under its influence they'd settled back in their chairs and were rehashing recent events, and especially the unexpected ending to affairs.

'Kevin, poor kid, was already in a blind panic when Sadie popped up and terrified him half to death. She did look quite extraordinary, not a bit witch-like really. She looked more like a deep-sea fisherman, all rigged out like that in yellow oilskins!' Meredith recalled.

She thought about it for a moment. 'But she still scared me for a few minutes because I had no idea she was behind me. Poor Kevin quite lost his few remaining wits. He really believed she was gifted with some magical power or other. What with that, the darkness, the lightning and everything else, his nerves were strung like piano wires. As I see it, he stepped back and turned to run, forgetting how close he was to the Standing Man. His shoulder brushed against the stone. But to Kevin, his mind in a whirl and filled with superstitious notions, it was as if the stone had moved and touched *him.* He jumped the way you do if you think you're alone and someone touches your shoulder, stumbled, fell and that was that. He just lay there, shaking and sobbing. Sadie picked the gun up. I hauled Kevin to his feet and brought him back in my car. Nothing would have persuaded him to get in Sadie's car. He kept gibbering about the stone moving and how he hadn't meant to do any harm to the sacred place.'

'Poor kid?' growled Markby. 'He might have blown your head off your shoulders.'

Meredith took the philosophical view. 'He didn't, so why worry? Unfortunately, the blast did chip a piece out of the other stone – the Wife. Sadie's terribly upset and I don't suppose English Heritage will be very pleased about it.'

'But what made the Warren woman go to the site?' Gill Armitage asked. 'I've always found her off-putting. Her eyes always look fixed, her expression miles away, as if she were in communication with some force the rest of us can't see, as if she's, well, permanently in receipt of spirit messages.'

'Spot on!' Meredith agreed. 'That's just what she insists it was, a sort of spirit message sent by the stones which were in danger. They were right too, in the event. Sadie leapt in her car and came careering through the night to protect the sacred site. That's her story and she's sticking to it. The truth may be that she came out there to carry out some ritual and just stumbled on Kevin and me. If so, she's not saying. I'll go along with the sixth-sense story. She definitely operates on a different plane to the rest of us. It may be self-induced and totally the product of her imagination, but they do say there are more things in heaven and earth than we know of.'

'Bunkum,' said Alan, the unbeliever, sturdily. 'The woman's got it down to a fine art, I'll grant you. But mumbo-jumbo, all the same.'

'My view is that she can believe what she likes,' said Gill Armitage. 'But if there are strange forces out there at work, hidden from most of us, I'm quite happy to stay in ignorance. One oughtn't to meddle.'

'Absolutely!' approved Tom Burnett. 'The effect of some of this stuff on weak minds can be catastrophic. I know of case histories where subjects have got involved in strange cults and gone right off their rockers. I wouldn't say no to another drop of your home-brew, Wynne. It's topnotch stuff!'

'Here's a peach liqueur.' Wynne unstopped a fresh bottle. 'This is a new one for me and I'd value your opinion.'

Glasses were stretched out as everyone gladly volunteered to give an opinion. The supernatural, as a topic, was abandoned, replaced by murmurs including: 'Oh, lovely, you must tell me how you made it' (from Gill); 'To be honest a tad sweet for my taste, but very pleasant' (Alan); and 'Blimey O'Riley, this stuff's got a kick!' (Rory).

'Poor Kevin,' Wynne picked up the thread of the conversation again. 'He was quite right in everything he said to you, Meredith. We did all know that Ernie led him a dog's life.'

'I didn't,' said Tom Burnett immediately.

'That's because you've not been here long enough and didn't have anything to do with the Berrys.' Rory drained his peach liqueur. 'But Wynne's right. Not that I knew just how bad it was in the early days. I had nothing to do with Kevin when he was a kid. But I suppose I'm making excuses because I could have worked out that if Ernie was beating him up at nineteen, it was something that had gone on for years. It was clear he *was* knocking young Kev around. He was always to be seen around the village with a black eye or split lip. Besides, you could tell Ernie was the type, a thug. I never liked the fellow. As for Kevin, it's my belief he troubled the village's communal conscience. So many people who'd passed by on the other side and felt uneasy about it. The way he was always called "Berry's lad" and never given a name. It dehumanised him, made him less of an individual and ignoring him less of a crime. "Berry's lad" was like saying, "Berry's van" or "Berry's anything else". It helped people deal with their bad consciences.'

Rory gazed into his glass. 'I used to console myself by thinking that if he was unhappy, then heck, he was old enough to leave Ernie and strike out on his own.'

'He couldn't do it,' said Tom Burnett firmly. 'A person who's been abused all his life like that, can't break free. His self-confidence has long been destroyed. Continual abuse becomes a habit – the abused become totally dependent on the abuser. It takes some quite significant change in circumstances to prod someone like that into rebelling. Finding Ernie dead released all the boy's pent-up hatred and longing for revenge. But prior to that, there's no reason why it shouldn't have gone on indefinitely.'

'Right enough,' Rory sighed agreement. 'Kevin couldn't walk away from Ernie, even when Olivia left him the money to do it. Do you think that was in her mind? She intended to enable Kevin to break free? If so, she miscalculated. All Ernie had to do was lay claim to it and the kid surrendered it, with hate in his heart, but powerless to resist. The poor little bugger ruined my car, but I can't say I can find it in me to blame him. He hated us all and had good reason.'

'Not Olivia,' said Wynne obstinately. 'He shouldn't have done that to the pony. I do hope it's true that he didn't push her down the stairs.' She glanced surreptitiously at Markby. Her expression begged him to say it hadn't been Kevin's doing.

'He says he didn't,' Markby said. 'No one can prove otherwise. I don't think he did, for what it's worth.'

Wynne looked relieved but Markby almost immediately destroyed her composure, saying, 'Janine might have had a motive, of course, if she'd known about the small legacy due to her under the will. But it's a long shot and difficult to prove.'

'Surely not!' protested Wynne. 'It was so little money and her job as housekeeper was ultimately worth more.' She shook her head and a hairpin fell out of the twisted topknot and tinkled down on to the table. 'But then, whoever would have believed she killed Ernie?' There was an accompanying murmur of assent.

Markby nodded. 'Oh, she killed Berry, right enough. The police had no trouble breaking her story of the visiting boyfriend she claimed had blacked her eye. They searched her place and found the knife which she used for the deed in the knife drawer in her kitchen. She'd washed it, but it's an old knife and there's a gap where the blade goes into the haft. Blood had seeped in there and she'd missed it.

'As to how and why . . .' Markby hunched his shoulders. 'Janine needed money. She worked for Olivia and did other odd jobs, but there's not many opportunities to earn money in a place like Parsloe St John. There's always one way, of course, in any community – and there's no doubt Janine was the village's good-time girl. Ernie was one of her regular customers. Market forces prevail in prostitution as in any other business. Parsloe isn't the hub of the universe and Janine's fee for services rendered was modest. But it all helped out her finances. Incidentally, a thought which occurred briefly to Meredith and might occur to others, Berry wasn't the father of her children. I'd better make that quite clear. We've traced the father and he's living two hundred miles away. He hasn't visited the children since they were babies. Janine received no contribution towards the boys' upbringing from him. She was obliged to do whatever she could.

'Then Olivia died. I agree Janine had little motive to harm Olivia, even if she knew of the will. Olivia's death was a big blow to her. She lost a steady job. Olivia had left her two hundred pounds – but also two hundred each to Ernie and Kevin. Ernie promptly took Kevin's and added it to his own. He'd got a new lady-friend over at Long Wickham, as Kevin knew, and he spent most of the money having a good time with his new love. What he forgot was that Janine comes from Long Wickham. Her mother still lives there and kept Janine in touch with what goes on in that village. She heard about Ernie visiting someone there and money being spent in pubs, on trips into town, of the lady in question parading new clothes and a lot of cheap jewellery around the place.

'Janine was furious. When Ernie hadn't much money, he'd come to her for a good time, and paid little enough for it. Now he was in funds so, as Janine saw it, he ought to spend it on her. There was nothing the Long Wickham woman could do for Ernie Janine couldn't supply. She felt he'd cheated her by taking his business elsewhere. Moreover, it hurt her pride. By his action he'd suggested that she, Janine, was only to be resorted to when a fellow was desperate and broke! I'd venture to suggest no woman likes it to be thought she comes cheap!'

'Dangerous ground, old chap,' warned Rory.

'Oy!' said his wife.

'On the fateful day,' Markby went on hastily, 'Janine had gone to Rookery House early in the morning to open up the place and let some air through. From the upper window, she saw Ernie crossing the paddock. He'd been living life to the full with his new love, had a hangover and was tired. He sought out a nice quiet spot he knew of, and settled down under the old chestnut tree for forty winks.

'Out of the blue, Janine appeared full of resentment, and started haranguing him about her grievances. Ernie wasn't a man to waste words on argument. He lashed out with his fist and struck her in the eye. Janine retreated and went home, filled with even greater rage and longing for revenge. At midday she returned in order, she says, to close up the windows again. She was afraid Ernie might still be on the premises and for protection – her story, at least – took a sharpened kitchen knife. She crept down to the paddock to see if Ernie was indeed still around, and what she saw was Ernie fast asleep under the tree. "Dead to the world" is the apt phrase she used. She says, she doesn't know what came over her. She took out the knife—'

Markby paused. Wynne said 'Ugh!' and Armitage muttered, 'Woman's barmy. Didn't she think about her kids?'

'She didn't think she'd be found out and charged. Murderers never do.' Markby gave a dry smile. 'In fact, she might have got away with it. But as she returned to the house after killing him, to close the windows as intended, she saw Kevin coming. She ran away and hid. She saw that Kevin was making for the paddock. He was looking for Ernie and he knew the chestnut tree was a favoured spot. Janine scampered off home in panic, leaving the windows open. Kevin found Ernie and we know what he did.'

'Yes,' Gill Armitage said in a tight little voice.

'All right, love . . .' Rory patted her arm.

'Perhaps the wound in Ernie's neck prompted Kevin in his actions,' Markby observed. 'Or it may even have called to mind the pub sign which would have been familiar to Kevin, and the pub itself, associated in his mind with Ernie.'

'So die all tyrants!' declaimed Rory suddenly. He added more mildly, 'Perhaps something like that was going through the kid's twisted brain.'

'Perhaps. At any rate, the cuts made by the larger knife, disguised those made by the smaller. Post-mortem examination identified the slashes as made by a broad blade. As the amputation was carried out only perhaps twenty minutes or so after Janine's lethal action – she saw Kevin arriving, remember – it appeared to be part and parcel of the same attack. There was no reason for the investigators to think that a hand other than the murderer's had done it. It was assumed the killer had begun to dismember the body but had abandoned the attempt after severing the head. A broad blade, fitting the wounds, was found with traces of Ernie's blood on it. No one looked for another knife. Why should they?'

He might have added, but didn't, that over-anxiousness on the part of Inspector Crane to find and identify the murder weapon had possibly contributed to the mistake. With the investigating officer standing at his side urging him to agree the machete blade matched the severed edges of flesh and bone, the pathologist had looked no further. Hadn't the path lab identified the blood as Ernie's?

Markby reflected briefly on a conversation he'd had with Crane the day before. She had been embarrassed and angry with herself over what she saw as incompetence on her own part. In vain he'd assured her that everyone makes mistakes and the great thing was to learn from them.

Her face white with passion, she'd informed him she had done the one thing she'd always sworn she'd never do. She'd allowed herself to become fixed on a theory and ignored any possible alternative.

Since she was in no mood to be consoled, he'd left her to

it. She would get over it, or not, as the case might be. He hoped she did. She was a good officer who had the makings of an exceptional one. But the learning process could be a painful one.

In the silence which had fallen in Wynne's sitting room, Nimrod eased himself to his feet and stretched, arching his back. He then turned to face in the other direction and settled down again. The summary executioner of numerous small mammals and birds, no one had ever charged him with misdemeanour – except for the occasional minor fuss over a bird. Humans didn't mind his killing mice but they were confusingly sentimental about creatures with feathers.

'What will happen to Bruce and Ricky?' Wynne asked. 'They aren't exactly little darlings, but this is a dreadful thing to happen to them.'

'Janine's mother has them with her over at Long Wickham. She's quite a young woman and well able to take care of them.' Markby smiled. 'Don't worry, Wynne.'

'I wasn't thinking of volunteering, you know . . .' Wynne said meekly. 'But after the business with Kevin, one feels that one oughtn't to turn one's head aside a second time.'

She turned to Meredith. 'Then you were right all along, Meredith. You said right at the outset it would all prove to be connected with Olivia's will and it was. Janine and Kevin both bore grudges against Ernie for his use or misuse of his legacy and Kevin's which he'd stolen. Olivia must have meant so well, leaving a sum to her housekeeper and her gardeners.'

'I think,' Meredith said slowly, 'that Olivia wasn't a terribly intelligent woman. She should have left Janine twice as much as she left the Berrys. She'd surely earned it, working on a regular basis in that house, cooking meals, running and fetching. If Janine had just received a little more, she'd have worried less about what the Berrys did with their share.'

There was the sound outside the cottage of a car drawing up. Doors slammed and male voices could be heard approaching the front door.

Markby got to his feet. 'In fact, Wynne, everything that's happened has been in connection with a will. Not just one will, however, but two wills.'

'Two?' Wynne looked puzzled.

'Two, and both made by Olivia Smeaton.' The doorbell rang. 'And here, if I'm not mistaken, is someone who can explain it all to us. I'll let them in, shall I?'

The arrival of Sir Basil Newton with Lawrence Smeaton caused a minor upheaval. The hostess having run out of chairs, two more were brought in from next door. Extra bottles of home vintage were exhumed from the back of a cupboard and dusted off by Wynne, clearly worried that she was going to run out. Like many makers of homemade wine, she tended to make far more than she needed for her own consumption. But the run on her stock by so many visitors of late had just about cleared it out.

At last they had all settled down again and a circle of expectant faces turned to the newcomers.

Lawrence Smeaton cleared his throat and took a manila envelope from his inner jacket pocket. With some embarrassment, he began: 'I hope this doesn't prove a mare's nest. I'd like to clear it up as much as anyone here – in fact, more so, being a family matter for me, as it were.'

'We're very grateful to you,' Meredith told him, 'for taking the trouble to come all the way down here and discuss it with us.'

Lawrence was fumbling with the manila envelope. 'You'll

understand that I didn't keep photos of Olivia. But I do have the photographs taken at my brother's wedding, showing Olivia, naturally, and the whole wedding party. Perhaps, ah, you'd like to take a look at them?'

The small sheaf of monochrome snaps was passed around the circle, beginning with Armitage, after Sir Basil had waved them by. Rory scanned them and muttered something as he peered more closely at one of them. He took another look at the ones already studied, and finally passed them all to his wife without comment. Gill glanced up at him as she looked through them, and then passed them silently to Tom Burnett. He raised his eyebrows as he leafed through them, and passed them to Meredith. She took them, in her turn, with unconcealed curiosity.

There was always sadness in looking at very old photos, the sitters either dead or aged, their world long passed away. These were, in their way, typical wartime wedding photographs. All the men were in uniform. The bride wore a dress with hem just below the knee, square padded shoulders and a series of tucks across the bodice. The material appeared to be georgette. To it was pinned a corsage of lily-of-the-valley. Her fashionable peep-toed shoes looked like suede and she wore a small round hat with a veil, tilted forward on her head. Her bridesmaid wore a severe tailored suit, similar corsage, and a hat like an up-ended flower-pot, set at a jaunty angle. Everyone smiled in a stressed fashion and the bridesmaid looked quite petrified. A scowling young man was identified by Meredith as a younger, stockier Lawrence. The scowl might have meant no more than that the sun shone into his eyes. Marcus, the groom, had been taller, thinner, of more academic appearance than his bulldog brother. He alone smiled confidently at the camera.

It occurred to Meredith for the first time that Marcus's

role in wartime might have been in intelligence. Lawrence's appearance, on the other hand, indicated a man of action. As children, the traditional roles of older brother protecting the younger might have been reversed. Lawrence, the younger, more outward-going, sports-loving type of boy, might have acted as protector of the older, bookish, unworldly Marcus. If so, Lawrence had carried on the role after death, tigerishly fighting to protect his brother's reputation at all costs.

She passed the photographs to Wynne, who received them last of all and spread them out on the coffee table.

They waited. Wynne said, 'Ah, yes – that's Olivia, all right. Don't you agree, Rory? Gill? Tom?'

The three addressed nodded. The two men looked ill-at-ease, Gill Armitage flushed, her eyes sparkling with ill-suppressed excitement.

Wynne reached out her hand. 'We're agreed, then. This person here, in the photograph – given that we knew her as an old lady – nevertheless we're sure this is the Olivia Smeaton we knew in Parsloe St John.'

And she tapped the picture where it showed the image of the bridesmaid, Violet Dawson.

CHAPTER TWENTY-FOUR

A word after dying

'LIKE MEREDITH,' Alan Markby began, 'I can't say for sure exactly what happened, but I can tell you what I think happened. With your permission, brigadier?'

They waited on Lawrence's reply. Smeaton had retrieved the photographs from the table and returned them to their envelope. He tucked the package away in his jacket, and meeting Markby's inquiring look, nodded.

'Go ahead. Get everything out in the open. Let's clear the damn business up once and for all.' He sounded tired, but determined.

Sir Basil, after a keen glance at his old friend, settled down with a bottle of plum wine at his elbow, content to be an observer.

'So then, this is how I see it,' Alan began. 'At the time of their marriage, Marcus and Olivia Smeaton made wills, each leaving everything to the survivor. Simple, straightforward documents, drawn up in troubled times with the minimum detail, insurance against one of them becoming a casualty of the conflict. Sadly, one of them was, Marcus, killed only months later, leaving Olivia a widow. Not, however, alone. From the beginning of the marriage, Violet Dawson, an old schoolfriend, had lived with the Smeatons in their home. A little unusual for newly weds, perhaps, but remember it was wartime. Many people had been bombed out and found themselves living with relatives or neighbours. A shared household economy also made sense in those days of strict food rationing.'

Markby turned to Lawrence. 'There are other kinds of attraction between men and women than the purely physical, brigadier, and if it's any consolation, I feel sure that Olivia loved your brother, even if her sexual preferences lay elsewhere. She was reportedly very distressed at his death. We don't know why she didn't make another will straight-away. Perhaps because of her grief. Perhaps because with the end of hostilities, it no longer appeared urgent. She was still a young woman, remember. Behrens, her solicitor in her latter years, has done his best but has been quite unable to trace any other will – until a woman claiming to be Olivia Smeaton came to him fifteen years ago and asked him to draw up the will of which we all know. It therefore seems likely that there was no earlier will replacing the wartime one which had been superseded by events. Between the death of her husband and the drawing up by Behrens of her last will, Olivia, or the person going by that name, was technically intestate. *That fact is all-important.*' Markby paused for effect.

Wynne urged, 'Do go on!'

'One reason why the real Olivia delayed so long to put her affairs in order may be because she'd moved to France with her friend and companion, Violet Dawson. Olivia may not have wanted to make a French will. There are some differences in testamentary law between the two countries, and this may have worried her. Violet had no money of her own but Olivia paid all the expenses and they lived very comfortably. Previous to coming to live with Olivia, Violet had led a wretched existence as paid companion to various unsympathetic employers. She wasn't trained to do any other kind of job.

'After a few years abroad, the two women decided to return to England. They set out and on the way across France met with a terrible and tragic accident. Inquiry has turned up that it was recorded, by the French authorities, that Violet was driving the car at the time. I doubt that. Knowing what we do of Olivia, it's hard to believe she was content to sit back and be chauffeured by someone else. In addition, in view of subsequent events, there's reason to believe Violet couldn't drive a motor vehicle. I believe Olivia was driving that car at the fatal moment and Violet was the passenger. The car was a write-off, the driver killed and there was considerable confusion. It was long before the days of seat-belts. The body may have been thrown clear. Perhaps the passenger, Violet, dragged her friend clear of the wreckage, hoping to administer first-aid, or fearing an explosion, not initially realising she was dead.

'The French police arrived on the scene and found the two women by the roadside, one dead, one nearly hysterical. As soon as the survivor was calm enough, they asked her to identify herself and the dead woman, and wanted to know who had been at the wheel. Violet Dawson, though still distressed, had had time to realise that Olivia's death meant, for her, a return to poverty. Possibly Olivia had intended to make out a will in Violet's favour on their return to England. We don't know. But Violet knew the only will was the old wartime one, only mentioning Marcus and out-of-date.

'In such circumstances, where a person has died without leaving a valid will, was unmarried at the time of death and childless, all possible efforts are made to trace blood relatives and the estate is divided up between these, according to established procedures. If all searches for kin fail and no one comes forward with a claim, the estate goes to the Crown.

'Violet wasn't a blood relative and believed she had no claim on Olivia's estate. She also knew that Olivia had no blood relations, so she wouldn't be defrauding anyone, as she saw it, if she told the French police that she was Olivia Smeaton – and the dead woman was Violet Dawson.

'Remember, years had passed by. The two women were of an age and had both been attractive when younger. Living together as they had for years, they'd probably grown more alike, adopting similar dress and hairstyles, similar mannerisms and attitudes, as sisters rather than friends. The dead driver – Olivia – almost certainly had severe facial injuries. It wasn't difficult for Violet to swop identities.

'When she returned to England, however, she didn't dare to live in London, where she might run into old acquaintances – or return to her native town where older people might remember the young Violet Dawson. She sought out neutral territory, the secluded village of Parsloe St John. It had an added attraction because the house, Rookery House, which she bought, resembled her childhood home. Violet, remember, was a parson's daughter. The picture which Janine saw her employer burn was of a large house near a church. No doubt it was the vicarage where Violet grew up, the only memento she'd kept of her early life. That last link was ruthlessly destroyed, as all else had been, when after many years, she unexpectedly received a letter from Olivia's former brother-in-law, Lawrence Smeaton. We can only speculate as to Violet's reaction on opening that letter. Disbelief, amazement, panic, anger – a moment of real horror to her. Knowing how vehemently Lawrence Smeaton had quarrelled with Olivia, Violet had never imagined that he would ever want to see her again!

'Smeaton wrote, offering to meet and put the old quarrel behind them. He too, forgive me, brigadier, was getting older and wanted to tidy up, as it were.' Markby made another break in his narrative and sipped at his wine.

'Let not the sun go down upon your anger,' Lawrence said. 'Bible, isn't it? I didn't want to go to my grave, nor let Olivia go to hers, still enemies. It seemed wrong. Marcus wouldn't have wished it.'

'Quite. But it terrified Violet in her role as Olivia. She couldn't have fooled you for a minute, brigadier. You'd known them both, as had your wife! She phoned Behrens and insisted he get in contact with Lawrence and make it absolutely clear she wanted nothing to do with him.'

Markby gave a rueful smile. 'You know, she might have got completely away with it. No one need have known. Two things let her down. One was that Olivia had been famous – or notorious – enough in her youth to warrant an obituary column in the press – and an experienced journalist was set on her trail!'

Markby nodded at Wynne who received the compliment graciously.

'The journalist immediately smelt a rat. She couldn't exactly say why, but instinct born of experience told her that somewhere in there was a news story! She thought it might have to do with the fatal accident of the fall down the stairs. But I believe that was truly an accident, due to worn-out slippers, as the inquest recorded. The crime, that of misrepresentation and theft, had taken place many years before! The creature which really gave Violet away, of course, was the pony.'

'How so?' asked Rory, puzzled.

'Brigadier?' Markby turned to Lawrence.

'Olivia was allergic to horses,' said Lawrence. 'My wife swears to it. Olivia couldn't be anywhere near them. Came out in a rash and other symptoms, rather like hayfever only worse.'

'Good grief!' said Burnett and whistled.

'So, you see,' Markby went on. 'Olivia would never have bought a pony and trap and driven around in it as Violet did for some years, much less keep a pony for a pet! But Violet loved horses. She even insisted that the last one she kept was buried in its paddock! Besides, she couldn't drive a car. For years, the trap was her transport and it was that need to be mobile which led her to take the risk and buy a horse, even though she must have known that Olivia would never have done it. She sold the trap as soon as she ceased to have use for it. Ernie Berry bought it and it's rusting away in his yard, even now. But the pony was a pet . . . She couldn't bear to part with that, and it betrayed her.'

There was a long silence as each thought it over. Tom Burnett's mind was running in one particular direction. He cleared his throat.

'Matter of interest . . .' He flushed as they all looked at him. 'Just wondering, what about the will? I mean, the one Olivia – that's to say, Violet – made out, leaving most to charity and small bequests to Janine, the Berrys, Julie Crombie, you, Rory and, er, myself? It wasn't her money to leave.'

'I have a view on that and I'd like to express it,' Lawrence Smeaton said loudly. 'Whether or not Olivia had a legal will drawn up in Violet's favour, I'm perfectly sure in my own mind she would have done so, sooner or later, had she not been killed in that car crash. Her wish would have been that

Violet live out her years in comfort. As a military man, I'm acquainted with soldiers' wills, of course, which may be oral, a wish expressed before witnesses. I realise that doesn't hold for civilians, although it's a great pity Violet destroyed all letters, because if Olivia had made clear testamentary disposition in Violet's favour in a letter, she might have been able to claim. However, my personal attitude is that of a soldier. One can't always be fiddling about with bits of paper. I believe Olivia's wishes were honoured, albeit in a peculiar manner! No one, as someone just said now, was defrauded. Olivia had no close kin. The loser, if any, was the Crown.'

He paused and Markby said, 'Ironically, had Violet been honest and followed the letter of the law, even the Crown might have been sympathetic in the circumstances and recognised that she was entitled to some sort of provision from the estate. But Violet didn't put it to the test. It was all highly irregular and lawyers would tut-tut over it. But I agree with the brigadier that the spirit of Olivia's wishes was observed.'

'Quite,' said Smeaton, 'and that, damn it all, is what a will is supposed to be for!'

'Besides,' Markby smiled and added, 'everything we've said remains speculation. We think that's what happened – but to prove it to the satisfaction of a court would be very tricky. To ask for a will to be set aside on the grounds of some very old wedding photos? The charities which have benefited from the will would certainly contest any attempt at that!'

'Exactly,' Lawrence nodded. 'As far as I'm concerned, the matter's been settled, all cleared up. We, here in this room, know the truth, and that's enough. There is no reason for it to go any further than these four walls. In fact, it would cause a dickens of a fuss and be most unwise. Are we all agreed?'

They were all agreed.

Later that evening, as light faded, Meredith and Alan walked down the road to Rookery House. They stood by the gates, looking through the wrought ironwork and down the drive towards the old Georgian building. In the setting sun, the stonework glowed with a mellow honey hue and the windows sparkled rose pink. It was a fairytale house, built of sugar sticks.

'It's very beautiful,' Meredith said quietly. 'But I could never live in it, not now.'

'No,' he said. 'Nor could I. It was just a daydream. Bit of a fancy.'

She slipped her arm through his. 'Perhaps, one day, we'll find somewhere else, just as nice. Not yet.'

He glanced at her. The sunset, which had coloured the windows, painted her brown hair with deep auburn tones. It was the nearest she'd ever come to accepting the idea they might one day set up home together. It wasn't much, but it was progress of a sort, and would have to do, for the time being.

'Wecome home!' said Paul, pouring out the wine. 'Glad to see you back in one piece.'

They all raised their glasses. Laura observed, 'I hope that means Parsloe St John has gone back to being the sleepy place it always seemed to us when we visited Paul's aunt. If I'm going to take holiday breaks in that cottage, I want to feel sure no psychopath is creeping around out there in the bushes!'

'Talking of nutters,' said her husband. 'What did they do with that dreadful youth?'

'As of the present moment,' Markby told him, 'he's undergoing medical tests. I suspect he'll be recommended for psychiatric help. I hope so, anyway. He needs it desperately.'

'Doesn't mean he'll get it!' said Paul gloomily. 'They'll shut him up for a couple of months, declare him cured and let him loose to roam the streets and jump out on innocent passers-by.'

'Nothing like looking on the bright side!' said his wife. 'Why don't you go and see to the roast?'

'Actually,' Markby leaned back in his chair and stretched out his legs, 'it was quite a good break, after all. I do feel refreshed. What about you?' He turned his head to look at Meredith.

'Mmn?' She was staring across the room and didn't appear to have heard his question. 'Laura,' she asked. 'How long have you had that picture?'

'Which one?' Laura followed her pointing finger. 'Oh, that! It was hanging up in the cottage at Parsloe and Paul brought it back here when Auntie Florrie died. He took a fancy to it. You must recognise it. Those are the Standing Stones where you met up with Kevin and Sadie Warren, Meredith. It's not a bad little painting, if a bit on the primitive side. Would you believe it? It was painted by the landlord of the local pub there, The King's Head, Mervyn Pollard.'

Laura pursed her mouth and considered Mervyn's effort. 'Not exactly my cup of tea. Can't think what Auntie Florrie was doing with it. Perhaps Mervyn gave it to her. I doubt she bought it. Still, no accounting for taste, is there?'